RUPTURED LIGHT

A Destruction of Gods

K.R. RICHARD

CONTENT WARNING

Ruptured Light is a Dark Fantasy Romance novel that is strictly meant for readers over the age of **18**.

It contains a wide variety of adult content that may be triggering for some readers. This is a list of those triggers, but understand that not all may have been listed.

If you find something that needs to be added to this list, do not hesitate to get in contact with me so I may add it in.

I ask that every reader takes this page seriously so that everyone's mental health is protected.

- **Adult Language**
- **Amputation of Genitalia**
- **Body Dysmorphia**
- **Child Abuse**
- **Child SA**
- **Dissociation**

- **False Imprisonment**
- **Forced Ownership**
- **Forced Sterilization**
- **Forcibly Muted**
- **Gender Dysphoria**
- **Kidnapping**
- **Mental Abuse**
- **Mental Manipulation**
- **Murder**
- **Physical Abuse**
- **Physical Assault with Weapons**
- **Pregnancy**
- **PTSD Flashbacks**
- **Self Harm**
- **Skinning Alive**
- **Suicidal Ideation**
- **Talk about SA**
- **Torture**

If you find yourself relating to any of the characters in my book due to their trauma, just know that I see you. You are not alone, and you are worth every breath that you take.

DEDICATION

*To everyone that was taught anything but "normal" was unacceptable.
I hope you burned all of those stereotypes to the
GROUND
and let the "normals" clean up the ashes.*

SYTHERAC
NO NAME DEEP
DESITAE
Shallow Grave
Passage
NO NAME DEEP
THU
Hedeft
UNIV
Xaxteen
RUNEA
Noctua Cartography - Cartographer Joshua

DARIA
Anona
Buron
ORICAL OCEAN
OCTOVAH
ER
ORICAL OCEAN
ED
kins - Stardustbookservice - 2024

THE LAWS OF SYTHERAC

As set by the five founders – Altairien, Hartland, Kav, Sandur, Nepatae – these laws are to be followed and upheld by all residents of Sytherac.

To never be challenged for any reason. To do so is to forfeit one's own life.

All worship of the old Gods is forbidden. Historical documents are to never contain any information about these Gods.

Each King is their own God for their own Kingdom. Once a King crosses territory lines into another, they no longer have jurisdiction in any aspect.

Each King is to help the rest, be it with textiles their region offers or food supply.

Each King's royal guard should always be ready to fight the only common enemy.

Wars waged between Kingdoms because of power struggles are punishable by death.

No one is allowed to call ownership over another being.

Mates are protected under the soul bound law, which states: "If two people are bound by the chains of the soul, then no person, no matter their status, has the authority to separate the two. Neither can they kill one just to get the other. If found doing so, their life will be forfeited."

To disrespect one's home means to disrespect the ground and sky for which all power is shared. You are to not bother what is not bothering you.

Under no circumstances is anyone allowed to sell any part of another being unless this consists of hunted animals.

Do not take more than what you need.

No female is to hold a seat with the Kings.

Each King can set their own rules and regulations in their own territory.

Everything that lives and breathes on land, sea, sky, and ground should be treated as equal.

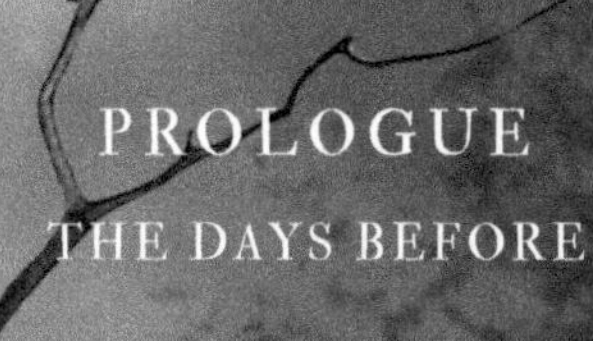

PROLOGUE
THE DAYS BEFORE

In the beginning, there were only two things, Light and Shadow. They are both nothing more than a great power that spreads across every expanse of known existence. Nothing is out of their reach because they are found in everything. The two great powers lie side by side in their own solitude. For the majority of the time, they never cross their boundaries, that is until the attraction between them is strong enough to drive them together. Light and Shadow cannot live without each other, and their time mixed together is always short-lived, once every ten thousand years.

In the moment they allow themselves to indulge in their love for each other, they create a life that is extraordinary. The life made from their embrace is all they have to remember each other until their bond grows too intense to set aside again.

Normally, only one life is formed every ten thousand years but that is not the case for the last. Instead of one they made two, a set of brothers, one almost exactly like Light and the other like Shadow.

The first to develop was named Lixtis, a name meaning Keeper of Souls. Light knew this brother would create beings made with pure hearts and bright souls. From the moment his body grew from the light in the stars, Lixtis found himself to be in Light's favor. Light saw itself the most in its new son and never questioned Lixtis' ability to judge good from evil. Shadow did not share the same faith in the older of the brothers.

The second to come was named Etbris, a name meaning Protector of Death. Light laughed at the name as Shadow bestowed it to the younger brother, who was smaller in size then his elder. Etbris came second because the darkness from which he was crafted decided to take its time while building the fundamentals of his mind. A luxury Lixtis did not receive from Light. Shadow did not worry itself with the laughter of its companion as it simply stated.

Everything needs a protector, even in death.

Light and Lixtis did not understand the meaning of the words but Etbris did, and that was all that mattered to Shadow. The darkness held no hope for its elder creation because it could see the seed of greed that was planted in his chest.

Leaving the thoughts of doubt behind itself, together Light and Shadow made a world just for their sons. A place they both thought would protect the pair as well as keep them content. Together the two powers named the world Arugo, meaning Home For All. It was a place sculpted by careful hands to ensure that it held everything the brothers would need to let their creativity run free. Light hoped that Lixtis would fill the skies with beautiful creations so it could watch the light dance around them. Shadow hoped that Etbris only made what he felt like he needed.

It did not take long for the brothers to start experimenting with their given powers, each one a gift from the essence that created them.

Lixtis wanted company in the form of beautiful bodies but with minds that did not question, so he created his first life using his own light. He made a body like the one he was made into. Something on two legs that held a torso, arms, and a head. The only difference he made were the wings that hung from the female's back of pure white feathers. He made her in his perfect image. Nothing was out of place on the female, and her mind was one that only thought of loyalty. Lixtis marveled at his creation while his brother watched with wary eyes as he could see the seed of greed blossoming in the other.

Etbris would watch his brother with the female he made, and instead of being jealous of their time together, he made his own company. Etbris did not like the idea of creating a body similar to theirs out of fear of temptation. He wanted a companion. Something that would choose him on its own free will but also something that would search for another greater than himself, if that ever came along. Etbris used his own shadows and created a species of beasts that could walk through any expanse of darkness. He called them Shadow Hounds. They would grow to have a terrifying representation of being masters of death, and it is of no fault of his own. His brother would be the reason for the misleading of their character, due to his jealousy of the bond they shared with his younger brother.

Lixtis would go on to make thousands of his first creation, an Angel, as well as his own Hounds. The Angels that he made from his own light fueled them with the same jealousy and greed that resided in himself. It was a silently moving disease among them that Lixtis could not see. It only showed itself in their fierceness and hostility towards anything that wasn't like them. Even the Hounds he made that shared many of the same traits as his brother's own would become the true definition of Masters of Death. Their sole focus on killing.

Etbris would go on to make hundreds of different animals that he would soon have to find a home for, Arugo being overrun by the Angels his brother crafted. Etbris was not bothered by the task of creating a space for what he saw as his creations, in fact it made him excited. He took expert care in crafting every detail that went into the new world, even small things like the temperature and color of the soil. Etbris mapped out the space so that every creator he made had its own climate and food to thrive. He never wanted his world to be anything but peaceful. Lixtis would soon ruin that for him as well.

The older brother watched his younger brother as he carefully put in every minor detail of this world. A small knot tightened in his center; Lixtis wanted the power flowing through his brother's veins for himself. He felt that if he had the same use of shadows that the other did then he would be unstoppable; nothing could destroy him. Even though Lixtis had no reason to worry about such a thing, the idea of being able to take the place of Light and Shadow filled his mind to the point of madness, and it was that madness that drove him to cause mass extinction of what his brother called his babies, the only things the other truly loved. A weakness Lixtis knew would always reside in Etbris.

Etbris could only watch as his creations were slaughtered one by one, each Angel taking aim at one of his animals. His brother's Hounds, made from bright white light, tore into the throats of even the biggest of what he crafted. The Shadow Hounds at his side tried to get away from Etbris's side to protect the ones they could, but the brother held them close. He was too afraid of losing them too. That same day after watching the carnage unfold, he created his first replica of an Angel, only the one he made had wings that replaced soft feathers for the texture of skin. He gave them the name Demonian and swore that they would only hunt the ones whose souls were tainted, stained by his brother.

Lixtis saw his brother's Demonians as an insult to the beauty that he created. The oldest brother found himself drowning in his own anger at the act of defiance from his small, quiet brother. Lixtis did not hesitate to use the loyalty of his Angels as he declared the Demonians an abomination and a clear sign of war. He was set to destroy anything his brother made from that point on, even if it meant destroying his brother along the way.

Etbris would not back down, not with the knowledge of his brother's madness. He could not protect his animals from their own death but he would protect everything else from his brother, so he built an army to match that of the others. Each of his Demonians had their own talents that set them apart from the rest, and he even made giant reptile-like animals that would be used as guardians.

It was at the mark of eight hundred years of being born that the brothers started The Eternal War. A war that would never end as long as one jealous brother and one vengeful stayed living. The years of fighting the same war against the same people caused many of the Angels to grow restless. The loyalty that Lixtis gave the Angels began to fade as they watched him kill not only their enemies but their own kind as well. The very first woman with wings he created was the first to develop her own feelings. She would help the others see the true nature of the one they followed so blindly into war, the one who had no problem killing their own. Some of the Angels even started to confide in Etbris as they saw his fairness and the level head that rested on his shoulders. Etbris thought about everyone and everything in the war. He made it his first priority that nothing made its way into death's hands without a helpful guide, a Shadow Hound. That is what made him stand out from his brother. It is also why Lixtis made the world his brother created into a prison.

Lixtis found another weakness of his brother's: Etbris was haunted by the extinction of his very first creations. Etbris would do anything to keep that from happening again, so Lixtis started placing injured Demonians into the world after ripping the wings from their backs, using them as trophies for each one he could steal away. Etbris would weep as he saw each pair of skin covered wings fall into his brother's hands. The pain he felt for his friends was met with his anger, and as the two mixed, he decided that he would keep his brother from accessing the world again.

Etbris used his own shadows to shield the world. The darkness of him engulfed the place until it was hidden from the light of his brother. Little did he know that Lixtis was not only dumping the discarded bodies of the Demonians on the soil but also those of his own Angels as well. Anyone that Lixtis thought was plotting against him, or anything that could cause his downfall was shunned to the world of many different climates.

The warriors that remained on Arugo kept fighting in The Eternal War out of fear of only one of their Gods and the wrath they would face if they stopped. Etbris became the protector of them all. It was their most kept secret.

As the years of war carried on, the first Angel created found herself with an unfamiliar feeling developing in her chest. The feeling was only felt when she would lock eyes with her biggest enemy, the commander of the Demonian army. The very first one created by Etbris. The commander felt the same emotions as the other, only he knew what it meant because it was his creator that told him. It was Etbris that shadowed the warriors as they met after their time on the battlefield, bloody and bruised, to mend each other. Both the Angel and Demonian would be the start of an awakening.

They would be the start of a wildfire that would spread across their world and to the other. It would scorch a path in the cosmos that would make it impossible for even Light and Shadow to mend, separating the two from one another for an additional ten thousand years.

A child would be born.

A child that would grow into a force strong enough to cause the destruction of Gods.

ORIEN

When the King sends Orien to complete a job, she works swiftly and with expert accuracy. Her reputation is excellent – she has never failed a single task assigned to her, leaving her the only person the King trusted to fulfill the requirements of the job.

Her face is set like stone as she wields one of her many daggers with perfect precision to peel the flesh off the nobleman's face who sits in front of her. She tied his body to an old, ragged wooden chair she found next to the front door of his house. Mud or boar shit coat the bottoms of each wooden leg, but it is not her place to question the man's living conditions.

Just like it is not her place to find out the name of the poor bastard she currently dissects. His time would not have been cut short if he had been more intelligent about who he considered his friends or who he voiced his concerns about the King's ruling to.

The man's blood curdling screams fill the rundown wood shack, and to Orien, they sound like a perfect melody, harmonizing just right with her skillful dagger work. The weight of the metal in her hand is as light as a feather, the black hilt specifically molded to fit her hand.

The blade is no longer silver but crimson, the ornate floral design along the shaft concealed under what she considers to be a rather decent visage for a man his age.

Orien has worked on removing the gentleman's face for several minutes now, and he has yet to pass out. It is one thing she finds surprising. Most of the time she can barely begin her work before her victim passes out from fear.

Her black pants and jacket now shine from the blood soaking through them, and her hands finally fill with warmth. The walk here from the Stone Castle was unforgiving this time of year. The Kingdom of Univier is currently in the late cold season which can cause the wind to become so rough it plants a chill deep in anyone's bones. Luckily, the blood soaking her hands is just what she needs to raise her core temperature back to normal.

Just as she flays the last bit of skin from his forehead, the screams turn into raspy sobs. The sound does not bother her but she has not found much that does these days; everything seems to run together in an endless loop. The feeling can be tiring at times, even for someone as shut off from herself as Orien.

It is not a surprise that Orien's face has not moved an inch during her meticulous procedure of skinning the man's flesh from the structure of his face. The sounds of agony have become the only thing that is consistent in her life now. As she holds up the wet slippery flap of skin, examining her work, Orien remains unbothered with anything else as she makes sure her work is nothing less than exact.

One thing for sure is that the female never allows herself to be anything less than perfect when it comes to any task she performs. It has been carved in the base of her skull for as long as she can remember, and it is all thanks to her upbringing in the Stone Castle.

Examining her work one final time, she slips her blood-soaked dagger back into the black leather sheath strapped to her left thigh. She will worry about cleaning it when she gets back to the castle after dropping the evidence of her duties to the King. Every shred of evidence of her ruthlessness would ensure that Alister Altair, King of Univier, was content.

The man that rules over this lively Kingdom of Orien's origin did well to keep his true wicked nature hidden behind a polite smile. Orien, however, knew the truth; not just from her upbringing in the walls of the castle, but from the marks that will never leave her skin.

She has watched as the perfect smile he gives everyone else falls from his face after long days of ruling. Because that is when his true happiness emerges as he carves into her skin.

Alister has used her not only for her talents but for his own personal punching bag for as long as she can recall. Orien has become accustomed to the beatings and abuse over the years. Only a small part of her body does not show the signs of the torment inflicted on her by this so-called "Caring King."

The man she was sent here to make a spectacle of has soiled himself in the time it took to work and now shakes uncontrollably. What was originally his face is now nothing but smooth, skinless muscle and tendons. No one would be able to recognize him unless they had seen him without skin before, and she doubts that has happened.

Folding the warm portion of skin into a perfect square, she then wraps it in a piece of black silk she'd stored in a pocket of her tight-fitting black trousers. The feeling of the smooth, almost waxy, fabric against her rough hands draws a long warm breath from her lungs. The sensation of silk has always been a preferred texture for her, but she cannot tell you why because she does not know herself. All she knows is it makes her skin feel nice when nothing else does.

Making sure the skin is tucked in tightly, she puts it back in another pocket. Now, it sits tucked away right over her heart, or the expanse of chest where a heart should be.

Orien is not entirely sure if she was born with a heart. The whole town thinks the same thing as well. The stories they tell always seem to become bedtime stories to keep the misbehaving children in line. It is true that she was not born at all but rather made into the perfect predator. A thing like her, so different then the humans and Fae she walks among. It makes the nobles of Univier sick to their stomach to even think her name. A part of her has always felt better than all of them. She thinks she will always be taller, stronger, faster, and that she will always be nothing like them. Putting the sporadic thoughts to the side, all emotions evade her.

"Please! I-I-I did not...d-did not!" The noble man sobs, making his shaking worse, and the old chair groans under him. Orien looks in his eyes and sees nothing but emptiness. She can taste every ounce of agony and despair racing through his frail aging body. The beast inside her feeds on the taste of the man's pending death. Sadly, she is not here to kill the man, just to make it known to anyone else what happens if someone tries to slander King Altair's name in his own Kingdom.

She has one last thing to do before she can head back to the castle and leave the evidence in the hands of the Kingdom's true monster. Reaching to her right thigh, she pulls out a metal surgical clamp. The weight is foreign in her hands, but the tool's size betrays the damage it can cause. The small silver U-shaped clamps are meant to seal wounds that cannot be healed by stitches or the healer's magic alone. She has seen the mender using the tools to do just that for some nasty gaping wounds on the many Knights that would come back from fighting some of their smaller battles around the other Kingdoms.

Most of them started over things like land and borders. All of them ended with the same outcome of tear-stained cheeks and more hate-filled rulers.

As she looks back at the raw face of the man, she knows it will hurt like a bitch. The shrill cries only get louder and more frantic as he sees her loading the clamps into the tool's base. His tears are mixed with his blood as they drip off his face and hit his naked milk white thighs. By his draining color, she knows he has lost most of his blood.

She reaches and grabs the man's lips, pressing them closed between her thumb and pointer finger. The connective tissues of his cheeks try fighting against her, but they lose the battle.

The metal surgical tool gets placed over his top and bottom lip, and when she presses the two silver handles together, the tool makes a click sound as the small U-shaped clamps close around his lips. They make a watery squelch as they bind together.

His eyes look like they are trying to escape from his head, and his cries are now high-pitched, filled with agony. She continues all the way across the expanse of the man's lips until all she can hear are muffled pleas trying to escape.

Orien returns the clamp back into the pocket attached to her leather strap around her right thigh. The same strap holds her other dagger, the twin to the one that pulled the man's skin cleanly off his body. She rubs her mouth on the sleeve of her jacket, forgetting that a muzzle is still a part of her own face.

A muzzle just like one used for the Wulves that once ran the streets inside town, only this one is built to withstand her. A gift from the one that raised her and the sorceress that he found to enchant the ghastly thing to her face. She is a beast. At least that is the picture that has been painted of her around the world they inhabit. The leather and brass rivets dig into her arm as she wipes her face.

The man has now passed out in front of her. Orien's body is numb as she studies him. His hair is a deep brown, his eyes, from what she can remember, are a dark blue. He had no facial hair, and the skin over her heart was home to many wrinkles. The rest of him matches with the same loose skin. She only knows because she cut off all his clothes before skinning his face so the cold prickling his skin would torment him as she worked. If she had to walk all the way here dealing with it and then turn around to walk all the way back, then he would feel it too. At least someone could share the same pain as her.

Taking one last look at the body, her eyes fall down between his legs. Disgust overcomes her as she looks at the thing that hangs there, resting on the seat of the chair. She does not feel much more than anger, but something about men really makes her want to set unnecessary things on fire. The existence of these creatures just makes life more complicated.

Finally, she leaves the shack. Fresh screams follow her on the way out. As she strides to the hill just to the side of the shack to start her trek back to the castle, she passes the man's pen full of boar and sows. Thinking back on it now, she decides it was definitely pig shit on the chair's feet. Nonchalantly, she tosses a pair of genitals over the top of the cage and does not slow her pace. She hears the pigs start fighting over who gets the treat, she just gifted them.

Her walk back is quiet and cold. She takes her time and decides to use the trees more than the road. She starts jumping from one tree branch to another.

Orien is tall and lean, but she feels weightless in the short distance as her body flies through the air. Her dull red hair has grown out from its normal cropped length, so it flows just behind her neck as she slings her body between branches. She travels along the main road that sits by the river just feet from the trees. Many small waterfalls line the way back to the main town that sits on the inside gates of the Kingdom of Univier. As her arms throw her body weight from one place to the next, nothing moves about in the night. Nothing but her at least.

The predator is out hunting so the prey will hide and try to keep safe. Unlucky was the prey she caught tonight.

It takes her two hours to get back to the center of town. She does not care how long it takes her either way because no one would dare stop her when they know what it means for her to be seen out of her hiding place inside the walls of the castle. It does not help she is also covered head to toe in now dry and crusted blood.

Dropping down to the road, Orien walks along one of two of the main bridges that lead to the castle just on the outside of the small, quiet town. The vines from the forest have made their way onto the stone pathways, making them appear more green than gray. Every other person would marvel at the way nature has taken over the built structures, but Orien could care less. Nothing has caught her eye as striking before.

The rushing river called Hedeft is the main run-off from the giant waterfall that sits at the west wing of the stone castle. The waterfall is the main source of life here. It provides everything needed for living a comfortable life. When the Fae nobles learned how to use its many currents to make what everyone now calls Water's Light, it changed everything for Univier.

The buildings all around are the same light gray as the bridge she currently walks across. The only thing that makes them all stand out to the eye is how the forest in which the whole palace is placed has found a way to engulf the stone.

The forest around the palace engulfs the stone of the entire structure, wrapping it in a verdant green and making it the only thing that does not blend into the rest of the gray all around.

The animals slowly start moving in with the forest as well. It is not odd to run into many unusual species walking, flying, swimming, or waddling their way to and from along with the humans and Fae. Sometimes you can even see some of the shifters in their animal forms playing with the young.

Orien sees it all, but it means nothing to her. She does not understand the meaning of beautiful things or the lives they all seem to live out in harmony. She never knew anything other than the anger and the stirring of the beast in her head. She is both the shadow of this town and its greatest, most feared thing.

Ascending the steps to the castle's main doors, Orien straightens her back to a perfect posture. She can already envision Alister's deep green eyes as he tries to mark any slight twitch or reaction as he inspects her work. It is all he does when she is in his presence. The joy it brings him to see how far he can push her is sickening.

Everything about the King is permanently engraved in her head like someone has branded it into her memories with a red-hot iron rod. The feeling is one she knows well from it being one of his favorite types of punishments. She has spent her life under his hand, and he is mostly the reason behind all the scars she wears on her skin. Each one with their own story and torment inflicted.

Opening the small servants' door that sits to the left of the two giant gold-plated entry doors, warmth greets her, coming from the many boilers built throughout the many rooms. Her skin slowly warms as she makes her way to the royal quarters on the far west side of the palace. All the small ornate hanging lanterns along the ceiling holding the Water's Light are out. She is not sure what the exact time is, but she knows it is close to dawn. Some of the morning singing doves have already started flying about outside, so their songs will follow soon.

She passes the kitchen, which is two corridors away from the entryway of the royal quarters. Water's Light shines brightly in the kitchen and the sound of thin metal trays banging around are a tell-tale sign that Fredrick already prepares the food for this morning.

Orien does not slacken her pace, but she knows Fredrick sees her. He is old and wears his age over every angle of his face, but his hearing is still one of the sharpest of the Fae. No one knows exactly how old he is, and no one to her knowledge has ever asked. He is full of stories and endless knowledge, but he mostly stays to himself in his kitchen nowadays. When she was a child, he was one of her caretakers and once a part of the King's Royal Guard.

Orien makes her way through the entryway of the west wing quarters and takes a left at the end of the hallway. She is met with two Royal Guards that are on watch, protecting their King from any threats, at least that is her guess. They look up at her and she down at them.

They are required to wear full suits of armor while on duty, including the tacky helmets that hide everything except the color of their eyes.

Orien looks at the bright white of their armor and thinks to herself, *what absolute buffoon would choose white when it will easily be stained in battle, or hell even if these idiots tripped over their own feet and face planted in mud. The suits are a monstrosity and deserve to be melted down, along with the King that designed them.*

The freshly polished gold of the intricate floral details also makes her question the brain of the man that came up with this design. Looking away from the outrageous armor, she sets her eyes back on the guards, now slightly trembling.

The guard on the right of the door knocks twice on the wood behind him, and a stern, deep voice that oozes every bit of confidence that his basic Fae body can contain answers in reply.

2

ORIEN

As the door opens for her, Orien steps into the room with one swift motion. The door thuds closed behind her and she is now left shut in the room with the man behind the voice.

Waiting just inside the office space, her eyes stay locked forward on the back wall behind the desk. Every time she finds herself in this space, her eyes always stare at the same tapestry that is hung proudly on the gray stone wall.

The title reads, The Five Great Kingdoms of Sytherac. Orien has seen all of the Kingdoms of their world and has yet to see the greatness of any of them. In fact, she finds them all to be basic and lackluster. They each share the same trait of power-hungry men sitting on each of their thrones.

Many of them are old and lack any common sense besides what they can gain from the young girls they can force into their sleeping chambers. The idea of the helpless servants being trapped in those rooms makes her hands ball into fists. The five men that sit on the thrones are too caught in their greed to recognize any of the common problems they all seem to share. Orien knows first hand about a disease that started in Thundaria, the Northern region of their world, and is slowly making its way from the territory. She has not had the time to study much about the sickness with how often Alister sends her to do his bidding, but what she does know is enough. It is said to be a sickness that can eat you from the inside out in a matter of minutes or years. No one knows where it came from. Hell, no one outside of Thundaria even knows if it has a name. None of the other Kingdoms have mentioned anything about sending aid in the form of healers to the frozen region, which does not surprise her in the least.

Orien often watches the young children as they run in the streets of Univier just to see if any of them have started showing signs of odd behavior. Her searching has come up empty every time which makes her shoulders rest a little bit easier as she walks the halls of this castle.

A throat clears from across the room, and Orien shifts from her thoughts on the Kingdoms and their ignorant ways to the male sitting at the desk. His dark green eyes are more sinister than sweet. They are rimmed with dark lashes and small wrinkles part out the outside corners.

His dark gray hair is slowly turning white, and it hangs in long layers across his head just to the end of his neck, always parted in the middle and shining from the oil he uses to keep it from falling out of place. His beard covers the bottom half of his face, and it too is put into place by the same nut-smelling oil.

The scent is one Orien has grown to recognize the moment he steps into a room. It has always been something that makes her nose wrinkle. Univier is covered in many different aromas from each different plant that resides here, so for him to choose such an odd smelling substance to mark his body has always seemed peculiar.

Alister does not have a single flaw that marks his face, but the small wrinkles creeping along his features are beginning to show his age.

She looks him in the eyes and waits for the command before she moves from her spot on the wooden stained floor. Every movement in his presence is muscle memory now, one wrong twitch could mean the process of regrowing fingernails. The last time it took them a full week to grow back in. Far less than the average four to six months that it takes for humans, but an annoyance, nonetheless. The King even went as far to add a slow growth serum on each of the nail beds, making sure they took their time to cover their normal resting place.

Alister seemed to prefer that punishment as of now for small acts of defiance. Orien wonders how his imagination has stayed fresh through her twenty-seven years. It can almost amaze her, sometimes, how he can keep finding different punishments for her. It amazes her even more how she can sit perfectly still while enduring the treatments.

"Come on now, I do not have all damn morning to wait on you. Sit down and give me what you need to give me." Alister is a man of many faces and right now he is wearing one that shows he is tired and frustrated.

It is one he wears often.

Not hesitating, she walks to the desk and pulls out the piece of black silk folded in her chest pocket. The fabric is soaked through and smells of iron and trees. Orien does not mind the smell, but the other scrunches his nose.

"Sit down," he says as he sticks his hand out.

Taking a seat in the tall, wide, wing back chair to the right of her, she puts the piece of the man in the King's outstretched hand.

The brown leather seat of the chair sinks down with her weight, the sound of the inner springs tickling her eardrums. Feeling the fabric under her, she cannot help but compare it to the face she just handed over. Both of which are smooth, cool to the touch, and are surprisingly durable. Orien likes very few things in her life, but comparing textures of different objects is one of them, as well as making sure everything has its place. She hates anything that is disorganized.

Sitting down, Orien still towers over Alister, and he hates the fact. She, on the other hand, does not. Her height has always given her an advantage over most of the men that reside in the castle.

Putting the folded fabric on the top of his desk, he begins the process of unfolding the perfect square.

"Next time you leave a job, clean yourself in one of the falls before returning to me. You smell like piss and," he sniffs the air, "is that pig shit?"

His face is set in disgust as he looks over her appearance. Something thumps in her head as she replays the way the animals in question fought over the set of genitals she gave them as a late-night snack.

Finally, he looks back at the laid-out fabric and the face that was concealed is now plain to see. It looks like it would make a perfect mask for one of the balls held every year here in this castle.

The slate complexion shows it has been gone from its host for some time, the outline of the lips is a dark blue.

The spot where eyes normally sit is loose and off kilter. Nose skin lays flopped to the side, resting against the left cheek. King Alister Altair smiles at the flesh in front of him and all his pearl white teeth are on display. Orien knows his green eyes are dancing with delight that she did her job to his liking.

"This is more than I expected but I assume I should not have thought so lowly of your skill set. I mean I did train you, so I would then be thinking low of my own skills and that is something I will never do."

He looks at her with the same unwavering expression on his face, and she watches his eyes. When she was younger, she would get lost in his eyes, searching for any signs of care. It used to make something in her chest hurt when she never found it.

His time spent with her was only meant for one thing and that was to make her stronger, which meant he would become stronger as well.

Looking into his eyes now was just her small way of asserting her own kind of dominance over him. It was something Orien knew he hated but that she also knew he did not let himself know that part of him, yet.

Passing her a piece of parchment accompanied by a quill and bottle of ink he asks, "Tell me, what all you did to our dear old Spence?"

So that was his name, she thinks to herself, grabbing the quill and dipping it into the ink. She writes out how she stripped him nude, peeled his face from his body, stapled his lips closed, and finally, how she cut off his testicles and penis, adding how she fed those to his own pigs just before she slides the paper over to him.

As he reads, a smile crosses his face. The change in expression is followed by laughter and the noise is enough to make her want to growl. Everything about the person in front of her makes her anger begin to bubble just like the giant pots of soup Fredrick likes to make on these frigid days.

"This is far more than I originally asked for and because of that I will think of giving you a day to yourself tomorrow or the next." Alister Altair's broad shoulders shake with his laughter, and it is enough to make his round stomach jiggle before he adds, "Before I forget, Orien, I do have another job for you. In the next week I will need to send an advisor for my Kingdom to Thundaria. The new King is being crowned, and I cannot risk not showing my face. Unfortunately for me, my leg gets sorer in the cold climates."

He pauses before continuing, "I will be sending someone in my place and that person will need protection. I cannot send my Royal Guard, so I will be sending you as a replacement." His laughing ceases, and he holds her gaze as he relays her next task.

She knows that no matter what, she will be sent on this ridiculous journey, and it is one of the last things she wants to do by herself or in the company of a stranger.

Alister is always content to use the excuse of his busted-up leg, given to him in a war long since forgotten, to get out of doing any actual work that needed done by a King. It is always advisors or trusted commanders sent to do his bidding.

"When I decide who I am sending, I will call you back. You are free to go for now. Go wash yourself before you come back anywhere near the west wing. You smell like a rancid ass, and it makes me sick."

Waving a dismissing hand in the air, he begins to fold the face of Spence back into the cloth. Not waiting a second later, Orien stands up and walks to the door. Before she can grip the gold-plated handle in her arm, Alister's voice carries to her from across the room.

"I guess we will have to push off your free day, since you will need to be in good physical shape for the journey North." She can feel the smile he wears as he speaks to her, never speaking to her, just in her direction.

Pausing shortly just before opening the door, she lets the words sink in. There would never be a free day for her, it was never something she even thought about.

Opening the door, she walks past the guards and back into the hallway. The dried blood starts to make her skin itch, so she decides to engulf herself with her shadows instead of wasting time walking to her bed chamber.

She moves with swift lightness through the shadows until she ends up in the middle of her washing room.

The shadows have always been a part of her, and no one is sure what they are. Orien knows they are more than just darkness because they do more than just shield her from sight. They tend to enjoy wandering around and sometimes they will even play with the small Wulve pups, the ones that chose to stay around here that is. The animals have kept her company many nights in the forest. Sometimes Orien finds herself looking for them while she is out.

The washroom is big enough for a soaking tub that can fit her seven-foot frame, a toilet, and a hand wash basin. The stone walls have very few vines clinging to them, so it is mostly bare. Only her and the color gray.

Above the small washing basin hangs a rough-cut circle of glass she uses as a mirror.

Bracing her hands on both sides of the circle bowl, Orien hangs her head and closes her eyes. Little was running around in her head other than the fact that she was to travel to Thundaria. The fact that she would also be the only protection over a stranger made the journey even more stressful for her. She loathed people and many other things that lived and breathed.

Pushing off the counter that holds the wash basin Orien strides the short distance to the tub. Twisting the small round gold-plated knob just above the tub, water begins to flow from the spigot just under it.

The whole Kingdom of Univier is equipped with a system of round hollow lines that feed water from the river to all areas of need.

During these few cold months, the water is always like ice but for a couple coins you can buy small glass jars of heating elixirs from the few sorceresses in town. Orien always keeps it in stock. She adds a whole jar to her bath as it fills to the rim.

Stepping away from the tub, the water now steaming, she strips out of her blood-soaked leathers, not even bothering to unstrap her many weapons. They hit the ground with a thud, and all that is left covering her body is her white underlings that sit on her waist and hug her to just under her ass cheeks.

When she had the things made for her several years ago, the sewist said, "You would rather wear something that looks like a boy would wear it, then something daintier and more attractive for a girl?"

The look on the lady's face was one of pure confusion, but she did not ask or argue anymore after Orien bent down face level with her and held her gaze.

The briefs made her feel comfortable and secure. It did not matter what anyone else thought about them because no one else had ever seen them. The women from the brothels she visited during her travels do not count.

Pulling the briefs down, she sets them to the side of her discarded clothes and starts to unfasten the tight band of leather around her chest. This is just another thing she does that causes questions.

It is also another thing that makes her feel secure and comfortable. Orien has never been one to like the feminine traits she has been given; oftentimes she feels like this is not even her body.

Letting the leather fall to the floor, she stretches her arms above her head and touches the ceiling with her fingers. It is low here but tall enough for her to stand comfortably. Steam trails along the room, clouding the mirror as she drops her arms.

Finally, she walks over and steps into the full soaking tub. The elixir has the water almost boiling, and it stings her skin and immediately turns it a bright shade of red. It is a welcome feeling.

The water stains a light shade of pink from the blood on her body as she sinks all the way in, and the room is filled with the sound of splashing water, but there is no one to care about the mess. There never is when it concerns her.

She lets herself stay under the water until her lungs begin burning just like the rest of her body, and the few air bubbles she has left in her mouth make their way to the surface.

After what seems to be hours, Orien walks out of her washroom. Steam billows out the door behind her, and her feet are soundless on the rug-covered floor.

She bound her full breasts down to almost flat with the leather strap before exiting the room. Making her way to the wardrobe in her sleeping room, Orien grabs another pair of white briefs, neatly folded and in line with the rest of them. Everything here has a spot and will never be out of place.

Slipping into her training clothes of black trousers, basic black blouse, and her usual leather boots, Orien decides she needs to see Fredrick to get her hair under control once again. He has been the only person she allows to cut her hair. The trust she has in the man has been built over countless years of give and take, what one would offer, the other would accept with no questions asked. Orien thinks it is because she knows he is a truly decent person and he is the only reason she has the handful of good memories she does. If she was going to let anyone near her head with a pair of shears, it would be him.

Walking out the door, she buckles the last buckle to her chest sheath, which she retrieved from her filthy, discarded clothes.

She slips in the waiting daggers she holds in her hand. The blades have become a part of her, and she has learned how to use them for many things, some of which are even helpful. Being without them is foreign for her.

Starting her walk down the corridor that houses her room, the black tentacles of shadow cover every part of her in a frenzy. Orien thinks they are being extra nosey today. As if she just spoke the words aloud, she is answered with a small rumble from around her.

31

3

ELISIAH

Across the castle in a small bedroom housed in the South Wing, Elisiah finds herself in a dream.

She stands in a blood-soaked field, bare-footed, her white night-slip still on. All the grass is dead and withered. Metal clashes on metal, the night echoes with screams of fighting, and the moans of dying are deafening.

Her golden-brown hands lay flat against her mouth, and her eyes are perfect wide circles in her head. They are not her normal chocolate brown anymore, instead covered by a milky white. She looks around the battle torn ground and takes in all the details of the bodies lying scattered.

All of them have wings.

Not just beautiful fluffy wings like she sees on the many birds flying around Univier, but so many that look more like bare skin.

She looks up at the sky and finds hundreds if not thousands of these same bodies flying and fighting. They are as fast as light and soundless as they tuck their wings and plummet to the ground to either give a finishing blow with their bright silver swords or to land and help a fellow warrior.

Blood falls like rain, but none of it touches Elisiah.

She stays clean.

Her hands fall to her sides, but her mouth still hangs agape as she looks down at her feet to make sure she is here and bearing witness to this massacre. When her eyes connect with her feet, a choking sob escapes her mouth.

She currently stands in the center of a completely empty chest cavity of a fallen soldier. Or what she assumes is a fallen soldier.

His eyes are cast over as he stares at the sky. To her it seems like he watches his friends continue their fight while he remains stuck on the ground.

His hair is a light dirty blonde; it reminds her of the dirt pushed from the water at the base of Hedeft. The sweaty blonde hair is cut close to his scalp, his mouth slightly parted. Small waves of smoke make their way from his lips.

Even in his death he is breathtaking.

He wears a black and silver suit of armor and has skin-like wings laid out behind him. His left wing barely hangs on, shredded from the battle, and dried blood streaks down its skin.

They are the same pale white as his hands and face; they must have been the same skin tone as the rest of him then. His ribs look like someone put them in a pulley and pried them apart, the pink and red protective membrane still wet with his bodily fluids.

Elisiah stands frozen in place, overcome by shock.

She examines just how perfectly everything in his chest has been cleaned out. He has nothing left in him, but his face is not set in agony. No, he looks at peace with the end he has met.

Elisiah does not understand how that is, but she does not have time to question it right now as another body falls in front of her. She gasps as the sound of crunching bone snaps her attention away from the chest she still stands in.

Looking up to the sky, trying to follow the path from where the body fell, she thinks she found the culprit of all these dead winged people.

Spotting a woman dressed in bright white armor with gold details along her breast plate and shoulders, Elisiah sees no protective helmet on her head, and the woman's red hair shines so brightly it is almost glowing.

It is tied back in a single braid that falls to the top of her backside. Her face is set in a snarl as she continues to swing her gold sword against another of a solid black.

The man she is fighting wears matching black and silver armor to the man currently under her feet.

The reality of the fact snaps Elisiah out of the trance she finds herself in, and she steps out of the man.

"I am so sorry, sir," she says to the corpse, her face scrunched as she thinks how stupid she is for apologizing to him.

She follows the line of bodies until she can get a closer look at the pair fighting in the sky, left alone by all the other warriors.

Something about the pair calls to her. It is a feeling she can feel running through her body, like a thread being pulled tight. No words can describe how unsettled she feels in the moment, but her feet do not stop their movement forward.

Now, close enough to make out the man's features, his smile shocks her. It is like he relishes in tormenting the female. He has deep brown hair; his eyes are solid black pits.

All she thinks is that someone with eyes that black cannot have a soul.

His wings are the same deep tan as what she can see of his hands and face. The man has small black lines going up his fingers and down his face, starting at his eyes. The black sword he wields oozes black smoke just around the edges. An ache in her chest grows at the sight of the smoke like wisps.

As their swords crash against each other again, Elisiah looks to the woman to see if she can make out the lines of her face.

Before she can look up at the warrior, her knees buckle under her, and she falls to them and the palms of her outstretched hands.

The heart in her chest completely stops while her lungs fighting for air.

The milky white that covered her eyes is no longer there.

She fights the heaviness on her neck to try and see what is happening, but she cannot move against whatever force keeps her in place. A swift, soft voice rings in her head like hundreds of doves, *"Do not fight against it and go back to where you came. This is not a place for you."*

Elisiah tries to apologize to the voice that keeps her planted in place. The only way she can describe the powerful cadence in her ears is angelic. Just before she can think of it any longer, her body lurches from her bed.

She pants as her hands begin to grab at her chest, ripping off the white night-slip to make sure she still has all her innards.

She does not know what she would do if she found a hollow chest like the one she stood in just moments ago.

Drenched in sweat, her head pounds like it will split open at any second. She plants her ass on the cold floor in hopes to calm her breathing. The only thing she knows to do is try to think about anything that makes her happy; flowers, baby animals, poems, Fredrick's beef and carrot stew.

The last one calmed her enough to open her eyes which she did not even know she had closed.

Looking over herself, she inspects her body as much as she can in the dark of her room. The only light she has is what is left of the moonlight coming from her bedroom window.

Everything is there as she counts her fingers and toes.

"One, two, three……eight, nine, ten. All ten fingers and toes. Okay. That is good, right? Oh, Gods, who am I even talking to besides myself?" She runs a hand over her face and lets out a deep sigh.

"Well, I am already nude. I guess I could get ready." Still, she did not know who she was talking to, but it gave her a sense of comfort after whatever the hell she had just been through.

Standing on shaky legs, Elisiah moves to her washroom and

turns the lever for the Water's Light to flicker to life in the lantern hanging from the ceiling.

The water for her soaking tub comes straight from the river by a system of hollowed out wood lines. It is a genius system put together by some of the same Fae that created Water's Light centuries ago.

Elisiah studied the way each piece of wood was carefully chosen, hollowed out, and then put together with the steadiest of hands.

None of the books she read on the topic has ever stated the name of the Fae that first thought of the idea, but they do state that he was a man of few words. A man who liked the quiet.

The water is far from hot, but with the amount of sweat clinging to her skin she does not care as she sinks down into the tub.

Stopping at the base of her head to make sure her long black hair does not fall into the water, she sighs.

The last thing she wants to worry about is heavy, wet hair, especially since it has been colder this winter than the one before.

Some of the female servants that walk the halls of the castle have mentioned that it is close to the temperatures of the Northern Kingdom, Thundaria.

Elisiah has never left the territory of Univier, so, to her it just felt brutal this season compared to the others.

Many of the nobles have caught winter sickness. It is the only illness that seems to spread in these months, and it is one of the deadliest, always targeting the young and the elderly.

All who die from it turn a nasty shade of blue, and the sounds they make resemble that of a dying rabbit. The few times she has been allowed to leave the stone walls of the castle, she has heard the dreaded squeals of the dying, and each time they have plagued her dreams with nightmares.

None of them could top the one she just awoke from, though.

Elisiah groans but refuses to close her eyes. Too scared to end up back in that place completely naked and end up finding out who it was that told her she should not be there.

She grabs the bar of compressed charcoal mixed with peony leaves and uses it to scrub the dream from her skin. The smell eases her muscles to a relaxed state as she tells herself she will not think about what happened until she is back alone in her room. The last thing she needs is for anyone else to know what she just experienced.

Rinsing off and stepping out the tub, Elisiah wraps a long piece of cotton cloth around her midsection as she walks back into her bedroom towards her bed.

Sitting on the edge of her bed, she reaches just under the ragged wooden frame that holds the thin matting she sleeps on every night. Her hand searches for her brown leather parchment book.

She just threw it on the ground the other day and hopes the thing has not become lost.

After one last sweep of her hand, it lands on the cool cover. Using the palm of her hand, she slides it from its spot before opening it to a blank page towards the end of the book. The smell of ink fills her nose.

Still covered by the cloth, Elisiah makes her way to her table where her ink and quill reside. Taking a seat in the small wooden chair, she scribbles out a picture. It does not take her hands long to work as her body releases some of the stress from her night onto the parchment. As she closes the book, a sigh from deep in her chest spills into the small space of her room.

Getting up from the table and heading to her wardrobe, she opens the doors and pulls open a small drawer towards the bottom.

The book thuds against the wood as it lands inside of the drawer.

After she shuts the small hideaway for her book, Elisiah grabs a blush pink silk gown trimmed in a soft, delicate white lace from the scarce selection of clothes she has.

The tulip sleeves sit just past her shoulders and the slit through the center gives her arms full range of motion. It is one of the nicest pieces of clothing she owns as well as the only gift she has ever received.

The pink dress was a birthday present from Fredrick, the castle's chief and one of her only friends.

She pulls on a pair of white cotton underlining that sits right at the base of her hips and ends right under her butt, much fuller than those of others around her. Her matching bra covers her petite breasts.

Her mother, Evadne, always says she should be ashamed of her body shape. The woman has never liked the curves her daughter has matured into, but neither of them can do anything about it.

Elisiah did not mind them which only further enraged Evadne.

Slipping the dress over her head, it falls to her feet like a ripple, and closing the small silver zipper on the side, she smooths the fabric over her skin. She smiles to herself at the way the silk feels against her palms. It reminded her of a flower's silk petals.

Reaching down, she pulls on her hard sole white canvas slippers before getting up and walking over to the small table once again. At the center sits a rough-cut mirror.

She combs out her hair as best she can with her fingers to not disturb any of the curls. She places some of her Woodsorrel, a small white and pink flower, through the curls and smiles just a little after looking at the flowers.

Her smile fades once she sees her eyes.

They look different to her. They look sad and distraught, reflecting exactly as she feels right now.

Her mind wanders back to all the dead bodies she saw and how the earth looked like it was dying right along with them.

Slowly, she puts down the little jar holding the flowers. "You can think about this later, Elisiah. You must smile, stand tall, and stay out of the way."

⁂

She stands up from the table and yanks a simple white coat from beside her bed. She does not let herself slow as she strides out the door, pulling the coat on to warm her arms from the faint chill still in the corridors.Making her way to the kitchen, in hopes Fredrick will have already started the pastry prep, she tries to convince herself that it will be a better day. Her hair sways with her steps, the smell of the Woodsorrel filling the area around her. The slippers on her feet are quiet as she walks the corridors.

Out of habit, her hand plays in the green vines along the walls.

You cannot really find a clear surface around the castle that does not bear some sign of life from the forest. All the hallways towards the outer part of the castle are open to the world by arched cutouts that look like they are missing windows.

It is nothing out of the ordinary to have some type of animal or reptile sleeping in one of those passages.

Elisiah uses the distraction of the vines and flowers to keep her mind away from her horror-filled night.

It is easier to not think about anything when she rounds the next corner and is welcomed by the sweet smell of different pastries. The bright aroma tells her they are just out of the oven. Elisiah's stomach growls as she draws closer.

Entering the kitchen's main archway, she finds Fredrick standing at the stove burner, stirring a giant bronze pot.

She stands in the doorway and watches him as his arm never slacks from the wood spoon in his hand, elbow high in the air at his side.

His hair turned white some time ago, and his soft blue eyes look tired.

When she was younger, his hair was closer to pitch black, and his eyes were always the same welcoming blue, until this morning.

His back is permanently hunched from his years doing just what he is doing now, standing over a pot of food. She is not sure how old he is, but she knows his hearing is one of the best of all the Fae she has ever met. His face is full of wrinkles and the veins in his hands are a bright blue now from how close they are to the surface.

Fredrick is much like a dad to Elisiah; he has taught her many things, and most of them she still uses every day. In fact, right now as she stands in the entryway, she uses one of those skills now.

Scanning.

He has always told her to notice every detail of a room. Never be caught not knowing every exit and entrance. Do not find yourself searching in the moments when you need to run.

He has always been her protector. That is until he became too old; now he spends his free time training her in combat. Elisiah has learned a great deal from the old Fae male, and most of it was taught to her from his spot on a stool in the corner of whatever room he decided was discreet enough for them that day.

Making her way to his side, Elisiah presses a soft kiss to his wrinkled cheek. She tastes the flour still stuck to his face from when he prepped earlier this morning.

"Good morning, Fredrick. You must have been up before the birds started flying to already be so far along."

She takes the spoon from his hand and motions him to sit down on his work stool by the table, full to the brim with different pastries and fruits.

He waves her off but sits with a plop, then lets out a breath and wipes his old tattered brown apron.

"Yes, my girl, I will never get to sleep with the way these young guards eat. I got woken up by a group of them in here taking the last loaves of honey oat bread. Been baking away ever since."

"You could have come and woken me! I hate that you had to do this all yourself. You can be such a stubborn old man. You know that right?" She continues stirring but turns her body to the side to face him.

She scolds the man, the centuries old Fae male who has seen and been through way more than she has.

Fredrick chuckles and rubs his white beard. "Yes, you do well to remind me at least once a day, my dear. I would rather die on this kitchen floor from work than come and wake you from your sleep. I may be a stubborn old man, but I am nothing but a gentleman."

With those words, he stands up with some assistance from the table and takes the spoon back from her hand.

Now it is his turn to move her to the small two-person table at the end of the room, stationed just by his own bedroom door.

Following his wishes, she finds a seat in one of the small chairs.

"You would not be any less of a gentleman, Fredrick. You simply choose to tackle all the work alone. It is no one's fault but the ones that took what was left. I would have been more than happy to come and offer my help; it is part of my daily duties anyway." She flattens her dress down on her legs and examines her fingers.

Trying to keep from fidgeting with her fingers, Elisiah would find anything to do with them right now.

Nothing helps her as she keeps circling back to that gut-wrenching dream. Maybe if he had come and woken her then maybe she would not have been sucked into it to begin with.

"Yes, we would hate for your mother to find out you were able to rest and not be disturbed with the task of replenishment." Fredrick rolls his eyes and finally stops stirring the contents of his pot.

Slowly he adds a mix of root vegetables and then places a heavy wooden lid to the top.

Fredrick plates a glazed honey spun bun, about the size of the palm of Elisiah's hand and puts it down in front of her. The warm honey dripping from the sides makes her mouth water.

She did not know hunger ate away at her until being faced with such a beautiful pastry.

"Eat and then get to the library for your studies." He takes the seat opposite her and cleans his fingernails with the tip of a small knife he pulls out of an empty mead glass in the center of the table.

She eats in silence as she looks around the kitchen.

At this point she could draw it from memory, but this space is the only one that makes her feel so calm.

The space is only big enough for what you can see.

The arch to her left does not house a door, so it is permanently open to all. Just in front of her is the worktable, which currently holds breakfast.

On the right wall directly behind the only workspace Fredrick has sits the open fire stove.

Nestled to the left of that sits a single rack set in a burner box big enough for all the pastries.

Then, by itself, on the furthest wall right across the room, there is a single hand wash basin. A couple shelves hang over it for plates, bowls, and glasses.

The silverware is always pushed to the very back of the table where she currently sits.

The same green vines grow along the ceiling, and some have made their way down the walls to the floor, but they all avoid the workstations.

Elisiah looks over at Fredrick and sees he has dozed off in their minutes of quiet, so she decides to slowly make her way to the library to start her studies.

Walking to the compost barrel set at the end of the table in the center of the room, she feels eyes staring at her. She pauses as all the little hairs along her body stand at attention. Gently, she slips the crumbs of the bun into the compost and moves to put the small white dish in the sink.

The eyes follow her every move. All that crosses her mind is how it felt the same way at the end of the night before she was thrown out of bed by her own body.

"If I die in this old depressing kitchen right now, I swear on everything that I love in this stupid world, I will haunt everyone in this castle," Elisiah thinks to herself as she turns and walks along the empty corridor.

She takes a deep calming breath as her legs run down the halls until she stands in front of the massive double doors to the library. Nothing could stop her feet as they pounded the stone on the way here, not even the fresh flower buds on some of the vines.

Using the wall right beside the doors, she props her hands and rests her forehead against the cool stone.

Her eyes closed, she suppresses the feeling of the tears building behind her lids and the burning starting in the base of her nose.

All she wants is a break. A break from her life. From the castle, her rancid mother, and the absolute too-handsy monster of a King.

Her sleep is not safe anymore, and now her body is turning on her too.

Was she really being watched or was it all in her head?

Pushing back from the wall and rubbing her eyes with the palm of her hands, she straightens her shoulders and opens the doors. If she stops herself from her normal routine, then she will only set herself further back.

Elisiah hopes with everything she has left in her body that she will have the whole library to herself.

It was not enough.

Hoping just was not enough as she comes face to face with her mother.

Standing tall and proud in her usual emerald green gown, the body it hides is thin and boney. Her dark ebony hands are clasped in front of her, like she knew right when Elisiah would be crossing the threshold.

She did and that is why the feeling of eyes set her in a panic. She would not put it past the woman to cast some type of shadow to track her.

Her deep brown eyes are set on the small flowers in Elisiah's hair, and her own long black hair is pulled back into a loose bun at the base of her neck. The gray of her bangs frames her face perfectly, but the two tiny silver chains running across her forehead clash with the dark golden brown of her skin.

Elisiah has always thought bronze or gold looks best with their complexion.

She kicks the thought to the side as she clears her throat and catches her mother's attention.

"Good morning, Mother. I hope you slept well." She does not move an inch as she looks her in the eyes.

"You have no interest in my sleeping, child, so do not waste your breath on things that do not concern you. I have come bearing a message from his greatness. You are expected to be in his royal office chambers the day after tomorrow at sunrise. No sooner. No later. Is that understood?" Evadne holds her daughter's stare, looking down her nose.

The slightest hint of disgust lines the shape and angular features of her face.

"Understood and heard." Elisiah steps to the side to hopefully pass her mother, but as she gets shoulder to shoulder with the woman, one of the clasped hands grabs the top of her arm.

Her mother squeezes tightly enough that a hiss slips from between Elisiah's lips.

She looks up at Evadne with blind hatred as she says through clenched teeth, "Get your fucking hand off of me."

"The next time the King calls you to his bed, you go and lay like the good little pet you are." Evadne slowly digs her nails into the white coat around Elisiah's arm, and the faintest bit of wetness starts to pool under her mother's nails.

"How about you get your shriveled up hand off my arm, you wrinkled bag of crap. I will not lay in that monster's bed even after I am cold and decayed." She yanks her arm hard to free it from the vice grip.

She looks down at the couple spots of blood that seeped through her white sleeve.

Anger fills her down to her core.

Elisiah knows she could deal the same punishments to her mother that she received from the woman, but if she did, it would cause suspicion on who had taught her. In the Stone Castle of Univier, whores were not meant to be taught anything.

It was out of fear of what they would try to do to King Altair if he pushed them past their limits. Elisiah fell into that category of the King's Whore, even though she has never laid with the man.

As if suddenly aware of herself, she feels a pair of eyes staring at the back of her head. The stare is so intense that it makes her want to start sprinting in the other direction.

Instead, she looks away from her mother's cold face and walks to her usual spot at one of the study tables in the far right of the library.

Do not show your emotions. Another one of Fredrick's lessons on basic survival around here.

She does not need to see if she is finally alone when the doors shut behind her with a loud thud and the feeling of eyes pressed to her back have gone with Evadne.

She spends her time crying softly to herself after being sure she is alone.

Already overwhelmed by the dream that replays in her brain, the spinning in her mind moves onto now feeling paranoid of being watched, and then a meeting in a couple of days with the King.

The same King who has called her to his bed many times since her fourteenth birthday. The same year she got her first blood.

Everyone said she should have bled sooner but she found that it showed up late. It meant another two years of safety from Altair. She often thanks any higher power that may still be listening for that safety.

Now, though, she spends her time hiding in small cloves among the castle walls anytime she gets word that the King feels any kind of emotions that will warrant a call to his side. Elisiah will live through thousands of those horrific dreams if it means she does not have to warm his bed.

Her mother will not try to help or save her. It sits on her chest that her impending doom lurks near.

She has never touched another person, besides a hug or swift kiss on the cheek. The thought of someone, not of her choosing, forcefully taking the only thing from her that she knows is only hers to give, makes her sob harder.

A feeling passes through her body, and the smell of embers and fresh water makes their way up her nose. Her cries die down, and for the first time, she realizes that as long as she is in this castle, her life will never be her own.

This is not the life she wants to live.

FREDRICK

Fredrick knows when Elisiah leaves the kitchen because he is not asleep. He could see the stress the girl held on her shoulders. It did not matter how she chose to try and hide it, and he knew she would find any excuse to stay to keep him company.

The old Fae enjoys her company more than he allows himself to tell her, but Fredrick knows she can see through his exterior.

Elisiah is easy to read once you spend time around her, and he has done plenty of that through his years.

Fredrick adores the young girl. She is a light in his life that he never knew he needed.

Every time she comes around, she brings a smile to his face; it manages to warm his heart more than he can ever expect.

Even after being around the world and meeting numerous beings, she still brings him the joy of unfiltered love. It is a gift she has but he is not sure if she knows she carries it.

As she put her plate away, Fredrick watched her leave his kitchen in silence. His brain races to try and find the reason for her suffering but an overwhelming feeling of someone else fills his senses.

It does not happen often now, but the feeling is still familiar. Fredrick does not rely on wishing often, but the feeling he just felt is one he wishes could occur more often.

The scent he catches on his way to the entrance is enough to tell him who is there with them. He cannot help the smirk that crosses his face as he asks himself.

"Who is standing in the darkness of the hallway, unseen?" Again, his old bones know right. No matter what, he would never forget the signature trail of one of the other children he basically raised.

Shaking his head now with a slight smile, he makes his way back to his simmering pot of meats and vegetables.

It is to be the afternoon meal for all noble guards and servants. It is one of the meals for these chilly days in Univier, some of the coldest they have had in the last ten years, if he remembers correctly.

Every time he leaves the warmth of his little kitchen, the cold surrounds him and all he thinks about is the home he left when he was just in his teens.

Thundaria is not a place he thinks about often, but it is his birthplace; a part of him will always stay true to the North. Fredrick would have never left his homeland if he knew that coming to Univier would become his prison.

The stories he heard of the wonderfully green land with a magnificent gray stone castle built right in the heart of a magic-filled forest were what blinded him at the time. He did not stop to listen about the horror stories some would tell about the King of Univier, or of the son he created who would end up just like him.

Fredrick walked up the steps of the castle the day he arrived from Thundaria. Then he made his way down the corridors with his head held high, shoulders squared, until he came face to face with King Alabaster Altair. The father of their current King, Alister.

Alabaster was a horrid person inside and out. He made his weakness clear for all to see and anyone who called his bluff would not live to see another day's light. His son on the other hand chooses to do his bidding behind closed doors, where no eyes can see.

That day, standing in front of Alabaster, Fredrick sold himself to the man. It was the only way he would be granted the right to live like one of the locals, as well as work.

⁂

As soon as the meeting ended, Fredrick was handed a ragged Guards uniform and told that he would serve Univier until the day he stopped breathing.Now, he stirs the contents of the pot as he fights his urge to beckon the invisible person back to the kitchen.

Oh, what he would not give to question them, knowing good and well they would not answer. Just to see the look in their eyes would be enough, though.

Fredrick smiles to himself and a slight chuckle shakes his hunched shoulders.

He had always hoped Elisiah would find someone to call a friend.

A person that was not him. Someone more like her. Someone who could teach her the things he could not, anything to add to her safety while she lives in this place. The time he spends with her teaching her how to wield small instruments like daggers and knives is just the base of what she needs.

Fredrick can only do so much from the seat of a wooden stool.

The girl also needs someone in her corner that can help her fight some of the battles she faces daily. Not just with the others in her life that make it miserable but with herself as well.

Elisiah has given him plenty of scares over the years that she has been around the palace. The way she can shut herself down completely is enough to make someone think she was dead. It is only her breathing that is the giveaway that she has not truly crossed into the endless sleep.

Twenty-four years is how long Fredrick has watched Elisiah grow into the young woman she is, and every single one of those years, he has made sure she knew what love was. Even if it was just from him.

He teaches her every trick he has learned in his long life and from the years spent as one of the King's Guards.

The old man has never had a chance to have children of his own, or a wife, due to his time with the Guard. So, his soft spot for Elisiah remains along with the one that is reserved for another who stays in the shadows.

The Guards of his time called him The Keeper of Children for how often he took them under his wing. In fact, some of those children walk among the warriors, and one has even made a name for herself. Is it a good thing? No, but at least she is still breathing.

Fredrick will always blame himself for her outcome because he knows he should have fought harder to protect her. That is why he has held so tightly onto Elisiah.

Every little hand that has held his has left a stain on his heart. A stain that makes his heart bright with color, where it would only be black without.

He cannot undo his wrongdoings while serving under the King's name, but dammit if these kids that came and went did not make him feel like he was doing something right.

Elisiah is not the first in the walls of this place to color a part of him bright.

No, he has had another do so as well. Only now he does not see the other as much as he would like. What can he expect from a shadow?

Some are just more haunted than the next or they choose to respond differently to threats.

The stories that are told by the townspeople and the King do nothing to sway the love he has. He only hopes that the day when he is finally called into the endless sleep that he can hold all those little hands again.

More than that, he hopes the two females who are still here will find each other.

The wicked Gods they used to worship are the only ones who know the truth about how much they need each other.

Fate has kept them apart for some time now, but he knows one day soon they will know each other's names. He only hopes he is here to bear witness to it.

5

ORIEN

ORIEN STALKS THE HALLS UNDER THE COVER OF HER SHADOWS. Her day-to-day life is spent engulfed in them, and her senses can relax as she is tucked away.

The constant heightened state of her emotions and thoughts, among other things can often make her feel a little unsettled. Unstable. Insane. The black she currently dwells in dulls every-thing, like a protective barrier. It is the one spot where she can let herself truly breathe, and the reason most of the castles and nobles do not know what she looks like.

A well-kept secret.

Orien stops just outside the kitchen's arched entryway to make sure Fredrick is alone. To her surprise he is not, so she leans against the far wall, crossing her arms over her chest.

Normally, this early in the morning, he would be alone and have plenty of time to run the shears through her loose curls. It has been weeks since she has last been in his company.

She can hear Fredrick complaining of food being taken in the night and the effects it had on his sleep. Then, a soft feminine voice replies to him, "You could have come and woken me! I hate that you had to do this all yourself. You can be such a stubborn old male. You know that right?"

Orien cannot help but agree with the other person but is soon caught off guard. The voice dances its way through Orien's ears and has her stepping closer to the entrance of the kitchen.

The movement is not driven by her own legs it seems but by a curiosity she has not felt before. If she had to describe it with one word she would be lost within her vocabulary.

She has not heard a voice so pleasing to her before. Normally, everyone sounds like they are an octave too high, and it makes for an awful screech. The sound is enough to make her teeth grind what little they can with her jaw immobile in the confines of the muzzle.

The old man continues his rambling, but all she can focus on is the soft, velvet, carcass of this new voice in her ears.

She can feel it run across every nerve ending firing in her brain.

"You would not be any less of a gentleman, Fredrick. You are just choosing to tackle all of it alone. It is no one's fault but the ones that took what was left. I would have been more than happy to come and offer my help, it is part of my daily duties anyway." The woman talks to the chef like she has known him for her whole life.

The thought seems impossible to her because she had known Fredrick the whole twenty-seven years she has lived in this castle. Surely, if this unknown woman lived in the same walls,

Orien would have known by now. She is an expert in intel for a reason.

Now leaned against the interior of the kitchen door, Orien looks over at the woman.

Altair has not mentioned anything about a woman of her looks before, and he would be the first to boast about her beauty. It drives her curiosity even more.

Looking over the blush pink ankle length dress, Orien cannot help but wonder how the fabric would feel in her fingers.

Ever since she was ten and able to sit in with the seamstress for lessons on fixing her own leathers, the feeling of all the different fabrics amazed her.

She still sits and rubs different textures between her fingers until the delicate fabric falls apart in her hand. Her favorite is the velvet made from giant worms found in the sandy hills of the Kingdom of Desitae, which lies to the West of Univier. A dreadful place consumed by sand, but their number one trading source for spices and fabrics.

The woman wears a simple white pull-on coat made from the basic materials found native to their home.

The woman's hair looks like the black cloth she used to wrap the face of the man known as Spence from last night. It flows in tight ringlet curls to the center of her back. Small white and pink flowers are set all throughout. Woodsorrel. Orien knows those flowers and where she had to forage to find them. The tiny flowers offset the dark shade of her hair well.

Her fingers tingle like they already know the feeling of the strands flowing through them.

She catches a glimpse of her eyes as she looks around the kitchen. Light chocolate brown. The color is a shade lighter than her skin, which she can only describe as an almost golden-touched mahogany brown.

Her cheekbones are high, but the rest of her face is soft and delicate. Every feminine thing about her fits perfectly, not like it does for Orien, or at least that is what she thinks.

Watching her eat the glazed bun is memorable. Orien has never seen anyone like her before, even in her years alive. It is a pleasant change from the utter repulsion she feels for every other being she has ever run into.

I would like to have a bite of that sweet bun.

Orien shakes her head at the part of her that is mostly dormant. Well apparently, until now. The sudden interruption from the thing in her head is not unfamiliar, and right now it is welcome.

"It would make you sick. We have not had the food we need for years now." Her voice sounds unfamiliar in her head. She has not spoken a word aloud since the muzzle got placed on her head at the age of four.

It has been the same amount of time since she has thought to talk in her head. She would usually let the thing go unanswered, but right now it is like she needs to say something.

The beast within her startles, but she can feel it perk up with interest. She should not have talked about the thing, but she is just as surprised by it as well.

Something about this person in front of her makes her feel like she is balancing on the tip of her dagger. It is a good thing she likes pain because if she does not balance herself carefully it could be dangerous.

Orien.

The beast says her name slowly and softly as if to make sure it is hearing right.

Orien ignores the thing as she watches the way the female's body moves across the floor.

Elisiah is at the sink now. She senses the eyes on her from the shadows since she got up to discard the remainder of her breakfast. If she knew how to smile, Orien is sure that is what she would be doing right now as she zones in on the faint bumps rising over the back of her golden-brown skin.

Elisiah hurries out of the kitchen and starts a jog to wherever she goes next.

Little does she know, the greatest predator has just caught an interest in her. A fun game of cat and mouse has just begun, only the ones playing do not know it yet.

Keeping her normal pace and stride, the shadows follow. Orien's eyes are set on the back of the female in front of her, such a small thing this person is. Smaller than the Fae females walking around the castle, and she did not notice any signs of pointed ears, so this one must be human.

Even though she does not smell entirely as bland as the average human.

The shadows slowly swirl around her body not like their normal hurried frenzy. They watch her too.

Coming to a stop right outside the library, Orien is perfectly calm as she watches the woman hold herself up on the wall of the library.

Her breathing finally slowing, she straightens to a perfectly rigid line. It is like the young woman is putting on an invisible suit of armor before battle. The look is all too familiar.

"I wonder what battles you fight, Little One," Orien thinks to herself. The shadows surrounding her pick up their pace as she pictures the golden skinned woman in her flowing pink dress, adorning herself with plate armor. The image leaves a sour taste in Orien's mouth, and the familiar vibrations flowing down her nerves tell her the shadows feel the same way.

Caught off guard by the display from the woman, Orien has not noticed the excitement coming from the other presence residing in her head. A sudden black streak crosses behind her eyes which brings her back to her senses. The beast in her seems to spin in a circle.

Orien, you used words. We can hear our own voice.

Orien slips in the library doors right behind this new person whose name she does not yet know and stands to the right of the double doors. Getting comfortable, she crosses her arms over her bound chest as she catches a glimpse of the older woman that walks up to the younger one.

"You have no interest in my sleeping, child, so do not waste your breath on things that do not concern you. I have come bearing a message from his greatness. You are to be in his royal office chambers the day after tomorrow at sunrise. No sooner. No later. Is that understood?"

Evadne Reindale. The personal, and only, seer of King Altair. She plays a hand in the torment Orien undergoes daily.

The sight of this sack of a woman grabbing someone as delicate as the other has the beast stirring behind Orien's eyes.

It wants to see it.

She does not resist, and the thing looks through her left eye. She does not need a mirror to know that the eye is now a black hole. All the worries about her voice ringing through her head have disappeared at the sight of the threat in front of them.

I cannot wait until the witch is ours to devour. Look at how the Little One looks at this old sack of bones with such discomfort.

The beast growls in her head.

Orien smells the tang of iron in the air, and her eyes immediately go to the hand wrapped around the Little One's arm and start a search for a wound. She finds small drops of blood on the white coat. Her eyes slowly track their way from the hand causing the marks to the person to whom it belongs. That hand will rip off its host; Orien has already decided that for a fact.

"The next time the King calls you to his bed, you go and lay, like the good little pet you are." The beast snarls and so does Orien at the words that leave that corpse's mouth.

Not a woman anymore but a corpse. She will not walk away from this conversation.

"How about you get your shriveled up hand off my arm, you wrinkled bag of crap. I would not lay in that monster's bed even after I am cold and decayed."

The small one rips her arm away and walks towards the library tables.

Hm, the small thing has a bark. I like it.

A chuckle rings in Orien's head, and she realizes it was the beast.

She cannot think of another time it has found something to be pleasing before.

She cannot think of it any longer as she moves to follow Evadne out the library. As the old witch walks down the hall, Orien wraps her in her shadows. She looks down at the petrified woman, who has begun to shake in Orien's snare.

She is smart to be scared. Orien has undergone a life of different torture, and a good chunk of it was caused by this woman. Orien let the beast come forward as she took a step back in her head like a spectator to her own life.

In here, she is the same as the outside, but even being in here, she never sees what the beast looks like that lives in this place.

"You cannot hurt me. The King will have your head! You know what happens when you disobey him, you stupid fool." She spits the words in their face, but the damage is already done.

Through the lenses of her eyes, Orien watches as her body grabs Evadne's arm in the same spot that she grabbed the woman's.

In an instant, Evadne is picked up off the floor, and the bones in her arm crumble like a stale piece of bread. Her screams echo through the shadows, but they are swallowed before they can penetrate the barriers. The pure hatred bleeding from Orien makes the dark wisp move faster and more sporadically. She swears from this vantage point they are like a pack of hounds, herding their prey.

The beast lives for this pain. It feeds a part of the thing that has not been fed in a long time. It is deprived of its basic nutrition, but so is Orien.

The years spent only allowing herself to drain the lifesource from small game animals that dwell in the forest have made this moment even more satisfying. She cannot seem to care about controlling herself like she has done her whole life.

Something has been switched on inside of her, and she is not sure what that is.

You think your precious Altair scares us? No one scares us. The pain you inflict only fuels us. We will eat you whole. You will be our first meal since we were four years old.

The beast talks right into Evadne's head.

The voice is that of a hound. It sounds like an echo engulfed by thunder clouds. It rattles bones and promises death. Orien has not heard such a thing her whole life even though it sounds familiar. At this moment, Orien knows she is about to let the beast feed for the first time since she was young.

She does not care what the punishment will be.

Evadne's mouth falls open as she hangs in the air by her limp arm, her deep brown eyes filled with tears and as big as a serving platter. The woman has been left alive for too long.

The shadows begin to swirl around them, and Orien immediately knows what the power has decided to do with the hag. She has not been so pleased with her dark side before today, but after hearing and bearing witness to how this woman would willingly make a person lay with someone against their will disgusts and infuriates her.

Orien can feel the black veins begin to spread from her eyes. It feels like her blood is being iced but also becoming electric at the same instant. Black veins trail along her face and down her neck, ending at her fingertips. Her left hand, now completely black, grabs the bare neck of the waste of flesh.

The shadows jump down her gaping mouth and make their way along her veins.

You do not deserve to suck another ounce of air down your miserable throat. I will leave you a husk of a human, then throw you in The Soul Falls.

Then the beast does just that.

All the life is sucked from Evadne's body, and the shadows, now a rich death-filled black, leave her and sink into Orien. She feels full for the first time since she was four years old. The life she has siphoned makes her feel stronger, faster. She feels powerful. More than she already was.

The knowledge that she could easily kill all of them that have done her wrong has always sat in her mind. She just never found an interest in it. To be honest, she liked the pain she went through. She even goes looking for that pain and adrenaline, and has since she was five.

Today was the first day she genuinely wanted to kill one of the people that had done her wrong, but it was not to benefit her. It was for the soft voice spoken from full velvet lips.

Full and satisfied, the blackness returns to its home in Orien's head. She can feel it curling up in a ball like one of the castle dogs she sees in the pastures getting ready for a deep sleep.

Her eyes are back to her normal honey color, and she keeps the shadows and what is left of Evadne around her until she gets to the open archway of one of the outer corridors just over the giant waterfall by the castle.

Without hesitation, she throws the shell of the woman's body out the window and finally lets the shadows subside.

6

ELISIAH

different types of flowers that could heal a variety of elements, but mostly crying, Elisiah finds herself back in her bedchamber.

Spending minutes in her washroom, splashing freezing water on her face, she decides to change out of her dress and into a pair of loose brown trousers, pairing it with a long white sleeve blouse for her top half that gets tucked into the waist of her pants.

She took the Woodsorrel out of her hair after her mother left her distraught in the library. White and pink flowers covered the table she occupied when she departed the dimly lit room.

The effect that woman had on her today was new; she normally has no problem blocking out the hateful words. She tells herself that it is only because of her experience last night. Not to mention the fact that she swears someone, or something, has been staring at her throughout the day. The thought sends a cold chill down her spine that makes her shiver.

Sitting on the edge of her bed, she pulls on her simple black leather boots. Elisiah's body brims with tension, she needs to find an outlet to release it. What she needs is to throw some punches at a burlap bag full of wheat while Fredrick watches from the side.

Standing from her bed, Elisiah decides to make her way back to the kitchen where she knows the old man can still be found.

Every step her feet make in the direction towards the kitchen, anger grows in her center. The nightmare she had last night weighs on her shoulders like one of the gray stone bricks that make up the castle's walls. Evadne's words echo in her head.

Bed whore.

Bed.

Whore.

Bed whore.

The words make one eye twitch and her hands flex by her side. Elisiah is anything but a bed whore. In fact, she is extremely intelligent; her time in the library is always spent reading as much as she can cram in her head.

To her, knowledge is the true source of power, and for a vast majority of the residents in the castle, it is something they lack. Elisiah has yet to meet someone that can challenge her mentally. Someone to make her work for an answer or a solution to a problem. In this place, she has no right to challenge anyone or let it be known that she is packed full of useful facts.

Fredrick is the only soul in her life that will sit and let her ramble on about any topic that catches her interest that day.

Rounding the corner that will bring her to her destination, a sudden scent brushes past her nose. Her feet stop in the middle of the step they were about to take as her eyes close and she takes a deep inhale.

Fresh water, embers, and a touch of leather.

Elisiah stashes the scent notes in her brain as a warmth fills her chest. Every racing thought has calmed down to a snail's pace as the aroma fills her body.

The same feeling of eyes on her is the only thing that forces her own eyes open and pushes breath from her lungs. There is no fear in her right now, only calmness as she continues the short distance towards the kitchen. Her need for physical exertion washes away with whatever that scent was in the hallway; now all she wants is to see one of her only friends.

Coming to a stop in the entrance of the kitchen, Elisiah spots Fredrick's frame by the table meant for two. The man sweeps what looks like short red hair with his broom from the floor. Walking over to him, she does not hesitate to grab the horse hair broom from his hands and finish his job.

"Girl! I am capable of cleansing my floor." Fredrick's actions do not match his words as he takes a seat in one of the brown chairs at the side of the table.

Elisiah does not hear him as she looks at the hair on the ground, reaching her hand down as she picks a clump of the strands from off the floor. Dull ginger red hair sits between her thumb and index finger. It is smooth but holds a slight curl. It smells like fresh water, embers, and a hint of leather.

"Fredrick, whose hair is this?" Her words are quiet as they leave her mouth, her eyes do not move from the hair in her hand. Slowly, she stands straight, using the broom to keep her from swaying back and forth.

Elisiah feels sick to her stomach as something snaps inside of her, like a rope being snatched tight. The smell in the hallway belonged to someone, and that someone has ginger red hair. Ginger red hair that is currently on the floor of Fredrick's kitchen. Her kitchen, her Fredrick.

She spirals into herself and cannot help but feel like she is drowning from the anxiety washing over her. Nothing has made sense since she was awoken from her sleep by that damn dream. The overwhelming feeling of not being in control of herself makes Elisiah feel weak, and now standing in this dingy stone kitchen with the freshly cut hair in her hand drives her over the edge.

There is a connection between her and the red strands. Just like there was a connection between her and whoever was watching her today, but she does not understand why. Elisiah is terrified that her body is betraying her.

Fredrick stands from his spot with concern covering his face. "My girl, what's the matter? Talk to me." He reaches a hand out and places it on her shoulder as the other makes its way to cup her cheek.

"Elisiah." Fredrick gently rubs her cheeks with his thumb and waits for a response.

"Fredrick." Elisiah's mouth is dry as she says his name. "Whose hair is this?" Her chocolate brown eyes connect with his soft blue.

"That hair belongs to a friend of mine." Fredrick does not stop his stroking motion as he says the words softly in the space between them. "That friend only allows me to cut their hair. They do not trust anyone else in the castle." He pauses for just a second. "Elisiah, I need you to talk to me. My girl, please talk to me."

Tears slowly build in Elisiah's eyes as she realizes the one person she has come to trust the most does not trust her with knowing who this person is. Her heart aches as she looks at him. She feels betrayed in this moment.

"No, Elisiah, do not think I do not trust you." Fredrick shakes his head from side to side as a small smile plants itself on his face. "It is not my place to tell you the name of the person who that hair belongs to, and if I did, I am sure you would think the worst of them."

"This hair." Elisiah holds the hair up between them as she pulls her eyes from the old man in front of her and focuses them on the strands. "This hair. Smells. It smells like something I have smelt before. I do not know how to describe it, Fredrick." She takes a steadying breath. "It smells like fresh water, mixed with embers and leather. The scent makes my brain calm." Her fingers stroke the hair as her words continue. "It makes something in me feel like I am being tugged towards something, but nothing is there."

Fredrick looks from the hair in her hand back to her face. The smile on his face spreads wider as he soaks in the information. Elisiah looks to him with pleading eyes.

"Please."

Fredrick gently shakes his head again. "No, my girl. Some things you need to find out for yourself."

Taking the hand from her shoulder he moves it to the hand that holds the hair. Elisiah follows his movements as the man takes the ginger red locks from between her fingers and places them on her palm.

"You are extraordinarily smart Elisiah, and I know you will find what you are looking for." As he says the words, he closes her hand around the hair and gives her cheek a gentle pat just before retrieving the broom from her other hand.

Elisiah is left looking at her closed hand as Fredrick finishes the job he was originally doing. She has no idea what he is talking about but she cannot find it in her to be mad with him. In fact, the feeling of betrayal has left her body completely. Elisiah can accept the fact the old man is protecting someone else's name; she is sure he does the same with hers, but now she is just lost.

The original plan to burn off her frustrations with physical exercise has been ruined by the smell in the hall. Just having one on one time with Fredrick in the kitchen was ruined by hair on the floor, and now all she wants to do is pass out in her uncomfortable bed.

"I need to get some rest," she says to no one in particular.

"I think you need to go for a walk to clear your head," Fredrick says from the other side of the room.

"You know I cannot leave the castle without the King's permission, and that would mean walking into his office." Elisiah's words are hollow as the words bed whore ring in her ears with the thought of being alone in that man's office.

"We have been training for any moment you are alone with him. Do not forget how powerful you are, my girl. You are a force to be feared and not many can say that about themself." Fredrick says the words as a reminder to Elisiah so that she does not forget what she has made of herself over the years. The young woman has worked relentlessly to become not only physically equipped for a battle, but also mentally.

Elisiah nods her head slowly as she takes in his words.

"Thank you, Fredrick. I love you." She turns so she is facing the man.

"I love you too, Elisiah." Fredrick moves from his spot by the compost bucket at the same time Elisiah moves from her spot by the table. They meet each other in the middle of the room and immediately wrap each other in a tight embrace.

Sugar.

Thyme.

Sea salt.

That is what Fredrick smells like. That is what Elisiah stashes away in her brain of the man holding her.

7

ELISIAH

Leaving the kitchen and Fredrick behind, Elisiah lets her feet take her wherever they see fit. She is too consumed with the feelings running through her body to even care about where she ends up. One thing she knows is that she wants to be outside.

As she walks down hallways and around turns and then upstairs, it finally clicks where her feet take her.

She has almost reached King Altair's royal office, but surprisingly knowing this fact does not slow her feet. She straightens her back and squares her shoulders.

As soon as she is to the top of his God's forsaken spiral staircase, she stops, the feeling of a stare hovering right at the back of her head.

Elisiah turns around casually like she might have changed her mind only to get a good look around to see if she can see anything that could make her senses a mess today. Other than the things she already knows.

Her eyes come up empty in their pursuit to find a culprit, and she begins the rest of the climb to the open corridor. Her hackles are still raised at the feeling of being watched, but she cannot let that hinder the scrap of courage she carries right now.

It is idiotic courage but courage nonetheless.

Walking up to the two guards standing post outside the door, she simply says, "I need an audience with his highness. Please, tell him it is Elisiah."

The guard to her right simply knocks twice and waits until the King gives his word to enter. As he opens and shuts the door behind him upon entry, the guard to her left looks right over her shoulder. Then he looks at Elisiah again.

She studies him with irritation displayed openly on her face. "What is it?" She snaps at the guard, but before he can answer, the other returns with permission to enter.

Leaving the door open, she enters and strides to the center of the room, keeping her eyes on the twin wingback chairs in his office. She does not have to look around to know exactly where everything is in the room.

She stands right on top of a beautiful, hand-woven, circular rug. It is composed of many different shades of green and brown.

The guest chairs sit right on the edge of it, and they too are a shade of brown wood with brown leather. The desk is the same-colored oak wood.

It is currently plastered with many diverse types of parchment, and to the center lies a flat piece of black silk. Something rests on it, but she cannot see what it is.

Altair sits in his chair, white shirt unbuttoned just past his chest, his gray hair parted down the center. His beard looks freshly oiled due to the shine it holds. His deep green eyes scan her body up and down.

She stops herself from audibly gagging. The last thing she wants is this man's eyes on her. You can see him undressing her in his mind. It makes her want to squirm and hide herself from him. She will not though, not today. The only small act she allows herself is pushing her thumb into her right palm where the hair from Fredrick's floor still sits.

Elisiah does not know why gently rubbing the thin fibers calms her nerves, but in this moment she will take what she can get.

She opens her mouth to speak when a little nagging thought crosses her mind.

You are brave for coming up here. Say what it is you need and then leave. He is not a nice man.

She has never heard her own voice sound like the one she just heard, but it must be hers if it is in her head. Right?

Clearing her throat, she looks the King in his eyes. They look hungry. A sweat starts to break along her forehead, and she thinks she just signed her own punishment by coming here. She curses that little bit of courage as it leaves her stranded now.

"Good afternoon, your highness. I am sorry for bothering you with no warning, but I was hoping I could speak with you on something urgent?"

Elisiah clasps her left hand over her right as her thumb continues to smooth over the hair. She wears a faint smile but nothing so big as to move her cheeks. The King's own smile spreads across his face, and he leans back in his chair.

He sets his broad hands in his lap.

"Yes, my dear, what is it I can offer my assistance with? I am happy to hear it." His voice is one of the most rancid things her ears have heard. She is not sure if that is because his voice is really that bad or if it is the fact that she just cannot stand this bastard Fae male seated before her. Reluctantly, she smiles at him and takes a step closer.

His hand lightly squeezes the thigh covered by his trousers, and she refuses to move another inch.

Disgust fills her core, and she wonders if she might just upchuck her breakfast, even though she barely ate anything. After leaving the library and finding herself distraught in the kitchen, breakfast was an afterthought.

The feeling from the stairs still lingers. It has not stopped or left like it did earlier today. It is like whatever it is, may enjoy the free show.

"I would like to ask if I could go explore outside of the town for an hour or two this afternoon? I am only asking due to needing to find certain flowers I studied today." Elisiah tries not to fidget with the fabric of her shirt as she continues. "I found two that would make a pleasant addition to one of my fever reduction tonics. I would just need to be gone for a little while, so quick you would not know." The weight of the fear in her stomach makes her realize that no matter how much she trains with Fredrick, she will never be able to face the man in front of her. King Altair will always strike paralyzing fear straight into her heart.

It is one thing for her to play out all of the ways she can hurt this man with her words or dagger in the safety of her mind, but actually facing him is a different story. Elisiah does not know if it is the look in his green eyes or in the way his shoulders square slightly as she speaks that make his intentions known.

She knows no matter what she says, Altair will not let her leave this office.

Not without something in return at least.

"You cannot leave the protection of the town's gate by yourself. It is maddening and dangerous to think that. Look at how small you are. How petite and inexperienced. Anything could snatch you up, or anyone." He stands up from his chair and rounds his desk and comes to stand in front of her.

The way he says petite and inexperienced riles her anger, but she holds her smile and moves her hands behind her back to hide their trembling.

She forgot how much taller he is than her. He is six-foot-eight, and his round gut currently fights the two buttons just by his navel. She looks up at him and he down at her. He smells of stale mead and cured salted meats.

Do not worry, Little One.

That voice is back, and she is almost positive it is not hers. Why would she call herself Little One?

The King says, "Tell me, Elisiah, what would you do if a strong male came up to you out there beyond my immediate protection? Would you scream and run? Would you just stay there and take whatever punishment he thought you deserved the most?" Pulling her from her thoughts, a long, thick finger reaches out to brush a curl away from her face, and her blood goes cold. His touch leaves a trail on her skin.

She does not swallow, fearful that he will see any movement as a free invitation.

She does look past him towards the wall directly behind his head. She memorizes the color of the stone as she waits for him to finish what he is already going to say.

"Come on. Be a good girl and use your words. I want to hear you say which one you are. Are you a fighter or one of the ones that just lay there and take it?" His one finger has now turned into his whole hand engulfing her face.

He grabs her right by the chin and now her eyes are back on his. The hand on her face scrapes rough and hard against her skin; it is not something she wants to feel anywhere else or ever again.

The King steps forward.

His body is now almost flush with hers and her heart beats faster than it ever has before. She would rather get the lashings from her mother than this torment she just willingly walked into.

Something shifts in the room, but as far as she can tell, he has not felt it. Not knowing what caused it petrifies her but not more than what this hundreds-of-years-old Fae wants from her.

He goes to pull her against his chest, cutting what little space left between them even smaller.

Just before they become flush, another hand grabs the top of her left arm. It is a gentle but firm grasp.

Before she can register what happens, she falls away from the King and hits a solid wall with her back, and the hair in her hand falls to the floor as it flies open.

Altair growls in his throat at whoever pulls her away.

Calm your heart, little one.

He will not touch you again.

As the words just spoken in her head sink in, she does just that and counts to five before her breathing evens out. Not sure why she willingly takes advice from this voice without a body she has yet to see, but for more reasons than she can count, right now she feels safe.

She refuses to look behind her though.

"You have no reason to be where you do not belong, girl! How dare you sneak in here with those deranged shadows of yours? Do you know what I already have planned for your ignorance and defiance?" The King vibrates with anger. His hands shake at his side as he looks up at the wall behind Elisiah.

He has to look up at whoever this person is that now pins Elisiah to their front.

Without thinking, she feels behind her gently with her hands that hang at her side. She finds soft fabric first, then her fingers graze against the warmth of what she thinks is the top of the person's thigh. The hand holding her arm tightens with her touch, and she sucks in a breath before she asks a question in her own mind.

If you're an actual person and not just a figure of my imagination, can you please get me out of here? She feels stupid asking a voice in her head for help, but it works. The voice chuckles and replies.

Of course, Little One, but hold on.

Two arms wrap around Elisiah, and suddenly, darkness is all she can see.

The darkness must have been curious about her because small little wisps keep reaching out to her.

She dares and sticks her pointer finger out so one can wrap itself around her. It feels like a cold caress. it is nice to feel, and it makes whatever the things are happy. She can tell from the way they seem to speed their circling around her.

After what feels like just a couple of seconds, the darkness subsides and she looks around to see if she is dead or about to be.

The answer is neither.

Elisiah finds herself in a very spacious room with its own separate lounge area away from the bed itself. As she looks around the room and notes all the black fabrics that cover every piece of furniture, it occurs to her that she still does not know who took her out of that monstrosity of a meeting she brought upon herself.

Slowly, she turns around and looks to the space just behind her. A gasp catches in her throat at the female standing in front of her.

Her arms are crossed over her chest, and she looks at Elisiah.

Her eyes are the same color as honey, her short, slightly curly hair is the same dull ginger red that she once held in her hand. Elisiah swallows as she studies the person in front of her.

She notices a splatter of freckles from the area she can see of her nose, but a leather mask sits in the way of the rest.

This female in front of her is tall. She is no shorter than seven feet. Her clothes are all solid black and she has daggers on each thigh held by leather straps. Two more peek out from under her arms on her chest.

"Holy shit, you are gorgeous. How tall are you? I could climb you like a tree." It slips out of her mouth faster than she can grab it, but she still slaps her hands over her mouth to try and catch the words. She can feel her cheeks flush.

The ease she feels in this room scares her and makes her question her sanity.

The woman's hands slacken but do not fall from their holding place.

No one has ever called us such a name. Explain to me what it means to be gorgeous, Little One. Orien will not tell me, but we could work out the tree climbing. We would gladly let you climb us.

"Orien? Like the King's assassin? The King's weapon? The same Orien that no one ever sees?" Elisiah's hands still hover by her mouth, but now she is more shocked than scared.

This is the person behind all the horror stories told to her since her adolescence. The ones meant to scare the children and reprimand the adults for not falling in line. Constantly, adults replayed the nightly tale of a hidden apparition sent out to eat young children who did not obey their mothers.

Or even the demon that, when summoned, would suck the life right from a brutish soldier skin for refusing to slay his own friends. Her milk maid would tell her a different one each night before bed.

They never bothered Elisiah though. She always thought of them as made-up stories by a sick mad man. In fact, she thought the name Orien even belonged to a man.

Looking the towering woman up and down slowly, she can only make out one scar. It spreads from her thumb all the way across to her pinky finger on her left hand. The expanse of the scar is raised, the color is a dull pink compared to the rest of her. Lingering on the jagged edges, she wonders what caused such a thing. All the others must be concealed from sight in the long shirt and trousers.

Orien shifts her body to the side and tucks her left hand tightly under her crossed arms.

Now, Elisiah finds herself growing hot from embarrassment. She stood gawking at this predator like she could not be killed just by being in her presence.

She takes a step back to put some added space between them.

Turning away and looking around the room, she finds herself not seeing a single window. Only a four-poster bed big enough for an abnormally sized Fae, two bedside tables, a wardrobe, what looks to be a worktable with all different knives scattered around it, and finally the room next to it, filled with plush couches and wingback chairs.

Everything here is black.

"I should not be in here," Elisiah says softly more to herself than anyone else but is met with a response, nonetheless.

Well, we brought you here, so we think you should. We protect you now, Little One. You will not be alone again.

The voice speaking into her head seems to prance around like it is happy or proud to have succeeded.

"Wait. Hold on. What do you mean, protecting me? I do not need protection! I am more than capable of taking care of myself." Elisiah's voice raises as her guard goes up and her heart starts pumping faster.

She looks Orien in the eyes but what is a beautiful honey now shows solid black.

"Oh, shit," she thinks and slowly backs up another step, but the lower part of her back bangs into the low frame of an ornate black velvet couch. She braces her hand on the couch behind her as she watches Orien.

The predator tilts her head and slowly takes a step forward. Her hands now lay slack at her sides.

Was it protecting yourself when you willingly walked alone into the King's office, knowing that all he wants from you is the prize you have between your legs? If we had not been in the shadows, you would have been laying on that filth covered rug, used and left to be carried off like trash.

Elisiah swallows the lump in her throat and holds back the tears that sting her eyes. Orien is now so close to her that the smell of fresh water and embers fills her nose. It is the same smell from earlier.

This close, she can see the many small freckles that grace the warrior's face. The pale red eyebrows that sit in the perfect arch and the full lashes that frame her almond shaped eyes. Her ears are rounded.

The fae have pointed ears.

It does not matter in the end if you thought you had it under control, because as of this morning, we are now in charge of your protection.

The voice sounds frustrated with her, or it is angry at what she almost caused herself.

"I did not give anyone permission to protect me! I do not need to live under someone's thumb more than I already do!" She yells now. Her fear turns into blind hatred.

She hates this palace, the people that live in it and the people outside of it.

As swiftly as she can, Elisiah snakes her way from the couch and then sprints to the door just a few feet away. If she is fast enough, she can get out of this dungeon of a room and haul her ass to the kitchen to hopefully hide.

Fredrick will keep her safe, but he also keeps Orien's name hidden from her.

Before she can even grab the doorknob, a hand grabs her by the back of her neck and picks her up like a feather. Shoved against the door with her face turned to the side and a warm, surprisingly soft hand pushing against her neck, she panics internally. She closes her eyes tight and waits for what will happen next.

In this moment, for the first time, Elisiah realizes she is the type of person to freeze when in harm's way. The realization snaps her back to being frozen on that battlefield.

do not run, Little One, we do really love a chase. Only against us, you will surely lose.

Orien's breath that escapes from the mask caresses Elisiah's ear and then her body gently lowers to the ground. She turns her face to the door and rests her forehead against the cool wood, her hands flatten against the door.

The tears she has held back fall down her cheeks.

The feelings coursing through her body do not make sense for the situation she is currently in. Her tears flow from the frustration of this whole situation, but her body is on fire, and butter-flies flutter rapidly in her stomach.

We will not hurt you. We only want to protect you, even if it is against yourself sometimes. We will not touch you again without your permission.

The voice goes silent in her head for a moment before adding.

It would not be wise to go roaming about the castle. Not after how that little meeting concluded. We will get your belongings from your chambers. For now, all we ask is that you do not leave this room.

Before Elisiah could process anything that happened, she is met with complete silence. Her head and the room behind her are left empty.

Turning around with her back to the door, she slips down the wood.

Her ass hits the floor, and she brings her knees to her chest and begins to sob into them. The thought of trying to escape weighs on her shoulders, but she knows there is no running from Orien.

How could she run from someone who seems to live in the shadows?

If she is honest with herself, she would admit that right now she has nothing left: no fight, and no care.

She is not sure how her day ended up like this, but she does know that now she has much bigger problems than just the dream she had last night.

8

ORIEN

Orien had to leave her room. She had given the hunger-satisfied beast too much free reign. Why did she grab the woman she now knew was named Elisiah like that?

The control she possesses to keep her hands to herself disappears when the new female is around.

She runs her hands down her face where they catch on the muzzle. The cool black leather adorned with brass rivets on each side of her mouth is a reminder of what can change if the King feels like she has embarrassed him. It has become another part of her over the years, but she still finds it hard to accept, which was the purpose for which it was made.

Alister thought it would cause Orien enough frustration in her day to day life that she would think back to the time she made him look weak in his own castle. The memory replays in her head most days, and for the days that it does not, she can almost imagine what it feels like to use her jaw again.

Orien does not think Alister would have enchanted the mask to her face if she required a normal eating schedule like others, or even a normal diet.

The young woman can go days, even weeks without eating, and not feel a single hunger pain. It is a benefit to having the beast live inside her head. They both crave the taste of the life that runs through people's veins, even though that cannot always be obtained. She normally keeps her meals to the game animals that reside in the Univier forest.

Lowering her hands in frustration, she walks down the halls almost blind to where she needs to go. "She will probably try to escape the room," she thinks. "Maybe I should have put a chest on the outside of the door?"

Where would she go?

The beast pauses.

She seems trapped in the castle just like she is trapped in our room. Surely, a hideaway from her King is more pleasing then where he can easily find her.

Orien listens to the beast while it rambles about Elisiah's current situation, but she cannot help the anger she has for herself in the moment. The lack of control she has shown in just a brief period makes her want to rip through the castle walls with her bare hands.

She has to get everything of Elisiah's transferred back to her quarters before the woman she left behind finds a way out. The idea of locking the door from the outside did not even cross her mind, so Orien may get back to the rooms and find them all empty. Even though the beast thinks otherwise.

What Elisiah does not know is that Orien would hunt her down even if she did escape.

Does Orien even know why she would go to such lengths to keep someone she just met in her reach? No. The answer is no, but she also does not care.

Elisiah is her problem now. A problem that seems like it will be fun to have.

"I suppose I could cuff her to my side. If she had free rein to walk around the palace then maybe I should change that. I know for certain that the bastard who tried to defile her will try again, if not today than another." Orien is glad that she had followed the woman who is now currently in her bed chambers to the King's office. Even though the sight of Alister placing his hands on Elisiah made her want to boil the skin from his bones in one of Fredrick's simmering pots. Orien is sure that the old chef would not mind. In fact, Fredrick would probably place his little wood stool right by the bubbling water just to watch the look on Alister's face.

What Orien would not give to pay the royal highness back for everything he has given her throughout the years. To see his body just as riddled with scars from the beatings she would make him endure.

The sight of Alister Altair's hands on Elisiah flash in her mind once again, fueling the anger she already drowns in.

Can we do more touching? Did you feel how soft her skin was? We could swim in it.

The beast sighs as if imagining what it would be like to be in Elisiah's skin. Orien rolls her eyes and tries to shut out the annoying plus one she has always carried around. The beast does not even listen to her right now, and apparently is not too worried about the fact she is still talking.

Oh! Let me smell our hands! Let me smell our hands! I bet it still smells like her.

This statement stops Orien in her tracks while taking a deep calming breath before she tries to stick her hand through her skull and drag out whatever it is that lives inside her.

"That is such a perverted request. I am not even going to acknowledge that you just spoke that aloud. Keep those thoughts to yourself." Orien swears she can feel a thump against the side of her brain.

It does not stop her from slightly looking down to her hand that held Elisiah against the door before she curses herself and takes another deep breath.

Well, we are we. I am not me and you are not you. We are we. One is the same as the other. Our thoughts are just that.

Ours.

This is just insane.

She realized years ago that she is certifiably insane. Now, she must come to accept that a part of her may be a tiny bit perverted. It is hard to comprehend because she has never felt like this. Orien knows she is a number of horrible things, but she never thought one of those to be a pervert.

The beast has never felt like this. Just seeing Elisiah in the kitchen this morning was enough to send both of them off the rails.

She could still smell the woman's scent in her nose and feel the way her body felt pressed against hers in the Kings office.

The way her slim hands touched her legs in curiosity. How she did not fight to get away when she was pinned against the door.

That would be something they would work on; she needs to learn to protect herself. A shiver runs down Orien's spine, her eyes closing at the thought of teaching the woman hand to hand combat.

Opening her eyes, she starts walking back toward the wing that holds Elisiah's scent the strongest, the South wing. The quicker she can gather the woman's belongings, the quicker she can get back to her.

It is not hard for Orien to find the room she needs. The essence of Elisiah is soft and her aroma allowed Orien to find her way so easily.

The beginning of her started as warmed vanilla and fresh pressed Callamon leaves. The leaves release a light beige oil when pressed firmly and can be used as perfume or in a tonic to aid a healer's gift.

When it is used in a perfume, the smell could only be described as sweet and spicy; it is pure femininity, but not a smell that will knock you on your feet with its strength.

Orien lets the scent warm her nose as she pushes open the small wood door. Her size makes the door frame look like it belongs to one of the dwarfs that live in the center of town. Ducking her head as she walks through the threshold, she takes in the small space.

The bed that looks like it would hold a small child sits in the middle of the room, its headboard against the left wall.

There is no way Elisiah can sleep comfortably on a bed of that size. Her back has to ache constantly if she holds herself to keep from hanging off its edges.

On the wall to Orien's left sits what she thinks might be the wardrobe. The wood box on legs looks like it can only hold four daily dresses. Too small for an adult.

Across the doorway, right in front of her, there is a wood desk with a stool. To its right is a window so small she doubts a rattle rat could come and go from it. The tiny animals spend their time thieving from any place they can squeeze their bodies into. Elisiah's room hit the bill of their go-to hiding spaces.

Walking further into the so-called bedchamber, Orien decides she will only take back what she can carry in her arms, leaving the rest for another day. So, she grabs what little bit of clothing hangs in the standalone closet. Noticing a couple of small drawers towards the bottom, she opens them to make sure she does not forget any undergarments. The small spaces look like they would be the perfect spot to tuck away the more delicate articles of clothing.

Checking the small drawers under the hanging bar, Orien stops in her tracks. Inside the bottom drawer is a medium-sized brown leather book. It is not what Orien thought would be in the space, but it makes for a good surprise.

The book is sealed with a single strand of thin leather that wraps itself around a thick brown sewn on button.

We are going to read it right? We would adore seeing what goes on in that small head of hers. The answer to why she willingly went to Alister's office could make sense if we did.

The beast cackles as Orien does not hesitate to unwrap the strap of leather, her finger flipping through the pages. The majority of what she skims is nothing but recipes for healing tonics and topical ointments. She knows Elisiah is a sorceress, but she has more knowledge of the flowers and vines that grow around the area than Orien gave her credit for. It piques her interest even more.

Continuing to look over the pages, she slows her pace to study the depictions of all the varied materials she has used in her studies. Sketches ranging from flowers, animals, and different types of jars fill the pages along with scattered sentences of information about each. The ink work is straight like a steady head painted onto the page with confident ease.

"She is smart and she can draw." The statement which she directs to herself, receives an answered nod in return.

In the very back of the book, one page catches her eye. This page is not like the others. Instead of filling every blank piece of parchment with knowledge and descriptive pictures, the single page depicts two sets of wings, drawn in thick black scratchy ink. The images are hurried, like someone was afraid of losing their mind's sight of them.

One set of the wings is covered in what looks like feathers, broadly set and outstretched. It feels like the wings could ooze power from the tips. At the base of them, streaks flow from the unfinished stumps like waves in a vast expanse of water. Over the top of the wings is a scribbled sentence that read:

"Wings as bright as Birth Light and as breathtaking as the sun."

Orien lets the sentence sit in her brain as she tries to understand the meaning. All she can think of is how bright and all-consuming the Birth Light is said to be.

She learned in her own course of studies from when she was a child that Birth Light has long since been gone from their world of Sytherac.

It was the main source of power for the Angels that fought in The Eternal War, given to them by their maker, Lixtis. He was a God at one point, but his name has since been erased from history. The arrogance the God had to start such a gruesome and bloody war was enough to make even his own creations turn on him.

He became so overrun by the thought of obtaining power that even his own brother gave up hope that Lixtis would some day change. Even the dead gave up on the thought of the salvation he promised.

The power that flowed through the Angels' veins was enough to scorch a Fae or mortal to ash with just one glance at their eyes. The few still living Fae warriors that told the tales of the great Astrial Angels said that they would often wear white silk bands to cover their eyes. It was the only way they could hold council with anyone not of their own kind.

For such a power, it was not strong enough however to completely demolish their enemies, the Demonians, but it was enough to cause enough damage that it would slow their heal-ing. Then they would give the final blow to ensure certain death.

Orien once read a passage about a female Angel who was the lead commander of the Astrial army. The female's name was Vanora, and it is believed that she was the first to be created by Lixtis. Some called her The Shining Star due to the amount of Birth Light the God of Souls gifted her with. None of the other

Angels have ever come close to the amount of rupturing light that Lixtis is made from, even his dearest Vanora.

The history writers, from which most of the books are written, say that only a true heir could match the brightness of the God made from Light himself. Orien is not sure if the being could even produce an heir. Better yet she is not even sure if someone would willingly procreate with the arrogant bastard.

Leveling her eyes to look at the wings under the words she has been studying, her brows scrunch.

Orien presses her free hand to the middle of her chest. An ache has set in, and phantom hairline fractures start breaking their way down each side of her ribs. Taking in a deep inhale of shaking breath, the creature in her head shrinks away into a dark corner of her mind. It does not hide completely, though. The beast is as curious as her; the questions rip through her brain and bounce off the confines of her cranium.

Before looking at the second pair drawn on the bottom of the page, she rips the parchment from the book, folding it into a neat square before placing it in the pocket of her trousers.

The shattering feeling in her ribs slowly subsides as her breathing evens itself out. After regaining her composure, Orien grabs what she can carry in her arms. The assassin raids Elisiah's small bed chamber with ease and precision to make sure she only grabs the necessities.

Using her shadows to project her back to her own rooms, she finds that her brain is on fire from the anger swirling through it as she thinks about all she has felt today. The wings and the reaction she had to them do not help her mood at all.

It feels like something familiar yet not at the same time. We have had to see such a thing before to feel as we did?

Slowly lurking back from the dark corner of her mind, the beast comes closer to her left eye and peers outward. They both look around the sitting room for the female they left here for what feels like not even an hour, but from the stillness of the castle, it has to have been longer.

Orien does not answer the curious question as she walks to the large black leather wingback lounging couch.

It sits directly across from the entrance door.

She looks around the space and does not see Elisiah. Slowly, she circles the room, smelling the scent coming off every piece of furniture and following it to the washroom. Pushing open the arched wood door, billowing steam hits her in the face.

A slosh of water comes over the rim of the brass soaking tub in the center of the room, and the body inside of it sinks down until all is hidden except her head. A tightness in Orien's chest eases at the sight of the other woman. Elisiah looks like she could be in a small body of water due to the size of the tub compared to her.

Stepping closer to the floating head, Orien's eyes narrow to slits, anger rushing to her surface as she thinks of the secrets this person is hiding. A million ways she could torture them out of her come rushing to her brain, but before she can bring them to fruition, a small, soft voice says, "Do not come any closer."

Orien's left eye turns completely black as the now feral beast fully takes in the sight. If that small part of her was not infatuated by Elisiah moments ago then right now, it overflows.

A small gasp comes from Elisiah, and the beast finally speaks in her head.

We could not find you in the sitting room, and your smell did not linger in the bedroom. The aroma came strongest from here, so this is where we came.

Both of Orien's eyes lock with the light warm brown of Elisiah's, and she feels a tug to move forward but instead her feet stay planted to their spot. Even the one that just spoke felt the pull, but instead of being its normal impulsive self, it agrees to stay perfectly still.

The feeling is new to both Orien and the beast; it is nothing like anything they have felt before. The only thing that comes close to describing it is being branded with a hot iron rod. Only in a different way from what has been done to her before; this was a welcome sensation that made her whole body burn with warmth.

"What is wrong with your eye and why do you talk like that? You are one person, but you talk like you speak for a group." Elisiah's head bobs in the water around her.

"Also, do you not know how to knock?" Each question is full of demand as she asks them with rapid fire. The water ripples as Elisiah crosses her arms over her chest and slowly raises her knees to cover her more delicate parts.

The questions snap both Orien and the beast out of their trance, leaving the burning that scorched Orien inside to slowly dwindle to smoldering embers.

Only the feeling does not completely die out.

This black is mine; the brown is hers. We are one physical being, but I am my own. My language is not one of your knowledge, so this tongue is second learned.

Why would we knock when this is our home? You are the foreign creature in our sanctuary. I speak for us to those that choose to listen, Little One.

Orien waits for the information to sink in as she stands perfectly still a couple of feet from the tub. Her chest does not even seem to rise and fall with each breath as both herself and the thing inside of her head stare at the new person in their space. The smell of vanilla and Callamon swims up their nose and fills their head with bursts of fragrance.

Elisiah does not know the leash she has on both of them right now in this small room; if she did, she would most likely run. Or she would take advantage of the situation.

The beast and Orien fight the urge to pull her out of that tub.

"Let me get this straight. I have not been talking to Orien but another person in her head. Does that mean I am willingly letting you in my head?" Elisiah's eyes are curious.

"If I can block your way let me know because I would gladly choose that path rather than this weird mind to mouth shit, and you know what? It is common knowledge to knock on a closed door, no matter where the door is. Especially if you think someone may occupy the room." The way Elisiah speaks tightens Orien's chest like a rope being pulled slowly around her. It strikes her as odd since she has not had the same feeling for anyone else. The only way she can describe it is how a mother Wulve must feel when the smallest of the pack brings back its first kill. Orien wishes she could understand how this person soaking in her tub can speak to her so bluntly but would not try to stop Alister from advancing on her.

Elisiah sinks her mouth under the water just enough to blow a string of bubbles with her frustration.

Orien's height allows her to look down at the top of the warm water, even though the steam flowing from the top of it blurs what is underneath the surface.

Orien is not sure which one reflects the Water Light more beautifully, the water in the brass tub or the deep mahogany skin just above the surface. She and the beast know that the brown eyes, a shade lighter than her skin, notice the shift in eye contact.

It does not stop their track from the expanse of skin they can see to her eyes rimmed with thick black lashes then to her long black hair, cascading down her neck and swimming in the water behind her. Orien envies the way her hair wraps itself around the base of her shoulders and sits against her narrow neck.

The tight ringlet curls are nowhere to be found, taken away by the weight of the water. It is a sight that makes Orien wish she had a photographic memory. Elisiah looks like a goddess in this moment, she even seems to glow just slightly compared to her surroundings.

Finally, she makes her way back to Elisiah's eyes but not before studying the sculpted cheekbones that frame the long slender base of her nose and end at full plump lips.

Orien has not talked to anyone since she was four. We do not remember the sound or cadence of our voice. The one you hear now is that of my own creation, and as for your mind, it has been open from the first moment we saw you.

That could be a problem but not one we cannot solve.

The beast chuckles at the curiosity and questions of the woman but it makes Orien nervous. What could she do with the information she learns about her? Even though Orien feels like there is something different about Elisiah, the thought of information being used against herself is still a fear.

Still, the voice continues,

As for us knocking, that is highly unlikely. We are not apologetic when we tell you that we are not nice. The last thing we concern ourselves with is the mannerisms of you soft-hearted mortal beings.

We have trained since before we can remember to be nothing more than a weapon. You will find that we lack empathy.

Now, your scarce number of belongings are on one of the loungers in the sitting room. We must go check on the business we have before we can go to sleep.

Enjoy our soaking tub.

With the last bit of sanity she has intact, Orien turns and leaves the washroom.

Shutting the door behind her, she rubs at her eyes. Taking off the clothes on her body and washing her freshly cut hair is all she wants to do. With the scent of Elisiah wrapping around her head and slowly blanketing her bones, she cannot do so in that room.

Orien walks to her wardrobe and grabs her loose black lounge pants and a simple black pullover shirt missing its arms. Clothes in hand, she disappears down to the smaller waterfall by the lower side of the castle to clear her head.

This waterfall is at the base of the Fall of Souls; this one is not important enough to warrant a name. Orien found it in one of her hunting lessons when she was ten years old and has grown fond of the small body of water.

She would find ways to sneak away from the confines of her bed chamber during her time trapped there, rather than wait to train and study in secret in the dungeons under the castle.

Everything about her existence is a secret. Even to herself she was a secret; Orien had no answers to any of the questions she had about her own existence. One day she learned to stop caring. It was the same day the muzzle became a part of her face when she was four.

The sudden memory makes her look down to her left hand that holds her clothes in a clenched fist. It makes the rough, ragged scar pull, growing wider across the expanse of the back of her hand.

One of Altair's golden rules when she was growing up in the castle was that she was to never be around any of the others. Only a select, trusted few had clearance to know of her existence.

It was the first rule that had ever been broken and the first scar she had ever received. It was not, however, the last time she would be beaten or maimed until a part of her was unrecog-. nizable.

Still, looking at her hand plunges her mind into the depths and replays the memory of that day.

She was left to eat her morning meal in the main dinner hall where most of the knights gathered.

Fredrick was to care for her that day as he was one of the most trusted captains of the King's army at the time. He was already aging significantly, and his movements were not what they used to be. He left her for what felt like seconds to gather the extra plate of food for himself on a serving cart that sat just inside a small hall in a servant's door which led directly to a passage for traveling unseen.

That small passageway joined to the same corridor as the kitchen.

In those seconds, a young guard, that she still does not know the name of, came through the doors. He immediately spotted her eating her portion of meal oats, a look of curiosity on his face.

Even from across the room she could smell the dirt on his hands and face from what she assumed was his morning training. The shining oil used to polish the white and gold of their daily armor made her nose wrinkle in protest.

She kept her head down and tried to forget that an unknown person had walked into a space that was supposed to be cleared of all life except for hers. This was supposed to be space to be out in the open for once.

The feeling of being watched set her skin cold, but the feeling also set her eyes to burning in their sockets. She knew about her beast even then at her early age, but she did not know about the control she needed to keep it at bay. It was all new to her.

She was just a child.

As the curious guard made his way closer, he chuckled and said, "Are you that little freak of a child the older captain talks about all the time? He cannot help himself, but he likes to talk about the power you already show at such an immature age. He is full of shit and would be better off rotting in the ground."

The way this man talked about Fredrick made her seethe with anger. The smirk that sat on his lips made her want to rip it off his face.

He came to rest at her left side and ran a dirt covered hand down her long red ponytail at the time. Orien could smell the thoughts running through his head. It was a mix of jealousy and hatred for a child he had never met before, and that was enough to tell her beast that he was not a person to leave breathing. If he could see an innocent person and hate them, then he is what made the word such an awful place.

Orien kept her eyes down, but her body was already reacting to the threat she felt in the air.

"He did fail to mention how pretty of a thing you are. How mature you look." He traced down the side of her jaw with the back of his knuckles, and his hand ended up circling around her chin.

His grip went tight, as he tried to turn her face to him.

Orien stayed as still as stone, her blood froze in her veins while her head and eyes only burned hotter. This was the first time her body knew she was either going to kill someone or die. For a split second, Orien felt fear setting in.

Sadly, for the piss poor excuse of a man, Orien could not die, and that fear vanished as soon as she remembered who she was. She could feel the little beast coming further to the surface, and all she wanted to do was escape from the moment, so she let the small untamed thing take her spot in the room.

Her head finally turned to meet him, and the way he pulled his hand back from her face like she had just bitten him made the beast smile.

Little did he know how hard and fierce her bite really was.

He put his hand on his dagger that was strapped to the outer side of his armor. "What the fuck is wrong with you?" His face was painted in disgust as he took in the sight of her black eyes that seemed endless and the matching veins spidering down her face.

The beast looked him in the eyes and said in a voice that wasn't Orien's own, "We thought we were beautiful?" The voice she heard would soon be one she would come to know but this was the first time she had heard it speak. The young boy cursed again and pulled out his dagger.

Orien and the beast looked at that small metal weapon and laughed together as they stood from her chair slowly. He made no effort to try and calm his heart rate as she walked towards him with a smile on her face that revealed a mouth full of needle-like teeth. They all sat against each other perfectly, but she had many more of them than she did her regular teeth.

Even her elongated fangs did not compare to the lethal things that now took up the space of her mouth. Without even a second guess, the scared guard lunged at the beast now in front of him, but it took no effort for the beast to move her body like liquid around the man jumping for hers.

Black shadows engulfed the room and took any light with them, the sinister veins turned her hands completely black and tipped them with claws. The same lethal needles as her teeth now adorned each of her fingers. Orien could smell the artery in the soldier's neck as he regained his footing and lunged close again. It caught her off guard because the beast became feral at the smell and quick pulse of his heart. She could sense the blood speeding in his veins and all the spots she needed to bite to cause enough damage.

Orien could smell the tainted spirit of his soul.

That little second of distraction was all he needed to slice completely through her left hand. The pain was almost unbearable, but to her surprise the coldness of her blood rushed to the damaged hand.

Blinding white light flared through her eyes like a bolt of lightning. When she did not feel the searing pain of her hand anymore, she looked down and saw that her hand was back together with nothing but the hair of a scar. The beast did not seem surprised at the burst of light, but to Orien it was something new.

When she regained her composure in her head, the beast had complete control of her movements. The culprit was pinned against the dining table, and her small body was hunched over him. She felt the warm slosh of blood as she realized the beast was ripping the artery from his neck. He screamed and begged as blood covered every surface around them. All he did was spur her to move faster.

The beast began to drink deeply from his neck and rip more bite size chunks from all the soft parts of his body. Even the foul-tasting armor did not stand a chance against being ripped to shreds under her claws and teeth.

Orien remembers when Fredrick came into the room and instead of screaming for help, he silently walked to her and placed a hand on her back. Fredrick knew it would happen sooner than later. He had once said something like, "You can only keep a wild animal in a cage so long before it bites its handler."

She continued to devour the now completely still man under her. Orien was lost in the hunger and anger that consumed every part of her. The pieces of him that did not make it down her throat landed all around them in harsh, wet, splats. She finished as quickly as it began and immediately the little part of her that controlled the massacre retreated to the back of her head and waited, panting.

Orien took in the slaughter with her own eyes for the first time. It did not make her feel anything, but she was completely satisfied for the first time and content that she had killed a threat. She had protected herself, and it felt nice to know what she could do.

When she turned, she felt the familiar hand resting on her back. Fredrick looked at the ground, but his face was laced with grief. She knew it was not for the man she just practically ate. No, he was scared for her and what the King might inflict on the young girl.

Later, that day when Altair made Fredrick bring her down to her usual chamber in the damp dungeons, the old man's fears came true.

The punishment she received was a permanent, thick, and hideous scar across her left hand that marked where the sword should have severed it.

Orien also received enough lashings with an iron tipped whip that her back looked like it had been torn from her bones. Her age did not matter to a King that wanted her broken and obedient, so the punishment for the one act he saw as rebellion and an embarrassment on his name has never ended since that day.

❖❖❖❖❖❖

The muzzle on her face is proof of that to her and Fredrick, who he made watch the entire time. Leaving her head finally, Orien shuts the mental door to more turmoil wanting to sneak past their confines and make her day even worse.

Stripping down completely, even removing the brown leather strap covering her breasts to immerse herself in the cool water, Orien checks her trouser pocket for the single piece of paper taken from Elisiah's notebook. Gently, she places the piece of parchment by her binding band that lays by the different sheaths holding her daggers.

Bathing in the waterfall gives Orien the feeling that she finally knows what it means to be herself. To just have one moment of being normal. Here, at the waterfall with no name, she feels like the others she has lived amongst and watched daily.

Even though her eyes see their world of Sytherac in dull colors, and her emotional skills are completely underdeveloped, even she needs a break from the life she leads sometimes.

After washing herself clean using some nectar from one of the native plants that grow along the waterside in Univier, Orien exits the water. She shakes out what is left of her red hair, throwing droplets of water around her.

Orien can stand on the dirt edge of the waterfall for hours completely nude if she chooses to; no one ever comes this way. The fishermen of the Kingdom think that no fish live in the small pond at the base of the falls, and it is their loss because the water creatures love the environment here.

Drying herself with the large piece of cloth she brought from her room, Orien leisurely pulls on her clothes. Her mind is at peace but she finds her thoughts trailing back to the woman that soaked in her tub and the beautiful skin that peeked out of the water's surface.

Gripping her soiled clothes from the day along with the single piece of notebook parchment, Orien lets the images of Elisiah fill her head.

From the first time Orien laid eyes on her silhouette while in the kitchen with Fredrick to the pure anger that shone in her eyes when Evadne drew blood from her arm. The way her fist pelted Orien's chest, and the salty smell of her tears.

Orien wants it all from Elisiah, from a woman she just met, and she does not know why.

Her shadows make their way from any exposed flesh as she runs her hand through her short cropped hair. The beast in her head has been content watching the visuals of Elisiah as they pass through their mind.

She is truly breathtaking.

Orien takes in a breath to clear her mind. "I know," she thinks to herself as the shadows take her back into the main sitting room of her safe space.

Orien finds the warmth of a fire in the hearth, filling the room. Keeping the scrap of paper tightly held in her balled fist along with her clothes, Orien does not bother looking for Elisiah. Not when she already knows exactly where she is simply by the way the tug in her chest tries pulling her body towards the lounging couch just to the left of the fire.

The tug is something that Orien just does not understand; it is starting to bother her. All she knows right now is that something in her has changed. In fact, everything changed the moment she laid eyes on Elisiah, and that was not something she expected.

9

ELISIAH

Elisiah watches Orien leave the washroom, sinking down into the tub completely submerging her head. She screams under the water until the last bubble leaves her mouth, then she reluctantly allows herself to float back up to the surface.

The Fae female is insufferable and more confusing than any potion or elixir she has ever had to concoct. Elisiah even thinks to herself that Orien may even be more complicated than her own ability as a Seer and what it takes to untangle what she sees.

Stepping out of the brass soaking tub, she dries herself with a medium-sized body cloth made from the fibers of a multipur-pose grass called Wyrkettle. It is a commonly-growing grass across the many Kingdoms that make up the world of Sytherac and is harvested for fabric-making. Wyrkettle is best used for drying cloths, infant tailclouts, and women's rags due to its ability to absorb more liquid than its weight.

Forgetting that she did not have anything to change into before getting into the water earlier, Elisiah now has to trust that Orien is not waiting in the sitting room. The smell of the King's mystery assassin and head warrior lingers around the space but is not as strong as it once was. She takes this as an approving sign that Orien left after exiting the washing room.

If not, then the woman is going to see her, covered only by the nude-colored body cloth. It would not be anything Orien did not see over the lip of the brass tub. Elisiah tries to keep her body cradled in on itself and hopes the elixir she dumped in the water will not wear off, taking the billowing steam with it.

As Elisiah steps into the room, she lets out a breath of relief when she is greeted by an empty room. What few belongings Orien brought back for her sit in the exact spot the assassin said they would be. Elisiah does not hesitate to search through the clothes for her white nightslip and matching underlings.

"Did Orien have to dig through my delicates?" Elisiah asks herself in a whisper as she holds her underwear in her hand. The thought makes her top lip curl as she sucks in a breath through clenched teeth.

After sitting with the cloth still wrapped around her, staring at her white underwear in her hand, Elisiah finally gets herself dressed.

Looking through the rest of her things to make sure all of the more important items made it back to her still intact, she finds her brown leather parchment book. Without hesitation, she brings it to her chest, relief washing over her body. Elisiah finds herself pleased that Orien managed to bring everything she needed or could want. Anything that is left in her room will not be missed because everything that held any significance to her is in this new space.

Satisfied with the outcome of a stranger retrieving her property, Elisiah takes a look around.

The piece of furniture under her is stunning and feels like sitting on clouds. Elisiah closes her eyes as she takes in the relief of not having a piece of broken wood stab at her through an old, tattered mattress. Soaking in the comfort swimming through her body, her mind wanders to what happened earlier in the washroom, as her hands wrap themselves around the book she still has not put down.

The way Orien looked at her was something she had never experienced before. It was a look of realization and disconnection at the same time. Elisiah is also aware that who she has been talking to is not the actual person standing in front of her, but something else in Orien's head.

The voice never matched Orien's face to begin with, but now Elisiah knows that she is never going to meet the real Orien, the one who makes her feel safe even when Elisiah knows she should not.

The feeling of those two-colored eyes staring at her makes her stomach swim, and the scent of Orien still wiggles its way up Elisiah's nose, especially as she reclines back on a lounger that had to be built for an exceptionally large person.

Elisiah has never smelled anything like her before.

Orien smells like a freshly lit fire burning in a field, damp with rain. Her essence is like that of safety and danger. Thinking about it made Elisiah's insides flutter. She could not think about the feelings she felt though, because as she looks around, she realizes she is stuck in this large room with nothing but herself and the materialistic belongings beside her.

It switches her thoughts from comfort into a burning hatred.

"Who does she think she is, honestly? She cannot lock me in her rooms, dump my things, barge into the washroom, and then just leave. This is insane." Elisiah is filled to the brim with rage as she talks to herself, sitting forward to rest her elbows on her knees.

The parchment book rests in her hands as she hangs her head. Looking up at her book, she sighs and tosses it on the top of a well-constructed table in the center of all the furniture.

The face of the male warrior she saw in her dream last night comes rushing back in her head as she rubs at her eyes to try and stop the unwanted memory. Elisiah has many things to figure out in her life right now, and the reality of it weighs heavy on her slim shoulders.

Wanting to try and ease the tension in her body, she decides to snoop through the spaces she is now confined to. Trying to escape is not on her mind since she has never truly been free anyway. This new place is just a part of the Stone Castle that Elisiah has not experienced before, and right now she wants to experience it all for herself.

Luckily, for her, she knows what it feels like to be the waiting prey for a stronger predator, so she does not panic. Her whole life has been spent in much smaller spaces than this one where if she were to make any sound she would have been met with consequences.

Most of the time it was always the same punishment for those things that were seen as acts of disobedience. Always a thin but resilient branch from a Wiliper tree, used to strike her back until it bled like many tiny rivers. The one to decide and administer her torment was the one that gave birth to her, her mother.

The hatred Elisiah carries in her body for that horrid woman equals the sickening level of hatred her mother has for her. Elisiah does not understand how a mother can beat their child or how they can hate their own flesh and blood so much. Elisiah has spent every night of her life thinking about what she has done to deserve the treatment she receives, but she has come up empty for an answer.

She has never known why her feelings stacked up on top of each other the way they do. Just that they do, and with no outlet to release all the pent up anger or sadness, Elisiah would find herself stuck in bed for many days. The young woman would not eat, bathe, drink, or even sleep.

She felt like a hollow shell those days.

It was like she stood on the outside of her body and the shell just laid there, staring at anything that would stay still long enough, unflinching under her unblinking gaze. Fredrick was always the only one to notice her absence in those days.

The old man would come by during his afternoons and offer her everything he had with him to try and muster a response from her. His face always looked so frightened, and she would make herself sick from crying after regaining herself back in her body. She hated herself more for the fact that she worried him so much.

Despite her body constantly being beaten, it does not bear any scars from her years of punishments, but her heart does. It did not grow hard and calloused, no, it grew bruised and tender like the flesh of a thrown-around fruit. To Elisiah, that hurt worse than anything else she had experienced. The heart is one of the most important organs, and hers is beaten and bruised by the hands of the woman that created it to begin with.

All that matters to her mother is that her body stays perfect and young, so that Elisiah is always appetizing to the one man she has been promised to since before her birth. Everything about her has been made and shaped into what he likes in his women, even if he is hundreds of years older than her.

Three hundred and ninety-one years older than her to be precise.

The racing memories and thoughts do not help to calm her body as she walks around. As she enters the bedchamber to the right of the sitting room, she stops in her tracks. The view makes her take a second look around the room.

In the center of the far wall, directly in front of her is a huge four-poster bed made of black stained wood. The bed coverings look like they are made from the darkest night skies. Under the bed, and covering most of the expanse of the dark wood floor, rests an oval shaped rug. Elisiah cannot help but walk over to the rug and rub her feet across it. She is delighted when the soft fur meets her feet. From what she can see, it is a chestnut brown color mixed with white and black.

Looking back at the bed, Elisiah runs her hand across the bed covers. As she rustles the coverings, the smell of fire and fresh morning dew fill her head. Every muscle in her body tries to pull its own way onto the bed. All her nerve ends spark like live wires as she balls her fist into the silken sheets. Closing her eyes, she lets the comforting smell take her thoughts away. Not sure how long she stands there enjoying the emptiness now in her head, she opens her eyes and realizes just what she is doing. She lets go of the sheets and walks away from the bed and plush fur on the floor. The coldness that comes over her is not just from the wood floor under her bare feet anymore, it is something else as well.

It is emptiness.

It is loneliness.

Rushing out of the bedroom, Elisiah covers her face with her hands. Her body feels like something that does not belong to her all over again.

Finding the fireplace at the other side of the sitting room, all she can think about is relieving herself from the chill that has planted itself in her bones. Elisiah takes the wood from the right corner of the room and pieces it together like a puzzle, making sure to leave a gap for air flow in the center. She finds the starter match just off to the same side as the wood. Taking the striking tool from the leather holder that keeps it from the elements of the room, Elisiah scrapes the metal bar against a slim stone that shares the space in the leather holder. Fredrick taught her how to light a fire in several different ways so that she would always be prepared for whatever reason. Elisiah also loves reading, but she has a vast amount of survival knowledge that she has not been able to use, yet.

The sparks made from hitting the metal rod and stone together set the dry wood ablaze in the small hole in the stone wall. Sitting on her knees while staring at the fire, Elisiah cannot help but think about what the next few days will bring for herself and Orien.

So much has changed in a day but also so little. It is just a new area of the castle and a new person over her imprisonment. She will undoubtedly have to face Altair, and that alone holds so many unknowns. The fear that streaks through her chest feels like lightning. It is enough to take her breath away.

Elisiah stands to her feet when she decides to walk to the small table in the center of the room to grab her parchment book. If her mind wants to race then she should focus it on something useful, like trying to figure out any key points to her latest dream.

Flipping the book open to the next empty page just after her list of useful flowers that grew around the circling Kingdoms, she searches for her ink and quill. Finding them both sitting wrapped in one of her billowy white button-down blouses, she pauses as she takes in how carefully Orien wrapped them. A small smile tries to show on her face but she will not let it form; it feels wrong.

Wetting the quill after setting the ink pot on the table, she begins writing down the main details that she can recall right off the top of her head.

I stood in a vast, open, blood-soaked field. The smell of iron was heavy in my nose but the sounds of metal striking metal was deafening. The body of the man I stood on turned my stomach, my beef stew from that evening fighting to come back up. When the bodies of fallen soldiers hit the ground, it shook like the beginning tremors of a world-shaking storm.

What seemed to plant in my mind the most was the way the man in black and silver armor, adorned with engravings of a hellish looking hound, looked at the women in front of him.

His face was void of any wrinkles or signs of long nights of fighting to the death; his eyes were solid black. They looked like they could swallow any light, and I felt a sense of familiarity in them. His deep brown hair laid over his ears and down part of his neck, slickened with sweat.

The black veins that took over his hands and slithered their way around his face made him look like he could have been infected with a disease. In his right hand, poised to block an attack, was a solid black sword. The smoke that rippled off the beast of a weapon danced in tune with the screams around them, like it was feeding and refueling.

He was a remarkable looking male.

Even more striking though was how his face was painted in what I could only describe to be pure admiration. I did not know why, but I wanted to find out how a soldier could admire their enemy. Just like I want to find out why it all felt so familiar to me.

Putting down her quill and closing her book, she is fatigued.

"Finally", she thinks to herself, but she has no idea where she is supposed to sleep or even where her captor ran off to. Her stomach makes an angry protest as she remembers she has not eaten since this morning.

Elisiah, tired, and drained from her day, flops herself down on the couch she has occupied since Orien first forced her into the room.

The fire cracks and pops as she lays her left arm over her eyes, and she stretches her legs in front of her. She has absolutely no clue where the kitchen is from here, and she has no clue how to get out of the room to even think about finding her way there.

As she lies in silence, listening to the crackle of the wood, Elisiah suddenly smells fresh water mixed with the cold scent of the air. Raising up on her elbows, she finds Orien standing in front of the fire she had lit. Nothing would have given away her sudden presence in the room if it were not for the way the woman threw her soiled clothes on the ground beside her. The female stands perfectly still, watching the flames eat away at the logs.

She finds herself watching Orien the same way as Orien watches the fire. The black semi-loose trousers traded places with a pair of black loose-fitting lounge pants and a black blouse with no sleeves.

Based on the raw edges, she guesses they were cut out. The arms that exit the holes are pale white, covered in muscles and small freckles. The long sleeve blouse from earlier did well to hide the pure strength that shows now in her arms. The way the shirt stretches across the expanse of her back reveals just how many hours she has put into her training.

The dull ginger of her short, cropped hair is damp with water, and it makes the earlier small loose curls fall in clumps around her face. Only the thick black straps of the muzzle are completely dry. Something aches in Elisiah's chest at the thought of Orien bathing someplace else and not in the comfort of her own space.

You need to get to sleep, Little One, it is late. Tomorrow we will need to speak with Alister.

The voice rings through her head like a delicate caress of a hand. Even thinking about sleeping brings the images of her dream swimming across her eyes once again. She finds herself again staring at the impressive size of Orien's back as she is still turned, facing the burning wood.

"Sleeping has been exceedingly rare for me here recently. I am fine with running on a few hours here and there for the most part, but who is Alister, and why do we need to talk to him?"

Sleep eludes the restless, and we hate to think of you being one of those, but one can never judge when they do not know the whole story.

The beast speaks in soft waves across both of their minds before taking a pause and continuing.

Alister is who you refer to as King Altair. We do not hold him in such regards however.

Elisiah keeps her mouth from falling open as she lets the King's first name sink into her head. She always wondered about the man's name but never found anyone that knew of it.

Alister.

A name that sounds like his parents knew he would be someone powerful one day, or a bastard she supposed.

Before she could ask again what they need to speak to him about, Orien is no longer by the fire. Looking around the room and not finding her made Elisiah think how someone could lose such a tall, broad, thing like Orien.

Getting up from her spot and walking to the main door of the room, she tries one last time to open it. Her hunger has gotten stronger, and she knows if she does not put something in her stomach soon, she will start to throw things around the room.

What she would not give for some of Fredrick's honey oat bread with melted margarine. The old fool is most likely going crazy in his little kitchen with no word or sight from her, but she cannot worry herself with that right now, because as the situation stands, there are more pressing matters to deal with first.

She still has a day and night before the official meeting with the King, but now she is not even sure if that will stand. With no word from her mother after her stunt today with the King, then being swept away by shadows means it cannot be good for her.

As she walks back towards the couch, Elisiah lets out a shrill scream as a towering figure suddenly appears out of thin air in front of her. Her heart lodges in her throat and her skin feels ashen.

"You cannot just do that to people, Orien! Good Gods, my heart feels like it just exploded in my chest!" Fueled in her frustration, Elisiah shoves at the chest in front of her. Not even budging, Orien only turns her frustration into anger and she begins hitting her with every bit of strength she has as she continues to berate her.

"I. Did not. Even. Ask. To." She takes a fast breath. "Be. Here! Why can I not make my own damn choices?! None of you people get to lock me away and beat me when you feel like it, not anymore."

Burning hot tears run down her face as she continues to shove and punch the hard wall of muscle before her.

Elisiah cannot control the words running past her lips or the sobs following them after. All she can think about is the pain she will most certainly endure from the hands of her mother when she sees her next.

A thud sounds on the ground beside the two of them, and before she can see what made it, Elisiah is pulled against the chest she just used as a punching bag. The strong uncovered arms encircle her, and they stay rigid like they do not know what an embrace is.

Giving into the warmth of the hug or what she assumes is supposed to be a hug, she rests her forehead against the hollow spot between Orien's ribs. Finally, Elisiah lets herself freely feel all the emotions she has kept trapped in her chest.

Anger, sadness, fear, disgust, pain, abandonment, and finally all the thoughts of making herself not exist anymore fall out her eyes and soak into the black blouse.

During her erratic crying, she wraps her arms around Orien's torso. Realizing what she has allowed herself to express and do, she lets her arms fall to her sides. Elisiah tries to back away from the female still holding her tightly to her chest. Orien's arms are not as rigid as before, and her chest rises and falls at a faster rate as the same voice sneaks back into Elisiah's head.

We will never beat you, Little One. No one will ever beat you again, not if we are breathing.

The voice fades, and Elisiah cannot help but breathe easier at the words just spoken to her. She can feel the promise in the words and the threat to anyone that tries to harm her. She will not ask why, not right now.

Finally for the first time in her life she felt lighter and all she could think was how thankful she was for the way she felt.

"Thank you, Orien, or whatever your name is in there. I am not sure which one is doing which so just thank you to both." Her cheeks sprout a shade of pink across her face, and she cannot bring herself to look up at the eyes she feels watching her. The arms drop from around her, and she is immediately left with a chill.

Looking around anywhere but up at Orien, she spots what made the thud against the floor. It is a metal tray stacked with bread, cured meats, and fruit. Her mouth is a waterfall at the thought of the flavors of them all. Without a second guess, she grabs the tray off the floor and sits it on the couch before shoving the warm bread and meat into her mouth. She moans slightly, but does not care as her stomach finally feels satisfied.

A low chuckle rings in her head as the beast speaks.

Do not thank us for anything when you are with us. Our priority now is your safety and well-being. Even if it means you need to take out any of your emotions on our body.

If the beast could send images through her mind like it could words, Elisiah thinks it might be smiling.

Also, Little One. Just know Orien is the primary in charge of our body and mind. As it stands right now, I am just the voice. Trust me when I say you would know if I had been the one holding you.

Elisiah stops mid chew and looks in the honey-warm eyes currently watching her devour the food in front of her. The shade of pink goes straight to red as she immediately brings her eyes back to the food and slowly begins to chew again.

Orien thinks the rose color of your cheeks when you blush makes your eyes shine like the night's stars.

Surely, the beast smiles now.

Elisiah understands why when she looks back at Orien's face and the woman immediately turns away from her and acts like the fire needs to be fed.

As the time ticks away and her stomach grows full, the tiredness she tried to push off all afternoon finally overtakes her. Slowly, as she lays back on the couch after moving the tray of food to the table where her book still rests, she says, "I think it would be easier if you had a name to go by. If you will be the one talking to me, then I would like to be able to call you something."

Slowly, the now welcome visitor comes back into her head like an overly excited dog.

Oh really! Yes, we would love that. We have never been one from each other, always the same but also so different from the other. I would love it if you gave me a name, Little One.

The beast pranced around her head, and she felt the smallest thumping against her skull.

Elisiah smiled at the excitement she felt from the beast in her head and glanced at Orien before she laid her head down on the couch. She fell asleep thinking of honey eyes, dull ginger hair, and a large body slumped in the chair across from her in the open space.

The feeling of eyes lingers across her body until the deepest of sleep pulls her into complete darkness, only hoping to not be bothered with the images of death and destruction.

ELISIAH

ELISIAH IS UNSURE HOW LONG SHE HAS BEEN IN THE DARKNESS OF her sleep, only that one moment she is peacefully adrift, and the next it feels like her whole body is weightless, free-falling through the space of her mind.

Frantically grabbing at nothing and trying to find anything that can tell her which way her body is going, fear clings to her body. No noise will leave her mouth, and she can feel her heart pounding in every part of her body.

There is no controlling herself in this moment or even how her body reacts. Elisiah knows that if she does not find a way to calm herself it will ultimately lead to a complete shock to her nervous system.

As soon as she tries to think of something that might calm her heart, a light zips across her right side. Not getting a good look, she turns her head from side to side to make sure she did not make it up. Just as she thinks another flash of light passes her, then another, and another. They soon come in fast bundles of little white light, and the faster she seems to fall the faster the lights come.

It is like she is traveling past shooting stars and with that new information, her heart slows to a normal resting pace.

Now at its normal rate, Elisiah can determine her body is falling down, towards the ground. As if compelled, she looks up above her and is amazed at the thousands of balls of pure white light flashing past; she knows that light, but she could not tell you its name.

Elisiah soon remembers that she is still actively falling, and she does not know if she will end up anywhere or if she will stay in this never-ending loop of falling and waiting. Her answer is coming sooner than she knows.

Just when she can make out things like a fading blue sky, discolored grass, and brown sticks for trees, she hits the ground. All the air expels from her lungs and her whole body screams, though the sound still sticks in her throat. Tears fall from her eyes and her nose feels wet.

Slowly, Elisiah lifts her hand to her face and feels her nose, and bringing it to her blurry eyes, she can make out the bright red blood.

Her tears fall faster.

The level of pain that racks across her feels like something is breaking every bone in her body and slowly putting them back together. The blood-covered hand rests back against the ground around her, and the coldness of it makes her shiver. Since the ground is cold, it has to be the snow months or close to them anyways. It is the same season in Univier as well, so she cannot be far.

The air slowly returns to her lungs, and they burn as they fill to capacity, the oxygen helping her brain to concentrate on her surroundings. With each slow, shallow breath, the pain in her body begins to become manageable. She tests her strength by propping up her upper body on her elbows.

As her eyes adjust the best they can, she realizes she is surrounded by trees.

Elisiah has landed in the middle of what looks like a grove of extremely large trees. These trees seem to touch the sky, and the canopies of leaves resemble clouds; she realizes just by the sight of them that she is not in Univier. Under her hands, the grass is a mix of a dark green and pale green. The colors mix like they cannot stand not to touch each other. It strikes her as odd.

The spot where her body landed is bare from the impact, and the dark brown dirt covers her completely. The white nightslip is ruined, and she realizes her feet are bare as her toes wiggle in response to her brain waves.

Slowly, Elisiah rises to her feet, and the pit in her stomach begins to grow. Looking around the space, she notices a light golden glow from across a field to her right. Against her better judgment, she starts walking towards it and hopes she is not walking into her own death headfirst. The fact that she knows she is not home is all too real, and it makes her take every step with extra delicacy.

Every crunch under her feet makes her jump, every other sound makes her skin crawl, and her head keeps turning to look over her shoulder.

Surely this is not another dream, she thinks to herself as she pushes forward and the light becomes more detailed.

It is a fire, and from what she can see, multiple figures sit around it, looking like they are made from the trees that stand around them.

Her feet slow, and her heart begins to race all over again. On the back of the figures she can see more clearly sit wings. The wings were made of matching flesh like the ones she saw on that blood-stained battlefield. Elisiah's throat wants to close off completely.

If she could make a sound in the moment, it would be a plea, a plea to whoever put her here to take her back.

This does not feel like a dream to her anymore.

The sensations this time do not match the ones from the first, and she fell from somewhere to get here. Surely this could not be her Seer magic coming to fruition.

She spends all her time on her basic sorceress training rather than on what it is to be a Seer; it is something her mother has not taught her yet because the King has not deemed it necessary. He is more worried about what lies between her legs untouched than actually teaching her about the main part of her that matters. It adds onto the reason she loves reading. Even in the thick books describing the many different powers that can be found in Sytherac, nothing says anything about whatever this is when it comes to being a Seer.

Not a single Seer in their history books has ever described a full body experience like the one Elisiah is currently experiencing. It makes her question herself and if she truly knows what she is. Could her Seer powers be a lie?

She pushes herself forward, this time with more urgency. If this is her ability to see into the past, present, or future then maybe the sooner she sees, the sooner she can wake up on that couch she fell asleep on.

Approaching the backs of the beings, Elisiah is confident they do not know she walks among them, so she slowly circles around them, only chancing a glance at their faces.

"Did anyone see where Cap snuck off to?"

Elisiah stops in her tracks as the voice booms around the group. It makes her hair stand on end all over her arms and she sucks in a deep breath and lets it out slowly. None of these men she can see wear any type of fighting armor, but they do all have scars, some even keep their swords by their sides.

Staying just by the tree line to the right of the group, she stops to see if she can hear anything else.

"No, I have not seen him. I bet each of you dickheads a whole bottle of Matryles wine that he is just finding a way to get his rocks off." One soldier agrees to the bet, and the others laugh and take swigs from their own mugs.

"On a serious note, man. Has anyone else noticed how every time we go to massacre those fucking Astrial Archs, he stays focused on Vanora? it is freaking me out." The one who speaks cleans his sword, and his long black hair is braided down his back. Elisiah waits for another to speak.

"Do not think about it too much, Hinchy. He wants this war over as much as all of us. He tries to keep her distracted so we can kill more of them off or something. You know better than to question the things he does; he has never led us astray." The man stares at the burning logs as he adds, "I last saw him headed to the infirmary tents."

Now she has some type of general location to start. Finding an infirmary war tent should not be hard, or at least that's what she tells herself. Leaving the group of men and their small talk, she tries to find what she thinks a medical tent looks like.

Walking blindly, she finds rows of nude cloth laid over large wood poles and beams. Men and women of all looks and colors walk around from tent to tent. Some laugh and others walk with their heads down. Most look defeated while others look like they need to bring life back into the camp. Conversations run into each other, and she can only catch a few words and sentences here and there.

We cannot keep up.

I am getting too old for this.

Cap's always gone.

That bitch Vanora needs to die already.

Why has he not killed her?

My mate is dead because of those Astrial fuckers.

The thought of losing your mate in such a brutal way makes her heart break for the male who spoke the sentence as she passed. She has to find this Captain they all seem to be questioning and growing tired of.

Maybe if she finds him then she can go home or wake up. Taking a left through another row of tents, she finds one that stands just a little taller and extends just a little longer. A tug in her core brings her to the front flaps of the tent. As she opens the way into the space, a woman's voice calls to someone else in the room.

"Mariem, please go string together the front covers. A wind just blew them open, and we cannot risk the ones in the back catching a chill."

A woman, Elisiah assumes is Mariem, walks to the front and ties the entrance together with a light brown leather strap. As she turns to leave from the perfectly tied bow, she stops just in front of Elisiah.

Slowly, Elisiah covers her mouth with her hands in hopes the tall dark brown winged woman will just continue to walk past her. After a few seconds Mariem leaves and returns to the side of the room where she originally sat.

The table is full of scattered papers and empty cups formerly used for hot beverages. Mariem sits down in an oversized wood chair and her eyes glance back in the direction of Elisiah, who still stands frozen in place with her hands over her mouth. The woman's eyes slant up towards her hairline at the sides, and they are such a dark brown they could pass as black. They look like they've seen years of battle-fallen kin and more hours healing than they have happiness and clear skies.

Her chest aches for the eyes searching for a presence she feels but cannot see, but as calm and quiet as she can, Elisiah moves further into the long tent. A variety of different size and color animals' furs cover the floor. Some are so big they take up much of the center space and the smaller ones go to the sides. With her bare feet, she savors the feeling of the warm plush fur. With everything she has seen and tried to make sense of, she forgot just how cold she was. Too scared to grab anything to cover her white nightslip in fear it would not be invisible as she apparently is, she keeps walking and observing.

The medical tent is just as she thought it would be. Two long rows of pop-up beds with basic brown coverings at the foot of the ones not in use. The majority of the beds do not have anyone occupying them, and she assumes that is a good sign. Getting just to the end of the rows, five beds lie full, each with their own winged warrior.

By the bedside of the last one to her right stands a beautiful blonde-haired male. His skin is tan and his eyes a dark blue. He checks a small bag of fluid going into the patient's forearm. Elisiah looks over the man now checking the pulse of the sleeping giant, and she looks to his back, searching for the same skin-colored wings, only she finds nothing. He has no wings of either that she had seen, the featherless or the feathered, and he looks smaller than the others as well. She thinks he looks human.

Surely, it is impossible for a human to live among these people, or at least she would have thought so not even ten seconds before if she wasn't now moving closer to the man. Elisiah can smell the sweat on him and see the small pinpoint freckles on his forehead. He does not have nearly as many as Orien, but he has them nonetheless.

Not knowing why Orien pops in her head and comparing her features to someone else's, she tries to see if his name appears anywhere. As she starts to try and find his work area, he stands and wipes the wrinkles from his black trousers. The movement makes her jump back, hitting a small moving cart she did not see as she walked over, lost in her curiosity. The man whips his head to the cart, and the woman that called out to Mariem earlier looks as well.

"Juroco, was that you?" The lady asks the pale-faced man, her voice full of wariness and curiosity.

"Ah no, wasn't me. I just stood up." The man who now has a name looks around the space of the cart.

"There is a presence in the tent. I felt it when I shut the tent's flaps and when I came to sit down. It does not seem to be malevolent, just a curious little thing," Mariem says without looking up from her work.

With those words, Elisiah speaks softly and mostly to herself. "You can feel me." She can feel her face turn a ghostly shade of gray when she gets a response.

"Well, of course I can feel you. You make yourself rather known. it is like you've never had to be quiet or mask yourself before." Mariem still tends to her papers while Juroco and the other one in the room, who is not currently knocked out, look around the space with wide eyes.

"Mask myself? What are you talking about, I do not even know how I got here. I do not know anything other than I went to sleep and woke up falling, and I think I must have died." Elisiah panics, and she cannot stop herself from trying to explain.

Mariem finally looks up from her work, right at Elisiah who still stands by the cart.

"If you say you fell asleep and then woke up here, I assume you are either dead or a World Walker."

Elisiah holds her breath for a moment before she feels composed enough to let it out. Across from her, the man named Juroco moves closer to the space where she stands, and slowly, he holds out his pointer finger as if he is going to try and poke whatever is apparently here. Elisiah reaches out and grabs his thin finger with her thumb and pointer finger. He jumps back, and a yell comes from his throat as he says, "Holy shit! It touched my finger!"

"If she can touch you, then she must be a World Walker. The dead cannot touch the living, at least not here." Mariem now stands and looks down at Juroco and his finger he cradles to his chest.

"You guys, I think I peed a little." Juroco slowly covers the crotch of his trousers with the hand that holds the one she touched.

Elisiah is too shocked to speak.

He should not be able to feel her touch, she does not think. She also does not know what a World Walker is, but she does not think this is what it means to be a Seer.

Surely, Evadne would have told her something about this, but then again, her mother is a heartless person who is too afraid of the helpless girl to teach her about herself. It is also another thing that is not in her books back at the library of Univier.

"I do not know what a World Walker is, but I am a Seer." None of this seems right. Her whole life Elisiah has been told she is a Seer. Everyday spent in the library has been dedicated to learning what she can about the gift. If she is not what she thought she was then who is she?

Elisiah's eyes remain on the dark-skinned woman almost in front of her. If she can get answers on why she is here, then this may be her only way. Mariem clasps her hands behind her back and looks down at Elisiah from where she stands on one of the big fur skinned rugs. Her face is lined with small wrinkles, most of which lie by her eyes and mouth, and her features are angular and sharp.

"A World Walker, my dear, is a being that can move through worlds. A key of sorts. Now, if you say you are a Seer, then you must not truly know yourself, because you cannot be both. If the word World Walker is new information for you, then I can only assume that you did not choose to be dropped into our place of resting. I can assure you though, you cannot be a Seer if you are a World Walker." The way the woman talks reminds her of the way the beast in Orien talks, the beast that still needs a name.

"No, I mean, I am sorry. I just went to sleep, and I ended up here, and now I do not know how to get back. I am sorry. I just do not know." Elisiah rambles and her palms begin to sweat. What does this woman mean by worlds? Where is she if she is not home in Univier?

Did she go to a different world?

What are those bright lights, then?

It is too much for her to handle, and she starts to hyperventilate.

"Calm yourself, child. All you must do to get back is wake yourself up. Focus on something in your time and place then let your memory take your mind back. If you have not learned about your ability, you need to know, for your body is taking you to places you do not belong, and your power can awaken something you do not want made known of your existence."

Elisiah slowly pats her chest right over her heart as she looks around the room and tries to gather her racing thoughts. If her body has somehow sent her here, then it must be for a reason. At least that's what she tells herself, and she starts to believe it.

The way she is reacting does not seem rational to her at all. She should have never talked to the woman that tries to teach her how to get back to her resting body. Surely, if she is in danger, her mind will not allow her to talk and make herself known so easily. Elisiah does not feel overwhelmed by the fact these people know she is here, but by the fact she has to leave with no answers about herself or why her mind brought her here.

There is no one back at her home that can teach her about any of this. Her own mother will likely beat the skin off her back for even admitting she started to project herself, even if it is against her own will. This is the last thing she would choose to do with her free time.

Thoughts of being back home start to make her feel lighter, and when she realizes that, she tries to stop them so she can ask more questions.

"Wait! Please, I have no one to teach me about what I am or what I can do! I have seen your kind once before. On a battle-field. I did not go to sleep thinking about any of this. Why am I coming back? I have so many questions, please answer them for me!"

Elisiah reaches out to Mariem and grabs her hand in hers. Tears run down Elisiah's face, and she can feel the warmth coming from the woman. Mariem puts her free hand over Elisiah's that is now cradled between them. The woman's kind eyes search the empty space like she is trying to figure out what Elisiah looks like.

"It is you who must answer your own questions. Your heart will not deceive you, and you should do good to remember that you must search in yourself but also in the others around you. Do not come back here, my dear, and if you do, think yourself wiser than to talk to the first voice that speaks." Letting go of her hand, Mariem turns back to her workstation and walks to the table. Her long white dress brushes over the floor and her wings tuck in tightly to her back. From a ray of light coming from a lantern, Elisiah can see the veins running along the bat-like wings.

A vision of Orien plays like a movie in Elisiah's head. She can see the tall woman sitting in the winged-back chair across from her in the sitting room, the way her arms rest on the sides of the chair. All she can do is watch the way her chest rises and falls with each breath.

Her mind is no longer in the world of the unknown but back in her own, in her body.

Go back to bed, Little One.

The voice is delicate as it speaks the words, and Elisiah tries to fight her eyes as they slowly close. Her body feels heavy as something warm gently rests on top of her. The smell of burning embers and dew-covered grass wraps itself around her, and she pulls in a deep inhale of the aroma before letting all of it lure her back to sleep.

II

ORIEN

Waking up the next day, Orien still struggles to come to terms with the actions she made the day prior and the decisions still to come today. She knows she needs to go to Alister before he has the chance to summon her. It is best to catch him off guard than give him ample thinking time. Orien gets dressed in her sleeping room while the woman that started this complete disaster sleeps on the lounge couch in the room over.

Buckling the last buckles to her sheaths while walking out the door, her eyes cannot help but find Elisiah in the space. The woman's frame curls up in a ball on the wide seat of the cushion. A thick black blanket covers only the bottom half of her legs, unlike when Orien placed the covering over her body last night.

Elisiah must have kicked it down in the early morning hours.

Orien studies Elisiah's resting face the same way she did last night, and still she finds her head swimming with questions.

How have they found themselves in their current situation?

Why does she feel everything about Elisiah like the woman is a part of her?

More than anything, Orien questions what she will do about the man that lives in the west wing of the castle. She knows that Alister is more than angry. He is more than enraged. Alister Farkle Altair, the King of Univier, is embarrassed and that is the worst emotion for a man like him to experience.

A weak man often spends his time worried about his appearance and how others think of him. He is someone who will do anything to make sure his name remains a symbol of power, and Orien ruined that for Alister. She single handedly took something from him that he had the audacity to stake claim over. Orien knows exactly how Alister feels because she has seen it far too many times to count.

Every time she has seen him insulted, she has been the one to feel his wrath. She is the one that wears the scars on her body from his embarrassment.

Orien tries to shove her racing thoughts aside but it is something the woman finds hard to do. It is strange for her; thoughts, and emotions have never plagued her like they do now.

Trying her best now to keep from pacing around the room, Orien's eyes focus back on Elisiah. Her curly black hair is everywhere. It reminds her of ink being spilt, covering the surface of fabric underneath her.

The smell of the cleaning soap she used last night in the tub fills Orien's nose, and for the first time, she truly watches someone sleep. Orien does not study Elisiah anymore, she only watches how at peace the other woman looks in their slumber. Orien could tell you every curve and crevasse of Elisiah from the time she spent filing the information away in her head, but she would not have been able to tell you what Elisiah's face looked like without any sign of emotion.

That is until now.

Until Orien actually took the time to simply admire how gorgeous a person could look while being lost to their own darkness.

This time, Orien feels like she is watching something more personal to Elisiah. The assassin feels like she is actually crossing some kind of invisible boundary that the other may have in place. It makes her feel like a stalker now, which to her is worse than a pervert. Which Orien is both of those things and a lot of other, worse things, if she is honest with herself.

Walking over to the sleeping lady on her couch, she gently sits beside her. Elisiah's breaths make her chest rise just enough to see. Her golden-brown face is blank of any imperfections or signs of distress. It is nice for Orien to finally see Elisiah's face so at ease instead of all the distinctive features it showed yesterday.

Against her better judgment, Orien grabs the sleeping woman by her shoulders and shakes her.

Elisiah's eyes pop open and her breathing quickens as she sits up almost immediately. Huffing and looking around the room with wide eyes, she says, "What is it? Who is there? Am I dying?"

Orien removes her hands from the panicked female's shoulders and stands while she shakes her head.

The beast stirs in her mind at the sudden commotion filling the room around them.

Crossing her arms over her chest, Orien inhales and releases a frustrating breath. The fact that these two can sleep so peacefully under the current situation sparks her nerves, and it is a feeling she rather dislikes.

The beast comes forward but not before it lets out a loud yawn in her head. Orien closes her eyes in annoyance; she cannot wait for the beast to go dormant again. If that will ever happen.

Is it morning already? We had just gone to sleep. We really need to gather a better sleeping routine. I need at least six hours or my beauty will fade.

The thing speaks to Orien like this is not something they have done daily for years. She cannot even think of the last time they have indulged in more than four hours of sleep at a time. Orien can feel the sluggish beast taking over her eye just as it looks at the woman in front of them. Elisiah is trying to gather her thoughts as she rubs her eyes.

Oh, good morning our Little One. I hope you slept well!

Elisiah looks up at Orien and investigates the solid black eye. A small grin grows on her face as she replies, "Good morning to you too, thing in Orien and Orien." Her expression changes into one of frustration as she says Orien's name. Elisiah pulls her nightslip down over her knees and adds, "I slept as well as I could, I guess. The fact I got woken up by being shaken like a damn maniac leaves a sour taste in my mouth, along with the fact that you already broke the no touching rule." Her eyes almost feel like daggers as she looks into the single honey brown one across from her.

We are pleased to hear that you slept better than us. A certain someone found it quite difficult to pull our sight away from staring at you all night. In fact, we slept in the chair just across from you.

Before Orien can think about stopping the insufferable terror that takes space in her head, the thing has already told Elisiah that she did in fact spend most of her night making sure she was well and safe. Elisiah tries to hide the horror on her own face, but Orien knows all too well the look of someone playing a part, so she turns towards the washroom before something else can come from her head.

Before Orien can enter the washroom and gather herself for the remainder of the day, a question comes from the couch. "What is the plan for the day?"

Without turning around, Orien tells the beast that it can relay the message of the plan to Elisiah.

We will be going to Alister's office first thing. The rest of the day depends on how that interaction will go.

"I was supposed to have a meeting with the King tomorrow. Can we not wait until then?"

The slight tremble in Elisiah's voice and the way her scent becomes tinted with the smell of spider ink tells Orien that she is truly scared. Nothing has happened between them but that means nothing with a person like Alister Altair, he is a possessive man.

Stopping in her tracks, the beast replies.

Sorry, Little One, the time must not be delayed. If we wait for him to call for us, then that just means more skin from our hide. We will be leaving in a few moments, so do get yourself dressed and ready.

She walks into the washroom and shuts the door before she gets a response from the couch. The thought of bringing Elisiah back into that room makes her blood burn inside her veins but she knows it must be done. The only claim Elisiah has on her is from the King, even if Orien knows that it is bullshit.

Walking circles in the space, she tries to gather her thoughts. The trip to Thundaria is approaching, and Orien cannot leave Elisiah here.

It is utterly ridiculous that Elisiah can have such an effect on the emotionless, supposed Fae, but it seems to stand that she in fact does. It leaves Orien constantly searching her memory if somehow they have met before, and that could be a reason she feels a need to protect and provide for her.

She is not even sure what Elisiah feels. Her scent changes rapidly, and what she shows on the outside Orien assumes never matches what she feels on the inside. Running her hands through her hair, she stops at the door and gathers herself before entering the joining room she left a few minutes ago.

Elisiah must have rummaged through her things on the couch, because some of her belongings have ended up on the floor while the others are spread over the back of the furniture. Orien looks around the room to find everything else just as spotless as she left it yesterday. The two people are completely opposite. Orien likes her space to be organized and clean. The way Elisiah's room was yesterday shows she is more of a grab and go person. Walking over to the mess, Orien starts to fold and organize the garments that cover the small area that was just occupied. She gently places the things neatly on the table in the middle of the room.

"Why are you touching my stuff?" Elisiah comes over and grabs the white nightslip from Orien's hands, mid fold. She brings it to her chest like it is a precious thing and looks around to the other clothing items that are folded on the table.

Orien's hands are frozen in the folding motion she had halfway completed before she yanks the nightslip back from the hands that snatched it away the first time. Holding Elisiah's gaze, she finishes her fold and places it gently on the pile. Now it is Elisiah's turn to stand frozen.

Orien likes a clean space. Excuse her brashness about the garment, but she has had a long night.

Orien wants to strangle the beast in her head. It is no one's business what she likes and does not.

"Well, I do not like my things folded by the hands of someone that has kidnapped me, held me against my will, and has put their hands on me." Elisiah's face has gone warm from the emotions Orien can see in her eyes.

"The same hands I know have killed many people for no good reason. Do not touch my things, and do not touch me! I do not need your help. I do not need your anything." Elisiah takes the pile of clothes and tosses them back on the couch as she spreads them out again. Her eyebrows are bunched together, leaving a little line creasing down her nose.

Orien watches her and clenches her fists by her side. Everything in her body wants to throw this childish human across the room and into the stone wall. Her hands have more blood on them then she or anyone will ever be able to comprehend. It has never bothered her, and this nice smelling woman will not change that about her. She has done what she has to survive, but that is something this tantrum-throwing woman will never understand.

The blood on our hands is something we do not have remorse for. It is something we will never apologize for. We are a monster, Little One, a monster that you just angered by acting like an ungrateful child.

Orien walks to the main door of the room and throws it open, walking into the hallway. Elisiah storms after her retreating form, sprinting to catch up.

"You do not get to call me a child! You do not know the first thing about me or what I have been through. It is not my fault you got dealt a shitty hand in life, but you are not the only one! The few things I have are all I have, and if I do not want you touching them, then you need to respect that! If I am a child, then you are a baby that was never loved by anyone." The insults flowing from Elisiah make Orien want to pin her against the wall and make use of the thick green vines growing along the stone.

Orien knows she has never experienced love but it has never been something she has needed. Love is a weakness. It drives men mad and puts women in early graves. She has seen grown men starve themselves just to provide what little they can for someone they love. Just like she has seen women crying under trees begging for death to take them just so the pain from losing their mate would end.

Orien has always thought if love is anything like what she has witnessed over the course of life then she would rather meet her end not knowing it at all. Elisiah's words are meant to hurt but for Orien they feel like a pinprick.

Elisiah grabs Orien by the wrist and stops in her tracks like a lead weight. Orien slows a little and starts to drag her down the hallway on her way to Alister's office. Orien is not sure if the man is even there, but it is the first place she would think he would be.

Every part of her wants to grab the small hand off her wrist and just throw her over her shoulders, but right now she is keeping her word of not touching.

Elisiah does not give up on trying to stop Orien from walking, as she is currently yanking Orien by the wrist and digging her heels into the wood floor of the hall. The brown pants she dressed in this morning stop at her ankles and her white slip-on slippers have blemishes on the sole from her determination to overpower the giant woman she hangs onto.

Her hair is pulled back and held in place by a leather tie, but it looks in disarray from her struggle. Elisiah's breaths are rough and ragged, but Orien does not pay her any mind, not as they get closer to the office. Orien straightens her back and ignores Elisiah as she comes to a stop in front of four of the King's Guards, currently in full armor, waiting in the corridor entryway.

"Orien. King Altair has called for your presence in the training room. He has asked that you go there immediately. Lady Elisiah is to go as well." The Guard who speaks looks slightly up at her and then down at Elisiah who still clings to her wrist.

Luckily, Elisiah has her breathing under control as her chest is not heaving as much as it was, but her eyes are full of worry. Orien nods her head at the Guard while turning her body back around towards the way they just came. They all walk together toward the training room that sits in the same wing as her room.

It also houses the Guards as well.

The hands around Orien's wrist tighten. She does not have to look behind her to know the frame now pressed closely to her back. The beast in her head stirs at the unease coming from Elisiah.

The four Guards circle the two slowly. Two at their backs and two at their fronts.

Orien knows what is about to happen all too well. She has had this same walk many times in her short life, and it will not be the last time she will do it. The only difference now is that the woman currently clinging to her could be in the line of fire, and that is one thing she will not let happen. If Alister Altair wants to hurt anyone, it will be Orien.

12

ELISIAH

Standing at the double doors of what Elisiah can only assume is the training room, the Guards stationed at their front open the wide, dark stone doors.

It strikes her as odd that these doors are the only ones not made of the same pale wood as the rest. Elisiah cannot help but think about how much each one must weigh as they open.

They make an awful groaning sound that makes her want to grind her teeth.

Orien's wrist has red crescent shapes all along the sides from where Elisiah has gripped it, and even though Elisiah can see her nail imprints on the wrist, she does not loosen her hold. She feels bad for leaving marks, but Elisiah is too scared to let Orien go.

When they ran into the Guards, all her anger left, and in its place she found dread and fear.

The fact that King Altair called both of them to this room that was unknown to her makes her feel queasy. Everyone was quiet on the walk here, and all she finds herself wanting is to talk to the beast inside of Orien, even if the last thing she said to it and Orien was cruel. Elisiah let her emotions take control of her in the moment, and all they wanted was to lash out and cause pain. It was pain that Elisiah now knows Orien did not deserve.

The room is as big as the throne room. You could fit a good two hundred people in the space and it still would not feel full. Right now, it feels entirely too empty.

Around its corners stand multiple different racks of weapons. Basic ones she recognizes like swords and spears but many she does not. One catches her eye, a long metal pole with a chain on its end that holds a large metal ball with spikes. Elisiah thinks back to her practice with Fredrick, but all the old man has ever allowed her to train with are smaller weapons.

"You never try to fight with something you know you cannot handle. Elisiah, you are at a disadvantage because you are smaller than most in the castle, so surprise is your greatest weapon. A dagger can be hidden easily while also allowing you to move quickly."

Fredrick's voice in her head soothes her as she recites his words from when he first allowed her to try her hand at dagger work. She was a natural with a blade, or so he said to her that afternoon.

Even though Fredrick has been working with her, the sight of the weapons makes her throat grow dry. She finds herself having trouble swallowing.

Elisiah freezes like she did in that office with Altair.

Her eyes are too busy looking around the room to notice everyone else stopping. Elisiah slams into the back of Orien; her fingernails dig further into the female's wrist. Everything about the way she feels is the same way she felt when her mother would come into her room with the wood whip. Panic grips her neck as the sounds of the wood tearing her skin echoed in her mind.

Do we have your permission to touch you if we need to protect you, Little One?

The voice is welcome in her head, and she has to stop herself from tearing up. Even with everything going on, she feels like she has a friend, even if it is just a voice.

"Yes," is all she can make herself say as she notices who is in the center of the room.

The King stands there with four more of his Guards, and in his hand, he holds what looks to be a metal tail.

It is long as it flows from his right hand like a smooth rope, the very tip just brushing the ground. Orien's free hand gently rests over Elisiah's hands.

The touch pulls her attention towards the tall woman. Nothing can be read on her face. It is like this is just another day for her. Suddenly, like a switch being turned on, Elisiah realizes that this *is* Orien's everyday reality. The scars she has been able to see from the little bit of skin Orien has shown should have been enough to tell Elisiah that torment is normal for her.

Elisiah cannot help the tears that swell in her eyes for the person she clings to. The person whose scent can make her feel calm and crazed at the same time. The assassin who saved her from being raped in that office. Who has said she would be protected from anything as long as they were around.

Elisiah knows nothing about Orien, but as she stands there, almost hidden behind this woman, she eats her words from earlier.

"Orien!" Altair yells from just across the space, "come here and take your place. You know the drill. Guards, grab the girl and make sure she watches everything."

Just as the King says, Orien lets go of Elisiah's hands as she begins to walk forward without a single look her way.

Two of the Guards behind her grab Elisiah by the forearms. She cannot bring herself to fight their hold as she tries to figure out what the weapon does and why Orien just walks willingly to the insane man waiting in the center of the room.

As soon as Orien stops at a stained spot on the floor that Elisiah just now realizes is there, Orien kneels in front of the King, raising her head just an inch to meet his eyes.

"You think you can come into my office and just take away something that belongs to me?" Alister raises his arm as he points a finger in Elisiah's direction.

"That girl over there was given to me as a gift from her mother, and she will do as I say. Neither of you are allowed to go against my orders. Neither of you will go without punishment." He pauses just enough to glance in Elisiah's direction, his arm resting back at his side.

"Since you thought it was best to take her away before she could finish her job, then you get the punishment you deserve, and she gets to watch." The King locks eyes with Elisiah as he says the last of his little speech, and her stomach drops at the words "belongs" and "job."

Is he really calling her his property in front of all these men and, on top of that, saying it is her job to lay down and allow him to rape her?

She cannot believe what she is hearing. Panic overcomes her as she watches Orien unbutton her black shirt.

Orien turns her back towards the King as her shirt falls to the ground. Orien's hands lay palm up just on her knees. Elisiah begs Orien in her head to tell her what is going on and what is about to happen.

Look away, Elisiah. Look away.

The voice is quiet in her head, and it makes her heart crack.

The whole time the voice has been in her head, it has never felt so small and quiet. She cannot cover her mouth to hold the sound of her frantic breathing. Elisiah pleads with the part of Orien to not just sit there, to get up and fight back.

Elisiah knows Orien can kill every one of these men, but she just sits there. The King smiles brightly at Elisiah and her display of distress.

Elisiah has never felt so useless and human until right now. What good is the power of a World Walker, or whatever she is, when you cannot even use it to help someone in need.

"Elisiah, I want you to watch what happens when someone touches what is mine. I do not like sharing." Altair lifts the metal weapon in the air to the right of his head before he adds, "And Orien, if you even think about moving an inch then I'll fuck her right here on this floor after its soaked in your blood."

Elisiah gasps at the gray-haired man as the vile words travel from between his thin, chapped lips. Before she can truly process the threat, the metal tail whips down in a harsh swing. A loud crack ripples across the room as the tip of the weapon rips through Orien's skin as easily as the pages of parchment rip in one of the old books from the library.

Orien does not even flinch as her skin is forced apart.

Orien sits like a statue, kneeling on the cold gray stone floor. A loud sob leaves Elisiah's throat as blood begins to flow down Orien's already scarred back. Elisiah's skin grows hot as the sound of her scream echoes back to her ears.

The sound of the metal whip slicing through the air is enough to make Elisiah's body shake. The way the skin squelches as it immediately pops open causes her to throw up all over the stones in front of her. Her throat burns, and her vision blurs from the tears trailing down her face. The speed at which they fall reminds her of the rushing water of Hedeft. If she could go anywhere, it would be in the waves of the river. Elisiah would cradle Orien in her arms the best she could and simply disappear with her.

Then she could say she helped in the moment.

As Elisiah looks at Orien's face, all she sees is that her eyes stay their soft brown color, and from what she can see, Orien's chest rises and falls in perfect, slow breaths.

Blinking her eyes to clear her blurred vision, Elisiah watches Orien's face, only to find the broken female staring back at her. Elisiah stares right back and begins to slow her own breathing. If the one getting their back shredded to pieces could sit and show some type of composure, then so could she.

Or she hoped so.

⬥❈❈❈❈⬥

Trying to calm herself, she starts telling Orien about the times she went foraging for different flowers and herbs in the forest. "One day, after my mother had just finished beating me, I snuck out of the castle through one of the openings on the outer wall corridors." Elisiah pauses before she continues.

"I spent some time watching the way the serpents would climb up the vines and make their way into the hallways. Well, I told myself if I never tried it then I would not know if I could or not. I climbed the vines all the way down to the ground that day, and I remember thinking to myself that I could just run away and never look back." She takes a steady breath as the whip connects to Orien's back again.

"Something in me would not let me run, though. I cried the whole way into the forest and my back still stung from the beating I received. That day it was just because my mother did not have anything to do with her time. She came by my room and made me lay over my bed as she pulled my dress up and whipped my back with this long tree branch that she wrapped in leather and horsehair. She would always use some herbs to heal the wounds before she left me. It did not stop the pain though." Another round of tears stain her flesh as she finds herself trapped in the pain of the memory.

"I made my way into the forest just by Hedeft, and I remember I saw a beautiful bush full of lavender flowers and bright green leaves. I had not seen it before, so I sat down beside it and cried. I just felt safe. It is one of the reasons why I love being with the plants. I always feel at home when I am with them, and I even talk to them sometimes. What living things would not want to be talked to?" Elisiah shifts in the Guards' grip as much as she can to try and relieve the pressure of their fingers on her arms.

Both of the men adorned in armor only tighten their hold on her.

"As I sat there, I calmed myself down, and the thought of going further into the woods came to my mind. So, I went further into the woods. I could not find it in myself to care if I got lost, or if I knew my way back.

"I am glad I went deeper though, because I found a single den dug into the side of a small hill. I walked right up to that den and asked in a low voice if anyone was home. I was greeted by a small Wulve pup. His fur was a deep brown that matched the shade of dirt he was surrounded by, and his eyes were black. The pup looked well fed, so I know he had a mother somewhere.

"I was not scared though. I talked to him, and he listened. He came and jumped up on my dress." Elisiah cannot help the feeling of a smile that crosses through her head. That Wulve pup may have been the only reason she stayed breathing that day, and she never got to thank him for that.

"I patted his head and smiled. It was the first time I smiled in years, like an actual smile. Not one of the fake ones I had grown so comfortable wearing. It was nice.

"I left shortly after that, but I did not climb up the castle wall right away. Instead, I went to that small waterfall by the bottom of the castle and stripped naked. I swam in that water for what felt like hours. I let the fish nibble on my feet while I laid on my back just floating on top of the still water. The flowers that surround that small body of water make the best washing soap." Elisiah pauses again as she lets the familiar smell of fresh water, embers, and leather take over her nostrils. Only this time the smell of iron mixes with the others.

"I still think about that pup. I have gone back to that den the few times I have been able to get back out, but he has never been there since that day."Elisiah rambles off the details of her memory like she is telling them to a long time friend.

The whole time she does not stop looking into Orien's eyes. Not until the whip stops screaming through the air and the blood stops pooling at Orien's knees.

Altair is sweating, his hair is hanging in clumps around his head. His teeth are on full display, and his elongated Fae fangs gleam in the Water's Light overhead. At this moment, Elisiah can only think about killing him.

Killing him so slowly that he begs for mercy, mercy he would not get from her.

The whip slows to a stop after a final strike and then the King drops the metal weapon to the ground by his feet. Slowly, Elisiah watches the King of Univier as he walks to the front side of Orien. Without hesitation, Altair kicks her across the face, her head snapping to the right. Elisiah promises to herself in that moment, King Altair of Univier, will be slaughtered.

"Twenty-seven strikes for twenty-seven years you have wasted my time. The kick because you got blood on my boots." Altair looks to the Guards that flanked his sides the entire time. "Clean the Fisherbone, and place it back in my room."

They waste no time in grabbing the metal thing that is now dripping crimson and take it away. Then he walks over to Elisiah who now holds her breath as her skin burns from a new anger that stirs to life in her chest.

"You will be going as my advisor to Thundaria. You were not going to leave until five mornings from now, but I want you out of my sight. Maybe some time on a horse going across the ice and snow will make you realize just how warm my bed is." Altair's breath is hot against Elisiah's face as he spits the words at her.

"If you so much as think about letting someone touch you, I will know, and I will find you. You will not be able to move your lower body after I get done with you." The sound of his voice makes her wish she could not hear at all. The smell of stale mead tries to force its way up her nose as his words linger in the air between them.

She wants to spit in his eyes but all she can think about is the woman just out of her reach, so she says and does nothing.

"Pack a bag, my doll. You leave tomorrow, and that thing bleeding out over there will take you. Do not think she will not kill you just as quickly as she has killed the hundreds before you." He grabs her by her cheeks and places his face just a few centimeters in front of hers before running his tongue across his lips.

"I cannot wait to get a taste of you."

Elisiah closes her eyes. Her heart rate quickens. The King smiles as he throws her head back. A pain shoots down the back of her neck, and Elisiah is sure something had to crack by the sound it made.

A growl comes from across the room, causing her and Altair to turn their heads out of curiosity.

Orien stands in her blood as her shoulders shake with anger. The brown eyes are gone, taken place by ones of black.

Elisiah notices the leather strap covering her breast, but it just barely hangs on due to the back being completely in shreds. The Guards holding onto Elisiah's arms slowly let go of her as they step away.

The King snarls back at Orien just as he starts to walk toward her. Before he can get a step closer, he stops in his tracks. They stand, their eyes locked on each other's, as black smoke-like tentacles rise from all around Orien. Altair takes a step back as his hands ball themselves into fists.

After a moment, Elisiah thinks that they may be speaking mind to mind. She cannot be sure, but it is what she would think is happening by the way they are both reacting while also not moving.

Altair blows out a breath, turns, and rushes out of the room while his Guards follow behind like the mutts they are.

Elisiah does not stop her legs as they break out into a run to get over to Orien. She does not even stop as her boots slap in the puddle of blood that pools on the ground. Her eyes are red rimmed and puffy, her nose has been draining snot, and her head is pounding.

Elisiah goes to Orien's back to inspect the damage just as a gasp leaves her mouth. She can see the bone of some of Orien's ribs. Slowly, she places a hand on Orien's side avoiding any of the lacerations. Orien's body tenses and then rests as Elisiah's hand lays softly on Orien's sweat soaked skin.

Circling back around to the front of Orien, Elisiah reaches a hand up to Orien's face and rests it on her cheek. Part of her hand is on the leather of the mask and the other on her freckled covered skin.

"How do I heal you? What can I do?" Elisiah puts her free hand over her mouth and does not care about the blood that could now be covering her own face.

Tears rain down her cheeks.

Do not do it. We are not worth any sadness or grief. We hate you had to see any of this. Just know he will never get what he wants from you. We will never let that happen, even if we must kill ourselves to do so.

The thing in Elisiah's head speaks slowly as Orien's eyes fade to brown.

We heal faster than most but we need a couple of days. We will only have the scars to show after.

The voice is comforting, and Elisiah shakes her head at the fact it is trying to comfort her right now. Orien leans her face further into the small hand resting there as her eyes close.

"Do not try to comfort me right now. This is all my fault. I was the one that went into that office not thinking about the consequences. Now your back is shredded, and I could have been raped right here on this floor. In your own blood." Elisiah's voice goes quiet as she thinks about what the King said.

Orien slowly reaches for her face but stops just before her skin connects with Elisiah's. Elisiah nods her head in approval just before Orien's large hand moves to hold Elisiah's face. Orien rubs Elisiah's cheek with her thumb and the beast speaks again.

Little One, no one will be taking you anywhere.

Elisiah turns her face so that her nose rests on the side of Orien's thumb and says, "We need to leave soon. This trip to Thundaria is a blessing in disguise. We can pretend not to be so broken."

Never pretend to be something you are not. Your broken pieces do not make you any less whole. You are the only one who can mend those and change what that picture looks like. Let everyone see you for who you are, and if anyone has a problem with who that is, then they can come tell us.

The beast is stern in her head, and it makes her smile slightly. She would much rather hear this side of the thing than the small, almost frail one she heard earlier.

Orien reaches down for her button up shirt, slowly.

Elisiah rushes to grab it and motions for Orien to kneel so she can easily lay the fabric over her shoulders and button the first few buttons. Orien stays still and waits until she is done. Elisiah eyes the leather band still barely hanging on but does not ask any questions. She will worry about that when the time is more appropriate.

Together they straighten the best they can and slowly make their way out of the double doors towards the rooms they both wished they never left.

Leaving the pool of blood to dry on the floor along with the vomit and tears.

13

ALISTER

Alister Farkle Altair has been in power over the Kingdom of Univier for hundreds of years now. The title of King has been his birthright since he was just a flutter in his mother's womb. His father, Alabaster, took him from the warm embrace of his mother as soon as the life cord was cut between the two.

King Alabaster made sure his son was taught the importance of what it meant to be a ruler, which made the boy into a little monster. The servants that helped raise Alister would say that he would be the downfall of Univier due to his arrogance and ability to manipulate anyone he came in contact with.

Manipulation was the power that he hid under his skin. He even hid it from his father until Alabaster was on his deathbed. Alister has used the ability to get his way in almost every situation he has found himself in, and has encountered very few people that his mind games do not work on. Those select few are the ones he likes to keep close to his side so he always knows where he can find them. If he cannot control their way of thinking to protect himself, then he would keep them under an invisible umbrella.

Better to keep his enemies close than to allow them to slip from his grip and attack from behind.

Alister's time ruling from the vine-covered stone throne has been easy for him due to his gift and nothing more. He is a direct reflection of his heartless, cruel father before him. Alister knows that about himself, and all he can see when he looks at his reflection is Alabaster, which does not bother him. Why should it bother him when he spent his entire life watching his father, dreaming of filling his boots when the time came?

Even though his father was a heartless man to the people he ruled over, he had a soft spot for his son. Or Alister had sunk his fangs of deceit into the old ruler at such a young age that Alabaster did not even notice he wasn't in control of his own mind.

The current King of Univier works hard behind his closed office doors to make sure the picture he paints to his loyal subjects is one that will not show his true face. The face of a monster.

Everyone has seen him as a fair ruler since even before he took the throne. His name is always followed by words like peaceful, fair, understanding, and even merciful. They see someone who holds a good head atop his wide, slightly round shoulders, and he never once questions his own ability.

That all changed twenty-seven years ago. The smooth flowing life he had become accustomed to was ripped from his fingers quicker than even Alister could see coming. It was the day an infant was left at his castle's doorstep with a single note that read:

Take care of her.
You owe us that much, Alister.

He knew from whom the child and note came from, and he immediately saw nothing but opportunity. Something that would make his rule stronger over the people.

Little did he know at the time that the child would be such a pain in his ass. Like yesterday when she decided to take what belonged to him, and today when that insufferable part of her threatened to hang him from the rafters of his own ballroom with his small intestine.

Beating her has become almost boring due to how she sits like a stone. His powers have never worked on her before, and that is something that makes his anger set his whole body on fire. If Orien were like the others, then she would be the perfect weapon for him. Alister spent so many nights when she was just a babe, fantasizing about the destruction she would cause, and the paths she would clear just for him. Orien was the ticket he needed to overthrow the other Kings.

Those dreams were short lived as she grew older and her mind could not be swayed. In the first two years of her life, Orien found joy in watching the leaves on the plants as they swayed with the current of wind.

Alister caught the ginger-haired girl laughing as animals found ways to flock to her. It never mattered where he hid her away because they always found her.

And she always laughed.

After those two years, Alister decided the toddler did not need to laugh anymore, so one day he took Orien into the Guards' training room. In that room, he let the different animals find her and all get comfortable around her.

He watched as predator and prey all laid together in harmony around Orien. He watched the young child as she took her time to pet each one. How she gave each a big squeeze around their necks, each animal resting into her touch.

Alister wore a smile on his face the whole time, even as his Guards emerged from the shadows around the room. The men hid behind the pillars that held the ceiling so high in the air, and when they appeared, the smile on Orien's face disappeared.

Alister watched in triumph as she sat in the center of all those innocent beings while his men used their swords to cut off their heads. Some men even went as far to just wound an animal and then watch it scream in agony.

Orien sat perfectly still during the slaughter, and by the time it was over, she was painted red from all of the blood. Alister knew by the look on her small, freckled face that he had won.

"This is what happens to things that you care about."

Alister can still feel the way the words felt when they moved across his lips and it still feels like a victory to him.

Now though, the reaction he has seen from Orien over this stupid human girl makes him nervous, but it does give Alister Altair leverage over Orien.

Every piece of him will enjoy playing with Elisiah just to get a reaction out of the monstrosity that he has housed and raised. The pleasure that thought brings to him makes him want to torment Elisiah even more.

As he makes his way back to his royal wing, he starts to rack his brain for any information that will cause them unrest on their travels to Thundaria.

"Malcom." He calls to one of the many Guards that walk behind him. "Find Evadne. Tell her I need her on an urgent matter."

"Yes, your highness."

Alister does not turn around as he hears the shuffle of armor behind him. If anyone can give him information about what to do next it will be that woman.

Making it to his bedchamber door, another Guard pushes the door open for him. Right now, he needs to wash and change before someone sees him. The last thing he wants to do is explain himself. Even though he loves telling a delightful story of his secret weapon that is nothing more than a blood-drinking monster.

If it were not for his stories, then the whole Kingdom would not be afraid to question his authority. He guesses that is one good thing about keeping Orien around; always having a fall back.

A throat clears from behind him as he starts to take off his boots.

"What is it?" The King says as he lets his boots fall to the floor with a thud.

"Your, highness, I just wanted to inform you that we have not seen or heard from Lady Evadne since you last called for her." The Guard is the youngest of all of them, and his voice wavers just enough to tell Alister that he is still scared to be in his company.

Such weakness from the boy.

He should not be left in charge of protecting a life, let alone a King's if he cannot even speak a sentence without his voice breaking. Alister turns his face to the Guards.

"Then where is she?" Alister walks slowly towards the young Guard as he shifts his weight from one foot to the other. Such weakness.

"We have looked for her, sir. Every place has come up empty. The last anyone saw her was in the library with Elisiah." The Guard swallows but holds eye contact.

"The one working the archives said Lady Evadne left after an argument, but no one saw her in the hallways after." He sounds confident with his information, and all Alister can think about is how someone can leave a room, never to be seen again.

Orien.

All the information points only to her, and if Elisiah and her mother did get into an argument, then it is possible. That big pain in his ass is going to get what she deserves, and he plans to use Elisiah for just that.

Walking up to the Guard in front of him, the one who reeks of cowardice, Alister smiles at him. Reaching up and placing his hands on both sides of the young man's white and gold protective helmet, the King slowly raises it off his head. The others keep silent and look straight forward.

With the helmet in his hand, he holds it down to his side as he says, "For that information I think you need a much-deserved break, soldier." The boy's shoulders drop just slightly, and his mouth opens to speak, but nothing comes out as Alister grips the helmet in his hand and swings it full force at the now exposed head.

The metal vibrates through his hand and up his arm as the sound of crunching bone fills his ears. Bright red blood splatters across his face as his smile grows sinister. A small laugh builds in his chest as he watches the youngest of them fall.

No one moves an inch. No one makes a sound as the metal of the suit of armor slaps against the ground.

"Your break will be taken in the infirmary." Alister drops the helmet on the ground by the boy's feet as he turns and walks to his washing room.

"Hershel, take him away and grab one of the servant girls and bring her my way. I need a much-needed stress release."

"Yes sir, your highness. Right away." Hershel, one of the King's longest working commanders is always by his side and has always been one with unfaltering loyalty. If the King cared about anyone, it would be him, but to his knowledge, no one knows that information.

As the commander shouts the orders to the others, Alister closes the door behind him. Left alone in the silence of the washroom, he runs his water and strips off his clothes.

Once he gets done cleaning himself up, he will have the company of a young female to warm his bed, and then he will decide what to do with Orien and her new plus one.

14

ORIEN

The walk back to the sitting room is one of torment for Orien. Pain claws at her back, but more than that her mind races with the memory Elisiah shared with her. She knows that as soon as she is able, they will be packing what they need for their trek across the two Kingdoms.

Thundaria is almost two whole weeks away, and that is with the weather being tolerable. The animals are a whole different factor, but Orien has made the passage several times now for a few varied reasons. It was never anything remarkable for her.

Orien found the blankets of pure white snow to be blinding. With Elisiah by her side though, maybe she can keep herself distracted which will make the time go by swiftly.

Getting back into her room, she immediately pulls off the half-buttoned shirt and the remainder of her leather binding.

Lying face down on the black couch that still smells of flowers and vanilla, Elisiah sits by her side as she holds out a hand over Orien's damaged back. The warmth of her palm sinks into the exposed flesh, and Orien's breath catches in her throat. It was not from pain but from the way her pulse quickens; she has never let someone so close to her when she is so vulnerable.

The only connections she makes with anyone are only from the women at the brothels.

It has already started healing, Little One. Get your things ready for the journey. As soon as this body can stand, we will set out.

The voice of the beast soothes Orien right now. It is a sound she does not know she needs until now.

It is normally not something surprising to her due to the beatings they have become accustomed to over the years. The beast always speaks to her during and after the times just to make sure Orien has not gotten too lost in her own mind.

Orien has only just started blocking out the beast during their times of torture because she feels like she owes it to the beast. It is the one thing that stays consistent in her life, and the beast has tried to protect her.

She managed to keep it at bay during the duration of the beating earlier, but as soon as Alister wanted to push the limits with Elisiah, she could not hold on anymore.

Everything in her and the beast raged in the confines of the cage that has been built in her mind.

All she could do was let the beast say what it needed to say and show the King that she would not back down so easily. The shadows on the other hand came of their own accord and have not been back since they felt the threat was gone. It was almost like they just needed to make sure Elisiah was safe before they went back to their hiding place again.

Orien cannot remember the last time she went so long without them being wrapped around her. It is like they think she does not need them as much now.

"Can I do anything for you? I mean you look really pale, well, paler than I would think you normally are." Elisiah sits on the very edge of the ornate lounger and folds her hands together in her lap.

She has not looked anywhere but at Orien's maimed, bloody back.

Orien cannot even find it in her to care that this woman sees more of her than anyone. A part of her feels comfortable being so exposed with her.

Alister, Evadne, and a handful of his Guards are the only other people who have seen her like this.

None of which was with her permission. Alister has taken many things from her and none of those things she will ever forget.

No. We will be moving in a couple of days. You need to worry about what you will need to keep you warm and comfortable.

The beast brushes against the space it takes up in Orien's head, like it is comforting a small creature.

Also, make sure you pack your boots.

Orien closes her eyes as the beast speaks to Elisiah, and all she wants is to see the light lavender flowers surrounded by bright green leaves and light brown bark again.

She does not know if the memory was meant to appear in her mind's eye when it was being told, but it did.

It was like she was there. The colors were vibrant and soft to her eyes. It was like looking through a separate set all together, because she has never seen the world as colorful as that. She could smell the fragrance of the multi-layered petals. Orien was sure if she reached out, she could have felt the touch on her skin.

The couch shifts, and it draws her out of the vivid world she desperately wanted to see again.

Opening her eyes and angling her head towards Elisiah, she watches the woman run her hands through her hair. The tips of her fingers get caught on many of the curls that have fallen from the leather wrapping.

"What all do I need to pack? I have never left Univier. Hell, I have never gone beyond the forest besides maybe only an hour out. What do we have to get through to get to Thundaria, and how many coats do I bring?" She rambles and her hands keep rubbing each other like she is trying to start a friction fire.

Orien knows this day has been absolute shit for both of them, but her mind has been made from stone, while Elisiah's has not.

She will try to never judge the woman in front of her, but Orien can feel how bruised and broken her heart is.

Her back starts to tingle, and she knows from the way her small hairs on her arms rise that some of the shallow cuts are closing themselves. The bigger ones, like the one that cuts down to bone, will take time. The others will heal rather fast or so she hopes.

Pack your winter attire and a dress or two. Any of your hygiene things as well. We will go to Fredrick before we leave to grab some satchels of basic foods, the rest for which we can hunt. Now, leave us to heal and go pack.

The beast sounds frustrated, and it does not mean to.

The pain and suffering that Orien has been through has of course run its way into the beast. For the longest time, it would try to seal her in her mind like she now does to it, but it never worked.

Orien is strong willed when it comes to something she wants. Most of her life, she wanted to feel the pain. It is the main reason she did not flinch when getting her lashings; a part of her still needs the pain to feel alive. She may not feel other basic feelings, but pain has always been the one she felt the most and until now her most craved.

Whatever she feels being around Elisiah is what she wants to feel every day until she stops breathing. It was not until she came around that Orien wanted to find a way to get her muzzle off; Orien wants to know her face for once. The thoughts of seeing what lay behind the mask scared her, but not more than the reason for wanting to reveal the mystery that it covers.

We will find the answers to the questions we ask, Orien. Do not worry, do not think. We need to heal so we can get Little One out.

Orien hears the beast, but it does not stop her now never-ending thoughts.

"Why do you call her Little One?" The answer she truly does not know but is curious as to why the beast gave Elisiah a nick-name. It chuckles in her head, and it sends a fuzzy feeling across her skull.

What else are we to call her?

"Well, I mean, she has a name."

Yes, she does, but Little One fits her. Does it not? Everything about her is little to us. Her hand on our face should answer the question for us. She is a lovely Little One.

Something taps the side of her brain again, and it makes her think that this thing in her has a tail.

"She is rather small I suppose, but her curves are magnificent." What did she just think about? She has no idea. Her cheeks grow warm, and Orien is baffled at the fact she is blushing. What is happening to this stone-hearted, cold-blooded killer? The beast laughs, and it sounds more like a howl than anything.

Remember the conversation we had about being a pervert? We are one and the same. Now we grow extra warm and something swims in our middle when we think about Elisiah.

"I am not a pervert; I just know something made by Lixtis's hands when I see it. That woman was made slowly and with all the care in that God's hands. Have you seen the way her skin seems to glow?" Orien has never spoken the name of the God of Souls before, but it is the only explanation for how this being could pop up in her life so suddenly.

The changes in the way she has felt in just these two days is enough to spin her head off her shoulders.

Do not speak of that absolute incompetent fool. He is better off forgotten for all the hardship he and that nebulous brother of his have caused. Centuries of war for nothing. It is a waste and a pity.

Irritation crawls over her skin, and she slowly sits herself up on the couch.

She cannot completely straighten her back, but the tingling has amplified, and the feeling of tugging is enough to tell her the large wounds are starting to heal.

Her healing has slowed since she was a child. No more bright white light, and no more instant healing. No one could tell her what it was or why it happened.

Now, she is left with what was left behind, but it is still a much faster process than that of a normal Fae.

Orien looks around the room and finds Elisiah on her knees folding her clothes in tight little rolls on the floor. The concentration shows in the way the lines appear between her eyes.

Her white blouse has blood streaked across the shoulders, and from what Orien can see, down part of the front. Grabbing the discarded shirt on the floor, she slips her arms in and starts to button the top buttons as she walks over to Elisiah.

She does not stop the rolling of her clothes as Orien steps to her side. Her face shines in the Water's Light from the tears cutting a path down her face.

Orien slowly kneels by her and gently wipes the falling tears from her cheeks. They are warm on her hands, and she can smell the salt in the air; a tug pulls in her chest.

At the same time she feels the tug, Elisiah looks up at her face and places a hand over hers. Orien breathes in the scent of her and looks into her eyes as she tries to find her own voice to tell her it will all be okay.

No matter how hard she tries, she cannot get that part of her back. She hopes Elisiah can see what she wants to say by the look in her eyes. One day she will be able to say all the words she needs to say, but that day is not today.

Elisiah takes a deep breath and closes her eyes.

A picture of steaming sticky iced buns pops into Orien's head, and she can smell everything about them. The warm smell of fresh baked pastry. The white sugar glaze lightly drizzled across the top. Orien is shocked by the sudden sweetness that overtakes her mouth. It tastes just like she imagined it would from the picture Elisiah created in her head. Even the familiar smell of the fire in the kitchen's burner does not compare to the small taste she just had of the sweet yet imaginary bun.

She watches Elisiah as her shoulders relax and she lets out her breath slowly. The light chocolate brown eyes open, and Orien's heart skips in her chest as she rubs her thumb across the beautiful brown skin and loses all her own thoughts in her head. She takes a breath in just like Elisiah and lets it out just as slowly.

Orien is not sure if Elisiah knows that she was placed in her memory during their traumatic time earlier, or if she knows that Orien can taste the sweet food she must be thinking about. Right now does not seem like the time to tell her, but it is the right time to get her stuff together so she can grab a whole tray of those buns just for their Little One.

I told you she is our Little One. Do not question me again about the things that I know.

The voice is smug in Orien's head, and with that smugness, she reluctantly pulls her hand from Elisiah's face.

Standing up and heading to her bedroom, she begins to pack a brown leather bag with all her fighting leathers and extra weapons. The beast may think Elisiah is theirs, but Orien knows that can never happen.

15

ELISIAH

Elisiah cannot help but watch Orien as she walks away. There is a tightness to her stride, and it makes her tears feel heavy as they fall down her cheeks again.

Between what she sees when she is asleep and now the images of Orien being beaten, she does not think she will be able to live through it.

Leaving her clothes where they are on the floor, Elisiah stands and walks into the bedroom just on the other side of the wall.

The door is open, so she steps through to find Orien sitting on the side of her bed, facing the far wall.

Walking to her side, Elisiah slowly sits down on the bed beside her.

Orien keeps looking at the wall with blank eyes, her hands resting on the bed. Elisiah places her right hand over Orien's left and sighs.

She cannot help but to look at her back again; her shirt is visibly damp from the blood.

Standing up from her spot, Elisiah turns to face Orien. The size of the assassin has them face to face, even with the taller one of them sitting down.

Her eyes are unmoving, solely focused on the same gray spot on the wall, as Elisiah gently unbuttons the few buttons at the top of the shirt.

Elisiah does the best she can to not look at the exposed breast in front of her as she slides the ruined fabric off the shoulders it covers. Orien should be resting, so that is what she will do.

"I promise I am not looking. This is ruined, and you need to rest. We can leave when you heal."

As she speaks the words, she begins guiding Orien's body towards the mattress, making sure not to let her back rest on the clean blankets.

"Come on, Orien. I am the size of an ant next to you." Elisiah grunts as she does the best she can to manhandle the body, so she is face down on her bedding.

We are tired, Little One. Orien has gone somewhere else.

The voice is minor compared to the other times it has spoken, and Elisiah closes her eyes to stop the tears from spilling over. Seeing the mess of Orien's back again, she knows that medical supplies are needed.

"After I get you laid down," Elisiah pauses to take a calming breath; she hiccups in the process. "I must get Fredrick. He will know what to do." She speaks to herself now.

Pleased with how she has gotten Orien laid on the bed, Elisiah grabs the blanket from the empty side of the bed and gently covers her legs. Taking a step back, she looks at Orien's face only to find her eyes closed, her breathing too steady and slow.

Taking that as a good sign, she leaves the room and heads to the main door that leads to the corridor.

Gently opening the door and peeking her head out slightly, Elisiah looks to see if anyone is in the area. Not seeing anyone, she slips from the door and sprints as fast as her legs will carry her until she reaches the kitchen.

16
FREDRICK

Fredrick sits at the small two-person table in his kitchen, whittling a small wooden figurine. The sound of pounding footsteps pulls his attention away from the knife and wood as Elisiah skids to a stop at the entrance.

As quick as he can, he stands from his spot. Her breathing is too fast, face stained with tears, and blood covers her hands and shirt. Fear spikes in his heart.

"Elisiah! What happened to my girl?" Fredrick crosses the space faster than he has in years, but as he grabs her cheeks to make her look up at him, he realizes she is physically okay.

He can breathe easier now.

Panic-filled brown eyes investigate his as she says, fighting her sobs, "Altair. He beat. He beat Orien. It is so bad."

Fredrick stiffens as she says Orien's name, and realization overcomes him.

"Are you hurt?" His voice is hard and stern. Right now, he feels just like he did when he was younger and in his prime.

He feels lethal.

"He made me watch." Elisiah grabs the front of his white shirt as her shoulders shake.

"It was awful, Fredrick. I could not stop him."

He holds her up as her legs go weak. Right now, nothing hurts him worse than what she had to see and what Orien had to go through.

Fredrick knows he has stayed sheltered in his kitchen walls for too long.

"Take me to her, Elisiah. I will try my best." He grabs her shoulders and sets her up straight as he leans down just enough to look in her eyes.

"You need to leave this place; do you hear me?" Reaching up to her face, he wipes her cheeks to dry them just a little, but his efforts fail.

"As soon as Orien can move without restriction, I want the two of you to go somewhere far away from here." The fear in his voice hides behind the growing anger.

Not for himself but for the ones he has watched grow since babies. He is not sure to what extent of damage Orien has been through since he retired from his service, and right now, he cannot bring himself to think about it.

"He ordered us to go to Thundaria in his place for the King's crowning ceremony. We are to leave as soon as we can, but Fredrick, she cannot move." Elisiah holds herself up now, and her tears have stopped. Fredrick knows the look well in her eyes.

The look of determination.

Elisiah is capable of remarkable things, and he has told her that all her life, but nothing he says makes her believe it.

She grabs his hands in hers and turns from the entrance where they have been standing all this time.

"Follow me." Demand sounds spectacular in her tone as the man grips her hand with his and follows on her heels the whole way to where he will find Orien.

It only feels like minutes when Elisiah guides Fredrick through the threshold of the tall wood door that brings you to Orien's rooms. Elisiah does not give the man behind her the chance to take in the view as he is pulled into a different room to the left of the main door.

As soon as he enters the room, he spots the bed in the center and the blood soaked back lying on top of it.

Letting go of the hand holding his, Fredrick hurries over to the left side of the bed to get a closer look at Orien's back. It does not take him long before a long line of curse words trail from his mouth, his hands resting on his hips.

"I did not know what to do. She walked in here, started staring at the wall, and then just passed out." Elisiah has one hand on her hip and the other moving through the air with her words.

Fredrick leans in closer to get a look at each of the wounds on Orien's back. He notices that each of the still open slices have a light purple tinge around the cut lines.

"Elisiah, what I need you to do now is calm down." The old man turns his head just enough to see her out of the corner of his eye.

"What good is the training we have been doing if when you need to use it, you completely lose your mind? You cannot panic in a time like this." Fredrick looks back to the body in front of him as his brain confirms that the purple ring around each cut is from a poison.

"Cannot panic? Fredrick, do you see the same thing I am seeing?" Elisiah's arms are spread wide at her sides as she looks at Fredrick with bewilderment on her face.

"I know this is brutal. I know you are overwhelmed, but right now it is not about you. It is about Orien and making sure we get this poison out of her system before it makes its way deeper." Elisiah steps to his side and begins to examine her back just like he does.

"Fredrick, I did not even notice the color changes of her skin."

Fredrick nods his head. "You would be surprised what you can miss when you are in a state of panic, my girl. Now, look and tell me what you see and how we can solve the problem."

Fredrick knows it is not the time to make this into a teaching moment, but it is the only way he can think to calm Elisiah's nerves. If he gives her a task that needs a correct answer then it will redirect her thoughts, keeping her in the moment with him.

She wastes no time beginning her search of the wounds to try and pinpoint exactly what type of plant could have been used. Fredrick cannot help but watch Elisiah as her eyes scan the expanse of the wounded flesh in front of them. It has always amazed him how she can learn so quickly; her mind seems like a never ending vault of knowledge to the old man.

"Since the color difference did not show itself until three hours after the initial strikes ended, and from the way the purple is branching off into her solid skin..." Elisiah pauses as she searches her mind.

"It is Popitee. Altair used Popitee to slow the healing process but to also make sure it would knock her out." Elisiah looks to Fredrick as she waits for his reply.

"That is correct. Now, we know Popitee can be lethal to Fae in a high enough dose, so what is the corrective for it?" Fredrick knows Elisiah knows the answer.

"Hollowsroot! it is Hollowsroot!" Elisiah sprints from Fredrick's side as the answer pops in her head.

He cannot help himself as he grins.

Fredrick is a very talented healer, or he once was, until his age started to catch up with his body. At one point in his life, he could have just laid his hands on Orien and healed her within seconds, but now he barely has enough strength to stand. He will still give it everything he has to heal her mangled back, but he will need all the help from Elisiah that he can get. This will not be a quick process for any of them, but it will be something that gets done.

17

ORIEN

Orien has been lost in her mind since she walked into her room. It only feels like seconds since she was just there. The last thing she could remember was the darker gray spot on the wall in front of her. Even the beast in her was silent.

As she drifts in this state of consciousness and unconsciousness, all she can think about is how she ended up here. She understood the beating and why she got the lashings, but she has not disconnected from herself like this in years.

The last time in fact was right after her first bleed. A time she remembers all too well but is not ready to think about again just yet.

Everything around her is pitch black, and it looks like it is moving. If she looks at it long enough, she could swear it watches her back.

"Who is it?" Orien feels delirious calling out into nothingness, but then again something feels so familiar about this place. It could be that this is in her own head but deep down she feels like she is not anywhere near herself right now.

Reaching up to her lips as she notices the odd sensation of her jaw moving, she pauses on the feeling of her lips.

The muzzle is gone.

As she waits for something, anything, to happen, she looks over the rest of her body. Everything is where it is supposed to be. Her fingers wiggle back to her, and her toes move in her black boots. A plain black shirt covers her torso, and she is sure that when she went into her room she wore a black button up.

This is not her own head.

Movement in front of her makes her whip her head up in the direction. The hair on her body stands on end, but she keeps her heart rate calm and her breathing steady.

"Who. Is. There." She speaks the word as a statement because she knows someone, or something is watching her back. "Come out or go back to wherever you came from."

A low rumble crosses the darkness, and Orien meets it with her own. Nothing will make her back away from where she stands, if she did, she would be weak. She is anything but weak.

You sound older.

The voice is smooth, warm, and soft. It is the only other pleasant voice besides Elisiah's. Something about it sends an ache across her center, and she feels slightly emptier than she normally does.

If you find yourself here then I take it you have found yourself in quite a bit of trouble.

Orien stands tall, locking eyes with a spot of darkness directly in the front of her.

"I do not know what you are talking about. I was in my room one minute and then in this place the next."

Everything around her shifts.

Yes, but the other part of you is not here, so you must know where you are going. You are not the type to leave it by itself for too long.

The voice slips closer to her. Orien's body grows warm, and her hair soothes, laying normally on her skin once again.

You always have favored that dark little beast and not the lighter one.

Confusion is the only thing Orien feels as this nothingness talks to her.

It is a shame you never gave it more of a chance. It could have healed you as soon as the first strike hit your back. Now, you're being healed by the hands of a human.

Orien's head clears at the mention of Elisiah.

"How do you know that? About anything that has happened to me?" A growl rips through her throat at the thought of someone knowing everything about her and nothing of them.

Because my little Orien, I am you.

Just as the voice speaks the words, a sharp pain burns down her spine. Her teeth grind against each other as it catches her off guard.

"Wait, what do you mean?" The words come out faster than she meant them to, but for as long as she has breathed, she has never known who she is.

Now not only does she have the beast telling her that it is a part of her own self, but this blank space is too. How can she be so many different things?

Only question yourself, Orien. I have been missing you while lost in this darkness.

Another pain shoots down her spine, and a gasp leaves her mouth.

Her whole body fights against her right now, and all she wants to do is close her eyes. She cannot leave whatever this is right now, she has too many questions. Before she can think about speaking again, a distant voice calls her name.

"Orien."

The sound is small, but she would know it from anywhere. It is Elisiah. As she recognizes it, so does the space in front of her because it shimmers a faint white.

Do us both a favor and protect that of which is ours.

With those last words and her name still being called from far away, her eyes close on their own accord.

Dull light is all she can make out when her eyes open again, and she is sitting up on her palms before she can stop herself.

A heavy object covers her shoulders, and a familiar smell fills the air.

"Orien, do not sit up!" Elisiah. It is Elisiah. Her shoulders drop with relief at the sound of her voice. Blinking her eyes, Orien looks around the room. Everything is the same as when she walked in earlier, except another smell also accompanies the room.

Standing in a hurry and shoving Elisiah behind her back, Orien looks to the end of the bed to the old man standing there.

"Orien! Damnit! Listen to me!" Elisiah is mad. Orien does not care as Fredrick stares up into her eyes. The same heavy feeling from earlier once again covers her shoulders. Looking down she sees it is one of her blankets and her chest is fully exposed without it.

Turning around to find Elisiah standing on her bed, she reaches for her face before pausing.

"It is fine," Elisiah says, watching her face, so Orien grabs her cheeks and begins to examine every feature and curl to make sure she is fine.

"I am okay, Orien." Elisiah rolls her eyes as she removes Orien's hands from her face. Orien watches her as she hops off the bed and walks over to Fredrick's side.

"Thank you, Fredrick." She leans in and kisses his wrinkled cheek. Orien notes how his eyes are bloodshot. Noting the curiosity on her face, Fredrick explains.

"Elisiah told me everything that happened. She got me as soon as you fell asleep, she was worried to death about you. It was only right that I come and offer any healing I could." Orien remembers in detail that Fredrick is a healer. It is one of the reasons he moved up so quickly in the King's Guard and why he was left to care for her. It was convenient that he could heal himself and others while watching a child who could only cause damage.

"Your back is on the mend now. I did not know what else to do, and I panicked." Orien watches Elisiah as she lowers her head towards the ground just slightly. She knows Fredrick watches her as he places his hand gently on Elisiah's shoulder, but Orien cannot pull her eyes away from the pained expression on the other's face.

A stirring comes into Orien's head and the beast says,

Oh, Little One, you did amazing. Do not feel like you overstepped, you helped us.

Orien is relieved to have the beast back with her, and the smile that shines on Elisiah's face tells her that she is not the only one either.

"Good because that was a lot of work. We healed you the same day you passed out and have been tending to your back for two days now." Elisiah chuckles lightly as relief sets into the lines of her face. Orien tracks the way Fredrick looks between them.

"What was that?" The old man studies Elisiah, then Orien.

"Can I tell him, and then I will answer any questions? I swear." The words cross into Orien's head like a small wave. The feeling is intoxicating. It is something Orien knows she will never grow tired of. As the last ripple of Elisiah's words leave the space they just filled, Orien cannot help but to take in a breath.

The beast gives its approval for Elisiah to fill Fredrick in on their mind games as Orien lets the fact sit in her head that she has been asleep for three days straight. She has never had that happen anytime before, and that place she went to. What was that place? Who was she talking to? The soft voice she has come to recognize, over every sound around her, pulls her away from her questions as it makes her shoulders rest easier.

"So, Orien has this voice or thing in her head. It can talk to me." Elisiah clears her throat and adds, "Like mind to mind. Orien herself does not talk though."

Nothing about Orien changes as she explains it, but Elisiah shifts on her feet. It is because of her nervous shifting that Orien notices not only does Elisiah wear a tight pair of brown leather pants, but her knuckles on both hands are wrapped with white fabric.

Fredrick's mouth slightly parts as he lets the words sink in.

Orien's eyes are trained on the wrapped knuckles of Elisiah.

Elisiah still shifts her feet as she watches Fredrick.

"Mind to mind? As in you can both always communicate with each other, without even talking?" Orien and Elisiah nod their heads at the same time, neither of them taking their eyes from where they are looking.

Fredrick scoffs in disbelief before placing his weathered hands on his hips, smiling.

Shaking his head he says, "I knew I was right about you two. I could feel it in my bones."

Elisiah smiles at him as Orien moves in front of Elisiah. Reaching down with her right hand, keeping the left gripped onto the cover around her, Orien brushes her thumb over the fabric.

What is this?

A small red dot, no bigger than the tip of a needle, has stained the top of the fabric over Elisiah's pinky.

"Oh, these." Elisiah swallows as she reluctantly brings her other hand up to show Orien. "My knuckles got a little banged up while I was training yesterday."

Orien's eyes shoot up to meet Elisiah's.

Training? Training for what? Wait, training with who?

The beast was just confused as Orien, and they did not like the idea of their person having bleeding, wrapped, knuckles.

"Yes, training." Elisiah's face turns to one of annoyance at the tone of confusion in the beast's words. "Training, Orien." Elisiah takes her hand from Orien's as she explains. "Self- defense. Learning how to fight so I can protect myself." Her words come out hurried as her annoyance starts to build beneath the surface of her skin. "Learning to fight back so I do not have to rely on *others* to protect me. I will not allow myself to be the damsel in distress anymore. I will not wait around for someone else to save me any longer."

The beast sits up in Orien's head as they both ask each other the same question in unison.

Are we "others"?

The use of the word feels like a slap across the face, a knife to the heart they are not even sure that they have. They would die for this woman in front of them without a second guess. They would burn this castle made of stone to the ground if she spoke the words. Orien and the beast would let Alister skin them alive, pour acid on their bones, pluck their eyes from their sockets, if it meant Elisiah was kept safe.

Then she said one word and it makes them both remember that they just met this woman. A perfect stranger that they took a beating for.

A beautiful nobody that feels like a wonderful somebody.

Orien cannot comprehend all of the unfamiliar things she is feeling all at once, but she does know that until her last breath she will protect the small woman in front of her, no matter if she wants them to or not. That is something she has known since the first time her eyes caught a glimpse of the prettiest thing they have ever seen.

Protect what is ours.

The words circle around Orien as she places her empty hand on Elisiah's cheek.

Tell us how we can help.

Even though Orien and the beast are still confused with the rush of emotions, neither of them can stop themselves from the urge to touch the golden-brown skin in front of them. Orien wonders if Elisiah knows her skin holds a slight glow that grows with each passing emotion.

F REDRICK IS FORGOTTEN ABOUT FOR THE MINUTES THAT E LISIAH and Orien have their semi-silent conversation. It is only the man clearing his throat that draws Elisiah back to their reality instead of being lost in the pale brown eyes in front of her.

"You can help by teaching me what Fredrick cannot." Elisiah stops herself from resting her cheek further into Orien's palm as she speaks the words. The honey brown eyes glance to Fredrick, who has been watching them the entire time, as Elisiah speaks the truth about who has been teaching her.

What has he taught you?

"I am decent with a dagger. He has taught me how to scan a room to know each entry point. How to scale a wall, silence my steps, hide my scent, basic guarding skills, and other things as well." Elisiah grabs a small wood-handled dagger from the band of her pants as evidence for Orien.

"She is not giving herself enough credit where credit is due." Fredrick rolls his eyes as he adds onto her earlier statement.

"The girl is as quick as a whip, as mean as one too. She can throw that dagger at the center point of a burlap head with her eyes closed." The old man pauses as he looks at Orien.

"She does need help with her strength, her arms are weaker than I would like them to be. Oh, she has a soft spot for anything sweet." Elisiah whips her head out of the hand still holding her cheek as she gapes at Fredrick.

"You are the one that always tells me I can have a treat after I finish!"

Fredrick smiles at her. "Yes, well, you are very motivated by food." Elisiah's mouth hangs open, her eyes wide. Orien looks between the two as the beast laughs in her head.

We are food motivated as well, Little One, do not think anything of it. Besides, you need fuel to keep your muscles strong.

"Do not dare speak another word." The beast chuckles as Elisiah's words echo through its space.

Yes, ma'am.

Orien turns her head towards the door of her room after the beast in her head says the words; they send a concerning feeling down to her core that she does not know how to take. Elisiah walks the short distance to Fredrick before speaking again.

Resting her hands on his shoulders, Elisiah looks into his blue eyes that are encased by wrinkles.

"Thank you, Fredrick. Thank you for everything you have done for me and the things I know you will continue to do for me. I would not be the woman I am now if it wasn't for you."

Fredrick's eyes shimmer as tears build around them. "My girl, thank you for giving me a reason to live."

Elisiah smiles at him as he wraps her into a tight embrace. She knows she and Orien need to head to Thundaria, and she also ·cannot wait to leave this castle.

"You are already behind on your morning duties since you refused to leave first thing this morning. Go. Do not worry about us. We will be by to gather some food satchels." All he does is break their hug before he turns for the bedroom door. Elisiah knows he will walk out of the room silently. It is what he normally does when he finds himself getting emotional; Fredrick has never been one to show his feelings openly.

Orien and Elisiah watch as the man they have both spent many of their years with in the castle leaves them together in the room. As soon as the main door shuts, Elisiah wastes no time in gathering her bag as she looks towards Orien.

"I did not know exactly what you wanted packed, so, I put basically the same thing in yours that I put in mine." Her eyes glance down to the blanket that Orien's left hand still holds.

"I am sorry I did not dress you. It was easier to clean your back and apply the salve while you were undressed." Elisiah ducks her head as she remembers the fear she experienced in the last three days. Watching Orien's body lay completely still on the bed just behind them was scarier to her than watching her get hit with that metal tipped whip; at least then she knew the other was breathing.

Orien watches Elisiah like she always does when she is thinking. Elisiah has noticed most of the ways Orien communicates even without using her voice. She cannot tell you when she caught onto the slight twitches that only barely make her eyelids move, or when her shoulders are just a hair's width out of rhythm with her breathing, but Elisiah notices.

Orien does not reply to her as she moves to the wardrobe just across the room. Elisiah watches her movements to make sure they are like they used to be. She would not be able to live with herself if Orien has lasting effects from the poison. As the covering falls from the broad shoulders of the back turned to her, Elisiah cannot help it as her body takes in a silent deep breath.

It has been a personal battle for her to be around Orien while she was so exposed, but the feelings dulled when Elisiah was only focused on making sure the other stayed alive. Now, the feelings burn at her skin, and it feels like she might just catch fire.

She only allows herself to watch Orien long enough to note that her movements are just a little strained but nothing that will not correct itself over time. Bags packed, both females leave the room and head towards the kitchen to gather a small sack of food for each of them. They both took turns cleaning themselves before they left, and Elisiah had to force Orien to let her help with the sheaths she now has strapped across her chest.

Orien's movements are still stiffer than usual, but it does not stop how her body moves like one fluid motion. Anyone else looking at her would not be able to tell that the woman just spent three days in the deepest sleep Elisiah has ever witnessed.

Orien walks with her head straight and her shoulders back; it is honestly very impressive to see how she has kept moving like the abuse was nothing.

Making their way to the kitchen, Elisiah cannot help but take a few glances to make sure no blood has seeped through the tight black slip over shirt, even though she and Fredrick did manage to keep the bigger lacerations closed. The fact that they could easily be busted back opened sits in the back of her head.

Elisiah has never seen a garment like the one the female beside her is wearing, but it fits Orien. In size and fashion.

When she came out of the washroom wearing the garment, Elisiah had to turn her head before her jaw hung open and rested on the floor. It hugs every muscle of her arms, back, and stomach. The way it lays across her chest does not give any sign of the new leather strap Elisiah knows lays there.

On the bottom she wears a pair of black leather pants. These are not tight like the shirt, but have just enough moving room for the many motions she makes as she moves. The daggers adorn her thighs and sides. She even saw her put a few others in the sides of her leather boots.

For Elisiah though, the day's wardrobe is a cream-colored scalloped top and a pair of loose emerald, green pants. Her boots cover her feet, and her simple white coat rests in her hand. Her hair is back in the leather band, but she has put little braids throughout. The last thing she wants to worry about is the mess of curls getting tossed in her eyes while on horseback. Elisiah picked out the things she feels the most comfortable in and hopes they work for riding horseback for days until they reach their first rest stop.

The smell of the meat Fredrick currently cooks for dinner finds her nose, and she cannot help but walk past Orien and head straight into the kitchen. Her face lights up as she sees the old man cutting away at the many different vegetables on his work table. It does not surprise her to find him back into his normal routine so soon after leaving them.

"Fredrick, what is that lovely smell?" Elisiah sniffs deeply as she walks over to the man like she did not just see him. "It already has my mouth watering, and I have not even seen what it is yet."

Fredrick stops his cutting and smiles at her. He wipes his hands on his tattered brown apron and pulls her in for a hug.

He holds her by her shoulders as he pushes her back and gets a good look at her to make sure she is all intact. His eyes stop on the brown pack thrown over her shoulder and the coat in her hand.

"You have everything packed that you need?" The wrinkles on his face deepen as he asks her the question.

"Yes, we have everything we will need." Elisiah places her hands at the old man's wrist and smiles softly at him.

She hopes he cannot read the pain that still lingers in her eyes. He does not hesitate as he takes off his apron and throws it on the now forgotten vegetables.

"It is heartbreaking that I will no longer have you with me in the kitchen. I can only hope that the both of you will be okay."

Before Fredrick can move an inch, Elisiah grabs his hand and says, "Do not worry about us Fredrick. We can protect each other."

Elisiah looks over to Orien who stands on the other side of the worktable, picking at one of the yellow peppers that has not been chopped yet. Fredrick follows her gaze, and his shoulders sink.

"Yes. I do suppose both of you will be safe. I know Orien has made the passage many times and can handle herself well in a conflict. I wish both of you did not have to go through this."

Orien looks down at the old man and spins the pepper in a circle as she watches his eyes.

Elisiah is not sure how someone can hold Orien's gaze so long. It is like she looks right into your soul. Elisiah does not mind it that much.

"It is much better traveling and seeing other parts of this world than being stuck in this castle all my life. You know I have always dreamed of leaving this place."

"Yes, yes, I know my girl, but it does not make it any less painful to watch you go. Let me pack your sacks." Before she can answer, he moves around the small kitchen, gathering different things and setting them on the board that currently holds the discarded chopping knife.

Elisiah smiles and shakes her head before she looks up and finds Orien shaking her head at the man as well. Orien grabs an extra leather bag she carried with her and puts all the things he has laid there in it. Once it is full, she sets it on her shoulder and looks at Elisiah.

We need to be going too, Little One. The stable boy will be leaving his post soon.

Elisiah nods her head at her and looks to Fredrick. He is looking between the two of them, and something is written on his face, but it is not something she can read. It is the same look he had just this morning in Orien's room.

"We need to be going now. I will write to you as soon as we settle in the new place and let you know how everything goes."

She pulls him to her and wraps him in a tight hug, the same as just a few hours ago. He smells of flour and smoked meats.

Elisiah will savor that smell because she is not sure how long they will be gone.

Fredrick pulls away from her embrace and wipes his eyes with the back of his hand. "You will always be like a daughter to me. Never forget that."

Elisiah holds back her own tears, but honestly, she is not sure if she has anymore left to cry.

She kisses his cheek and walks to Orien who has not stopped watching the two the entire time. Something like familiarity crosses her mind, but it is soon washed away by a hand landing on the small of her back as they both walk out the kitchen's entryway.

The touch sends a spark into her stomach as her throat goes dry. Elisiah can feel every outline of Orien's hand while it rests on her back, and each connection sends waves of heat straight into her spine. Each heat wave makes her head feel fuzzy, but she walks along like nothing is wrong.

What is it? You smell of lavender. You have not smelt like that before.

Elisiah feels Orien's eyes burning into the top of her head, but she shakes her head as she tries to stay as calm as possible. "Nothing. It is nothing."

It is a blatant lie to herself and the one next to her. The feeling she has right now is one that cannot be put out on its own.

She has had this same feeling very few times in her life, but when she has, it always goes away after some alone time in her bed. It has never been from another person's touch, though.

The first time she felt it was right after she had her first bleed. She was reading a book before bed about a knight who saved a princess, and they shared a passionate kiss. Elisiah found herself exploring her body that night and many more after.

The urge to find a quiet, empty room nags at her head as they walk to the stables even though Orien took her hand from its resting place as soon as they were out of sight of the kitchen.

The warmth of her touch still lingers. The stables sit at the bottom of the castle on a few squares of open field. The holding barns are made of wood to her surprise, but every other building is, of course, made of stone. It does not matter to the forest though, because even the wood stalls are covered in vines and flowers.

A tall, slender boy sits just on the outside of the barn.

He jumps to his feet as he sees the duo approaching him. Orien walks past the boy as if she does not even see him, but Elisiah smiles at him before saying hello.

Just before Elisiah can tell the boy that she needs a horse, Orien walks out of the wooden barn with a massive animal.

The creature is so big that even seven-foot Orien cannot see completely over it. Her eyes stop just at the center of the horse's wide back.

It wears a black leather saddle, and Orien tosses her leather packs over the horse's rear end. The dark gray coat makes the animal look like it has just rolled in soot from a fire. Its long black mane and tail lay in perfect straightness down its neck and backside.

"Surely this cannot be a normal horse," Elisiah thinks to herself.

The stable boy takes the pack from her own shoulder and hands it to Orien. Elisiah watches as the female in front of her moves like fluid around the horse. Every time Orien has to cross in front of his head, the animal gently snaps his teeth at her, and each time, Orien simply narrows her eyes toward his.

Elisiah finds herself wishing she knew what the two communicated to each other. After Orien finishes latching the last few buckles to make sure all of their few belongings are held tightly, she jumps right on top of the animal.

Elisiah is still mesmerized by the sheer size of the animal.

"Will I be riding with you? I know how to ride a horse." Elisiah is confused by the fact that another horse has not been brought out for her.

If we put you on a separate horse then how will we keep you safe? We cannot stop the mind of an animal if it wants to run or toss you off. On here with us, it cuts down on our worries.

Not wanting to argue, Elisiah walks toward the mountain of a horse and the person currently sitting tall in the saddle.

Lifting her hand to Orien, she is met with a strong grip as she is tossed on the back of the horse. She adjusts her position on the back and tries not to bump into Orien.

His name is Samuel. He will be gentle to only Orien and well, now you, so do not worry about him.

Elisiah currently sits on a horse named Samuel, and she is leaving the Kingdom with the most feared assassin known around this Kingdom and others. Elisiah feels like she should laugh right now at the situation she finds herself in.

You need to come closer and wrap your arms around us. The track from the castle has many hills, and if you fall from the top of Samuel, you will be more than bruised.

Slowly, Elisiah scoots forward just enough to wrap her arms around the torso of the wall of muscle in front of her. The burning feeling comes back due to all the various places their bodies touch. Elisiah closes her eyes and says, "Okay, I am ready."

She is not ready; not at all.

With that information, Orien kicks Samuel's side, and the horse jerks forward before he starts in a brisk walk down the cobbled road of the castle. The movement makes Elisiah hold on tighter to Orien, as the sway of the horse's body under her is going to drive her insane.

Just relax, Little One. You will give yourself riding sores if you do not control yourself. You need to find balance and stay there.

Elisiah tries listening to the beast, but her body sends her too many different signals to know what to do with herself. She shifts her body slightly forward, and her breast grazes the back in front of her. She can feel Orien tense, and Elisiah feels terrible if her movements cause Orien's back to start to hurt again.

After getting used to the sway of Samuel, Elisiah loosens her arms from around Orien, leaving them to fall to rest on the Fae's thighs. Now, Elisiah is too consumed by the way the land flows to even think about the way she was just fighting the nerves of being so close to the body in front of her.

Orien squeezes the reins tightly in her hands, and she takes a few deep breaths before her shoulders relax again. Elisiah is completely immersed in the beauty of the land which makes her forget about the companion she travels with.

The nobles walk about, getting their daily tasks completed before sunfall, and even the animals of the forest carry supplies on their backs.

Elisiah has always found the balance between the people and the forest to be inspiring. If she could go back and see how it all started, she would. The lack of information she has about the start of the Kingdom of Univier sometimes consumes her brain, but today she just soaks it all in. The books that would have told her what she needed to know about her homeland cannot be found in the small library of Univier due to one of the laws put in place by the first founders.

Many nobles stare at them as they pass and gasp at the sight of Orien or the horse; she is not sure at this point. The fact snaps into place as they make their way out of the town and past the large arched gates.

"Orien, you did not hide yourself."

Not today. Hopefully never again.

"The people should know the truth. Maybe if they did, the bedtime horror stories would end."

Both females remain silent after their exchange, and it allows for some much-needed reflecting time for Elisiah.

19

ORIEN

THE SUN HAS ALMOST SET, AND ORIEN STILL RIDES RIGID ON Samuel. The trio makes it out of the immediate territory of Univier not too long after crossing the gates.

Samuel's gait made for quicker travel than that of a normal sized horse, but it did often make certain terrain harder for him.

For instance, when the pair was assigned to hunt down a shifter Fae that lived in Xaxteen, Samuel would sink knee deep in the mucky bogs that surrounded the place.

Xaxteen is a small town just outside of the Runearied Kingdom, which is always flooded by rain. The whole territory smells of mold and wood rot; Orien hated her time there whenever she had to go. She always spent hours after leaving in any clean water she could find to scrub her skin raw from the smell of the place. Orien does not understand the need to live in a place like that even if it is the favored place for unlawful activity.

The territory in which the Fae shifter hid is known for its long-standing underground market for selling the more unorthodox things.

It is a place that you only go if you have good cover, as well as eyes in the back of your skull. Many people say that the market even partakes in selling various parts of all the beings that live in Sytherac; the more exotic, the more frequently requested.

For a brief time after the founders of Sytherac built their settlement, many suspected the wings of some of the unlucky outcast fallen warriors were the main selling point in the market. No one has ever found evidence to support that statement, but that did not mean no one believed it.

Orien did not bother with such a place though; she simply went to get a job done and return to the warmer climate of her home. Most of her time in Xaxteen was spent chilled down to the bones, so the heat was something she looked forward to.

Elisiah stays quiet after her last talk with the beast, but the feeling of her hands resting on Orien's thighs does not subside. Orien is not sure if the training Elisiah went through with Fredrick is enough to prepare her for the actual thing. Being out in the elements, away from the comforts of your room can be a complete shock for some. It does not matter how much you train in a controlled environment, because once you leave that space, it all becomes real.

Orien knows her companion will need some advice when it comes to what is needed while on the journey, and that is what makes her nervous. Orien is not the best equipped to teach others, and she tends to be impatient in situations that she feels need to be done in a certain way. The fact she also has never had to teach another living thing how to keep itself from dying is also another reason for her unease. To Orien, survival is a skill she has always had and thought was second nature for everyone. She can only hope Elisiah already has some of those skills.

Being such a particular person is not easy for Orien, and it is not something she chooses for herself. It does not just make her mad when something is not done perfectly, it makes her skin crawl. The feeling is so overwhelming that it can make her see spots, and it has been that way for her for as long as she can remember.

Orien will try to teach Elisiah, but she holds no promises that she will not throw something in the process.

The weight of Elisiah's body against her back makes her turn her attention behind her. Elisiah has fallen asleep, and her cheek molds to Orien's back.

Looking at the surrounding forest, Orien decides that they can stand to go a little further before finding a place to roll out their beds for the night as the sun finally blinks out and the moon takes its place in the sky. The air cools with the setting sun and rising moon, and it makes her think of the woman behind her. She wonders how long it will take Elisiah to grow cold with no fire, and the thought makes Orien want to get to the first rest house they can find.

They will travel on the main trading road that leads into the next town over. The small town does not have a rest house, so they cannot pay for a bed but once they get closer to the Thundaria territory they will find a place to rest properly. She just hopes the air does not turn Elisiah to ice before then. Orien is not concerned with herself though, she finds herself always cold. Her luxury in life is a scalding hot bath after her long days.

Sleeping in a rest house would be a much-needed recharge just before the crossing of the snow flats that lead to the great frozen castle of Thundaria.

"Are you asleep?" Orien asks the beast in her head as she rests the reins in one of her hands and puts the other hand on her upper thigh, just above Elisiah's hand. The warmth from the small hand on her leg radiates through to the rest of her. If all it takes to warm her skin is Elisiah's touch, then Orien will make sure that touching is a necessity.

No, just enjoying the view. It is nice to see the forest come alive at night and not be forced into that corner we are so often in.

"It is a forest, what makes it nice? I have seen it many times and it all looks the same."

Yes, that is true, but we have never seen it with the likes of her. Can you not feel what we feel? Everything seems brighter and more alive.

Orien is almost positive the beast is being delusional.

"I feel the same as I always do. I do not know what you are talking about, and you are getting on my nerves with all this *we* talk. I am myself, and I do not see how you can be any part of me, the things you say do not line up with how I feel." As Orien says the words in her head, she cannot help but think back to the conversation she had in that dark space from her deep sleep.

Then why is it that every time she touches us our body lights on fire? Why does her aroma calm us and keep us centered? Her voice is soothing to our ears, and her features are soft on our eyes. It is moments like this that really make me think we are blind. At this point, we do feel like two different things just sharing a space.

Frustration floods her body as she listens to the beast speak about what she is supposed to feel, and part of her does feel it. That is what frustrates her more than anything. How is she supposed to know what she is feeling or who she is?

"Well, good. Now you can stop referring to everything as ours and us. That shit is annoying, and quite frankly, I am over it. From now on, you will talk for yourself, and I will do what I need to for me."

The beast inside of her seems to grow with anger, but it quickly turns and retreats to the back of her mind.

Orien feels slightly guilty about making the beast mad, but at the same time everything that has happened recently has driven her to the end of her sanity.

If it were not for the words of that empty place flooding her head, then Orien knows she would not have been so harsh with the beast inside of her. Everything has become a jumbled mess in the last couple of days, and now not only does she have one thing trying to tell her she does not know herself, but even the beast in her head is doing it too.

It does not help that even before any of this, Orien still could not tell you what she truly is, or who she wants to be. It was never a choice for her. She was not given the opportunity to be anything but what Alister wanted her to be, an emotionless monster.

Drawing herself from her thoughts, she looks around the dark traveling road, surrounded by dense trees with a mix of high and low canopies. The only ones that still hold onto their leaves in these cold months are the evergreens, which are the home for most of the small animals of the forest. The wind blowing through them makes the ones with leaves sing. The sound is the only thing Orien wants to hear at the moment because it allows her to clear her mind.

If it weren't for the added songs from the small birds called Nightferrows, Orien would not find herself slowly drifting from her body at all. It seems like the only safe place for her is beyond the confines of her own self, even though, right now she would rather be nothing at all.

The small birds only sing at night, and the stories say that no person or Fae has ever seen one. They almost seem like a myth to some but not to her. They did not need anyone to lay eyes on them to sing their melody every night. The creatures of night knew who they were, and it always made her think about herself. What she would give to be like one of them.

Orien does not know who she is, and every day she grows more consumed by the idea of finding out. Even if it were not for the cruel upbringing of Alister Altair, she feels it in herself that she would not be much different.

Accepting the fact that she has murdered more living things in her life than she has saved does not bother her. That is all she needs to know to tell her that she is a shit person. The beast in her is also more proof of that because it sees nothing wrong with the blood that stains their hands. Orien often finds herself wondering if the other part that lived in her at one point would be as accepting of their time spent killing others.

It has never made itself known other than healing the body she occupied when she was young. It did not stay around long enough for any of the feelings to stick in her head like with the other. Since the first day the thing made itself known, Orien can tell when it is awake, hungry, or even angry.

The light that would come and help her in her time of need did not leave so much as a trace of itself. For a long while after it would appear, she would spend time in her rooms cutting along her arms and legs. It was partly to see if she could get it to come back, but also because she began to crave the pain.

After years of beatings, lashings, ripped out nails, and even being burned with red hot rods, the feeling became welcome. The days when Altair decided he did not want to see the skin tear away from her muscles, she would find some way to feel that feeling, mostly from her own hands. Now, she is left to heal herself and to question if it was all just in her head.

The sound of a river grows louder and drowns out the song-birds. Orien is released from her thoughts but is now left with the lingering tingle in her skin that always comes before it gets split open by one of her daggers. Cracking her neck to release some of the tension in her body, the river comes into view. A river she does not remember being here.

The rushing water runs across a bed of large boulders and even some smaller trees. Ripples radiate back and forth through the water that tell her that it has different currents. They can cross easily, but to make sure none of their supplies gets swept away, she decides to get off the back of Samuel.

Something does not feel right about this new water source, but her mind is too crowded to think more about it.

Samuel stops just before the ground turns to soft sand while Orien places her hand on Elisiah's forehead to keep her head from hitting the saddle horn. Slowly, she slides off the horse while also lowering the head full of soft black hair down to rest on the seat.

Surprisingly, Elisiah does not wake up.

Standing with her hands out for a moment to make sure the sleeping woman does not tumble off the giant horse, she slowly brings her hands to rest at her side.

Inspecting the river and the width across, Orien grabs the leather straps of the halter that currently lay on the side of the dark gray coat of Samuel's cheek. Samuel huffs out a warm breath at her touch, and Orien gives the animal a good shoulder to the neck.

They have a mutual understanding between them that he will not bite her, and she will not bite him back. Since she bought the horse, they have often found themselves leaving each other's company bloody and bruised. The damn thing is a viper in a four-legged body, but its rider is also something in disguise as well. They make an effective team, but they fight more like siblings.

Together they walk towards the rushing water, and the body on his back does not flinch once. Orien notes that as odd.

"It must be nice to be such a heavy sleeper," Orien says into Samuel's head, he throws his own to the side in return. Her arm jerks with his movement and makes one of her still healing wounds pull open. It must have been one of the deeper ones that Fredrick and Elisiah could not heal completely during their time working on her.

The smell of her blood hits her nose just as they step into the water. It runs warm over her feet and legs and stops Orien in her tracks. Water in this climate should be almost freezing. Her brain starts trying to piece together the things she has seen on their way here, but with the songbirds' singing drifting her into her thoughts, she cannot remember much.

Her nose did not notice any scents besides that of Elisiah as she slept against her back. She curses herself as she tries to back out of the water, but her feet are planted in the stream. Samuel neighs by her side and tosses his head from side to side, almost hitting her on the side of hers. His muscles work to pull his hooves free to no avail. Orien looks behind them and finds four sets of glowing green eyes watching them; her eyes immediately find Elisiah.

Putting a hand on Samuel's cheek to try and calm him down, she calls to her beast. "We are being watched and trapped."

Nothing answers her, but she can feel it circle and lay back down. Anger rises in her chest.

"I need you to speak to Elisiah and wake her up. She is not safe asleep on Samuel's back."

Still nothing.

"Gods dammit, you're a tantrum throwing thing."

The eyes get closer, and Orien knows what they are by the way they move with perfect tandem.

The nobles that live on the outside of the gates call them Dream Weavers; they say that the entities are nothing more than green floating eyes. The tales that are told say they manipulate reality so that your dreams or nightmares come to life in front of your eyes. There are even some instances where the things can even make up their own reality for a person if they cannot find anything in that person's mind. Dream Weavers move with the night, using the darkness to travel from one place to the next. The only form anyone has seen from them is their green iridescent eyes.

Orien watches the four sets of eyes as she thinks of a way to protect Elisiah. Dream Weavers love to play games, but most of all, they love to watch their prey squirm. It is why they love to trap them.

Right now, they are trapping, but little do the beings know, you cannot trap a shadow. Just as the Dream Weavers draw closer, Orien wraps herself, Elisiah and Samuel in the black embrace of her shadows. The tendrils pull in the darkness of the night and blanket them. It is clear the only help she will get is from herself now, but she cannot bring herself to whisper her voice in Elisiah's head.

Her anger at its boiling point, Orien rips her feet from the ground that was just water and walks to the sleeping woman still laid on her horse's back.

Not hesitating, she grabs Elisiah under the arms and yanks her down from her spot before letting her ass hit the ground. Elisiah's eyes open and look right into Orien's, only her light brown eyes are solid white.

A white so solid it reminds Orien of the time she read a description in one of the first history books of the God of Souls, Lixtis. She only read the first few sentences before it was taken from her and burned over a fire by Alister.

Orien bends down to Elisiah's level and looks into her eyes. Elisiah blinks, and the white is replaced by her normal brown. The sitting female startles and then looks around at her surroundings. Not giving her time to make a noise, Orien puts her hand against Elisiah's mouth and shakes her head slowly. Looking behind Elisiah, she searches for any sign of the green iridescent eyes, but she finds nothing.

Even if the Dream Weavers did move through the night, they could not move through her shadows. The blackness that lives in her veins is a different kind of darkness than that of the night. What lives in her seems to be more alive than anything around her most of the time.

Feeling comfortable enough with their surroundings, Orien looks back at Elisiah. Her eyes swim with anger, and the sight of it makes Orien snarl low in her throat. Elisiah's breathing picks up, and the palm of Orien's hand grows warm, still pressed against Elisiah's pillow-soft lips. Their eyes lock in a silent battle to see who will back down first.

Before Orien can even think about removing her hand, two others wrap around her wrist and pull it from its resting place. A sharp pain shoots down her arm and ends at her elbow. Sucking in a breath and looking at her hand, she sees that Elisiah bit down just below her thumb.

Elisiah's eyes still watch Orien's as she says, "I thought we talked about no touching."

The feeling of teeth and the warmth of Elisiah's mouth brings Orien to her knees in front of the aggressive female.

The thing in her head finally uncurls from its corner and walks to the front of her head. Sheer excitement consumes the beast as it takes over its usual eye. Elisiah looks to the black eye and then back to the honey brown. She bites down harder, Orien leans in further.

Oh, Little One, if we—

The beast pauses, and Orien swears it looks at her brown eye before changing its words.

If Orien had not dragged you from the horse and cloaked us in shadows, we would have been dead.

The beast pauses as it watches her alongside Orien.

While you spent your time in your own dream land, the rest of us were being hunted. Oh, but do not let that stop you from biting harder.

Orien cannot even thank the beast for not putting them in the same box for the first time in her life. She is too consumed by Elisiah, the way anger suited her, the way her lips feel like soft butter on her skin. It is enough to make her feel everything all at once.

This is the first time she has been touched by someone out of anger apart from Alister and Evadne. It is so overwhelming that she does not even think she is breathing. Elisiah sinks deeper into her hand and blood trickles down the sides of her mouth. Something flutters in Orien's stomach at the sight.

"I will bite off a chunk of your hand if you do not keep your hands to yourself. I do not care if I were to die. I do not care if anyone ever sees me again, and I do not care about you or this stupid fucking trip to another fucking Kingdom."

Elisiah's heart pumps hard enough for anyone to hear it. Orien does not understand what is wrong with her or what could have caused a reaction like this.

"Every single one of you can all go fuck yourselves. I am done. I am leaving." She lets go of Orien's hand as soon as she finishes her rant, and the Fae female is utterly pissed.

You do not get to die. That is not your choice anymore, it is ours.

The beast does not lie, because to the both of them, Elisiah will not so much as skip a heartbeat without them having a choice in the matter. Everything for Orien has changed since Elisiah came into her life, and she will not let that go without a fight.

Biting us is doing nothing but making both of us excited, Little One, and if you think you can leave, then you must not know who we are.

Orien can feel the sinister smile paint itself across the beast.

We love playing games. So, if you want to play chase, then you better run and run hard, because when we catch you, you will not like us.

Orien snatches her hand free from Elisiah's mouth and blood drips from her fingertips. Her breathing is calmed but Elisiah's is frantic.

Elisiah looks around the forest and stands up from her spot on the ground. Orien crosses her arms over her chest as the beast says to Orien:

Do you think Little One wants to play?

Just as the words bounce around in her head, Elisiah bolts into the trees as quick as a wild hare.

The beast chuckles, and a wild feeling completely consumes Orien. It makes all her senses hone in on Elisiah, who is now her prey, as she runs through the forest.

"Looks like it," Orien replies as she sends her shadows to follow the escaping female as she twists and turns through the trees. They can play this game the whole way to Thundaria if it pleases Elisiah, because it more than pleases Orien.

Letting her get a head start while keeping the beast at bay for as long as she can, Orien darts from the open sky of the road to the covered canopy of the trees.

Orien's only purpose right now is to capture the woman responsible for turning everything that she is into dust at her feet.

20

ELISIAH

HER HEART POUNDS IN HER CHEST, AND THE GROUND UNDER THE soles of her boots echo with every drop of her feet. Why did she run? Elisiah has no idea, but at the time she just wanted to get away from everyone, even herself.

She does not remember falling asleep on that massive horse, but she remembers the ground meeting her ass as her wake-up call. Running only makes the throbbing in her cheeks worse. The sudden spark of reality tore her away from the place she visited in her sleep, and it made everything in her brain feel like a beaten egg, and she spoke without thinking. Her actions were solely based on fight or flight.

The sense of danger does not bother her, but the thought of living to see the future does.

If whatever she witnessed while she slept is any indication of how every single life will end, then she does not want to be here to see it. Only a fool would think they can change something like that. It was not long after they left the castle that Elisiah was sucked from her body once again. Only this time, it was not the battlefield or the camp. She found herself in a different body than her own, and it was a body filled with so much resentment that it made her sick.

Elisiah knew the person she found herself in was a man because his voice was one of the deepest she had ever heard; it rattled everything around him. She was stuck behind his eyes as he went over his plans in great detail with a female that she could not see.

The man talked about an extinction of all races that were not of the ones he made.

"Everything would be right in the world again without the pests running around to infect it. I could finally kill that bastard brother of mine, and everything will go back to how it was meant to be. He was never supposed to be born. I was supposed to have everything. He took that from me, and I will finally take everything from him."

The woman spent her time only agreeing with him, and Elisiah only wanted to leave wherever she was. The extinction he spoke of wasn't just a mass murder; no, he wanted to make a game out of it.

He wanted to hunt.

He wanted to torture.

He wanted everything to suffer from his own hands. Elisiah had never felt as terrified as when that man described the pain he would inflict to her world, to her people. It is all she could think about when she came back to her own reality.

That would explain why she tastes blood in her mouth, her lungs burn in her chest, and she has no clue where she is going. She does not think about biting Orien, but she wants someone to feel as hurt as she had when she was trapped wherever she was. The opportunity showed itself when Orien's hand did not move off Elisiah's mouth, so she took it.

The tastes of fresh water, spiced fruit, and a hint of metal still sit in her mouth from Orien's skin. When she drew blood and the first drop hit her tongue, her mind went fuzzy, and Elisiah swore she was floating. Orien's eyes spoke to her in that moment, and fear set deep in her chest; all her body wanted to do was flee. Looking back on it, she wanted to throw herself off a cliff.

There was no noise around her, except for her own breathing as it became labored due to her stupidity. Orien must be getting close, or maybe she did not even come after her. Who would miss a nobody like herself, and who would go through the trouble of chasing her? Even when the thing that lives in Orien's head told her they liked to play games, she did not think either of them meant it; well, until now.

The cold slices its way across her face, and the top of her ears feel numb. Still, she pushes further into the unknown.

From the corner of her eye, a swift black line passes by.

"Fuck, fuck, fuck," Elisiah says between strained breaths. She pushes her legs harder and swings her arms faster. Her legs have never carried her so fast, but even now she knows they are not fast enough.

A pit starts to open in her stomach at the uncertainty of what could be stalking her in the darkness. Another fact she did not think about was what else could be living in this place. Being hunted while she slept should have been enough to scare her away from this mistake, but in some situations, Elisiah did not make the best decisions.

The black line passes her again, but this time it is closer. If she could focus then she could defend herself from the threat, but her heart is working itself too hard to calm down, and all she has done in the past is freeze. What good has training done for her if she cannot even use her skills to actually protect herself? Alister is all that crosses her thoughts as his words repeat on a loop from when she asked him the one and only time about learning to protect herself.

"What good is a bed whore if she knows how to throw a man from the top of her?" He laughed at her that day, and after that she never brought it up again.

Bed Whore.

The words blur her vision as they keep repeating over and over, only now they begin to sound like her mother's voice.

Now, the black line begins to circle her as she runs blindly. How she has not tripped over a rogue tree root? She does not know. Come to think of it, she had not run into anything that she would think to reside on a forest floor. Looking down for a split second out of curiosity, she finds she is running on what looks to be a flat path, and around her ankles are flowing black ribbons of darkness.

"Why did I run? Oh, Gods I am a complete fool." Her words come out in a whisper, and her eyes burn with the tears she has been holding back.

Her body screams at her to stop, and her mind screams right back that she cannot. She is engulfed, drowning in a tidal wave of emotions, the main one, fear. Everything starts to blur as the water continues to pool around her eyes and the blackness that circles her has stopped right in front of her.

Not seeing it while she wipes the back of her hand across her eyes, she slams at her, full speed, into the chest of the only other person in this forest. Well, she hopes so anyway. She could die with pride at the hands of the most feared assassin in their world, but to die at the hands of some random person roaming the trees at this hour gives her cold chills.

The wind and every thought leave her body as she lands on her back on the ground and a silhouette leans over her. No air resides in her lungs and her heartbeat pounds against her skull. Strong legs straddle her upper thighs and squeeze her legs tightly together.

She is being pinned down on the chilling solid floor of the Earth, and the way her body reacts does not seem right for the moment. She needs to fight back.

Fresh water and the same perfume of spiced fruit dances across her senses. Orien. A familiar pressure starts to build between her legs, and heat creeps up her neck. She should not feel like this, not right now. Her breathing is out of her control, and her heart pounds against her chest as Orien's hands pin her own above her head. She feels so exposed even though she is still fully clothed.

Orien's face comes into view and her eyes are solid black holes. Elisiah gasps softly and the buds on her breast harden against her blouse. Orien looks so threatening when her eyes are fully consumed by the beast, but it sends a thrill down Elisiah's spine.

She thinks she must be losing her sanity. To find such a Fae this attractive when they can kill you with just a couple of fingers.

Elisiah tries to kick her legs as much as she can while pulling her wrists towards herself. The legs around her only tighten like a vise as the hands holding her wrist dig their nails just slightly into her skin.

The face above her slowly looks over her body as she tries to control her reaction to being studied so closely. Being examined by anyone else has always made her want to vomit, but right now she feels like a star shining in the night sky above her. If she could fly, she is sure her place would be right there with them. Embarrassment does not even touch the surface as the eyes cross her hips and every dip of her body.

Black eyes stop on her chest where her hard nipples push into her top. They slowly make their way to Elisiah's face, and her mouth parts slightly at the sight of the red hair against the pale skin. Orien's beauty is breathtaking and unique. A mix of masculine and feminine encased in a tall, lean body.

The black mask is harsh compared to all of it.

Not being able to see the lips underneath it makes her feel a rush of anger and need. Elisiah will find a way to get it off and see if the freckles on the top of Orien's nose grace the rest of her face.

Until then, she will get lost in the eyes watching her burn the details of the face inches from hers.

Orien lightly ghosts the tips of her fingers down the fabric covering Elisiah's arms, and the back of her head digs into the ground under her. The pressure builds over her whole body and her mouth opens wider as she starts to lightly pant. The fingers stop just at the base of her arms and start to trace towards her exposed neck.

Neither of them breaks eye contact as Elisiah gets to watch as one eye fades from black to brown. It is transfixing to witness.

Orien's large hands find Elisiah's throat.

She finds the strength to stifle a moan. As one keeps lightly squeezing the base, the other finds its way down her body, stopping just at the swell of her full breast. Elisiah lets out a breath, and the pressure stops abruptly. The feeling makes her want to groan, but she does not allow herself to give the Fae above her the satisfaction of her distress.

The pace at which Orien's hand travels is honestly painful, and the pressure being held against her throat is not enough.

Elisiah needs to feel her strength.

Elisiah wants to feel every ounce of what Orien can do.

Orien puts more of her body weight on Elisiah, and her hand tightens around her throat. Elisiah's back arches from the ground, and her eyes close as her head tips up to allow more room for Orien to grab. Not missing the invitation, she moves her hand from the base to the middle and squeezes the pressure points on the sides.

Elisiah cannot stop the moan that comes from between her lips. The hand resting by her breast slowly moves to the ruffles in the middle of her blouse. Her hands, no longer pinned on the ground, do not move from their resting place.

Parting the buttons and slipping her hand inside the fabric, Orien's calloused, scared covered hand makes Elisiah forget any fight to conceal her moan. Elisiah is overcome with need as she tries to move her legs an inch, so she can release some of the pressure growing between them at a rapid pace.

It works to no avail as Orien tightens the grip she has with her legs, and the hand on her chest finds the mound of her breast.

As soon as Orien grazes a fingertip over a hard nipple, a low growl comes from her throat, and Elisiah feels like her back is going to break with how far it has arched. Her whole-body aches for more, her whole-body aches for a connection with someone.

If she is to die, she does not want to die not knowing the touch of another person.

Her mind screams Orien's name and begs for anything, but the words will not leave her mouth.

Orien pinches her hard nipple between her fingers and lowers her face to Elisiah's. The muzzle grazes across the captive woman's lips, and Elisiah cannot help but to wet them with her tongue, imagining what Orien's lips look like and how they feel.

When she opens her eyes and looks at Orien's face, her eyes are closed, and her nose rests next to her own. Her face rests in a way she has not seen before; all the tension normally rooted there is no longer present, and in its spot is something that resembles peace.

The grip she has on her legs loosens just enough, and Elisiah can finally bend her knees.

Slowly, Elisiah rubs them together. Feeling the movement, Orien lifts her head just slightly and shifts her hand from the peak of her breast.

"Please." The word is hoarse as it comes out of Elisiah's throat, still held tight, and her eyebrows scrunch together as she investigates Orien's eyes. As soon as the word leaves her mouth, Orien's hand that holds her throat releases.

A growl releases from Orien as her eyes close again.

"Please." Elisiah begs as she says the word again. All she wants is for Orien to explore every inch of her body in the middle of the forest. Elisiah does not care about anything else other than what Orien's hands feel like on her body.

Orien moves her hand from the white ruffled shirt, and rests it on the ground next to Elisiah's side.

Moving her legs away from Elisiah's, she rises up to her knees. Orien's shoulders sink in, and her head falls back so she looks up between the canopy of the trees.

We would never do anything you do not want us to, Little One.

The voice is soft and gentle in her head, and she knows it tells the truth. The words leave a trail of flames inside her that mix with the shame she feels from thinking something good would come from this.

"I never said I wanted you to stop." Elisiah can feel how red her cheeks burn as she lays her arms by her side.

No, you did not, but we did.

Elisiah looks into her eyes for answers as Orien watches her face.

"I do not understand." She did not know what else to say now, but she did know she wanted clarity. If she could shrink down and crawl into a hole she would.

You do not want us. You want a distraction.

Orien's hand wipes across her face, and her chest rises with a deep breath as the beast does its best to explain.

We are many things, but a distraction is not one of them.

Elisiah shakes her head in disbelief at what she is hearing. "I am not asking for a distraction, Orien. I am just asking to feel something. Something other than the hell I have been feeling."

Orien sits on her knees, still straddling Elisiah's legs, her arms draped lazily across her black covered thighs.

You want something that will take you away from yourself. That is a distraction. Until you know the difference between that and us, we cannot go any further.

Nothing makes sense to her, and all she wants to do is get off this forest floor and start back on their journey; forget this ever happened.

"I need to stand up." The words are short, and she refuses to let any emotion show in them. Orien does not hesitate as she rises to her feet and reaches a hand out for her to grab.

Elisiah ignores the hand as she gets to her feet. Quickly she dusts off her ass and legs before turning back to the way she came, or what she thinks is the way.

Honestly, she cannot tell the difference in the directions right now.

Little One, do not ignore us. You need to understand for your sake and ours.

The air feels colder now that she is not filled with the burning from her body, but she continues walking straight as she pretends the giant shadow behind her does not exist.

Orien stays just a few paces behind her on their way back to Samuel, and Elisiah cannot help but distance herself from reality.

She is not sure how long they walk in silence before the horse comes into view again, just off to the side of the narrow red dirt road. Samuel knows there is something going on between the two as he walks over to Elisiah, pushing his front hooves forward so his shoulder drops, making him closer to her level. She gives the animal a small smile as she slips her boot into the stirrup and plants herself into the seat.

He stands to his full height and begins walking down the road, leaving Orien on her own two feet. Elisiah tries not to laugh aloud at the shock on Orien's face, but if she had to guess, Samuel has just picked a favorite. The trio keeps walking that way until daybreak the next morning.

21

ORIEN

the pair walking beside her. Elisiah is still riding on Samuel's back, and both of them are doing a perfect job of ignoring her. If the one in the saddle cannot listen to reason, then she will not waste her time trying to get the beast to explain it.

Orien has never met anyone like Elisiah before, and understanding her has been a task the assassin was not properly prepared for.

Well, she is not just anyone. It would make sense that we cannot understand who she is as quickly as we can others, Orien. She is not others.

The beast has been restless since their time deep in the forest, and Orien cannot blame it. One of the hardest things she has ever had to do is turn Elisiah away. It actually makes her muscles ache from how she has to restrain herself from constantly touching the woman.

Everything about their situation last night was perfect for her. Everything, except for the way Elisiah felt, because it completely overwhelmed Orien. The mixture of Orien's own wants, mixed with the Elisiah's need of forgetting, was just too much. The beast could not even tell if what they felt from Elisiah was genuine.

What Orien felt for Elisiah since the moment she saw her has been real. It has been extremely confusing for her, but it is the one thing she can say is real. Orien cannot bring herself to take it any further with Elisiah if she does not know if the feelings are reciprocated. She does not want to be a distraction for Elisiah.

"I know she is not just some other person to us, but we do not even know what she is to us either. Now, she has taken our horse while also giving us the silent treatment."

That is true, but we did just turn her down while she was her most vulnerable. That is enough to warrant the treatment.

Orien rolls her eyes as the thing speaks. She knows everything could have been avoided, but nothing has ever set her spiraling more than that mouth biting down on her.

Elisiah clears her throat, and Orien looks at the side of her face.

"Samuel, how much longer do you think we have?"

"Is she really talking to the horse? Like the animal can speak back to her," Orien thinks to herself, but she looks ahead to see if she can spot any signs of the town.

We will not be coming into the town until after sundown.

The beast speaks in place of Samuel as Elisiah sits up straighter in the saddle; that makes her seem much smaller than she is.

"Samuel? Did you hear something?"

The horse blows his breath as he shakes his mane, which gets a smug smile out of the one on his back. Orien cannot believe this grown woman is acting the way she is.

Brat.

The beast in Orien is getting just as annoyed as she is, and satisfaction fills her as Elisiah snaps her head to the side to shoot daggers her way. She stares right back at the female.

"What did you just call me?"

We called you what you are acting like. A brat.

"How dare you call me that! I am not a brat!"

Could have fooled us.

Elisiah pulls the reins tight in her hands stopping Samuel in his tracks just before she slips out of the saddle and walks right up to Orien. Pushing a finger into Orien's middle she says, "You do not get to call me anything, do you understand me?"

Orien can see the steam coming from her ears.

What if we do, brat, what will you do?

She moves closer to Elisiah, the single finger pushing harder against her.

"I will make you walk the rest of the way to Thundaria. You will be kicked off Samuel the whole way." Elisiah means it, but she does not know that Orien has walked much further many times before. This is only child's play to her.

Orien grabs her wrist so she cannot move her hand, and Elisiah flattens her palm against Orien's shirt as she takes a step back.

Her eyes look between the hand covering her skin and the face looking down at her.

Before she can think better of it, Orien wraps her free arm around the smallest part of her waist and pulls Elisiah in so she is flush with her chest. Elisiah's wrist is against Orien's throat, Orien's hand wrapped around it as she looks into the soft brown eyes.

Are you really saying you can overpower us? Should we replay last night?

"Why? Just so you can turn me down after getting me worked up?" Something like hurt crosses Elisiah's eyes, catching Orien off guard.

We were not trying to hurt you, Little One. We just do not want to ruin you.

"Ruin me? Orien, how could you ruin me?" Elisiah goes slack in her arms, and Orien tightens her grip.

Little One, we are stained by blood. We have killed more than we can count, and all those deaths are on our hands. If we do anything more with you, then we risk staining you with that burden as well. You are too beautiful to be ruined by red.

As the beast speaks the words, Orien wishes she could have said them instead. Every word it says is true.

Only Orien should have to answer for her actions when it comes to her affairs, not anyone else. Especially if that person is Elisiah; this woman can change the world. She has felt that deep inside her from the very beginning.

"You do not get to tell me what burdens I choose to carry. Neither of you do. If I want to drown myself in crimson, then I will. No one can stop me; this is my life." Elisiah's words are strong, and her pride slaps Orien in the face as they sink in. She is right. No one gets to tell her how to live her life and how she chooses to spend it, even Orien.

"If I want to be properly ravaged after I run through the forest in the dead of night then I will do that on my own free will. No one can stop me. If I want to be held against a chest by strong arms–" Elisiah inches her face closer to Orien's, "–no one can stop me." The words are a whisper against the muzzle.

A soft rumble crosses Orien's chest, and her hand grips Elisiah's hip as the beast says,

Oh, Little One, I do not think anyone would want to stop you.

"Good. Now, put me down." Elisiah gently places a kiss against the smooth black leather against Orien's face. "And do not question me again when I am begging."

Her arms slacken from around Elisiah, allowing her to gently fall to the ground, landing on her feet. Shock and something else are clearly written on what can be seen of Orien's face.

"Samuel," is all she has to say, and the horse bends down for her to throw herself back into the saddle. Her cream shirt is more of a light brown from their night of chase, followed by sleeping on the forest floor. She grabs the reins, and the two start walking again, leaving Orien in the same spot as she tries to wrap her head around what just happened.

This time she was the one at a loss for words.

She is going to be the death of us, and we have just only met her.

The beast does not try to hide its interest in her, and at this point, Orien does not know if she can either.

22

ELISIAH

THE PAIR MAKE IT TO A SMALL FARMING TOWN JUST ON THE INSIDE of the Thundaria territory right after sundown. Both of them are tired. Elisiah wants a warm meal, and she also fears what will happen if she falls asleep.

It is not hard for them to find a resting house because it is also the town's tavern. The first thought Elisiah has when she sees the place is, "Please, let Orien behave." Each person they pass as they walk down the small dirt road immediately finds Orien. None of them have looked Elisiah's way, which makes her glad.

She must look dreadful after everything that has occurred.

They pay for a stall just outside the building that will hold Samuel for the night. Luckily, the young boy who shows them the proper stall also agrees to feed the horse. Samuel obeys the boy with no signs of irritations, even when his boney knuckles brush against his coat to unstrap the saddle and bags. Orien makes sure to be there to catch the bags as they fall.

The sight of the boy makes Elisiah sick to her stomach. He stands level in height with her, his eyes sitting back into his skull. The color of them seems dull from what she imagines to be a bright blue. Grey outlines the perimeter. The bones of his cheeks cut into the pale white flesh that covers them. What remains of his hair looks to be a light shade of blonde and arranged on his head in patches.

So many questions run through her head as she watches his slow, jerking movements. Questions she would not ask, too afraid to know the answers.

It is all she can see as they make it into the small room that holds the tavern. Not many patrons sit in the mismatched chairs around the water-swollen tables. They look like someone yanked them from a sunken ship or even a flooded building. Not a single soul looks their way, and Orien never looks theirs.

It is a relief from the curious, fear-stricken looks they got from the others outside. She starts to breathe easier, now, as the elderly man behind a small counter hands a small metal key to her companion. Elisiah has no idea what to call Orien and herself, but she knows it is madness to call her anything but a stranger. Even though she has already been more vulnerable with her than anyone else. It is all she can think about as her body follows Orien's through the small space of the tavern as if being pulled by a string.

Elisiah stays silent as Orien opens the wooden door to the space they will occupy for the night. She does not care about what her surroundings look like as she makes her way across the squeaking wood plank floor. Her body is sore and an ache has set in behind her eyes.

Now as she stares at the wood plank ceiling, her eyes fill with tears. Elisiah has never felt as disconnected from her emotions as she does in this moment. The pace of the last few days traveling has left her feeling like a ghost, like a shell with nothing inside.

She does not know peace during the day, and nights have become full of nightmares. Not the normal ones she has grown used to since the age of five; no, these were real. When her eyes close, her soul is either sucked from her body and sent spiraling to another world, or she sees inevitable death through the eyes of some power-crazed man.

As the water slides down the sides of her face and onto the rolled blanket under her head, Orien gently places a hand on her cheek. Turning her head to see the face close to hers, Elisiah smiles slightly.

What is it, Little One?

The cadence of the voice is soft as it blankets her jumbled mind. As it finds its resting place, everything Elisiah shuffled through gathers itself. Everything is now in order, but the stack seems massive.

"It is everything. So much has happened in such a brief time, I do not know what is really happening." Taking a deep breath, the tension in her shoulders fights the muscles in her neck.

"I do not trust my own feelings or thoughts anymore." Elisiah looks for answers in the light brown eyes searching her face in the dim light of the moon, glowing into the room from the only window.

I know. It feels like everything has been turned upside down. Like it is all slipping past you, no matter how hard you fight and you cannot grip any of it. We feel like that too.

Orien looks to her eyes as she wipes a tear from her damp cheek. Every touch of Orien's hand feels like a new experience every time. Elisiah wishes she could understand that.

"I have so many questions, but I do not know if I want to know the answers. I do not even know who to ask or where to start. Leaving the castle was supposed to be a clean slate. A chance to live my life for once. All I feel is confusion."

Ask us. Ask us your questions, and we will give you the answer. If we cannot, then we will hunt for them until we can.

Elisiah knows the beast is telling the truth, but she does not want someone to have all the answers for her.

No, she wants to be responsible for finding her own answers and learning along the way.

"Orien, I do not want you to hunt anything for me or be the one responsible for taking care of me. I want to learn and grow. I am so tired of being weak. I am so tired of being told how I need to speak and act. I cannot become better if someone is always there. You cannot always be there." As the words leave her mouth, her tears come faster.

Elisiah is mad, so mad.

The way Orien sits up on her elbow tells her she can feel it just like Elisiah can feel the growing joy in Orien. Of all the things Orien could be feeling right now, joy is not what Elisiah expects.

Little One, if you want to be better then you better give up now, because you will never be better than who you are in this moment. Do you know how big it is for someone to accept that they are not the best version of themselves? That is a monumental realization. We will be whoever you need us to be in any way, Elisiah. We can teach you what you want to learn, and if we cannot, we can do it together. If you are growing, then so are we.

The beast pauses shortly before adding.

We will follow you in any decision you make.

Orien nods after the beast says its piece, and Elisiah laughs.

"I still need a name for you. I need a name for the other voice that also takes up space in my head." Her laughing stops, and she looks into Orien's eyes as she asks, "How did it get in your head?"

Orien moves her hand from her cheek and holds her fingers in her hand as the beast in her answers.

She does not know the answer to that. All she knows is that I have been here for as long as she can recall. She has always had a voice in her head, which only grew the longer she acknowledged me, then before she knew it, I had taken up permanent residence. She says I am always commenting on things, looking from our eyes, and even eating.

Silence grows between them as Orien looks down to their hands.

I was once just a feeling. I do not think Orien knew what I originally was. With what she has experienced in her short years, I think everyone would need a friend. She made me that for her, even if she does not agree. Sometimes I was the protector, but mostly I was just the voice when she felt alone.

Orien does not move as the voice talks to them both, soaking the information in. Elisiah grips her fingers and whispers, "I can be another friend."

No, Little One, you have already become so much more. So, much more.

"We just met. We are basically still strangers. I do not know the first thing about either of you except what I have been told."

Orien wraps her fingers around Elisiah's as she traces the length of her arm with her eyes. Orien speaks so much with her eyes.

A picture of Orien getting ripped open by that ghastly metal whip plays in her memory, and Elisiah sighs, "Strangers, and you got beat because of me." She could feel eyes burning into her skull as she examined a loose thread on the ragged blanket under her.

She would put herself in the line of any fire if it meant you got away safely. She knelt on that floor that is stained by our blood and took every single lashing because she knew he would be too tired to try anything with you.

If you think for one God damn second that she would let Alister, or any man, put their hands on you then you have got the wrong idea. Elisiah, we will gladly kill for you or die for you.

Orien takes a breath before the beast adds.

You may say we are strangers, but to us, we have always known each other. From the first time we saw you, the first smell, and the first hint of attitude, all we have done is grow. We feel more when we are with you than we have in all the twenty-seven years we have been alive.

"But why?" It is the only thing Elisiah can think of.

That is a question we will have to answer together.

Elisiah cannot say anything, so she speaks in her head.

"Teach me how to be better. How to fight like a warrior. Teach me how to take care of myself, so I can protect you like you have me."

Anything.

Orien leans forward and places her forehead against Elisiah's.

She relaxes at the pressure against her head and the warm breath mixing with hers. So many questions to answer and even more feelings to line out, Elisiah's body feels like it is made from lead as she gently kisses Orien's mask and falls back against the rolled blanket.

The soft rhythm of a heartbeat lulls her to sleep, and she prays to whoever may be listening that she can stay just where she is. Surrounded by the old wooden walls of this moonlit room, on the top of the small tavern underneath. With the one person she should be terrified to be alone with, only to end up being the one person she only wants to be with.

Tomorrow they will continue their journey, and Elisiah will have more than enough time to ask questions.

23

ELISIAH

It seems like immediately Elisiah plunges down the same black hole. With the same bright streaks passing her by. All she wanted was one night of peace.

Lack of sleep is going to be the first thing to take her out if it is not something else.

As she descends through worlds this time, she does not make a sound and even manages to somehow put herself upright, so she now falls feet first instead of on her back.

She should have some control over how she lands this time since she is calm and in a more fitting position. It does not feel like an eternity either as she falls through space and time.

The ground becomes visible faster, and as it rises to meet her, she tells herself she will land on soundless feet, and in a way that will not break her legs.

As if the cosmos can hear her, she meets the ground with a

lightness to her she has not felt before. All she can think about now is finding the healer's tent.

If she has been brought back here again then she will get answers to her questions before she leaves again.

Her body moves automatically, her legs taking her toward the dim orange glow of flames. She is grateful for it now because the feeling of fear does not have time to plant her feet in place.

Elisiah's brain swarms with questions.

Questions for beings she cannot even recall the names of.

As she approaches the woodline, her senses are stronger than the last time. The wood spitting embers on the ground hums in her ears. Somewhere a wild pig is being roasted, and she can see the silhouettes of the massive wings hanging behind backs.

I guess being calm really does make a difference.

Elisiah talks to herself and waits for a response that will not come.

The lack of intruders in her head as she walks into the dark woods in front of her makes her feel small. Hiding behind a tree just outside the view of a few warriors walking past, Elisiah inhales a deep breath as her eyes close.

Just as she steps out from behind the barrier of the trees, her eyes open. Horror wraps itself around her throat as a large male body stands planted in front of her. Almost walking right into his chest, she freezes.

The breath traps itself in the passage of her airway as she fights to keep her heart rate down. Slowly, she looks up at the man's face.

Her neck aches from how far she must tilt her head back just to see his features. Elisiah's eyes grow wide, and she takes a quick step back as the image of the angel in solid black armor aligns itself with the face of the man in front of her. This person has the same face as the other. Their body is home to the same broad set shoulders and tan colored wings.

Oh. Fucking Gods.

Her shaking hands slowly move to her mouth to keep any potential noise contained. The heart rate she fights to keep calm now beats like a hammer in her chest.

The chestnut brown hair on his head looks black in the night, and the cast of orange from the fire shows the man has not cut the hair growing from his face. Elisiah cannot move from her spot as he lifts his nose in the air. She watches as he inhales a deep breath and slowly lets it out.

His dark colored eyes search the spot where she currently stands like he knows the person behind the smell.

Elisiah is sure the man does not know her smell. Confusion replaces the fear, and she takes a small step back toward him.

With every step she takes, he grows taller. His eyes begin to move frantically around the space, and his chest rises and falls more noticeably. Elisiah wants to speak to him and ask him what bothers him, but before she can, another male walks up next to him.

"Hey Cap, are you going to come eat with us?" Elisiah recognizes the voice, and the realization makes her look his way.

Hinchy.

That is this one's name, and his long black hair replays the memory in her mind. He stands just a few inches shorter than the one he called Cap, and his arms look to be slimmer as well.

"Save me a leg. I need to talk to Mariem about the progress of some of the others." Turning away from the one she knows is Hinchy, he walks towards the rows of tents.

Hinchy raises his left hand and slaps it with his right. "Good job, Hinch-man. You got him to talk, that is a win in our book." He smiles like a child as he compliments himself, and it makes Elisiah smile as well.

Propping his hands on his hips, he looks around at the trees and sniffs. His nose wrinkles and she can see the white of his teeth.

"It smells like sweaty ass over here." Elisiah's mouth drops open, and her arms fall slack at her side. Sure, she has not had a proper bath yet, but she cannot smell that bad.

As he turns to walk off, the black plait swinging against his back, he yells at another, "Hey, Matryles! Did you wash your ass after today? It smells like you over here." The warrior by the fire throws a stick at Hinchy's head as he gets closer, and laughter rings out around the two.

Blinking and closing her mouth, Elisiah recovers from the insult. She knows where she needs to go and hopes she has not wasted precious time standing in the same spot.

❦❦❦❦❦

Breaking out into a sprint, she weaves between the abnormally tall people to find her way back to the long tent. If she cannot catch up to the man called Cap, then she does not know what she will do. Skirting around a group of sitting women, she finds the tent in question. Slowing down her pace and looking around before slipping between the flaps of the entryway, Elisiah is again met by the same person. This time his back is to her, and he speaks to the woman that told her the way back home last time.

"I am positive of what I felt. Even what I smelt felt like confirmation." Mariem stands just in front of him, a simple beige dress draped from her shoulders just hitting the floor.

"I am not denying what you felt, Bashtian, I am simply saying it is just your worry. Our minds can do strange things to us when we let our guard down. Some people even allow themselves to drift into places they do not need to be." Elisiah looks at the older woman's face only to find her already looking directly to the spot where she stands. A pit forms at the base of her stomach.

Bashtian runs his hands through his messy hair and follows her eyes to Elisiah.

"Is something wrong, Mariem?" His husky voice runs down her back like claws, a familiarity soothing the scratches on their way down. Something about this person in front of her sets off every alarm bell she has in her body, but Elisiah can only connect him with the first time she saw him in her dream.

She is not sure if that was a dream now.

"No, Bashtian, everything is okay. You need rest and a hot meal. You should go eat with your men; they have been missing you during your time gone. They need to see you among them again." Her eyes are back to the one standing in front of her and Elisiah follows.

Now that he is in better light, all his details come in full force. His dark eyes look almost black. His square jaw line is covered in black stubble, and his dark chestnut brown hair is a mess of loose waves. Every inch of his face has some type of scar, one of which cuts through his right eyebrow.

Every muscle on his body seems to bulge just enough to see, and the tips of his fingers are black. Elisiah studies him as closely as she can before he says a final word to Mariem, turning to leave out the shut flaps.

"I told you not to come back. It is not safe for you here, and you will get yourself killed." Elisiah looks at the woman as she turns her back to her and walks over to her worktable.

Her hair is up in a high tight swirl on the crown of her head.

Elisiah follows her. "He could smell me. I thought only a few of you could?"

"Yes, well, he is complicated. As are you, now."

"What do you mean by me?" Elisiah looks around the tent to find it empty.

"Your smell has changed. Did you know that?"

Orien's face crosses her eyes, and the feeling of her hands around her waist floods in.

Mariem sighs as she says, "According to your reaction, I assume you know exactly what I am talking about."

Elisiah's cheeks grow flushed. "I just want answers to my questions. Nothing that has happened in the last few days makes sense, and I do not know who else to go to. I was not planning to come back here tonight, or ever."

"Yes, well, you're here now, and with that new scent laced into your life force, I assume I could answer some questions." Mariem has already sat down in her chair and begins looking through her sheets of parchment. Elisiah does not wait a second longer.

"That man, Bashtian, I saw him before. The first time was on a battlefield. He wore black armor, and this woman fought against him. All I saw of her was her white armor and a voice in my head telling me I did not belong there."

"That man is the captain of a God's army. One I do not think you know the name of. If you did you would not be as confused as you are. Ignorance becomes you."

"Was that an insult?"

Did she just insult me?

"Can you please just help me understand some of it? I feel like I am drowning, and all I want is to sleep."

"It was the truth; do you not have books where you are from? It would do you good to pick some up and read. Expand your mind and such." She stops rummaging the papers as she turns in her chair to face Elisiah. "Tell me why your scent has changed."

Elisiah nervously pulls at the arms of her top as she fights the urge to throw something at the woman in front of her. What she feels for Orien is confusing. She does not even understand it herself.

"I am on a trip with someone. I guess their smell has rubbed off on me."

"No, their smell would stay with your physical body. Your soul, your essence of life, carries the scent as well. Do you know what that means?" Her hands clasp shut in her lap, and her back is straight as she speaks at Elisiah whose brain feels like mush.

"You mean to say this person I am with has been tied to me? Like to my soul?" Shock fills her as she runs her hands across her face, and her feet take her in circles.

"Yes, your soul, dear. Mates naturally do that when they find each other." As soon as the word leaves Mariem's mouth, Elisiah sinks to the ground. The animal skin rug underneath her is warm and soft on her backside.

Mates? Orien cannot be my mate. I would know as soon as I saw her if she was. My body would call hers and hers to mine. This is crazy, I just met her. I just met her. Oh, Gods, Orien. Orien is my mate.

The sudden realization makes everything clear for her now. All her mixed emotions and the way she does not feel or act like herself.

Elisiah cannot help the tears that run down her face as everything becomes clear in this moment. She has cried so many tears in her life but never the amount she has shed in the past week.

"You have a lot to learn. I hope you learn it quickly."

"How did he smell me?"

"He did not smell you."

"But. You said–"

Mariem cuts her off before she can finish. "I said your smell has changed. That change in smell is what caught his interest. Not just yours, but the one now mixed in with it."

"Orien." Elisiah says her name softly to herself as if saying it would summon her to this place.

Right now, all she wants is to go back to that tiny room with that tiny bed, and curl closer to the woman she feels safe with.

"I have not heard that name in years." Mariem looks past Elisiah as if she recalls something in her head. She wishes she could see into other people's brains just to understand.

"So, he smelled her on me and what? He knows her?"

"Oh yes, Bastian knows her. Only I and one other know of her as well; the rest are left in the dark."

"How does he know her?"

"That is something you will need to find out for yourself. My answers are done for now. Please, get yourself under control before you get lost."

"Get lost in what? How?" Elisiah stands up in her spot as her heart rate accelerates. "Please tell me what that means, Mariem? I am begging you. I will not be anywhere near a library for days, and I need sleep." Elisiah walks to the woman and grabs her hands. "Please, you're all I have right now."

Mariem sighs as she gently pats her hands. "Before you go to sleep, tell yourself you will not leave your body. Convince yourself that you are better off in your own world. You must believe it; you cannot come running back for answers."

"Okay, I will try. Will Orien know who Bastian is?"

"No, she does not know any of us, or this place. Do not tell her anything until you know for yourself. You are her mate, Elisiah, she needs you more than you may know. Now go."

Mariem releases her hands and turns back to her work.

Elisiah steps away as the word—mate—floats around her head. It makes her feel light on her feet.

The sound of Orien's voice comes into her head like a soft song for the way home. Without hesitation, Elisiah closes her eyes as her life source finds its way back to its shell.

Only some of what she needed to know cleared itself up by the time her visit was done, but she now knows what she needs to do when they make it to Thundaria.

That is the only Kingdom with vast knowledge of all their history. If she would find it anywhere, it would be there.

24

MARIEM

Mariem sits in her chair and waits for the small girl to return from whence she came. In the many centuries of being alive, the older woman has never felt such unease until Elisiah started coming around.

She has only known of one other World Walker, and he was not a pleasant man to know. The God of Souls was notorious for his ability to walk between their world of Arugo and the other of Sytherac until his brother put a stop to that. Mariem has never heard of another person being able to transcend their body across the plains of time, but then again Elisiah does not seem like just an ordinary being.

The first night she walked through the entrance of the medical tent was enough to tell the true purpose of her presence in that moment. Not only could the old Demonian woman sense the shift in air from other presences, but she could also use that heightened skill set to read their energy.

It wasn't something she was born with, or bred for, it was something she mastered on her own through much research.

Elisiah was terrified when she first walked between worlds, but the young girl was also curious and searching. She just does not know what it is she truly seeks. If she did then she would not be worried with small questions like why Bashtian could smell her. Elisiah needs to be asking the question of how she is able to walk on the soil of Arugo, and if her being here sounded an alarm for the one responsible for the suffering of thousands.

Mariem knows Elisiah does not know what she seeks for or even how to find out for sure, but she knows even now that the girl will figure it out. Now that she is tied to such a strong familiar scent, she has no choice. If this so-called human does have true feelings for the person Mariem is sure is the same Orien that still haunts her dreams, she needs all the knowledge she can get.

Elisiah coming back to Mariem tonight is not a surprise. The thought is that she ran into Bashtian, not once, but twice.

If that man recognized the scent in the air, then she is sure nothing will be left standing. Mariem knows for certain that nothing in either of their worlds will stop him from finding that female.

Getting up from her seat and exiting the warmth of the tent, she follows the sounds of boisterous laughter to the end of the camp. There, seated around the same fire as every night, the most feared group of Demonian warriors sat, eating a whole roasted boar.

As she stops just in the light of the flames, she looks around to make sure everyone is accounted for.

Hinchy, the youngest of the group, and the most comedic, sits by Matryles. He is the brains for all the men and spends most of his time sitting amongst them all in silence.

Bashtian is seated in the middle of all his fellow brothers and is the captain of this whole army. He was specifically made for bloodshed and battle.

To the right of him sits Torrein the Insane, as all the others call him. When he is on the field, no one can stop him, and nothing is off limits for a kill. Seeing him is enough to make any enemy run for the hills, but that is not to say he would not catch them and use their innards for a necklace first.

Lastly, the smallest one in the group is Zorro, and what he does not have in muscles he makes up for in speed. Quick like lightning and the shadows of death follow him, the man can rip a head from a neck in a blink of an eye. No one picks on him but Hinchy.

Mariem has watched every single one of these beasts grow from younglings and even spent time teaching them wound care for the fields.

"Ma M!" Hinchy yells to her from his spot on a tree stump as he waves an arm in the air like a small child. The rest of the men already look at her in silence.

Bashtian has dark eyes trained on hers.

"What have I told you about calling me that, boy? I am not your mother." Mariem makes her voice stern and cold but inside she smiles at his foolishness. Hinchy never has understood authority.

"Well, I do not have a mother, so I claim you as mine now.

Nothing you can do to stop me, old woman." She watches as he crosses his arms across his chest and puffs out his cheeks.

He has so much growing up to do, and she hopes he does that very soon. Their future has just turned dark.

Placing her arms behind her back and clasping her hands, she spreads out her dark wings, using them as a shield behind her back before saying, "I find it best that I tell each of you something important. Do not take this lightly. Most of all do not tell anyone else, or anything." She makes a point to look in each of their eyes as she says the words.

Each man sits up straight as silence stretches between them. Bashtian stands from his stump as his arms lay slack at his side.

"Our future has taken a turn, a turn for the dark. Every one of you needs to be ready. I am not sure when this will happen, but it is coming, fast. A shift has occurred." Mariem looks deep into Bashtian's eyes as the words leave her lips, his shoulders stiffen.

Slightly, she nods her head in his direction, and realization flashes in his eyes; he takes a deep breath.

As the men stand and turn to face their commander, she turns on her heels, tucking in her wings, leaving them to plan as they see fit.

Mariem only hopes she did the right thing as she makes her way back to her quiet place in the tent, and that the one responsible for their change in fate will get the news to the other side.

25

ORIEN

Orien watches Elisiah sleep on the inappreciable bed in the far corner of the room. She has not left her spot in front of the wooden window close by the door. After their encounter with the Dream Weavers, unease crept its way into her middle.

If her history knowledge is correct, then those specific beings only stalk their prey when they actively hunt on the commands given to them by a master.

Orien cannot recall how a person can become anything of the sort, but that does not mean it has not happened.

Everything that she has read and even the stories told say that if they are roaming on their own free will, they do not wait to make their attack. Orien knows they are toying with her and Elisiah. She would even bet that the one giving them their orders has required them to make their hunt enjoyable for themselves.

The Dream Weavers are invisible serpents of the night who do not even have to sink their fangs into your flesh to wrap your veins in poison. The green eyed things can lure you into their dream state and make you kill yourself if that is what they choose. Nothing is off limits to them when they get a hold to your mind while stalking through the darkness of night.

Orien knows for a fact they would use her against Elisiah if they got the chance to trap them again. The Dream Weavers now know that Orien has the ability to call upon something that is darker than them; it is something they will never forget either. She revealed one of her greatest abilities to them, and that is now one of her weaknesses to them, in the same way Elisiah is as well.

The beast in her has been telling her they are being watched, and she agrees.

Everything in her is rigid. It is something she has only felt one time before, and every time she takes off her shirt she is reminded of that day.

A day she will never speak about and a scar no one else has seen.

Across the small farming town in a freshly plowed patch of earth, the same iridescent green eyes glow.

"I knew it. They are hunting us."

Who do you think has sent them?

"If I had a guess, it would have to be Alister. We embarrassed him and took what he claims as his." Orien refuses to take her eyes off the green ones staring back at her.

We have precious cargo on this journey, Orien, we cannot move during the night.

The beast in her stalks to the front and watches.

It is the only time they can hunt. The more ground we put behind us during the light the better.

"I know. I already sent a messenger to the new King; he should send someone to meet us halfway. I cannot see her teeth chatter another minute longer out there."

Hartlander is really to be crowned King, then?

"Yes." Orien has not seen the snow-white male since she first visited the Kingdom of Thundaria.

They were both children then, no older than four and seven. It was right before the mask was placed on her face.

The first time they saw each other was a shock for both.

Orien can see his pale white skin and hair perfectly in her head, his bright cyan blue eyes will never be easy to forget. It felt like every gaze went right through her.

Hartlander was the only other kid she had ever seen or been in the company of besides herself.

For Orien though, her hair was long then, down to the base of her ass, and the red was a shade brighter. She was taller than he was even if she was only four at the time.

The two bonded over the lives they got dealt.

Both wore scars from the ones that raised them, and they both could kill before they could even walk properly.

On her last trip as an adult to the ice-riddled place, she did not run into him. She did not even think of him that day.

If it were not for the one sleeping in the corner and the green eyes of the Dream Weavers still locked with hers, she would have never even sent the bird.

Orien felt weak asking for a buggy at the halfway point, but she briefly mentioned the fact that she carried with her an ambassador for Alister.

Does it not worry you how our Little One does not move while she sleeps? It is like she is a rock, or dead.

Orien turns from the window and takes a few steps to the bedside before sinking down on the edge. The pile of feathers covered in cloth buckles under her weight.

Placing a hand on Elisiah's shoulder and stroking her hand down her arm, Orien leans her head to hers.

Her breathing is steady, and her heart is strong. She could have known that from anywhere in this damn building, but to feel it so close to her body makes her mind drift from the present.

"Why do we feel this way? I have never been so confused before, but I also have never felt so content in my life." Orien asks the beast in her head in hopes it will have some answers.

We are not meant to know. It might be for the best if we do not, not everything is supposed to make sense. When has our existence ever not been anything but confusing?

The beast in her head is calm, collected. It has never been like this before.

"You have been so calm with her. Even when our body was pressed against hers, you did not even try to take control."

Orien, she is ours, even though you will not accept it right now. It is true. I feel it. I think she does as well.

Silence fills the space, and the feeling of eyes leave.

You did not say your body. You said our body.

The beast sits up in her head, and a distant thud sounds. Orien rolls her eyes at its reaction to her slip in words.

"Do not get excited, you insufferable fool."

If you would just accept that I am a part of you then you might just get some type of relief.

"All I would get is a bigger damn headache." Orien curls her body around Elisiah's small frame and her eyes close.

The sweet scent of vanilla and wildflowers welcomes her as she drifts to sleep. She cannot recall the last time she got any rest; she just hopes they do not oversleep.

They both need to wash before heading out or they risk smelling worse than the holding house for the horses.

Elisiah nudges closer to her chest, and a soft moan leaves her mouth.

Orien wraps her tighter in her arms, and all she wants to do is speak to her. She has to find a way to remove this muzzle.

As she drifts off to sleep, a giant green field comes into view in her head, with what looks to be the glow of a fire just in the tree line. As soon as her eyes adjust to the only light in the dark, it all disappears.

Orien is met with the blackness of her mind just before she falls asleep. The image is all but forgotten.

26

HARTLANDER

AS THE TWO WOMEN SLEEP THROUGH THE REMAINDER OF HOURS before daybreak, the messenger bird lands at the double doors of the soon-to-be-crowned King of Thundaria.

The bird pecks at the frosted glass doors as it hops from one clawed foot to the next.

The cold is harsh in the heart of the Kingdom, but to the ones that live there year-round, this is their considerably warmer summer.

Footsteps echo over the elegant dark blue tiled floor, and just before they reach the door, a gust of wind blows them both open at the same time. Taking flight just before the cold breeze can touch its white and gray feathers, the bird hovers in the air, meeting the face of Erwin Jay Hartlander.

"Come. Drop the note." His voice is smooth like silk and as light as a feather. Many say his voice is a true deception. It draws you in with kindness just before he can cut you down with his sword.

Dropping the letter in his open palm, the pigeon rests on a lone chair on the balcony. As he rolls out the parchment, a woman calls from inside the room.

"What is it Harty?"

The woman's voice is as soft as his, but nothing gives way to harm.

Slowly, he looks over the letter, and a small smile crosses his face as he calls back to her.

"We are going to have company, snowflake." Hartlander's smile grows wider, and he is overwhelmed by excitement.

"You better get your notepad and quill ready because you will love to study the likes of who is coming to our home."

Hartlander sends the bird off to its warmer home, turning to walk back into his own.

Too excited to go back to sleep, he hands the note to his bed partner and slips into his more comfortable attire. He must send someone their way immediately.

"Everything I have told you about her, you will get to see first-hand. I cannot wait for you to meet her. She is just who we need right now! I must find a way to pull her to our lines on the field." He speaks fast, and his hands start to shake.

The petite woman sits up in her spot and smiles up at him.

She loves watching him get overcome by his emotions, but sadly it happens more than what is needed most of the time. It is the main reason some of the Kings say he should not rule.

"Go, Harty. Send someone and then plan it all out. I will go to the library at first light to find any information I can that may help." Hartlander rushes to her side and kisses her forehead as he places his palm against her slightly swollen womb.

She beams at him as she covers his hand with hers.

27

ELISIAH

Waking up, Elisiah feels like her whole body has been beaten. Every muscle is sore. All she can think about is her time in that other world. As she tries to stretch her aching body, she is swiftly met by failure as she realizes her body is held snug to a wall behind her.

Warmth seeps into her back and a familiar arm lays across her waist. She cannot help but smile.

Her mate.

The fact seems ridiculous. She is nothing but a human, and even though they say Orien is a Fae, she is not so sure. She would not find herself questioning what the other is if it were not for her time spent in that other world.

Every time Elisiah looks at Orien, she is flooded by the familiar features she sees in the others from her sleep. The first time she saw the female's black eyes, all she was reminded of were the black eyes of the warrior dressed in black armor from her first dream. The warrior she now knows is named Bashtian, who also knows her mate, Orien. She has to be missing something, she knows she is missing something.

Her mind swims with questions but a voice echoes back to her.

Only you can find the answers.

The library would have what she needed, but she is not sure how much longer they need to travel.

Shutting her eyes, Elisiah, lifts the arm just enough to turn towards the body behind her. Orien's face is smooth, empty of all feelings, as she sleeps. Her lashes are mahogany brown, like the color of Bashtian's hair, and freckles cover most of her skin's surface.

Her hair is not just a dull red; it has dark blonde strips. Even some brown. The curls are smooth and loose.

But, the muzzle is thick.

"I really need to get that damn thing off," Elisiah says to herself as she lifts a hand and gently slides her fingers across the leather.

It is cold but smooth underneath her touch. She cannot wait to see the rest of what she is certain is a perfect face underneath.

Anger builds as she thinks about the years it has been in place. How does she eat with it on? Does she clean her teeth?

Elisiah stops her movement as she realizes she has never asked anything about it before. She cannot recall seeing Orien eat or drink once in their time together, no matter how short it has been.

As if in answer to her pondering about how the other nourishes their body, her stomach rumbles just as two very warm brown eyes open. Elisiah lets herself show a partial smile before she quickly removes herself from the body still pressed to hers. She is still mad at the female for the way they have acted; she cannot let the beautiful face sway her from that.

Or the fact that this other person is her mate. The information does not sit exactly right with Elisiah; her whole life she has been told humans cannot have mates. It was the only explanation Evadne gave her when she asked who her father was.

"Humans will never mean anything in this world. If the Law did not state that all living things are to be treated as equal, then we would simply be unpaid slaves." Her mother would always pause, and her gaze would go some faraway place.

"Not that we get paid much of anything for all we do." Elisiah can hear her mother's words so fresh in her ears, she cannot help but wonder what that monster is up to.

The questions still flood her head, and she cannot wait to reach their destination. More importantly she cannot wait to set her eyes on massive shelves full of information she has yet to explore. Being surrounded by the leather-bound pieces of parchment in the small library of Univier has always made her feel like she belonged somewhere.

Elisiah keeps a vast amount of her knowledge under lock and key in fear that the two people who oversee her life will see it as an act of rebellion.

What type of bed whore needs to know the difference between a Dragon, Wyrm, and Wyvern? More importantly, their inner workings from their eating habits, sleeping, and even where to find the proper scales to deliver a killing blow. Elisiah was not even sure if Altair even knew that some of the giant flying animals were awake.

The Dragons and Wyverns of Sytherac have all mostly been dormant for many years now, but something slowly wakes them from their slumber. It has been the number one cause of most of the deaths reported around the other Kingdoms. None of the newly awoken dragons have been reported around Univier or Thundaria though, not since the last time she checked their movements.

The Sand Wyrms of Desitae are a different story on their own. Those giant beasts never went dormant, in fact, they are the main protection for the Kingdom made of sand. A majority of the locals from Desitae build bonds with the Wyrms, using them for things like riding, hunting, and building, and they will even make homes under the sand with the animals.

Elisiah found herself curious one afternoon and discovered that the Wyrms dig out tunnels under the sand and then use oil from their skin to harden the sand around them so that it does not crumble in on itself. If you pair that with the magical abilities of the people that live there, then you get a complex system of living and surviving underneath the desert sky.

The thought makes her wish that she could have seen the beasts that hunted them in the forest, but it was her unfortunate luck that her mind took her someplace else. To see a Dream Weaver with her own two eyes would be terrifying, but it would be a story she could tell. A story of an adventure. Of a time when she faced death and lived to tell about it.

Deciding to leave her train of thought behind, she moves to stop herself from staying in the confines of her own self. Elisiah moves from her spot on the mattress.

Just as she reaches for her brown leather bag lying just to the side of the door, the bed creaks from movement. Looking over her shoulder, she watches Orien as she sits up and plants her still booted feet on the floor. The female runs her scarred hand over her face, pushing her fallen hair from her forehead. Elisiah is not just aware of her anymore. No, she is overly aware. So much that when Orien's fingertips brush the red strains, Elisiah is slapped in the face with her scent.

Her body's answer to the smell is to cover her exposed skin with small bumps, and Elisiah shakes her head slightly before looking back to her bag. If she is going to make any sense of this mess, then she needs to dive into any book she can.

Grabbing one of the thicker, long-sleeved, wool dresses she has brought accompanied by a pair of lightly lined riding pants, she straightens to her full height just as the smell of her own filth-covered skin hits her. Scrunching her nose, she looks back to Orien, who now stands by the small window.

She must hold in her laughter at the sight of her.

The seven-foot frame is currently bent in half as she looks out the window, arms crossed across her chest, feet spread slightly apart. If she had a photographic memory like some, she knew this would most definitely be one she went back to from time to time.

"I need to clean up," Elisiah simply says as she suppresses her amused smile. I am mad, she reminds herself as Orien turns around from her current position, straightening to her best ability while also not hitting her head on the ceiling rafters.

Good morning to you too, Little One.

The beast yawns in her head as she rolls her eyes.

"I am being serious. I can smell myself and I do not like that fact." Elisiah huffs as she lightly kicks the bag out of the way of the door.

Yes, we can smell you.

Elisiah freezes with her foot stretched out in the direction of the bag, and slowly her eyes rise to meet the ones across the room.

"And what does that mean?"

Orien uncrosses her arms and holds her hands up to the side to show her innocence.

We smell horrid too, Little One, it was nothing personal.

The beast chuckles before it adds.

The washroom is just down the stairs to the right as soon as you get to the main floor.

Bringing her foot to its resting place beside the other, Elisiah turns her head towards the door. The thought of using a washroom that was not inside the room she occupied terrifies her.

"Anyone can walk in." Her eyes do not leave the door as she listens for any noise made by other patrons.

No, not anyone. Just us.

Orien drops her hands to her side as she walks over to her own bag just by Elisiah's.

"You're going to stand by the door to make sure no one enters, right?" Elisiah glances in her direction as Orien gathers her own clothing for the day ahead. In her hand is a smaller bag.

"What is that bag?"

Orien unzips the small bag and pulls out a heating elixir and a bar of scented coal body cleanser. Cursing to herself, Elisiah takes a few steps to her bag and gathers her own cleaning products. After she makes sure she has everything, Elisiah looks to Orien and waits for an answer to her earlier question.

Looking at her full arms, Orien turns for the door just as small sweeps of shadows leave from the wood. The door creaks open a second later.

"Did you use those to open the door?" Elisiah watches as the tendrils find their home in the tips of Orien's fingers. That will be something she studies while in the library; she cannot recall reading anything about shadow magic.

Her knowledge of the common magics passed down from bloodlines is strong as well as the unordinary ones that seem to pop up once every few generations. None of those have any relation to shadows or the blackness that seems to reside in her companion.

No. They sealed the door last night while we slept. Otherwise, we would have not slept at all.

The beast says this as a matter of fact as Orien starts descending the stairs. Elisiah follows closely behind her without being too close to step on her heels.

"Wait, how does that not make you even more tired? Do you not use energy when you use them?" As soon as Elisiah asks, the shadows grow up the walls of the unlit stairwell. Even though the rising sun rays light their room, this little passage remains dark.

Elisiah runs a single finger down the wood as she watches them swirl around the tip. She cannot contain the smile on her face.

Each time they lightly graze her skin, a small surge of energy runs down the digit.

They are more of their own thing. Orien can control them but only if they agree; it has always been a decision on both of their parts. When it is dark it takes nothing from either of them but during the day it can drain both fast. The recharge is grueling.

Orien's footsteps cease just at the bottom of the stairs, and Elisiah stops just before hitting her back. If she runs into the female one more time, she will die of embarrassment.

The shadows roam to her feet as her fingers disconnect from the wall.

They like you.

The feeling of a purr vibrates in Elisiah's head, and it feels quite nice as she looks to the door to what she assumes is the washroom.

Orien opens the twin doors to the one that houses the room they slept in last night; Elisiah slips into the space. To her surprise, she is followed inside.

Turning around, watching the door close and shadows cover its expanse, Elisiah looks up at Orien.

"Are you not going to wait on the other side of it?" She swallows as her nerves swim in her stomach.

We cannot protect you if we do not have eyes on you constantly. We are currently being hunted by things that strive in the dark, so to answer your question, no. We will stay right here until you get done and then you will do the same until we finish.

Elisiah gasps. "So you are going to watch me bathe?" She cannot believe what she is hearing.

No, we will turn around, or the shadows can cover you. They do not mind.

The voice in her head sounds bored, like this makes perfect sense.

"Are you forgetting what happened between us not even twelve hours ago? How you turned me down and now you want me to get naked in front of you?" Elisiah rears back like she just got smacked across the cheek.

Orien shifts all her weight to her left leg as she watches her.

Little One, we have not forgotten anything, and we did not turn you down. We do not want to ruin you.

Orien's eyes search Elisiah's.

"Ruin me? You think that your touch will ruin me?" She shakes her head as water starts running behind her and shadows cross over the floor. What she feels at this moment is hurt. Her own mate thinks that her touch is something of destruction. Something that will stain. It makes her heart physically hurt.

"Orien, I need you to listen to me. You cannot ruin me. You cannot make my value any less than what it is now. Your touch is not life-ending for me. It may be that for others, but it is not for me." Shadows gently swoop the small circular elixir jar from Orien's hand and disappear behind her.

"I know you have killed more people than I can imagine right now. I know you think their blood stains your hands, and if it does then, so what? That does not magically transfer to me."

Steam starts to cover the wood-planked floor as Elisiah bends down to unlace her boots.

"Until you understand that, just forget that I even wanted you." Frustration laces every word, and tears burn her eyes.

If Orien cannot get over the fear of turning her into something she is not, then she would not know Elisiah is her mate. If the woman truly knew that information, then Elisiah knows she would not question anything about the feelings between them, but she wants Orien to come to terms with it by herself.

Boots now off, Elisiah starts to strip off her trousers with Orien, still standing in the same spot, eyes still on the woman in front of her.

"Turn around or wait on the other side of the door." Elisiah does not hide the pain and anger in her voice as her clothes fall to the floor, leaving her only in her more delicate attire.

Not waiting for a reply or to see if the set of eyes has looked away, the white fabric falls to the floor just on top of the others. Turning to the steaming water, Elisiah steps in, one foot at a time, as she unties her curls and they fall onto her back.

Sinking into the water, she cannot help the moan that leaves her throat as the hot water calms her aching joints. Her eyes close just for a second before she turns her head in Orien's direction.

"I said to turn around." She is not surprised to find those same honey-colored eyes still trained on her, only now they look hungry. Triumph is the only thing Elisiah feels as Orien growls slightly before turning her back to her.

If the world's most notorious assassin wants to deny her feelings, then Elisiah will do so as well.

HARTLANDER

28

SINCE THE MOMENT THE NEW KING RECEIVED THE LETTER FROM one of his oldest friends, the castle has been running wild with his demands. No one is safe from his constantly going mind on any regular day, so the fact that he will be setting his eyes on the one and only Orien for the first time since he was seven has his need for perfection heightened to new highs.

Everything in his castle made of ice looks to be less than perfect. Racing thoughts consume him by the minute and tell him of how he will fail at the things to come.

You are nothing but a failure Erwin.

All your work is for nothing.

No one respects you; you are too young.

You are not the man your father was.

Orien will see right through you.

This castle is nothing to look at.

Your mate will leave you.

The child in her womb will grow to hate the man you are.

You cannot save your people.

You cannot even save yourself.

You.

Are.

Nothing.

Being left with his own thoughts is one of the most dangerous things for Erwin. Only a few know of what he goes through daily as he fights the invisible demons in his head. There is more than one time he has been watched over like a small child because he would become too consumed in the darkness of his mind. Some of his worst thoughts are often thought while in a room bustling with people, and no one understands that.

No matter where he goes or who he has with him, they never stop, never go away. The only relief he has from them is when he can hold his mate, but even then, they do not completely go away.

Hartlander chews at his fingernails as he paces the floor in a straight line, back and forth, in front of his throne.

His fingers are one of his favorites when he needs a distraction from his own self. When his mother was still alive, she tried anything she could think of to get him from gnawing the nails down to nubs. None of it worked.

After being beaten for the action by his father, he would find other ways that did not draw much attention, like chewing the inside of his mouth and cheeks. That worked best in large crowds, and even while being watched on the throne. When that was not enough, and he could hide his hands, he resorted to scratching whatever he could. He has dug holes in countless chairs right here in this room over the years. Ice is fun for him to chew on as well, and the people think he is just eating.

On the other side of the room, a small servants' door shuts, drawing the man from the racing in his head. Hartlander brushes the front of his plain white top and smiles at the old woman who has just entered the large room.

"Erwin, dear, what have we talked about when it comes to your fingers?" The woman responsible for the last few years of his upbringing before he was seemingly adult enough to rule says as she crosses the space between them, holding a silver tray.

"No chewing my fingers if I cannot stop myself before they bleed. Yes, I remember, Rissa." He wants to roll his eyes, but knows if she sees him do so, she will melt the ice from under his feet. The last time she did it, he almost busted his head; it was his fault for calling her old. Rissa spent weeks apologizing to him.

Besides his mate, Aneira, she has been the only person to ever take accountability for their actions with him.

Everyone else marks it off as he deserves it. Even when he was being beaten long before he could talk. How does a toddler deserve a leather strap across the face for just entering a room?

You will be just like him.

Your unborn child already hates you.

You deserve everything that happens to you.

"Do not use that tone with me, young man. You may be my King, but I am the one that has kept you alive some years." Rissa's voice snaps his awareness back to her as she stops in front of him.

Sitting on the silver tray in front of him is a bowl of steaming oats with sugared dewberries. It is one of his favorite morning meals; the sight makes his stomach grumble.

Grabbing the bowl from the tray, he walks to the only table currently set in the center of the room. Once the day draws closer to his guests' arrival then the rest will be in their positions.

"Thank you, Rissa. I did not know I was starving." He chuckles as he does not hesitate to dig straight in, the oats slightly burning the roof of his mouth.

"It is hard to know what your body is feeling when you get so consumed with the thoughts running through your head. I wish you would take the root powder I made for you." Rissa sits on the other side of the table, facing him. Her eyes are always set with worry when she finds him far away. One thing that terrifies her is the thought he will be responsible for his own ending.

"I wasn't consumed in my thoughts." That is a lie. "I was simply making sure everything has been set into motion for when our guests arrive." The spoon does not stop shoveling the food into his mouth.

"Yes, well you have not tried this hard to impress the others. I know these from Univier will be the first to arrive for the ceremony, but you have been completely focused on only them." The woman across from him straightens out the white shawl that hangs over her round shoulders.

"Rissa, one of them is not just anyone." Hartlander looks up at her, his spoon forgotten in his hand as his whole face grows with yet another smile.

It is the one expression he seems to always wear; even when he is mad or sad, the smile always remains. "This is Orien!" Excitement shakes his hands, and the spoon hits the side of the bowl sending a light ding echoing through the room.

Defeat changes Rissa's features as she takes in the young King in front of her.

"Erwin." She reaches her hand across the space between them to hold his spoon hand steady. "You must remember that it has been twenty-three years since you last saw her. People change my dear, and from the stories we have heard, some are not always for the better."

His smile does not falter as he stares at her pale green eyes. The same color as Aneira's, her daughters, and his most precious person.

"Do you not understand? That is the point. If I can get someone with her strength and ability on our side, then everything we have been working toward will be that much more successful." The spoon falls from his hand as he grips Rissa's instead. "If the stories are true, then we need her."

Rissa faintly smiles at him as she blows out a breath. "Yes, well, we can only wait and see now, can we not?" Her eyes fall to the half-eaten bowl of oats.

"Aneira is in the library finding anything she can about the powers Orien wields. Anything she can find to help us understand is all we need." His shaking subsides, and the grip on her hand lightens. "Rissa, I promise that this will work out."

The plump woman looks into his eyes before saying, "I know, Erwin." With those words, he lets go of her warm hand and resumes his shoveling of the oats and berries.

They sit in perfect silence as he finishes the food, and just under their feet, in the deepest part of the castle, a beautiful woman with bright green eyes, pale yellow hair, and a growing womb searches through the ancient archives for any information on the beings that created everything before them.

If the couple is on the right path, then they may live to see their child become an adult.

29

ORIEN

That is the only question Orien asks herself as their morning flows into midday. After their time in the washroom, they both just wanted out of that small, steam-riddled room. The pair did not even stay long enough to eat the warm breakfast offered to them by the innkeeper.

Orien made sure to offer up some of the salted cured meat that Fredrick had given them, and she may have even shoved just a couple of glazed buns in the sack.

The freshly washed female in her dark green wool dress did not hesitate when being handed the pairing of meat and pastry. Before they even made it to retrieve Samuel, you could not even find crumbs on Elisiah's hands.

It is hard for Orien to remind herself that humans do have to nourish their bodies regularly; it honestly seems like a chore. Yes, Orien also has to eat, but since having the muzzle placed over her mouth, she tends to just let the beast take control when they need it. Often, that means hunting for small game animals in the forest around the castle, but they only sustain her body for two days at most. Evadne made for a much larger meal that will keep her full for just over a week.

As Orien saddles Samuel, she cannot help but notice the way Elisiah's face twists with concern as she watches the stable boy. Everything about the child tells her that he has been in contact with someone infected with the disease spreading from Thundaria.

She did not know much about it, but she knew the warning signs. The boy would not be there when they passed on their way back. Orien wonders if she needs to explain that to her companion.

Elisiah has been everything but approachable which makes Orien retreat into herself, like usual.

It is not out of the ordinary for the Fae to prefer the confines of her own self. Even if she did not know what it felt like yet, she enjoyed having company.

What Elisiah wants is something the other is not capable of giving just yet. Not when all her years have been spent doing nothing more than killing. This is the longest she has gone without committing the act of murder.

That is her problem.

She needs to find an outlet for everything she hoards inside but does not know how to discuss.

Orien wishes she could pluck the woman off the back of Samuel as she walks beside them and drop Elisiah into her mind.

Elisiah's hands could untangle every knotted thread in her head, and Orien would let her. That is the problem Orien cannot understand at first; how did this one person come into her life so abruptly and still manage to turn everything upside down?

As the ground grows denser, the air drops colder. Orien glances to her right and she can see the slight tremble of Elisiah's hands. Not hesitating, she shucks off her thick black coat and tosses it over her trembling shoulders. Elisiah stiffens under the weight of it, and her scent changes the air. Orien can feel something tight in her own chest, but cannot pinpoint the reason for it. The sensations keep growing the longer she is around the woman riding Samuel.

Even though it all sits in her head, she cannot focus on it right now. Every question and thought of confusion will have to wait; she does not have the luxury of being distracted. Even if it is by a beautiful face.

They are being hunted during the night hours by beings many think are only legends. If the people only knew that they were real and nothing but black smoke holding green eyes, then no one would be out after dark. No one knows when they are out on the prowl until they find themselves sucked into a dream-like state. Even the shadows that find solace in her veins cannot catch their trail. It is the main reason she sent word to Erwin Jay Hartlander.

The being that made the damn things seems to like the idea of them never being found. Which makes them excellent spies.

The actions of them traveling in a pack only solidify what she and the beast thought last night; they have been summoned. Orien is not even deranged enough to fool around with the type of dark magic it takes to bind them to you. That is the only way to bring the solitary apparitions together, anymore.

The stories say they have refused the pack mentality they originally were made with because of the pain they suffered when their beloved Demonian family member finally met his final days in Sytherac.

This Demonian warrior named Morzon, was the first of his kind cast to this world by his God and maker.

Etbris, the God of night and death, is one of two of the only beings in the Nether, a place no one has seen and many have tried to erase from history. It is believed that from this God's hands, he creates all things opposite of the other, who brings light into the world. Everything is said to be made by them, even the world they currently inhabit. It is their love for creating that caused them to divide. The worst wrath is that from a jealous God; everything living has felt that wrath since the beginning of time. Even the ones that should be closest to them.

Morzon paid the price for his crimes against his own kind and faded away along with all the tales from Before Creation.

All her thoughts completely block out the rest of the world; all she sees is what is in front of her and the sound of nature playing its part in her ears. A throat clearing from beside her draws her out of that place in her mind.

"Hello, is anyone home?" Elisiah looks at Orien as she waves a hand in the space between them. Orien rolls her eyes at the gesture and looks around them.

Clouds slowly cover the sky and what little bit of sun they have, which means they need to get to the next town over before the sun is completely covered. She does not want to deal with the four Dream Weavers, but her body aches for action.

"Orien!" Elisiah yells her name, and it rattles her ear drum as her head jerks away from the sound. The beast jumps to attention as it rushes forward to its eye.

You do know we can hear grass grow, right?

It growls in her head as the ache in her ear reaches the darkness behind her eye. As Orien looks back at Elisiah, the anger that rested on her face earlier has disappeared.

"I am... I am sorry, Orien. I have been trying to ask you a question, but you never even looked my way." Her hands go slack from where they hold the saddle horn in front of her. She and the beast cannot bring themselves to care about a question when their whole head feels like it has been shocked.

Normally, Orien can dial down the sounds around her on her own so she does not react to them, but something about Elisiah has everything messed up. She feels like she needs to find a way to distance herself from the woman, but just thinking about it makes her blood boil in her veins.

So many conflicted thoughts and feelings.

What is your question?

The beast is still ruffled, but it cannot leave its Little One looking so distraught on the back of Samuel.

"I was just asking if we will make it to another rest house before those clouds hit?" Elisiah looks up at the clouds as they slowly get closer to covering the traveling road.

Deciding they really need to make progress today, not just

because of the clouds, but also because, if the message did make it, they should have a coach at the halfway point.

The pair still has five days on their own before reaching the mark, but at least it is not the full twelve.

Move forward.

Before anything else can be said, Orien mounts the stirrup with one foot and swings her other leg across the saddle. Samuel does not stop his steady stride as she mounts him, but Elisiah gasps as Orien pushes her into the horn.

Grabbing the reins in her hands, encasing the body in front of her the beast says,

Relax, Little One. We will not be able to make good time if you stay sitting like a pole.

Elisiah slowly inches herself to a relaxed position against Orien's mid-section as the reins slap against the horse's thick neck pushing him from a walk to a canter.

Having her so close is truly a temptation.

The beast says to Orien as it retreats from its spot in the front of her head, moving to the center.

"Yeah, tell me something I do not know." Orien tries her best not to lock an arm around the small waist in front of her. She knows all the temptation currently resting on her torso.

We should talk about why we have turned her down. I know we do not want her to be burdened with what we have and will do. Then there is the fact we do not want to be a distraction for her, but she has a point.

"What point?"

What if we do not stain her? What if we are not just a distraction for her? She said she wants us, Orien. Us.

The beast lowers its voice at the word "us" like it contemplates the reassurance of it.

"What if what we feel is just lust? We both know it is more than that for her. I cannot even say what I am feeling because I have never felt any of this before." Frustration fills the space between her and the beast that lives inside of her. What she would not give to be able to talk to someone else. To be able to talk at all. Her jaw aches at the thought of moving it.

Orien, you talked to me for the first time in half your life after just one glance at this woman, and you are telling me you do not know how you feel? You do not have to be able to describe it, to feel it. The one person who we both know can help is sitting right there.

The thing is right, and Orien knows that but what it is talking about is something dangerous.

Orien has never cared for anyone. The thought of not just caring for someone but also being intimate with that person is outlandish to her. Orien already has more targets on her back than she can count; putting Elisiah in the mix would only make her one as well.

She is not a good person, and has never claimed to be, but any harm coming to Elisiah is something she will never allow.

Without realizing it, her left arm wraps around Elisiah's waist and pulls her closer. The wind picks up from the storm clouds rolling in, and Samuel begins to move his legs faster until he runs along the road.

With the horse's speed, they should be able to make it to the next rest house before the sky turns completely black.

"Orien, your heart is beating really fast." The soft voice dances across the nerves in her body, and they all spark to life.

I told you. We never feel like that.

The beast is smug in her head as it bristles with the caress of Elisiah's voice. Orien shakes her head as she blows a slow breath out her nose, filling the muzzle with the warmth of it.

Do not worry about our heart, Little One, Orien is fighting a great inner battle.

The thing smiles, and Orien growls in her chest. The vibrations make their way to Elisiah, and she straightens her back, rubbing against Orien.

Orien's hand grips her side and pulls Elisiah's body closer, closing the last inch of space between them just as they pass a small house.

Elisiah gasps from either finally passing a lived-in structure or from the grip that currently surrounds her.

"Does that mean we are getting closer to the town?"

Yes, Little One.

Snow starts slightly drifting from the sky as Orien curses herself.

Wasting no time, she kicks Samuel just before his back leg, and the horse picks up speed, which seems almost impossible. Even he knows they cannot be out in the dark, and he knows what he carries on his back as well. Orien is sure that the giant thing would leave her to rot on this road if it meant he got the other somewhere safe. She likes that about the horse.

30

ELISIAH

T HE CURRENT EMBRACE SHE FINDS HERSELF IN MAKES IT HARD FOR Elisiah to remember why she is angry at the Fae.

She finds the snow falling from the sky to be one of the most magical things she has ever seen. Since Elisiah's life has been spent in the Stone Castle, she has not had the pleasure to experience what the other Kingdoms hold.

She has heard many say that Thundaria is a miserable place with constant bone-chilling temperatures, but that has not stopped Elisiah's desire to experience it for herself. As they get closer to the heart of the Thundarian territory, Elisiah cannot stop herself as she builds images in her head as to what the castle looks like.

Just to say she has traveled is good enough for her, and to say she stayed inside the ice castle is purely bragging rights. Of course, she could only brag to Fredrick, who is one of the people that says the place is one of misery. Elisiah asked him one afternoon how he knew what it was like to live in Thundaria, when she found out that the old man is originally from there.

It explains his white hair and blue eyes.

What she could never get him to explain though is how he found himself working in the kitchen of the Kingdom of Univier, or why he chose to stay for so long.

Look, there.

Elisiah follows the path Orien points down as the beast's voice rumbles into her head. She almost falls off Samuel's back as her eyes catch what races besides them.

"Is that a Wulve pup?" Elisiah's eyes stay locked on the small white thing just in the treeline across from them. It runs alongside the trees with as much grace as any adult Wulve.

A smile spreads the width of her face, a laugh following after. The pup looks over to her with its tongue hanging out of its mouth, snow falling around them all.

Quietly, she thinks to herself, you are so beautiful.

"I know."

Those simple words spoken back to her match the small bark that comes from the pup. Her hand covers her mouth as tears burn her eyes; all time is lost.

Did you hear me? she thinks to herself again. Surely, she imagined this small white pup talking back to her. If not, the number of intruders that have access into her brain is incredibly sad on her part.

"Yes, that is why I answered back."

A sassy little pup. Elisiah laughs in her hand, and her body shakes against Orien's chest.

"My mom says I am."

This is the best moment of her life. Her whole life can never top this moment right here.

"I would not be able to speak to you if it were not for the one behind you."

Elisiah is not sure she heard the Wulve right as her hand slowly moves from her mouth.

"Do not make that face, it makes you less beautiful."

Did she just get insulted by a dog?

"If it were not for the one at your back, I would not be able to talk to you. I know you know about her bond with the Wulves of your home."

She did hear her right.

It is Orien.

How can she open a line of communication between two distinct species? Another question in her mind that she will have to ask later, when they are not running alongside a Wulve pup.

You are not from our home though, are you?

Orien eases her grip from Elisiah's side and slowly reaches for her hand that is still out in front of her face. Her hand warms as it is engulfed by Orien's and placed at her side.

"She is bound to some, so that makes her bound to all."

The tears fall from Elisiah's eyes as she looks away from the pup. Turning her head and part of her upper body, she looks up at Orien, only to find her eyes already on her face. Removing her hand from around Elisiah's, Orien reaches up and brushes the tears from her cheeks. It seems like all Elisiah has done is cry, leaving her companion to clear them away.

"Thank you, Orien. This is magical, I will remember it for the rest of my life." Elisiah does not know what else to do but to give Orien a proper hug. To the best of Elisiah's ability, she turns the bottom half of herself to match the top. Orien's hands rest lightly on Elisiah's waist as she moves on top of Samuel. Elisiah wraps her arms around Orien and buries her face into the wool shirt she wears.

Seeing you smile is what counts to us.

One of Orien's arms wraps around Elisiah's shoulders as she soaks in the familiar smell while also feeling the strength in Orien's back under her hands. The abdominal muscles under her cheeks are solid, and the height difference has never seemed more noticeable to her than right now.

A spark ignites and sends a tingle down her spine. Elisiah only allows the love she feels for Orien to rest in her soul for a split second before she pulls herself away. She will not allow herself to be hurt like she was only a few days ago.

Hurt is all her body has ever felt and she does not trust the feeling of love she feels with Orien. The stories of mates that she has read about play in her head as Orien does not fight her from turning back around.

Elisiah knows what she feels, but it confuses her when she tries to make sense of Orien's actions. She keeps telling herself the only thing she needs to focus on is their journey ahead, and how she will get along with the new King.

Houses are getting closer together as Samuel finally slows his racing pace. The wood structures look like small huts compared to those in Univier. Each one she can see is adorned with a blanket of snow on their roof, and each has a chimney with a steady stream of smoke billowing from the top.

The view only stops her wandering thoughts for the minutes it takes Samuel to pass by the small homes.

If the hurt she feels right now is simply from Orien not understanding her feelings and not knowing they are mates, then Elisiah never wants to know the feeling of those who have lost their mates.

The tears that still run paths from her eyes now fall for a whole new reason. She just does not have anyone to share that reason with. She will not share her feelings again with Orien for the fear of looking more foolish.

As they enter the town, Elisiah notices the people do not even look their way. No curious glances for the massive horse or the Fae from made up horror stories on its back. She is not mad about it, but it is surprising to her.

"Do you know where the Inn is?"

Yes, it is just past the town's circle, to the left.

"No one is staring at us like they did in the last town."

You will find the further away we get from Univier, the less the people actually care to listen to his stories.

Elisiah is relieved to hear the beast say those words and finds herself taking in the small town with a new set of eyes.

The small houses are now nestled in with shops, stables, and markets. All of which are made from the same deep brown wood with some type of thick white clay between the logs. It looks like someone has taken the falling snow and fused it to the wood. They made the snow into a binder that now holds their homes and markets together.

It is amazing the things people can produce for survival and comfort.

Children dressed in thick coats and trousers run up and down the road, some of them even run with more Wulve pups. It will always amaze Elisiah how the animals and people have become so close with time and patience. The snow-covered street echoes with the sounds of laughter, warm welcomes from the shop keepers, and the chatter from the animals that make their way to different places. Elisiah takes in as much as she can of the place as they make their way through.

As they pass a fountain in the middle of town, Orien halts Samuel just before sliding from her place in the saddle.

Reaching a hand out to Elisiah, which she does not hesitate to grab, her eyes scan over each open and closed door around her. As she brings her leg over the saddle horn, the hem of the thick fabric of her dress catches there.

Before she can fight the fabric, Orien untangles the dark green wool from the brown leather of the saddle. Placing one arm under Elisiah's knees and the other behind her shoulder, she gently removes her from the seat.

Elisiah is not sure what is going on with Orien, but her behavior now is completely different than when they started this morning. If only it would continue. If only she could get into the mind of Orien and figure out what was going on. Somehow, she will figure out all her mysteries even if it takes her to forbidden places.

31

ELISIAH

JUST AFTER PAYING FOR THEIR ROOM FOR THE NIGHT, ORIEN leaves the rest house after making sure Elisiah is comfortable to be left alone.

Elisiah makes sure to convince Orien she is free to leave her with no worries because she needs the space to clear herself of every bad feeling trapped in her mind. It is not long after Orien disappears from sight that Elisiah walks back down to the small kitchen area on the main floor.

She is starving since all she has eaten today is the cured meat and bun this morning. Eating is one of her favorite things to do, and Elisiah has never gone so long without a proper meal.

Her mother has always told Fredrick to stop feeding Elisiah. It has always been said that the food she eats is what causes her hips and backside to grow to what they are, but Elisiah knows that it is not the truth. Fredrick knew so as well and has continued to feed her whatever she wishes.

Elisiah regularly goes on runs around the castle halls just to clear her head, so her stamina is fine. Her physical strength is fine everywhere except in her arms. It is the one fault she finds in herself when training with Fredrick, but she has always found ways around what she lacks.

She was serious about having Orien train her to become a better fighter. Elisiah wants to not only know how to protect herself, she wants to protect the ones around her as well. The training has not happened yet, but she can only blame herself for that.

Her time has been spent worrying too much about others and not on herself. What would she do if Orien were not here and someone tried to get to her? Would she pause like she did in that office?

"What can I do for you, miss?" The gentleman just behind a small half wall made of the same dark wood and white paste as the rest of the town says to her with a warm smile.

Returning the same smile, she cannot help but take in the beautiful color of this man's face. Elisiah can only describe it as a rich deep brown; it reminds her of the morning drink Fredrick prefers, made from ground beans.

Even though she lives in a busy come and go Kingdom like Univier, Elisiah has not been able to roam about freely on the roads. Seeing anyone that looks like her makes her feel a fullness in her chest. Her mother preferred that no one else in the castle resembled them.

"It makes us unique."

At least that is what her mother would tell her when she felt alone as she ran along the corridors hoping to find a friend. That dream never came true, along with so many others.

"Hi, how are you?" Her hand outstretched in front of her in the man's direction, she does not wait on him to answer before continuing.

"I am absolutely starving."

The man does not hesitate to softly grip her hand with his. As soon as skin touches skin, a splitting headache races across her head causing her to jerk her hand back. Elisiah places her hands on the side of her head as her teeth grit from the pain. A flash of the night sky from above the town crosses her eyes.

"Miss, are you okay?" The man jerks his own hand to his chest too, and he cradles it like it is a small child. Shock mixes with fear on his perfectly round ebony face.

As the headache dulls, she is consumed by the images of bright blue flames eating away at rows of small houses. People of all kinds run along blood-stained dirt paths, everyone is screaming, small children are crying. She can feel the panic as it enters her own body, her hands are shaking as she sees the same fountain as the one that rests in this exact town.

A deep rumble enters her head that matches the male's voice she heard while on the back of Samuel. Whoever the man is, he laughs at the destruction that plays in her mind's eye.

Looking just over the top of the crumbling fountain, Elisiah sees a beast she never thought she would encounter. A White Tail Dragon.

One of the many varied species of the Dragons that live in Sytherac, the White Tail Dragons have not been seen by the eyes of anyone for more than one hundred and fifty years. Their bodies are light gray with many different patterns of white down the expanse of their back and chest. The fire that they breathe is one of the hottest of the north, with bright blue flames that do not even have to touch your skin to melt it off the bone.

What she is seeing cannot be true. The only problem is that it is. Elisiah knows her eyes are cast over by white as they stare off to the side of the man's head. Her body has not left the spot where she finds herself standing, but the scene she watches seems like it is all currently happening.

The male's laugh coats her head as she realizes he is showing her what is to come of this town, of these people. Elisiah is not sure how he knows where she is or if he even knows who she is, but he must know that she found herself in his head the other night. She heard what he planned to do to Sytherac, but how was he able to find it? All she knows to do is warn as many of the Nobles as she can.

"White Tail. Coming." Her hands shake worse with each word, but she must warn these people. They need to run. Elisiah is not sure if the babies and older children will get out in time, but she can give them as much warning as she can.

"What? White Tail? I do not know what that is." The voice that passes her ears is hoarse while it shakes.

"Dragon." One single word makes all the residents around them pause and look her way with wide eyes.

The screams that pound in her head and the pictures of the scorching blue flames do not stop as she repeats to anyone that can hear, "Dragon!" No one moves as her sight slowly comes back to the present.

"She must be a Seer," someone behind her whispers to their neighbor before hurrying out the door. How can she tell them that she is actually a World Walker?

As she looks around the small expanse of the rest house, all she can see is the rush of moving bodies. Elisiah has never experienced anything like this before, it has her body on high alert at an invisible danger. Nothing in the moment tells her when the attack will occur, but her body knows, and she trusts that.

Without even having to tell her body, she jumps into motion towards the main door just behind her. She will be no help if she stays in the building. She would also not be safe either.

The wails of babies still in her head immediately send her feet in the direction of the doors that line the cold, snow covered, dirt road. People of all walks of life are throwing bags over their shoulders as they grab the arms of children and unhook the tied-up horses.

As if the animals of the town heard her warning as well, they run between shuffling legs, looking for anyone left behind in the chaos. A sleek white fox runs past her feet with a small boy's shirt gripped in his teeth, it chitters back at him as tears shower his cheeks. Elisiah's heart tightens at the sight.

A deafening roar rings across the sky echoed only by the haunting sound of wings slicing through the air.

Elisiah cannot stop to think as she throws open doors and amplifies her voice over the noise as best as she can, "MOVE! GET OUT NOW!"

No one stops to question the stranger invading their space as certain death only draws nearer. She has not seen Orien since the woman left their rented room only a couple minutes after they sat down their travel bags. The thought of her weighs heavy, but her body is focused on the safety of the others.

No infant or child will be left to die if she has her way. Elisiah will not be able to live with herself if she does not try everything to get these people moving towards safety. Does she know where safety is? No, but she will not stop until her body has told her it is enough.

Just as she steps back on the almost deserted road, scorching blue flames rain down from the sky, burning a line of more than seven houses. Elisiah is transfixed at the sight as the flames part from the wind of wings. All that remains of the once-standing houses are mounds of ash.

If it were not for the flames lighting the sky in an eerie blue glow, she would not be able to see the monumental animal opening its jaws, a bright white light building from its throat, eyes locked on her. Realizing she is the next target, her heart skips, and the feeling of dying seems familiar. The ball of light grows just as she turns towards the sparse wood line where she talked to the young wulve pup just some hours ago.

Even moving as fast as she can carry herself, it does not seem like enough as flames whip at her back, cutting their way through the top layer of wool, a scream rushing from her throat. The voice laughs louder in her head as her pain becomes palpable.

The crackles from the burning wood seem to match the fury of the bellow followed by the flames. All her time reading about these beasts does nothing when you're faced with one. The adrenaline filling her body does not give any room for coherent thoughts.

The White Tailed Dragons went dormant just over one hundred and fifty years ago, and it was not unheard of for the four-legged serpentine creatures to fall into a lifetime of sleep. The time spent sleeping brings them back to their full strength and even allows for the youth to age peacefully. If the history books are correct about what the people know of this species, it is currently on the hunt for a quick meal, and the Dragon will be at full power after its slumber.

Waking up from the death sleep leaves the beast ravenous but also at its most dangerous. The power that collects in their core builds to such strengths that if they do not release it, they stand a chance of being burnt from the inside out.

Elisiah's back throbs as she pumps her arms, her hair whipping behind her, the ends burnt where the fire met it. The shadow of wings envelopes her, but she does not stop pushing herself forward. She will not die this soon after leaving the castle.

The blackness in front of her ripples as it parts for Orien, long daggers held in both her hands, her eyes locked with the gray and white scaled dragon.

"RUN, ORIEN!" Elisiah pleads in her head and out loud for the person in front of her to turn around and move to a safe place. No response sounds in her head.

The sight of Orien grows closer, and she seems to grow in height. The blackness around her comes from her hands, clutching the blades, as they part into individual wisps and start taking a shape. Elisiah cannot bring herself to focus on what the mass of black is turning into, yet another call of anger swallows the space around them.

Light grows brighter behind her back. Elisiah knows another line of fire is about to head in her direction, and her feet seem to move quicker. She cannot stop herself as she repeats a string of words to herself.

I will not die today.

I will not die today.

I will not die today.

I.

Will.

Live.

Black streaks race past her straight into the path of danger, but she does not stop moving. Her lungs feel like the same flames that touched her back now wrap themselves around her organs. Elisiah's breathing is harsh, and her temples are pounding.

She never wants to feel this way again.

Orien is gone from in front of her, and in her place stands six figures all shaped like hounds. Black tendrils flow from the sockets where their eyes should be. Where paws meet ground, the same substance flows into the soil, staining it black.

Elisiah would rather meet her fate from the likes of whatever is standing in front of her than what flies at her back.

The ground quakes under her feet, causing her to lose her balance. Elisiah skids across buried rocks in the ground, and they cut and tear away at the front of her dress and skin. As her body slows to a stop, Elisiah stumbles to her feet before turning around. What she expects to find is not what is there.

Instead of being face-to-face with a hungry mouth full of razor-sharp teeth and steaming breath, she finds the White Tail Dragon, standing on all fours with its head swinging back and forth, as it watches the person standing in front of it with a pack of black hounds behind them.

Standing in place to gather any information she can about the scene in front of her, the six black masses stride up and encircle her. The one closest to her stands at her right side and looks over to Elisiah.

Elisiah freezes, stunned at the size of what can only be described as a hound from the depths of darkness. Something created by the God, Etbris, himself.

It lowers its head just enough so that she can look at its face without straining her neck.

"Were you made by Etbris?" She needs answers for whatever she is watching unfold in front of her as Orien crouches close to the ground. The dagger in her left hand is raised blade up behind her back, her right hand fisted around another as it rests on the ground for support.

The shadow hound's long snout nudges Elisiah's hair, taking her attention away from Orien. Looking into the pits of black, the hound simply nods its head in the direction of the now lunging figure in front of them.

Dread consumes her as she watches Orien fall from the air in a quick black streak, straight towards the neck of the mountain-sized Dragon. Nothing is left standing of the town behind it as its white tail, armed with two rows of spikes on each side, whips through the air in Orien's direction.

The black hounds act at the same time as they release themselves from their spots on the earth, hurtling towards the wings and feet of the beast.

The white of the Dragon is stained black by the hellish hounds finding their mark and slithering their way into the scaled skin of the screaming beast. Orien lands on the thick neck just moments before the first couple of hounds sink under the pale white and gray skin. Slowly, black lines start snaking their way along the expanse of its body as more make their way in. Dark red blood runs from every entry point of the Dragon.

The hounds by her side do not even bristle as they watch the others absorb into the Dragon. Elisiah cannot even begin to comprehend what she is watching.

Orien makes her way up the spiked neck in a full sprint, using her daggers for traction every time the animal swings its head, trying to dislodge her body. Snow-colored wings begin to beat as the dragon tries to jump towards the sky only to let out a wail of pain.

Reaching the massive expanse of the head, Orien drives a dagger into its left eye as deep as it can go before pulling it out. Elisiah watches in horror as Orien shoves her hand in the hole she created in the Dragon's eye.

Elisiah stomach flips as she watches Orien's arm disappear into the socket. Elisiah puts her hand over her mouth just in case her empty insides find something to vomit back up.

The Dragon begins shaking from its legs all the way down its tail and wings. The hounds have made their way to its spine by the looks of the black veins. Orien retracts her arm in one swift motion, long strings of crimson clutched in her grip, as clear fluid flows like a river down the scaled cheek of the dragon.

Elisiah gags as she realizes that it is the muscles of the eye her companion holds in her grip before tossing them to the ground. She is glad that the sound of a pain-laced roar masks what she knows was a wet slap from the inner workings of the beast's eye.

The hound at her left moves closer as it ducks its head so her hand rests on the top, gently. Elisiah's hand strokes the shadows making up the thing as tiny wisps curl around her fingers. The small act reveals that these are not something just created by The God of Death. They are also created by her own mate, Orien.

The hounds flanking her sides lean against Elisiah as her knees grow weak.

Orien jumps to the ground after removing the other eye from its natural resting place. No fire builds in the throat of the Dragon as blackness seeps from between the teeth. As Orien's booted feet hit the earth, the Dragon in front of Elisiah falls to its side, less than half its original size.

What once were hounds standing beside Orien fade into nothing more than black lines as they flow right into any open expanse of skin on her tall, lean body. The six that stayed with Elisiah remain in their spots as they all wait for Orien to walk their way.

Elisiah is still fully supported by two other hounds that have not left her side, and her legs are completely numb underneath her. Watching the display of pure, raw power, Elisiah finds only one question residing in her head at the moment.

What is Orien?

ORIEN

32

As she walks up to the woman being held by two of her shadow hounds, all Orien can feel is the vast amount of power that has now made its home in her body. Whatever the shadows touch, they drain. It is how she survives without the need for physical food, even though she does wish she could taste some of things she comes across.

Elisiah looks like she is the one whose life drained from her veins rather than the shriveled corpse behind her. Fighting a White Tail Dragon is not something Orien wanted to do tonight, but when she heard the beat of wings off in the distance from the Wulves den, she cursed herself for even leaving Elisiah's side.

Just like it was not her idea to fight a Dragon, it was not her idea to open the passage of communication between the pup and Elisiah. It was the pup's. Going to the den after making sure everything was in the room, including the one staring at the remains of the animal, was a mistake on her part.

If she had been in town instead of gallivanting deep in the woods, then she could have met the beast before it was able to come into the small town. Orien's body yearned for the feeling of being among those that accepted her; that is the only reason she left. That single white pup, Glace, changed her plans as soon as Orien felt his presence.

Thinking about the way she feels at ease with the oversized canines of the woods makes her question if Erwin has already heard the news about the attack.

The village that lays in smoldering embers behind them is called Buron.

Orien had not shared that information with Elisiah and now to do so only seems ridiculous. She really needs to work on her communication.

Orien finds herself wanting to see the thick fur-lined suits the Guards of Thundaria normally wear outside of social occasions; she is not entirely sure why, but the desire is there.

Reaching a spot just in front of Elisiah, she looks over the expanse of her body. Orien and the beast inside her growl at the same time. Elisiah is bleeding from what seems to be every-where, her once green dress now a mix of brown and black. Her hands are scraped, her nails are broken, and she smells like burnt skin.

Is she burnt?

The beast says as it paces the front of her skull. They both know the answer to that because they heard her screams; they felt the pain that ripped through Elisiah. They also feel the desolation in her chest as she stares at the shriveled corpse.

Orien reaches her hand towards Elisiah to relieve the hounds of her weight, even though she knows it is nothing to them. The shadows only move a couple inches as her hand loops around Elisiah's small shoulders. Bending down enough to loop her other arm under her knees, she scoops Elisiah off the ground in one fluid motion.

Stay out. Help keep watch.

The beast commands the six hounds flanking Orien's sides, and they ripple in agreement. Without a second thought, they all turn and make their way through the rubble. If this place is gone then they will go on to the next.

Orien knows the villagers are safe because the animals from all around came to lead them to safety. The nobles share a good relationship with the wildlife which means they all look out for one another. They will find shelter in a cave made by some of the Bergsmed, a race of short statured men that find their homes in caves or surrounded by stone.

They make the best weapons.

The daggers she favors are made by one who lives in the mountains of Runearied. The man told her he added the floral design along the blade and hilt as a last-minute idea and said she would know its reason soon enough.

She still has not understood his reasoning.

33

ORIEN

Orien walks until the sun breaks through the clouds in the sky. Elisiah still in her arms, and the hounds still at her side, the ground behind them is stained black from their leaking, black paws.

She never understood why the shadows always seemed to ooze until one day she discovered that when so much power flows through you, it can break you. Releasing what will slowly eat away at your existence can be the only logical answer, and frankly she is grateful for that residual energy in herself to return from where it came.

It was taught at a young age that you never take more than you need; it is even one of the Laws of Sytherac, so the abundant amount of power she siphoned from the dragon was truly only meant to go back into the earth.

The woman in her arms has not moved since her eyes closed just beyond the outskirts of town. Under her feet, the snow grows thicker, but the sun makes it easier to keep some heat on her cheeks. Everything they had was destroyed in the rest house.

Orien knows Elisiah will be hungry when she wakes. She needs to hunt, and a fire would not hurt either, but she will not wake up the blood-stained woman in her arms. Now she understands why she would not mind seeing The Guard of Thundaria walking by right about now. They still have days before they make it to the meeting point.

Orien can use her shadows to quickly get from place to place, but only when she clearly knows where she is going in her mind. Truthfully, she has never gone further than from the expanse of Alister's office to her rooms with another person. That was the first time she had taken someone along with her, and she had hoped it would be the last.

It looks like it was only the beginning though as Elisiah shivers in her sleep. Orien cradles the woman's small frame closer to her chest as she looks around to the shadow hounds walking by them.

"Should we try putting some much-needed distance in today?"

Orien asks the shadows in her mind, and in a blink, five of them merge into the one at her right side. The lone hound becomes a darker black and stands more than twice the size of Samuel.

"I will take that as a yes." Talking in her head has become normal for her now, but with the company she keeps, the ability to use her voice would be extremely helpful.

The part of her that has become an annoyance since setting eyes on Elisiah has been asleep for hours now, it always needs rest after being forward for so long. The silence in her head is welcome.

Just as she adjusts the body in her arms so that Elisiah's head rests against her neck, the power beside her loses its shape and engulfs the pair. All that she allows herself to think about is the larger town midway to the castle.

It is built close to the Orical Ocean and used for trading.

The image of the dock plays in her mind until she can count exactly how many rings line each board down its path. As soon as it sticks in her head, her body moves under the power of the shadows.

It feels like nothing to her now that she is older, but when she was younger it would make her sick. She learned the trick after a long day of physical training which included scaling the castle's bare walls with only what she had on her body, her hands, and feet.

When she reached the top of the wall, her skin hanging from her hands and feet, she pictured her bed. As soon as she saw the blankets lying over that giant bed of hers, she began to feel like she was falling through the sky, only to end up on her bed just how she imagined herself.

Now, it only feels like she is weightless. The weight of the body slumped against her is the only thing that lets her know she is moving; she hopes towards a place safer than where they have been.

Orien cannot remember the name of the port town, but she does recall that it is one of the biggest of the territory besides the one that lies in the direct territory of the castle. Thundaria is encased in a wall of frosted ice, much like the castle itself. When she first saw the intricate work at four years old, all she wanted to do was stare at the walls for hours. It was amazing to her at the time what could be created by the hands of the ice-magic wielders that sit on the throne.

The fact that Erwin Hartlander now sits on the same throne as his ruthless father, Edmon, makes her feel like he had some type of victory. Edmon was known for his harsh treatment of prisoners, and even his own wife and son.

He made it known that anyone without royal blood in their veins was worth the same as the humans. It was one of the long-standing laws decreed by the founders of their world that everything should be treated as equal, but for a majority of the Fae, that law is seen as obscene. The topic of the value of humans is often discussed in the Kingdoms. Orien has found that every royal she has been in company with is full of voices that only hold arrogance.

As for Erwin and his mother, Blythe, they only knew their father or husband as his reputation suggests.

Blythe met her end quickly for the lifespan the Fae normally lived. She died at one hundred and fifteen. Erwin was only nine at the time, if Orien's information was correct. Blythe was known for her beauty in all of the surrounding Kingdoms of Sytherac, but Edmon did not care enough for his wife to notice. He only noticed himself.

As Orien's feet meet the water-soaked boards that make up the walking path of the dock, the shadows sink into her neck, face, and hands. Normally anything that would take her more than two hours to walk would drain the energy from her, but after the abundant meal they shared earlier, she does not even feel the slightest bit drained.

The excess power flows back and forth through her skin, leaving it plastered with small bumps that raise the smallest of hairs.

Her mission now is finding Elisiah a safe place to sleep, wash, eat, and a mender to heal what has been broken on her skin. The blood from her many cuts somehow found its way into her silky black hair and managed to clump her curls together at the ends. All Orien wants is to break them free of their confinements and watch as they take their tightly coiled form.

Those curls are one of the most beautiful things Orien has ever laid her light brown eyes upon. The thought of them being soiled by anything makes her see red.

It does not take much for her to become angered in general, but her emotions have become more than foreign to her now. They have been consumed by the one in her arms. Everything Orien feels now is directly related to Elisiah.

HARTLANDER

It is not long after the attack on Buron by the White Tail Dragon that Erwin receives the news from one of the shifter Fae that resided in the village. The man rushed from the safety of one of the caves nestled alongside a small, snow-capped mountain that sits towards the West of the region.

The shifter flew to the castle in his falcon form. As he reaches the entrance of the castle, he collapses with exhaustion from the travel, but he feels like it is the only thing he could do to help his little village at the moment.

The Guards standing by the double front doors have to lift him off the ground as he demands to see the King.

"It is urgent," he says as he grabs the thick jacket of the Guard to his right. "A Dragon." He looks to the one on his left. "Black dogs killed it." The Guards try to soothe him the best they know how as they use their bodies to shoulder open the doors.

"It burnt. It burnt everything." His slim body shakes with a mix of fatigue and sadness. The hair on his head is soaked in sweat and it drips on the dark blue floor as the Guards carry him into the warmth of Erwin's home.

Erwin heard the commotion from where he sat in his throne room since sleep eluded him as it so often does. The young King finds solace in the vast empty space in front of him when he occupies the room by himself.

That night, his mind is quieter than normal, but it is short lived as the double doors open and take his peace. The Guards relay the information they received from the falcon shifter, and for the few minutes the man stays conscious, Erwin Jay Hartlander, hears enough.

He knows Orien killed the dragon; all he needed to hear was the few descriptive factors that immediately took him back to her from their childhood. The red hair and pale skin are enough for him; he has to get her to this palace as soon as he can. If she is the reason for these black dogs that helped kill such a beast like a Dragon, then she is exactly what they need.

Erwin knows that from the very beginning, although everything they have been working towards will be for nothing if they cannot get this extraordinary Fae on their side. They will not stand a chance against Orien if she chooses to unite with the others already against him.

If it were not for his pregnant mate, he would have already left to grab Orien and the one with her.

The thought of leaving Aneira and his child is not even an option for him. The bond between mates is the strongest thing in Sytherac, and that soul tie only deepens when a child is brought into the mix. Both Aneira and Erwin are more than thrilled to be able to have a child since mated pairs tend to not be able to conceive so soon after the bond is accepted.

No one really understands how the souls choose their match, but then again, no one has really looked too far into it.

Some believe it is because when the two people are created, they come from the same strain of light used to make every soul. Since not everyone is destined to have a mate, it could stand true that sometimes the God of Souls, Lixtis, may become complacent with his job.

When Erwin thinks about the God and the ways of the universe, he finds that it would not surprise him if the being did become lazy and just start throwing souls around until something like a tie was created.

The King is grateful he has Aneira because he would not be who he is today without her; he would be dead. If he were left to his own devices in this world, with his mind, he has no doubt he would have killed himself by now.

His wife, his queen, saves his life every single day just by smiling at him. The thought of her rejecting their bond when it was first founded could have driven him mad if it were not for her taking the first step in consummating the relationship. It is the only fact everyone knows for certain about the life-altering tie; any person can reject the bond, and it normally will end with the rejected half dying. Erwin has witnessed the strongest of warriors lose his life at the hands of their other half.

To die of a broken heart seems like the worst way to go.

His thoughts of his mate take him away from his reality for a fleeting moment before returning to the here and now. He must send a group of his knights to help the villagers of Buron as well as clean up a dragon corpse and find Orien and the plus one with her.

Without letting himself sit still for another moment longer, he sets course from the throne room to the knights' cabins built at the back side of the castle. They were originally built in the isolated place to keep distractions, such as women, away from the men, but it now has become home to only those that choose to stay there.

It is not his place to tell these men who are responsible for protecting his life and his peoples' lives, what they do in their spare time. They have lives to live outside of being a part of The King's Guard. Just like he has one outside of being the soon-to-be King of Thundaria.

The rule has been in place since before he was even thought about, but that did not stop him from changing it to better the Kingdom. Many of the men came to him and expressed the struggle they had between wanting a family and protecting their home, so he found a way to make it easier for everyone.

It was the first traditional rule he broke after his father's death, and he would be lying if he said it did not make him feel like he just spat in Edmon's face. It is a feeling he wishes he felt when the man was still alive.

Making his way across the castle, he feels like his body is on autopilot from how he can tell you exactly where he is even if he were blind in both eyes and walking backwards. It gives Erwin time to think about what he wants to do to correct the situation. Not just for the people but for himself as well.

Send the new recruits to the town, and then send your best to find Orien.

No, even the best could not locate someone like Orien.

You do not know unless you try.

Well, you do know because you have already tried finding her.

No one can find her; she is a ghost.

Just go yourself!

You cannot leave Aneira, what if something happens to the baby?

The child will not like you anyways, what does it matter?

Are you sure Aneira even likes you?

God, do you even like yourself?

Maybe letting himself think was not the best option at the moment.

The fact he can start on one topic and end on something completely different never ceases to amaze him, and now his fingers are chewed raw, again.

"Harty, my love, please stop overthinking. I am trying to read." The sound of Aneira's voice feels like a cloud floating in his head, and it brings her light with it.

"As you wish, snowflake. Enjoy whatever has caught your attention." The smile that plants itself on his face as he thinks about her, sitting in one of those old wooden chairs, hunched over the table, books sprawled out in front of her, makes him have to adjust his pants. The effect she has on him, even in his imagination, speaks to the level of intensity their bond has created.

His reaction wastes no time as it travels down the link of the bond.

"Get your mind out of the ditch, Erwin Jay Hartlander. You have important business to attend to, and I am preparing for when you go and bring back our guest." Aneira's tone takes on that of a mother scolding their child. Erwin finds it suitable as she is currently making one of their own.

She said, "You go."

That is permission.

If you leave her here, the castle will melt on top of her.

So, the last thought is false, and he knows that, but now his eyes look to the walls around him as different images flood his head of the castle melting around him.

"I will be perfectly fine while you find this friend of yours. The library is where I need to be right now." Reassurance fills his veins as she speaks to his mind.

Just another benefit that comes from a mate bond. Being able to feel what the other is feeling is also an added bonus. He loves when her feelings wash over him as she feels them.

"Okay, I will find her. I promise to be back as soon as I can." He stuffs his hands into the pocket of his overcoat as he reaches the small clear door made of even more ice that leads to the wooden houses just on the other side.

He has never questioned why the houses are all made of wood instead of the same ice and snow as the castle, but now as he looks at them, it seems odd.

"I can guarantee I will be right here with the same books when you return." Aneira speaks the truth, because that is the only place you will ever find her unless she needs to sleep. Most of her meals are even eaten at the same table where she currently sits.

"Take Kemp with you." She adds the sentence quickly before shutting the link in their minds, stopping the male in his tracks and cursing the air.

He should have known his brother-in-law was back from wherever it is he runs off to on the rotating off days.

Kemp is Aneira's older brother and Rissa's only son. Since Aneira has been raised in or around the castle from the time she was an infant, Erwin had time to know who she was. Meeting new people has always been hard for him, so he liked to take some time learning them before approaching them.

When the male first came to live with his mother and sister in the castle, Erwin had hoped it would be easy to gain him as a friend. As it turns out, he was mistaken. Kemp hated his life in Thundaria, and rightfully so, hated Erwin.

Aneira knew what she was doing when she told him to go. She knew he would take her up on the offer and it would give her the clear shot to demand he have to spend time with the one person that hated him.

Chills run down his spine as he thinks of the way the male stares at him when they are forced to be in the same room as the other. Hartlander has no ill will towards the brother of his wife, but he can think of hundreds of other things he would rather do than have him tag along on a hide and seek mission.

· · ·

Break your foot, then you cannot go.

That's too easy, the menders can fix it.

Cut a testicle off, they cannot fix that.

He would rather cut off his own manhood than deal with the stagnant air that fills the space between Kemp and himself.

That is pathetic.

For once, he agrees with himself.

35

MARIEM

Mariem stands in line, waiting for her food rations to be set in the separating compartments on her round plate, when the familiar presence fills the space behind her. The woman lets out a heavy sign as her eyes close and her chin lifts towards the sky.

She knew Elisiah would be a problem for her, but an annoyance was something for which she did not account. It feels like yesterday that she gave the young girl the life-altering information that she has a mate, but apparently it was not something that altered her life enough to stay in her own world.

Opening her eyes and walking up the line, Mariem smiles gently at the young girl serving the food today. Her mother must be the one cooking this afternoon then.

The girl still stands behind her as Mariem feels her every movement match her own. Leaving the line before she can finish gathering the rest of her meal, Mariem heads back toward the same tent where she always is.

She will not forgive the girl following her for making her miss all the food intended to fill her plate. Now, she will have to finish her night with only the bare minimum to keep her appetite satisfied.

The inside of the medical tent is still empty as she pushes through the flaps that hang open a full minute after she already makes her way to the same worktable she constantly occupies every day of her life now.

Before the army was given their new orders to push back from the front lines of the main fighting ground of The Eternal War, all the men and women surrounding her had made perfect homes just on the East side of the killing field. You could walk into actual wood-built homes, children ran wild with friends, there was always laughter, and most of all she always wore a genuine smile.

These tents are all they have now, and it is all thanks to the God that decided to make them. The one who abandoned them when they all needed him the most, Etbris has never disappointed her before, but right now as she thinks about every person she has helped raise because of the feud between him and his brothers, she finds herself filled with displeasure.

It is because of this higher power that she has lost the only person she has truly loved. Not a day passes that Mariem does not sit and think about her wife. Zoe was everything to her, and she died on that death-stained field along with all her life-long friends. She can never forgive their maker for that.

She thinks he knows that too. At least she hopes he does.

As she sets her plate on the bare spot in the center of her space, she runs her hands along the backside of her skirt to keep any wrinkles from forming as she takes her spot in her chair.

Elisiah, the supposed human, is standing just off to her left side. The feeling of eyes watching Mariem does not even make her eyes wander. If anyone is used to the feeling of being put under a microscope, it is Mariem.

Deciding to be the first to speak, she clears her throat and looks in the general direction of her World Walker.

"What can I do for you, Elisiah?" Mariem clasps her hands on her lap as she waits for a response.

"What the hell is Orien?" The anger rolling from her invisible form is palpable in the room. It is nice to know the being can feel anything other than sadness and confusion, but she will not be getting any answers from her mouth.

"I take it you have yet to read any books like I told you to do on every other unwanted visit." Mariem cannot help but feel like she has been repeating herself to Elisiah every time they have one of their encounters. She could not care less if the invisible woman in front of her is traveling. If Elisiah wanted answers as badly as she is saying then a library would be top priority. Using the excuse of their travels is just that, an excuse.

Elisiah moves closer to her. "Oh, I am sorry that I have not had the time to think about finding a book when I am too busy running for my life as I get chased by a fucking Dragon!"

Mariem stares at the space in front of her, waiting to see if anything else is going to come from this.

"Do not even get me started on how Orien, my supposed mate–" She stops at the word before continuing. "–killed the damn thing WITH shadow hounds!"

This information makes Mariem sit up straighter in her seat. "What do you mean, shadow hounds?" The older woman knows exactly what she means by shadow hounds, but surely, she is mistaken. Shadow hounds only live in the realm with Etbris. They can only be brought forth by him.

Her thoughts pause as she thinks of the history of the things. It is said that the hounds of the Shadow Realm cannot be called to the living world unless by the God of Death himself, unless the beings feel that someone else holds more power than their creator.

"THEY WENT INTO HER SKIN!" Elisiah's words tumble around the tent as Mariem slumps into the chair, a breath leaving her mouth as she stares at the half-full plate of food in front of her.

She needs to find Bashtian.

"On top of that, they killed a White Tail Dragon in less time than it takes me to get dressed in the morning. By the time they left from inside the animal, it looked like a shriveled berry."

That is exactly the behavior of the Shadow Hounds said to reside in the Shadow Realm. Mariem definitely needs to tell Bashtian.

"Hello, are you listening to me?" Air whips across the side of her cheek, and it draws her from the horror playing out in her head. The energy of Elisiah flaps her hands around the air. It makes her look like a chicken trying to catch flight.

"Yes, I am listening to you, girl. Give me time to process some of this." Mariem takes a calming breath before adding. "What you are describing are Shadow Hounds."

The arms stop flapping in the air as Mariem speaks to her. "Shadow Hounds are real? I just called them that because that is what they looked like. I originally thought they were the hounds from hell." Elisiah sounds ignorant as she speaks the words, but she also has not read any books about anything that has been happening to her, so what can Mariem expect?

"Go home, find a library, and read a book. Read every book you can find on all the subjects you have questioned me about and learn for yourself. I cannot help you if you do not try to help yourself." Anger again becomes palpable in the space around them.

"Have you not been listening to me? I. AM. TRAVELING. TO. A. DIFFERENT. KINGDOM. What forest or snow-covered field HAS A FUCKING LIBRARY?"

Mariem watches as Elisiah's energy walks towards the entrance of the medical tent. "Elisiah, find any way you can to get yourself and Orien to a place of learning. That is all I can tell you."

"Fuck you."

Elisiah's energy source leaves Mariem's world, taking all the anger with it. The woman turns to her plate of cold food and sweeps it into the trash can on the left side of her space. Her appetite is nonexistent as she stands from her chair and starts her hunt for the man responsible for this, Bashtian Ivor Etubious.

36

ELISIAH

Waking up in a bed, Elisiah does not remember going to sleep here. She does not even remember going to sleep. The last thing she recalls is being held up by the two hounds, a wrinkled Dragon in front of her, and Orien's hand dripping liquid from the eye she took from his socket. She shudders as the picture replays in her head.

Sitting up in the bed, she looks around the room. The four-poster bed sits in the middle of the warm, well-lit room.

Straight in front of the bed, there is a single door and a matching one nestled in the wall to her left. The walls are covered in a soft white paper with dozens of small wisps that reach from the ceiling to floor.

Looking at the floor, Elisiah gasps as she realizes it is completely covered in a thick white fur. No spot that she can see is not covered by the mass of the animal shed.

The lanterns holding the Water's Light hang from the perched ceiling by four different silver strings of metal, each one meeting a large round clear bowl. Nothing else takes up space in the room besides a table on either side of the bed, both of which match the frame of the bed.

Looking down at the blankets covering the bottom half of her body, she does not even realize that her top half is completely naked, her breasts exposed to the warmth of the room.

Running her hands gently across the soft material, her stomach growls, catching her by surprise.

We are bringing you food.

The beast in her head is warm just like this room and the blankets. It all feels comfortable. For a fleeting moment, she forgets that her time asleep was spent away from her body, yelling at a winged woman.

The anger from their encounter runs down her body in a rush, and she feels the peaks of her chest heat with the air around her. Elisiah is horrified as she looks down at her body, finding her torso nude. Slowly, she raises the material on her bottom half to find everything is bare. Bile burns the back of her throat as she thinks of someone undressing her.

Her skin is clean. Someone washed her. She lifts her hand to her hair and gently pulls a lock of curls to her nose. It does not even have to get closer to her nose to smell the floral fragrance dancing from it. The pain that resided in her back is gone as she moves, and her hands are free of any cuts. Someone has healed her.

Throwing the covering from her body, she jumps from the bed. Elisiah hopes the door in front of her is the bathroom and not the door to wherever people may be. Surely, no one would put the bed in front of an entrance door.

Thinking better than to risk running into the opening fully nude, she rips a blanket off the bed and wraps it around herself before quickly walking to the door.

Grabbing the round handle, she gently pulls it open an inch so she can peek out with one eye just as she lets out a calming breath for the fact that this is the bathroom door. The other door behind her closes with a light click.

Elisiah slams the bathroom door and jumps off the ground as she screams. Turning around to see who has just broken into the room, she finds it is only Orien.

Orien, who currently holds a tray of steaming bowls with a side plate of bread. The delicious smell coming from the bowls on the silver tray makes Elisiah's mouth water. All she can focus on is how empty her middle is and how appealing whatever is in those bowls must be.

We said that we were bringing you food.

Elisiah does not care what the beast in her head says. She does not care about the fact that she is naked or even the fact that she just experienced the full range of emotions in less than five minutes. All she cares about is getting that food in her mouth.

Walking over to Orien with the blanket clutched to her chest to keep it closed, she uses her left to balance the tray she takes from Orien's hands as she walks to the side of the bed.

Instead of sitting on the bed to eat, Elisiah slowly eases herself to the plush floor that feels like soft grass under her feet. Bringing herself into a crossed-legged sitting position, she rearranges the blanket so she has more room to move as she places the tray of food on the floor in front of her.

The shining tray has two bowls resting on it which are accompanied by a small plate of bread. The first bowl she finds is filled with a light red liquid with little green leaves on the top. It smells earthy but also holds notes of fresh cream.

The one off to its right has chunks of seared meat mixed with what she can tell is strips of carrot. This stew does not smell nearly as delicious as Fredrick's, but right now it will do just fine.

She cannot stop herself from grabbing a piece of bread and dipping it straight into the bowl filled with red. As it hits her tongue, she is welcomed by the familiar flavor of tomato. Her eyes close, shoulders go slack, and a soft moan leaves her lips as the velvety texture warms her throat.

Orien has been forgotten in the moments of her first bite until desire stirs in her chest, but the feeling is not hers.

Straining her neck to look up at the Fae in front of her, she realizes that Orien has been watching her every move, and the female's throat shifts with a swallow. Elisiah smiles as she realizes it is not her feeling of desire, it is Orien's.

Looking away from the eyes watching her, she does not hesitate as she picks up a piece of meat along with the bread and takes a bite. Another moan leaves her mouth as pure bliss envelops her tongue from the taste. Desire grows stronger in her chest. She repeats the act.

Stop making that sound.

The voice in her head is rough, like it is restraining a growl. The sound makes Elisiah laugh in her mind.

"What sound?" She keeps her eyes on the food in front of her as she tears a bigger slice of bread in half. She licks the side of her lip to clean off some gravy left by the stew. A low growl vibrates in her head. This time, the quiet moan that passes her lips is not from the food.

"Stop groaning in my head."

Stop moaning at the food.

"The last one was because of you." Elisiah cannot believe she let those words slip, but damn if it was not the truth.

The desire in her chest is matched with her own. If she can feel Orien's, then there is no use hiding hers.

She lifts her eyes back to Orien's.

"You can feel it though, can you not?"

Orien's shoulders straighten but her throat swallows again.

"I know you can because I can feel you." She releases the hand clutching the blanket and it slowly falls to just under the base of her breast, her hand moving to cover where her heart lives in her chest. Another growl graces her head with its vibrations, and she sucks in a breath.

"I feel you right here, all the time." Elisiah's heart picks up as the standing female lowers to her knees in front of her.

She notices that Orien still wears the same filth-covered clothes, but she does not care. Not since the top of Orien's shirt lies open just enough to see her collarbones and the very top of the leather band covering her cleavage.

Their eyes do not leave each other's as Orien's hand reaches for the one resting on Elisiah's chest. The thought of the Dragon's eyeball juice does not even bother her at this moment. All that bothers her is their lack of contact. Skin touches skin, and both seem to suck in a breath at the flood of want that overcomes them.

Slowly, Orien takes the hand off Elisiah's chest and turns her palm over so that it faces her own body.

With her left hand, Orien pulls her shirt over just enough for Elisiah to see not only more of her freckled skin but more of the wrap as well. She places Elisiah's hand over the exact spot it is on her own chest and holds it firm.

This is where we feel you, Little One. We feel you right here. Always.

A single tear runs down Elisiah's cheek as Orien places the hand that was held to her chest back in Elisiah's lap and stands. All Elisiah can do is watch her as Orien turns and walks into the bathroom.

Not long after the door closes behind Orien, Elisiah hears the sound of water running into the empty tub. Elisiah stares at the food in front of her. The desire mixes with sadness.

"I cannot do this," she says to the empty room as a soft splash comes from the bathroom. Before she can think better of the idea, Elisiah stands from her spot and the blanket is left empty on the floor as she takes a few brisk steps to the door separating the two.

Opening the door and walking inside the steaming room, Elisiah finds Orien sitting in the tub with her knees to her chest, resting her forehead on her crossed arms. Elisiah knows Orien knows she is in the room, so she does not stop her legs as they carry her across the floor and into the water. Slowly, she reaches for Orien's arm and gently rests her hand on her wrist as she pulls it from its resting spot. Orien's head lifts as she unfolds her arms and watches Elisiah.

Elisiah pushes slightly on Orien's raised knees; she hesitates just a moment before climbing over the side and finally resting on Orien's bent legs. The tub is too short for them to stretch out properly, but it is wide enough to allow Elisiah to straddle Orien's hips as she lays the top of her body flush with the female under her.

Orien's heart beats rapidly, and her body stiffens as Elisiah rests her right ear over the expanse of chest where her hand was just moments ago.

Wrapping her arms as far as they will go behind Orien, Elisiah lets out a long breath as her eyes close. Orien's heart slows, and her arms envelope Elisiah's body, as she rests her muzzle-covered mouth on the top of her hair.

Nothing matters in this moment to either of them as they lay in each other's arms in the hot water. Elisiah does not think about Orien's bare body under hers, and most importantly, Orien does not think about everything she is exposing herself to.

It is something the assassin has never thought of doing with anyone. Hiding herself from Elisiah was not an option.

Not when Orien feels like she finally has a home.

A place where she belongs.

The invisible thread of Elisiah's soul that has been reaching out for Orien's finally has something to grab on to as just a little part of the female under her accepts the feelings between them.

"You feel like home." It is all Elisiah can say as a spark lights deep inside her and her arms grip tighter as she presses her ear closer to Orien's heart.

37

ELISIAH

The two of them sit holding each other until the steaming water turns chilly on their skin. Elisiah moves from her spot on top of Orien, making sure her eyes stay averted from the places she knows the other is not comfortable with. Even though she felt every curve and dip that made up the expanse of her body, she still wants to respect her boundaries.

Orien follows not long after Elisiah, both wrapping a drying cloth around their own bodies.

To Elisiah's surprise, Orien went and found a shop that carried the proper size attire for both of them, something simple for their continued travels.

The cold soup and stew still sit in the same spot where they were forgotten, but Elisiah cannot find it in her to care for the substances, not when she catches a glimpse of the bare back across the room.

It makes her turn around so she faces the uncovered skin on the other side of the bed. Neither has spoken since her last words in the washroom, but right now words are not needed; they both have said everything they needed.

It is not a secret that Orien's back is scarred; Elisiah saw her get whipped with her own eyes. Helped heal her wounds too, but it does not stop the rage she feels when she cannot even find a centimeter of unmarked skin. Scars cross over the next, some even layer right on top of another. They range from long and narrow to short and wide, some even make different shapes, like someone purposely wanted to use her skin as a parchment page.

Elisiah cannot stop her eyes as they follow some rogue, longer scars that trail up her neck and disappear into her red hair.

Orien pulls on the long sleeve black shirt she grabbed for herself from whatever clothing shop she found wherever they are. As she turns toward Elisiah, she flattens out a few wrinkles that rest on her flat, muscled stomach, and her chest is once again laid flat.

The leather piece she discarded in the washroom earlier was beyond saving, and Elisiah does not ask what she found to take its place as she remembers every inch of the seven-foot Fae in front of her. Orien does not try to hide herself from Elisiah, which feels like a win.

"I am sorry if I overstepped earlier." Elisiah bends down to lace up the leather ties of her same brown boots. They are the only thing she has left from her original belongings. The thought of her things buried in that brown bag makes her head snap up to look at Orien, her eyes wide in terror.

"Samuel! We left Samuel!" Elisiah did not even have time to think about the horse when all hell broke loose in that small town, and now all she can think about is the fear he had to feel being left on his own.

"We left the horse." Her voice lowers, and her right hand rests on her chest, covered in the same black fabric as Orien's, clutched tightly in a fist.

What kind of person just leaves their horse when there is a Dragon?

Orien runs her fingers through the top of her hair to move fallen curls from her eyes before she closes the distance between the two. She does not hesitate to pull Elisiah's hand from her shirt and hold it in left as her right uses the same brushing motion to smooth the angry scrunched fabric.

Come on. We need to show you something.

Elisiah can tell the thing is smiling as it says the words because she finds herself smiling as well. Everything has become a link to each other. She still does not know if Orien knows what it is. Elisiah finds herself too scared to tell the other.

Will she hate Elisiah for not telling her sooner? Will Orien reject her? The question itself makes every grain of her existence feel weaker and broken.

Nodding her head as she looks up at the female in front of her, she shoves those feelings of rejection into a tight vault in her head. If she locks them away, they cannot come back to hurt her. That is how she has managed to survive so long. It must work.

As they walk to the door, Elisiah cannot help herself as her mind floods with questions.

"Where are we exactly? Do you know where Samuel is? I really hope he is okay; I cannot believe we both just left him." Her head shakes back and forth as they enter the hallway.

Both sides of the walkway have more than ten doors on each side. The room they occupy is the last door on the left side of the space, and it ends in a dead end just to her right.

Every elaborate detail that she found in their room flows into the hallway as well. The same plush fabric adorns the floor for as far as she can see, even as they get closer to an opening at the far left.

We are in a port town not far from the immediate gates of The Ice Castle called Anona.

The beast tells Elisiah this as Orien watches her take in every detail of the space where they are.

As for the horse, he will be okay.

"How have we made it so close to Thundaria if we were just..." She pauses. "Five days. Five days from the halfway point."

We Shadow Walked.

The term is said easily in her head, but the memories of her visit to whatever other world Mariem resides in feels like a slap in the face.

"Shadow Walked? Is that the same as having shadows leave your body, turn into giant hounds, sink into a Dragon, and then leave it two times smaller then how it began?" Elisiah stops in the middle of the turn that leads to a flight of stairs; even those are covered in the fabric.

The walls, to her surprise, have changed. The paper in this area has turned to a dark red with thousands of white, pink, and orange flowers. It is hideous compared to what they just left.

Exactly.

That is all she gets in response. Her hand is still held in Orien's as she gently gives a squeeze. Looking behind them and to their sides, Elisiah realizes people walk about in every which way. Elisiah understands Orien's gesture to not speak too loudly.

"For another time then," she replies in her head as frustration flows along with it. Orien's eyes narrow on her as her shoulders straighten just slightly at the new emotion now flowing in her body.

Any question you have, Little One, we will answer it. Right now is just not the right time.

"It seems like it is never the right time to ask anything," she scoffs out loud. "Next you're going to tell me I need to find the answers myself like Mariem did." Elisiah shuts her mouth even though nothing left her lips.

She tries to shut the link in her mind that allows for her thoughts to travel so freely. Orien tilts her head slightly to the right as she looks right into the center of Elisiah's eyes.

I guess you're not the only one with questions now.

The voice rumbles across her body as dread fills her stomach at the idea of having to try to put what she has been experiencing into words.

She does not worry about sounding crazy.

She worries about what Orien will say. If her name is known in another world then she must have some recollection as to why, and if she does not, then what does that mean?

All she wants to do right now is get to the Ice Castle, as the thing in Orien called it, and read any books she can find.

The pair start back walking again, still hand in hand, only this time Elisiah's fingers are intertwined with Orien's. Her hand could be invisible by the way the other swallows it. A smile plays on her cheeks at the sight.

"I really need to find a library."

And you will have one.

The voice is soft in her head as it chuckles, and admiration passes between them.

Walking into an open space full of people, Elisiah pauses to take in the sight in front of her. The room they have entered is bigger than the ball room in the Stone Castle of Univier.

Details can be found everywhere your eyes wander; no spot is bare. Metals varying in every shade she can think of have a place in this area, different color paper cling to the walls, the once white fur is now an array of browns.

The amount of Water's Light that hangs from the ceiling is matched by the amount that sits on tables in large bowls.

Bodies come and go in every direction, some leaving to walk into a bustling street on the other side of a wall of clear glass.

Orien walks toward a half wall in the center of the room, and Elisiah follows along, her arm outstretched from falling behind as she tries to catch every minor detail. Reaching the wall, Elisiah seals her mouth as tight as she can so it does not gape at the woman behind it.

Elisiah has never seen a Merfolk before since they do not like to travel too far from the sea, but she has never imagined someone could be so breathtaking.

The woman in front of her has juniper hair that looks like it is fresh out of the water but it is not dripping. She has perfect round eyes the color of sand, outlined in long black lashes, and no eyebrows grace her face, instead, gray scales cover most of the surface.

Each time she turns her head to greet anyone that comes to her working spot, the Water's Light catches the fingernail-sized armor on her face and casts an iridescent glow on the top of the wood under her webbed hands.

"Orien, this came for you earlier from a messenger Pixie." The voice that greets her mate is soft and sensual. Elisiah hates it.

Orien reaches for the rolled parchment with her free hand just for it to be caught in the clutches of the gray webbed hand. A growl runs down their link followed by repulsion.

Before Elisiah can stop her motions, she pulls her hand free from Orien's and grabs the dagger from the sheath held at the thigh of the body next to her. Raising to the tips of her toes, Elisiah slams the blade of the dagger into the wood just between the webbed fingers holding Orien's hand captive.

A squeal leaves the Merwoman's mouth as the thin skin between her fingers is held to the wood by Orien's long dagger.

"Orien," Elisiah says through clenched teeth, "does not want your slimy scales touching her." The sandy eyes snap to hers, and Elisiah smiles as she continues, "Remove it or I will do it for you."

Pulling the dagger from the wood, she angles it so the tip indents the skin of the Merwoman's wrist. Elisiah's smile never leaves her face, and her eyes show every ounce of anger in her body.

The woman removes her hand and shoves the message towards Elisiah instead of who it was originally intended for before she turns from her spot, leaving from behind the desk. Droplets of dark blue blood rest on the wood, along with the indent from the blade of the long dagger.

Gripping the paper in her free hand, Elisiah slips the dagger back into its home at Orien's side before handing her the message.

Her smile disappears as she looks up at Orien who still has not grabbed the paper held out in front of her. Elisiah finds slackened shoulders and a vibration in her core as she stares up at Orien.

"Are you going to read it? It might be about Samuel, maybe someone found him." She did not think someone would care to message someone like Orien about some random animal.

We should have taken all of you in that tub.

At once, Elisiah understands the feeling sitting in her middle as the beast rumbles the words.

"Is that just you, Nox?" Elisiah uses the beast name for the first time in her heated question to Orien. "Or do you speak the other part of you as well?" Elisiah draws closer to Orien's body as the new name flows between them.

Orien's eye changes to solid black as it normally does when the beast, now named Nox, comes forward. Orien's arm wraps around Elisiah, picking her up so they are eye level. The same shadows that created the hounds wrap around them.

Elisiah hears several gasps from the bodies around them, but right now it is just them, all three of them.

Did you name me?

A small tear falls from the black eye, and Elisiah wipes it away with her thumb.

"Do you like it?" Elisiah watches the face in front of her with caution. She knows both are fine with the name, but it is nerve-wracking for her to say it.

I fucking love it.

It does not escape Elisiah that Nox referred to itself as singular. It only makes her laugh in her throat. Their foreheads meet each other's as their eyes close. The swirling shadows around them take turns brushing against any piece of Elisiah they can get close to.

You have us all going crazy, Little One, we cannot wait to taste you.

The arm around her waist tightens, and the other grabs a handful of her ass, covered by the twin black fabric of Orien's. The shadows brush across her legs wrapped around Orien's torso.

"We have to get this muzzle off." Elisiah's words are shallow as she speaks the them over the spot where Orien's lips lay under the leather.

I will tear it to pieces if it means I get a chance to have you.

Orien's brown eye is replaced with the black of Nox's.

"Nox." Elisiah pauses as she studies the eyes looking into her. "I cannot wait for the day I get to know what it feels like to kiss you and Orien."

Nox purrs at the sound of its name on her lips, and the thread between them twists together until they are a finely interlocked string. The feeling makes both tighten their grip on the other, and Elisiah gasps slightly. If this is how it is supposed to feel to have a mate, then she does not want to feel any other way.

"Nox?" Elisiah asks, her eyes closed and lips parted.

I know, Little One.

"Orien?"

Yes, but she is complicated.

Elisiah takes a reassuring breath as what Nox says sinks into place.

38

FREDRICK

 the substance in his pot to come to a boil. He has been staring at a small, discolored spot by his booted feet. The old man dug up his old uniform boots to remind himself where he started in this Kingdom.

He was a man that held power. He was respected. He was feared.

It is his own fault that he ended up being stripped of his title and thrown into the kitchen, but damn if he has not been seething since learning what he had from two of the girls he helped raise. Univier will never be good enough for those two.

Fredrick hopes they do not come back to this place, unless something happens to Alister Farkle Altair. Such a ridiculous fucking name. Just having that name in his head is enough to make him ball his hands into fists, his knuckles turning white.

His kitchen has become cold and silent following the days of Elisiah and Orien's departure, and it only gives him time to think and plan. He has lived in this world for far longer than he has cared to.

The two people that have made his life feel like it has had any meaning are gone, sent on a fool's errand. Everything that he had left to give was written in a letter and dispatched to his home region of Thundaria just this morning. With any luck, Erwin will get a chance to relay the message.

Fredrick cannot fathom the idea of either of his girls thinking he left them to fight the fight they do not know anything about yet. The couple will know soon enough when the time is right.

As he stands from his favorite sitting spot, he makes his way across the cold stone floor. The King requested carrot and radish soup, so that is what he will get, as will all his loyal puppets that have the audacity to call themselves *Knights*. If his own Lance was still living, then these new boys would not stand a chance.

He tests the temperature, making sure the soup is hot enough to properly dissolve the fine black powder Fredrick has kept under a loose stone under his bed.

He knew it would come in handy when he needed it the most, and right now he needs it more than any other time he can think of. Unplugging the nude cork from the glass neck, Fredrick proceeds to dump every single grain into the pot of soup.

He even goes the length of spooning some carrot and radish soup back into the jar and shaking it around before adding back into the pot. All it would take is a drop to take down a fully-grown Griffin, but you can never be too sure when it comes to beings the likes of Alister.

Fredrick portions the soup into their bowls and leaves it to rest on the cleared work table behind him. Arranging the bread neatly to the left side of all the bowls, he waits for the first of the Guards to trickle in.

Slowly, not even four minutes after he has cleared the pot of the liquid, the first male comes through the door.

"His Highness has requested his share." The boy does not even try to make eye contact with the old man as he relays the message with demand in the undertone of his voice.

Fredrick ignores the boy as he places a bowl in one of the knight's gloved hands and a plate of bread in the other. Looking into the odd-colored substance, Fredrick cannot even tell anything extra was added. Perfect.

He watches as the armor-clad body leaves his kitchen with dinner for the King of Univier. He does not allow himself to smile until there is only one bowl left on the table in front of him.

An ear-piercing alarm sounds through the castle, and debris falls slowly around him as he picks up his own bowl of specially-made soup. Screams fumble down the halls but only those of the men.

Fredrick sent word that all women and children should take the next two days to go visit their family. The ones who do not have any received two pounds extra of their normal pay. All of which came from his own. He would not be needing it anymore, not after today.

Thunderous echoes overpower the scream of the alarm as a full pack of Dream Weavers swallow what light is left in the corridors.

As soon as Fredrick overheard that Alister had made a deal with four of the dark beings to hunt down the only two people who could make a change, he took matters into his own hands.

This man will not hurt his girls again. Fredrick will hate himself even after his death for allowing those two females to suffer at the hands of Alister. It was the only thing he could think to do for them after they left, so he sat in the kitchen, plotting his revenge. The old man just hopes it plays out in his favor.

Just as he finishes his bowl of soup, Fredrick is met with the familiar glow of green eyes and a fire building in his middle. As he stares at the form in front of him, he nods his head in approval as he says, "All hail the new Queen of Univier, Orien Ather Altair. May she rule with grace and vengeance. Spreading the truth with all."

39

ORIEN

The change Orien feels goes deeper than just her heart. It is a feeling she has never felt once before in her life, but now that she has, it is something she never wants to lose. Nox and Elisiah held in their embrace for four minutes until they finally parted.

The note left for her was from Erwin Hartlander himself.

Orien,

I know you went to Anona. Stay there, I am coming to pick you up.

Since nothing can seem to go right, I'll just do it myself. Stay in the city! Do you know how hard you are to find? I do not want to hunt for you again, especially since I was forced to bring my own plus one. Oh, before I forget, tell your plus one I said hi! See you soon!

E.J. Hartlander
P.S. I am going to be a DAD.

All she can do is shake her head as she reads the letter before handing it over to the "plus one" at her side. Elisiah finds the message to be just as humorous, as does Nox.

Now, sitting at a table in one of the local food shops, watching the one in front of her eat some sugar-filled pastry, she cannot help but question the now named beast in her head.

"You said she was ours when we barely knew her after the first time we saw her."

Yes, I did. And?

"You knew she was our mate."

Nox grew silent in her head.

"Answer me."

Well, technically, you knew so I knew.

Nox sits up in the back of her head.

You must accept it, Orien. Will you allow yourself to feel something if it means you get to keep the woman in front of you?

"I think I already have." Orien reaches a hand across the table as she lays it on the top of Elisiah's.

The woman still tearing into her sweet-smelling treat pulls the plate away in a flash before realizing Orien just wants to hold her hand. She and Nox laugh together in her head. As the sound of her laughter rings in her head, both Nox and Elisiah abruptly stop what they are doing.

SHE FUCKING LAUGHED!

Nox screams in her head and down the link. Orien immediately stops herself as she realizes what she has just done.

"Orien. Is that what you sound like?" Elisiah covers her mouth as her eyes fill with tears.

Orien does not know how to answer her, and now she is scared to try. What she would not give for Erwin to pop his head into this shop right now.

Elisiah! She laughed! Elisiah!

Nox is jumping around in her head like one of the Wulve pups when they are excited to play.

If one is over the moon and the other is almost in tears, then she guesses an answer would not be too much. Orien is terrified to speak to anyone or anything that is not Nox, and since that person is also her life partner, it adds a whole new level.

"Yes." The word sprints down the bound.

"Nox, shut up. You are insufferable." Nox sits in place in her head as they both wait for Elisiah to respond.

"Orien?"

"Hello, my Love." That is all she can think to call the beautiful golden-brown woman in front of her as she finally speaks to her.

Elisiah's shoulders shake as silent tears fall from her eyes. Orien lifts her hand to wipe the tears from her face, but Elisiah's small wrist grabs hers as she presses her soft lips in the center of the palm and gives it a kiss.

"You sound as beautiful as you look."

She said we are beautiful.

Nox smiles, and it causes a small laugh from both people at the table, and soon both of their minds are filled with the melody.

Just as Orien and Elisiah go silent with Orien's hand cradling the other's face, the door swings open, and the few others in the small seating area all stand.

"His majesty!" rings out among the crowd, and Orien turns her head as everyone stands, bending at the waist with their eyes on the ground. She and Elisiah are the only ones not doing the same. The young King finds Orien as soon as he enters the room, and he immediately walks up to her with another male trailing behind him.

"Orien!" His smile stretches from ear to ear, and he is just as pale as she remembers him. He stops short when he sees the muzzle on her face.

Elisiah stands from her spot and moves to Orien's side. She gives a small bow before putting her hand on Orien's shoulder.

"She does not talk." The statement is short, but she says it with a small smile that sends a low growl down the line from Orien.

"Do not smile at him."

Ooohh, someone is jealous.

Nox laughs in their heads.

Elisiah ignores both as she speaks to the King of Thundaria.

"We are so happy to see you, your Majesty."

Erwin offers his hand to Elisiah, and she extends hers to him. Orien shoots from her chair as she pulls Elisiah to her and lowers her hand, so it is held in hers.

A growl moves from her throat and forces itself past the confines of the mask. The Guard behind Erwin pulls a knife from behind his back as Elisiah speaks at the same time as Erwin.

"Holy shit, you're tall."

"She is just protective."

Elisiah looks at the man with a knife and says, "If you know what is good for you then you will put that toy back where you got it from."

The dark-haired man stares at Elisiah with accessing eyes.

She and Nox do not like it.

Nox moves to its own seeing eye, and both men in front of them take a step back. The people that were here are now all gone.

"That is Nox." Elisiah says, trying to defuse the situation. Pleading to both beings in her head, she says, "Can you both please calm down? This is weird for me, right now."

Nox grumbles and retreats to the back again as Orien thinks about what she needs to do. Slowly, she loosens her grip on the body in front of her as she moves her head side to side to loosen some of the tension in her body.

"Tell them that we are mates so that one does not end up dead before we leave this room."

Elisiah whips around as the word mate reaches down the bound.

"Tell them, my Love."

The two men stare at them from their spot nearly across the room by then.

"Orien said to tell you that we are mates." She pauses as she turns back towards the two. "Also, if you touch me or try to undress me with your eyes, she will kill you."

Elisiah smiles wide, and Erwin begins to laugh with the knowledge. The dark-haired man, on the other hand, walks out the door with his knife still drawn. It is not exactly what she told Elisiah to tell the males, but it did get the message to them clearly.

"I have a mate too!" Erwin walks closer to the pair still standing by the table they occupied, and his face lights with excitement at the statement.

Nox matches his expression in her head as Orien holds out her hand towards the boy she once knew. It does not surprise her that he takes her hand in his with ease. His skin is cold to the touch and matches the snow on the street just outside the shop perfectly.

If his hair did not have a soft shine, then it would not be noticeable on top of his head. Orien remembered him perfectly even after twenty-three years apart. How could anyone forget the likes of him? They shake hands as he slightly tilts his head to look at her eyes.

"So, the stories are true."

Orien holds his gaze as she tightens her grip on his hand. She does not know what Elisiah has heard of the stories that find ways to linger in every region of this place. Erwin tightens his grip with hers for just a second before he gives her a barely noticeable tilt of his head. Elisiah clears her throat from beside her.

"If the stories are the same ones I heard growing up, then for the most part, yes."

Both of them look at Elisiah as she answers.

"She is insanely tall, broody, angry, strong, quiet, full of unstoppable magic, but I have not seen her kidnap misbehaving children from their rooms, so I am going to assume that is false." The woman extends each finger on her hand to keep track of her list as she names off just some of the main points in the stories that circulate.

"Oh, she did kill that Dragon." That fact flows from her mouth as a satisfied grin makes her lips close.

Orien shakes her head as she watches her mate. Erwin laughs at the statement that she has made just before he pats Orien's shoulder.

"Come on, we can catch up on the way back home. I have a pregnant wife waiting for me." The fact did not slip her memory from the letter he wrote her, she just chose to ignore it.

It is not a subject she likes to talk about or even think about. Elisiah grabs her hand as they walk out behind the new King of

Thundaria. No crown sits on his head and his clothes are not the least bit royal. Orien silently gives the man just a hair of approval in her mind for the action.

"Kemp and I came on horseback. If you two do not have a horse, I can grab one from the town's stable." Orien tucks the information of the dark-haired man's name as they meet blistering wind head on.

"We have one of our own. Thank you for the offer." Elisiah burrows herself against Orien's side as the wind whips into her face. Erwin smiles at her as he looks to Orien before raising his hand as if in question. She nods her head in approval. With one quick flick of his hand, Erwin puts a blocker around them. Elisiah's hair falls immediately, and she does not wait to flick the curls from in front of her face.

"What happened to the wind?"

"I put a wind block around all of us. It will repel the currents around us instead of allowing them to go through us. Makes for easier travel." The male is very pleased with himself as he brings one of his pinky fingers to his mouth, biting the side.

Orien recognizes the act from when he was a small boy. As far as she knows, he has always found something to fiddle with.

The one named Kemp stands by his brown mare as the three of them start toward him. The knife he removed from his fur lined trousers still rests in his hand, only now he uses it to clean under his fingernails.

Out in the open, Orien can finally make out the details of his face as he looks their way. His dark brown hair is shaved close to his bronze skin. Dark blue, almond shaped eyes stare at her as they stop just in front of him.

He is taller than Erwin by two inches, but still not as tall as her. Compared to her seven-feet, the man, Kemp, stands six-foot nine inches, leaving King Hartlander at a whopping six-foot seven.

Only one of them seems to notice or care that they both have to look up at her, but she is used to the men around her trying to live up to her height instead of theirs. She only hopes her longest friend will prove different in the matter.

"Kemp, this is Orien and..." Erwin looks to Elisiah as he scratches the side of his head, his cheeks slowly growing with color

"Elisiah. My name is Elisiah." Orien grabs a stray curl that lays on the opposite side of her hair and puts it in line with the others on the right side.

"Kemp, this is Orien and Elisiah. Orien, Elisiah, this is Kemp. My brother-in-law." Erwin looks just as uncomfortable as she feels with the introduction. The man by the mare looks familiar to her, but she cannot place him in this moment of time. The feeling nags at her.

Nox moves forward to its normal eye as it takes in the face across from them.

He has the skin of those in Octovah.

Nox is right. The way his skin seems to glow in the bright white around them makes it apparent.

"We have not been that way in a while. I doubt we know him from there."

Yeah, I assume not. Oh, well. Let us get Samuel so we can get to that castle. I am starving but not for food.

Lust runs down the bond as Orien and Elisiah look at each other. Elisiah's smile mirrors back exactly what she thinks as she lightly waves at Nox's dark eye. A throat clears as they both look from each other to Erwin in front of them. His ice blue eyes are wide in his head as he holds his breath.

"God, please keep it in your pants until you two are far away from me. I can smell the sex in the air, and you two have not even touched each other."

Elisiah laughs as she adds, "Three. The three of us. If you do not count the shadows."

That's our girl.

Nox replies with a smile as Erwin tries to keep his mouth closed by the shock of the statement.

"Let us just get going." Kemp's voice is deep as it slices across her ears. Orien cannot help the rumble that grows in her throat. She does not know what it is about this male, but she does not like him.

The look he gives her says he returns the feeling.

4°

ANEIRA

It has been two days since Erwin left the castle and his wife.

Aneira has only left her spot in the heart of the library long enough each day to eat, sleep, and wash the smell of ink from her skin. The heavily guarded underground room is her happy place; it is where she feels the most like herself. Aneira has always felt like she belonged within the walls of the knowledge filled tomb.

No one can disturb the peace that surrounds her while she sits at the oak table meant for a group of people as large as eight. It is only her that occupies it though, Aneira, and at least ten stacks of books, each no less than six books tall. She has been reading the thousands of ancient relics for two decades now and still has not managed to make a dent in the vast amount of knowledge awaiting in the unread pages.

It is something that will haunt her even after her expanded life-span has come to an end.

411

Aneira thrives when she is constantly challenged with finding new things to research. It is one reason she has been studying anything she can about the ones that created what they call their home.

Sytherac has always been one of her favorite subjects in which to immerse her mind. Everything about their world intrigues her, but most of all, she questions what came before them. The world that could have held creatures like Gods and all of their secrets. The denser her brain becomes from absorbing information, the longer she finds herself pulling more books from the plentiful thick oak shelves that line the two straight walls to her front and back.

The library of Thundaria is one of the only places where you can find the secrets that the original five founders tried to have cremated just before they each met their last years. It is only because of a bookkeeper named Neo who made his way around to every library outside of Thundaria to transport each original text to his own haven under the castle he grew up admiring since he was an infant.

Each man that built the Kingdoms originally wrote their own versions of what they were before they were sentenced to Sytherac until their last days. Neo made it his personal goal to secretly invade each library to hunt for the books.

He was a skeptic who shared his theories openly to whoever would listen. Not many gave him more than a look of judgment but his daughter. The little girl would follow that bookkeeper down into the quiet room, filled by dimly-lit sticks of Water's Light.

The flames are still covered by cylinders of frosted glass to be sure nothing disturbs the flames flickering inside; they are still his daughter's favorite thing to sit and watch when she cannot follow the lines on paper.

Neo would walk with her up and down the neatly lined walls of books, telling her everything he could about each one, making sure she could grow into his shoes one day. After he died from a sickness that invaded their Kingdoms' lands, his daughter refused to leave the place she felt the closest to him.

She was ten when she watched him take his last breath, his yellow hair completely abandoning its place on his scalp. The same way the weight filling his body vanished, leaving only his muscles to nourish the rest of him until finally they too dissipated to nothing. No one is sure where the sickness comes from or how it chooses its host, but everyone knows that when it does, there is no living through it.

This illness forces your body to eat itself from the inside out, drinking every ounce of nutrients it can get from you. That is how it got the name, The Sapping Sickness. It still spreads unchecked in their Kingdom with no hope for a cure. Symptoms have even been spotted further from the immediate territory of Thundaria, and the next place it could travel would be to Univier.

King Edmon Hartlander tried to warn King Alabastor Altair of Univier, but it was to no avail. The man was too arrogant even after hearing about the death of the other King.

Every healer across the Kingdoms has been working together on finding a solution to the sickness, but they have found trying to treat it only makes it move through the body faster. The pain that comes from the rapidly-moving disease is horrendous to experience, but to outsiders, it only looks like the person is in a deep sleep. It is only the ones that have The Sapping Sickness that can tell you how the slower it moves the less pain you feel, and the faster it spreads the more intense the suffering.

Neo once told his yellow-haired daughter that it was a curse from the God of Death, Etbris himself.

For the bookkeeper, his sickness moved over his body over the course of several years. He was lucky to be one of the few that could continue his daily activities as if nothing was wrong until it finally had enough of him. The weeks leading up to his death, everything seemed to move quickly and in a blur. One minute, he was up organizing his books, and the next he was sucked into the deepest of sleeps.

It only took one person to lift his body off the floor where his body fell. Neo had become so frail that his ten-year-old daughter, Aneira, could lift him from the dark royal blue floor on which he rested.

Aneira did not leave his side until he took his last breath, and even then it took the help of her best friend, Erwin, to get her to move. After that time with her father, she found herself growing quieter around the people with whom she would normally express herself the loudest. Her time above ground in the castle became scarce, and her relationship with her mother was strained.

Aneira did not know how to comfort a person when she could not even do that for herself, so it felt best in the moment to remove herself from everyone entirely. Her time was spent with her nose shoved between pieces of parchment as her photographic memory carefully placed each bit of information into the correct compartment of her mind.

There is nothing she cannot tell you about The Sapping Sickness from reading every scrap of detailed healers' notes going back to the first reported case, and now there is nothing she cannot tell you about Sytherac.

Except how Altairien, Hartland, Kav, Nepatae, and Sandur came to originally find Sytherac. Each man writes that they were cast out of their original home, but none of them share the same stories on why or how they found the one they made their home.

Aneira has gone back to every book to only receive the same information her brain already stores, and all it does is make her question everything she knows even more. It is why she looks forward to their company that should be walking into their home in the next ten minutes.

Orien is the only person that Aneira has heard about who shares the same characteristics as some of the first founders, and if what she hears about the woman's powers are true, then it could mean a complete change in their history.

41

ELISIAH

The two days it took the four of them to enter the castle walls felt like a lifetime. Elisiah has never been so cold in her life, and the miles of blank white expanse of ground they had to cross made her eyes feel like sandpaper. She found herself wondering if anyone has ever gone blind from staring at the reflective surface.

King Hartlander's horse stayed close to Samuel's side so the man on his back could steadily talk to herself and Orien. Elisiah is still processing how the animal managed to not only help the people of Buron but also help itself.

It was almost immediately after the attack that stories started spreading from the small villages of not only a tall figure cloaked in black, but of a giant dark gray horse. What they have heard is that Samuel carried any he could on his back, while holding infants wrapped in thick wool blankets from his mouth. They say he left as soon as he made sure there was no one else left in the rubble.

Elisiah is proud to have Samuel as one of her companions. A horse that saves countless lives without a second thought is better than many of the people she has met, especially when one of the men they are traveling with has already pulled a knife on Orien.

The dark-haired man, Kemp, kept his distance from all of them, and Elisiah caught him staring at her from time to time. It took everything for her to keep her mate and Nox calm when the feeling of repulsion would travel from her body to the one riding behind her.

Something inside of her screams that Kemp is untrustworthy, and it is something that she will not ignore. Orien feels the same way about him, and she does not understand it either.

The time they spent trying to rest at night along the journey was never long-lived because of the frigid cold, but also because Erwin was more than ready to be back in his wife's arms. It is all they have heard about since the morning they saw the large walls framing the castle, but Elisiah did not mind his rambling as he bragged about how smart his queen is. Kemp on the other hand threw a variety of harsh words at him.

No one cares, Erwin.

Shut up, already.

Good Gods! Do you ever shut up?

If I hear about my sister one more time I will knock you off that horse.

My ears are bleeding.

· · ·

Elisiah found herself throwing her own insults back at the man for taking away the light in her new friend's eyes. She saw no fault in a person being happy in their relationship, and the fact Kemp found it necessary to make that feeling into a negative was enough for her to decide she did not like him.

As the four of them make their way closer to the castle made of ice, Elisiah cannot help but gape at the beauty in front of her. Thundaria has always been described to her as a place of misery. You only hear the details of the cold days that grow even more frigid at night, how at least once a day, white powder falls from the constantly overcast skies, and most of all how this region is the only one that spreads sickness.

Every bad detail she has heard about this place washes from her head as she takes in her surroundings.

In the heart of the frosted ice walls stands a monumental castle, glistening from the few rays of sunlight breaking their way through the thick clouds. To Elisiah, it looks like a crystal that has just been polished, set out to be admired by anyone that passes by.

Each place where wall meets wall is adorned with its own turret. She can make out fifteen just on the front side of the structure itself. She is sure the number of them grows as you work your way around the castle, and the height of which the palace stands has to make it one of the tallest places she has ever seen.

Five levels of ice, each built on top of the one before it, make the very top turret seem like it rests in the clouds. Elisiah does not try to keep track of every window and pane of glass she can see as they grow smaller compared to it. She feels like a minuscule insect as the doors in front of them seem to elongate. She has not paid any attention to the dozens of houses and stores that make a crescent moon around the front of the royal palace. Even the people and animals in the busy street cannot break her attention away. She is consumed by the beauty that stands in front of her.

The Stone Castle of Univier is revered for the way it shares the space with the Earth around it, but The Ice Castle of Thundaria *is* the Earth. Someone with delicate hands had to have shaped every piece of snow and frozen rain to make this masterpiece. She wishes she could have met that person just to laud their remarkable skill set.

Approaching the giant double doors of the grand entryway of the castle, Elisiah rests her hands on Orien's thighs for balance as she strains her neck, looking to the very top point of the doors.

Each one is frosted until midway up as they slowly fade to transparent, elaborate appliqués that resemble snowflakes dancing through the wind, each of them a different size. The center of her head rests on the torso of the body behind her, but she does not even realize how everyone's eyes are on her, not just Orien's.

Erwin watches her reaction to his home with a warm smile on his face, clearly enjoying how the craftsmanship makes others feel. Kemp stares at her as well, but his look is one of curiosity and judgment.

Elisiah could care less about either of them as she whispers, "It is beautiful."

A hand comes to rest on her right side, the thumb stroking the fabric of her overcoat. She still wears the same black outfit picked out by Orien, and she was given the coat that rests over her shoulders before they left on Samuel the same day Erwin found them in that shop.

The layers are thick, keeping every possible ounce of body heat in her, but the chill still nips at the tip of her nose. The hand on her waist and the body pressed behind her make her feel like she is floating over the ground as a smaller door to the left side of the grand doors opens for them.

The sound of Erwin's feet meeting snow draws her away from the details in front of her. Her head comes to its natural resting spot, but she cannot focus on the conversation he has with the Guard in a light gray uniform. Her nerves have lit like a match, and all she can focus on is the warmth behind her and the hand holding her waist. Elisiah cannot stop her hands from moving further up the thighs they still rest on, and desire is the only thing that she feels in that moment. A low growl rings in her head that makes her breath catch.

Is someone needing something?

Nox lightly laughs as Orien's hand tightens on her side.

"You know what I need." Elisiah cannot help the way it sounds like a plea when she speaks in her head.

Orien drops the reins she holds in her right hand as shadows slowly make their way from the palm of her hand.

As they blanket them just enough so the others will not see, Orien grips Elisiah's waist as she picks her up just enough to turn her. Now face-to-face, Elisiah wraps her legs around Orien's middle as her hands hold tightly to Elisiah's ass.

"Tell me what you need, Love." Orien's voice is smooth like silk as she speaks the words straight into Elisiah, causing the female to shift slightly so her body presses closer to the others.

"You know what it is, Orien." Elisiah brings her hands to the back of Orien's short cropped red hair as her fingers make their way between the strands. The hands on her backside grip tighter, pulling a whimper from her mouth.

"Use your words, Love." Orien's eyes center only on Elisiah's as one of her hands trails its way between her thighs. Elisiah gasps as the warmth and pressure send heat straight to her center, and desire races down the bond at the touch.

"Words, Elisiah." Desire meets with demand as Orien speaks to her mind. As the palm of Orien's hand rests on the bottom of Elisiah's ass, her pointer and index finger slowly rub the fabric between her legs.

Elisiah sucks in a breath as she bites her lower lip. The conversations around them do not stop as the shadows slowly make their way around the pair on top of Samuel. Neither of them find it in themselves to care as they lose themselves in each other's touch.

Orien fights her need to feel Elisiah's smooth skin under her hands. The other just wants to be able to see the face under the muzzle and feel the lips on hers.

"I need you." Elisiah says the words against the shell of Orien's ear as her hands grip the hair still held in her hands.

"I will always need you." Slowly, she trails her lips along the curves of Orien's ear, and her eyes close as she memorizes the touch so it is tucked away deep in her soul. Orien's hands move from their resting spot, and her arms wrap around the female pressed to her body.

"Elisiah, you are my home." Orien's words are met with a soft purr from Nox in her head.

I knew that as soon as we saw you, Little One.

Elisiah chuckles lightly as the beast speaks, and she can feel the annoyance radiating from the Fae holding her.

"Of all the time in the world, you pick right now to be a pain in my ass?" Orien snaps the words at Nox making Elisiah's whole body shake with laughter.

Well, I could not let you have all the love, dammit. I need love too!

Nox fires back the words as Elisiah replies.

"I love you, Nox." She pulls back from the embrace as she moves her hands to hold Orien's face in her hands, making sure she has all of her attention.

"I love you, Orien." Orien freezes, even her breath is still as she lets the words hang in the air.

I love you too, Little One!

Nox's excitement swims into Elisiah's veins, but her face is still as she watches the one held in her hands. It feels like minutes tick by before Orien's chest rises and falls again.

"I love you too, my Love." Elisiah's smiles so wide her cheeks ache.

Orien lays her forehead against Elisiah's chest as the string tethering their soul bond grows thicker from another thread falling in place.

She loves me.

Nox prances in circles around Orien's head, making her chuckle in her mind at the thing and the fact that someone can actually love her.

A throat clears to the side of them, making the shadows quicken their pace.

"Orien." Erwin's voice has a hint of panic as he says her name. "Orien, the things around you are looking at me." A nervous chuckle comes from him next.

The shadows come to a stand still as Orien releases Elisiah from her grip.

"Orien! It has a snout. Orien! It is looking at me!" Erwin's words are followed by the same panicked laugh as Elisiah slides down from her spot on Samuel with a helping hand from the body still on his saddled back.

As she steps from the shadows, the slim black face of one of the hounds looks her way before taking the complete shape of one of the hounds that held her upright the other night.

"They will not bother you as long as you do not bother us." Elisiah raises her right hand to rest it on the hound's head. The Shadow Hound lowers its head to make it easier for her to reach.

Erwin stares, wide-eyed as he takes in the thing in front of him. Kemp's jaw clenches as his left hand rests on the hilt of the dagger at his side. Footsteps echo from inside the castle walls, pulling everyone's attention towards the small door that still stands open, and the Guard's mouth hangs open at the sight in front of him.

Orien stands at Elisiah's side as all the shadows except for the single hound across from her make their way back into her face and neck just as the footsteps cross the threshold. The trio by Samuel's side takes in the sight of the slender woman with golden yellow hair as she runs into Erwin's outstretched arms.

Elisiah watches as the male grabs her tightly as they spin in a small circle. Orien's hand comes to rest on her shoulder as she also watches the happiness radiate from the couple. Her eyes catch the resentment coming from the man standing just behind her longest friend. As the two slow and separate from their embrace, Erwin looks towards Elisiah, Orien, and the Shadow Hound.

"Orien, Elisiah, shadow dog thing. This is Queen Aneira of Thundaria. My wife and mate." Aneira smiles slightly at Elisiah before it disappears as her eyes move to Orien beside her and then to the hound. Elisiah smiles at her as she introduces all of them.

"I am Elisiah. To my right, this is Orien, my mate, and to my left, this is one of her Shadow Hounds."

Its name is Roe.

Elisiah is taken back by the comment, but adds it in anyway. "The hound's name is Roe."

The hound looks at Elisiah before its tail of shadow wags behind it. Elisiah smiles at Roe as she strokes her hand down its head.

Aneira looks over each of them, taking all the time she needs to study their bodies, before looking at Erwin with light green eyes, and her soft voice fills the silence.

"Do you know what Roe is, Harty?" The young King looks at his partner, and his eyes narrow slightly as his face floods with confusion. Aneira does not look away from him as he thinks about his answer. Before Erwin can come to his own conclusion, another's voice cuts through.

"That *thing* is a Shadow Hound, made by Etbris himself. *It* should not be here. *She* should not be here." Kemp bares his teeth as he spits the words from his mouth, his right hand lifted from his side as his pointer finger is pointed directly towards Orien.

Elisiah steps forward as she grabs the dagger from the right thigh sheath secured to Orien.

"Her name is ORIEN, and you will not talk about her like she is not standing right here." Elisiah raises the dagger in her hand as she points back to Kemp the same way he still points at her mate. Roe takes a step so that its head is beside Elisiah's. Black wisps flow from its eyes quicker as it picks up on the anger flowing from the person beside it.

"That thing does not deserve a name! Nothing about any of them feels right." Kemp's feet move forward at the same time Orien's do.

The male stops in his tracks as he looks up at the other whose eyes are replaced by black pits. Elisiah moves so she stands between them, her hand placed on Orien's stomach, the dagger still raised towards the vile man.

"That *thing*," Elisiah says the word with venom, "is my mate. Disrespecting her will be the last thing you will ever do."

Kemp's blue eyes lock onto Elisiah's browns, and a small smile spreads across his lips. "Yeah, your mate. We will see about that." Everything about the man in front of her reminds Elisiah of the King of Univier. Kemp is easy on the eyes, but under his appearance is something ugly. It seems like every man she meets is all the same, except for the few that have actually proved themselves to be decent, like Fredrick.

A growl rips across the stone ground they all stand on just outside of The Ice Castle. Kemp looks back towards the person behind her and the shadow by her side before he scoffs, turning in his spot and walking back towards where they had just come from on the horses. Elisiah watches him as he walks away, and a pit opens in her stomach as his words bounce around in her head. Even Aneira's question finds a way to echo in the space.

Do you know what Roe is, Harty?

We will see about that.

She has no idea what that means, but the way he said it makes her feel like it was a promise to something that is to come, and if Aneira is asking Erwin that question, does that mean she can help with what she has been dealing with? Before she can stop herself, the hand resting on Orien curls into a fist as she turns her attention to the couple behind them.

"You asked Erwin if he knows what Roe is. Do you know what Roe is?" Elisiah's face twists with anger and confusion. She is tired of the questions piling up in her head. They take up too much space. Her head pounds as the place where she has been shoving them bursts open.

Aneira stares at Elisiah with a straight face. "Of course I do. Do you?" The females watch each other as Erwin wraps an arm around his wife's shoulders.

"We have a lot to talk about, Elisiah. As do Orien and Erwin." As she says the words, she turns towards the small door and begins to walk inside.

"We cannot do that out here in the cold, though, and all of you need to clean yourselves. I have smelled compost barrels more pleasant than the smells that come from all of you."

Erwin kisses her cheek as Elisiah gapes at the woman's back in front of her. Orien grabs the hand that still holds tight to the dagger and leads her towards the entryway. Roe follows behind them on silent paws.

Walking into the castle, Orien notes that everything is the same as it was when she was four. Erwin is not one for change, so it does not surprise her that nothing has been touched since his father's death two years ago.

The Kingdom of Thundaria had their steadily-spreading sickness to thank for their late King's death. Edmon Hartlander was fierce, and he made sure everyone knew it. He was the complete opposite of Alister, and a part of Orien was grateful for that. Edmon did not use his son to hide behind like Alister did with her.

Elisiah's head is on a swivel as she tries to take in every detail of the space where they currently walk, the dark royal blue floor underneath their booted feet. Orien cannot help but watch the woman as the hair on her head coils down her back in thick layers.

The Water's Light, held on the snow white walls by silver sconces, makes the black of her hair shine like a gem, her golden brown skin absorbing the light seeming to make the planes of her face glow.

Erwin points out small details to Elisiah as they walk towards a set of doors that take up the height of the wall they rest in, the throne room. The doors open with a small gust of wind as all four of them, plus Roe, make their way into the mostly empty space.

"I thought we needed to get cleaned before we spoke?" Elisiah says to Aneira who currently rests a hand on her slightly swollen stomach. Orien watches her hand as it gently strokes down the fabric of her blue dress. The flash of a memory makes her hands clench just slightly.

⚜⚜⚜⚜⚜

"Hold her down!" Alister bellows at the group of Guards surrounding her as her body is strapped down by thick silver straps to a stone slab. Ten-year-old Orien fights with everything she can muster, even with the diluting serum flowing in her veins.

Evadne is the one responsible for her lack of strength and mental clarity as she is the one who concocted the poison that currently attacks her insides. Orien does not know what she is capable of just yet, not completely, not after the bright light that lived inside of her left. She does not cry out because the muzzle on her face feels just as tight as the silver on her wrist, ankles, chest, and forehead.

The stone under her is cold against her bare body as she lies with her legs spread and her arms raised above her head. Orien has never felt as helpless as she does at this moment. She feels what fear is for the first time in her ten years of existence. Everyone around her yells orders to the other as they work their way around her to make sure no part of her can retaliate.

"A thing like you should never be able to bring another life in this world," Evadne whispers in her ear as a sharp pain shoots its way down Orien's neck and spreads across her body.

"There." The woman moves from her naked body and looks to Alister who stands at Orien's feet.

"She is fully restrained but also fully aware. She can feel everything." A smile spreads across the woman's face as she clasps her hands in front of her, looking at her King for approval. Alister does not so much as look her way as he walks to Orien's side and says, *"A weapon of mine is of no use if it has to worry about the possibilities of children, so we will take care of that for you."*

His face is calm as he speaks to her, but Orien can see the satisfaction in his green eyes. She has never once thought about children, but she knows it should be no one's choice but hers if she is to have any or not. Now that choice is being taken from her.

Alister nods his head to someone out of her line of sight, and her heart rate picks up as much as the diluting serum will allow it. The Guards around the room watch her like predators watch their prey from the cover of bushes, and it adds to the fear she already feels.

The thing in her head fights to get past the effects of the substance flowing through her body, but it is to no avail.

A man with a brown leather apron comes into her view as he immediately starts pressing on her lower abdomen and on top of her pelvic region. Orien already knows what is about to happen, and all she can do is try to take her thoughts to other places.

"Besides, who would want any more abominations running around in our world?"

Alister Altair stares straight into her eyes as he delivers the sentence, and the man with the leather apron pulls out a small tipped knife. As *he pushes the tip into her skin, Orien can feel it split apart and the warmth of her blood as it flows from the cut. Her body tries to raise up as he drags the knife straight across her upper pelvis. She can feel every inch of skin as it parts, making room for the man to move further down until he has sliced through nerves, muscles, and what little fat she has. Her eyes burn, her throat constricts from the need to scream, but her body will not allow it.*

Orien watches as a bare hand moves to grab something inside of her. She watches as his other hand flicks with the knife. She feels a part of her being removed. She feels the empty space that is left behind. As the man brings out a handful of small pink organs, Orien knows that this part of her will never grow back. It is something that will always be lost.

"Is that all of it?" She cannot pay attention to whose voice fills the room around the sounds of her body's squelchings from the intrusion.

"That is all. I can stitch her up, now."

"Do not worry about how it looks, she will never show anyone."

"Yes, your Highness."

Evadne stands over Orien's face as she smiles down at her, and Alister moves his way across the room as he says over his shoulder to one of the Guards still planted at her feet, "She is yours to deal with now."

Orien knows who he is before he appears directly in her line of sight. Since her incident at four that left her with a permanent face accessory, all of the Guards have wanted revenge. It does not matter to them that she is still a child. These protectors of the King only see her as the thing Alister has made her to be, a monster. Men can do cruel things to anyone or anything when they do not see it as equal, and unluckily for Orien, she has never been seen as equal.

The Guard grins at the approval he has apparently received from his King.

It only takes the one Orien assumes to be a healer five minutes to stitch her body back together before he wipes the blade of his knife on his apron and says his farewells to Evadne.

The woman stands in the corner of the room just past Orien's right foot as the Guard at her feet smiles at her bloodied body.

"The man you ate is the reason you have that." He points to the muzzle on her face as he moves closer to her body. "He was my brother."

Orien's eyes burn from the heat rising in her body. The pain that she felt has only fueled her anger, her hatred. She could not fight off the Guard from taking what he thought she deserved in return for killing his sibling, but she could sink herself deep into her mind for the moment.

Orien could not tell you how long she laid on that stone slab after being dissected and then stolen of her virginity. She did not care to tell anyone either, just like she did not care when Fredrick ran into the dark room and found her still strapped to the surface.

"Oh, my girl, my girl. What did they do to you?" The man who has been the only one concerned about her life sobs as he unbinds her restraints with shaking hands.

"I am going to kill him. I am going to kill him." Fredrick speaks out loud, but Orien knows he is talking to himself.

As her body is released, it is gently lifted into solid arms, and warm tears drop on her forehead as he carries her from the room.

"Let us get you to your room, my girl."

As soon as the memory fades to nothing, Orien pulls her eyes from Aneria's belly, her hand still gripping Elisiah's. Looking to her side to make sure the female is still close to her, she is met with white glazed eyes. Slowly, the glazed eyes return to their soft brown as Elisiah stares at Orien, tears streaming down her face, her mouth slightly parted.

"Orien." Her voice is hoarse as she speaks her name.

Orien looks into her eyes as she realizes that as she could see Elisiah's memories, her mate could also see hers. Without thinking, Orien drops the hand being held in hers, turns back towards the doors, and walks to the same hallway she remembers from her childhood. She cannot face Elisiah after what she has seen. No one was supposed to see that part of her.

Orien knows Roe has stayed with Elisiah, because the added security she would normally feel is not with her. It does not bother her that the thing has chosen to stay behind. It actually makes her feel better knowing the woman will be protected when she is not there. Her feet do not slow as she walks with only the memory of running down these same halls with Erwin. Nox is uneasy in her head as it also drowns in the memory they just shared with the one person they need to be the strongest for.

If Orien was not strong enough to shield her scars from Elisiah, then she knows she is not good enough for her. If the blood on her soul from all of the murders she has committed were not enough to ruin Elisiah, then it will be her personal life that does just that.

Her hands flex as she makes her way down the dimming hall. The shadows begin to leak from her palms as her pace quickens. Nox paces behind her eyes at a matched speed to her own.

Everything in her wants to scream, but the fucking muzzle is still attached to her face.

Her breathing starts to quicken. Her heart pounds so loudly in her chest she can hear it vibrating the walls around her. She needs to get out of this place. The ice is too perfect to house a person like her. A monster should not be able to be in a place like this. A monster should not be able to touch skin like that of Elisiah's.

Orien, we have to get out.

Nox has stopped its trail behind her eyes, and the words shake with worry. Orien does not understand what has startled the thing, but she knows if she does not get out, this castle will become a tomb made of sparkling ice.

She will not let herself crumble, at least not right now. As she takes a sudden left turn at the end of the long hall, she is met with a single door. The walk down the expanse of floor and walls seems to be a lot longer than she remembers, but seeing her way out, she makes her way towards it with the comfort of being back in the open. Making it to the door, it strikes her as odd that it is made from wood.

The same wood as the ones that you find in Univier. As she reaches for the gold-plated knob, Nox jumps into the front of her head as it yells.

Orien! That's Elisiah's door!

Before she can retract her hand from the already twisting handle, the familiar door swings open, taking her with it.

43

ORIEN

As the door swings open with a harsh phantom wind, Orien cannot keep her grip on the knob. Her hand slips from its surface, and she begins to fall through darkness. Her body hurdles so fast she feels like she is not moving at all. There is no sound that she can pick up on and no light making a break in the blackness around her. Nox claws on the same spot it jumped on earlier as they both try to get a grip on what is happening to them. Everything they thought they knew feels like a lie at this moment.

Did they really allow Elisiah to see one of their deepest memories?

Are they still in the throne room?

The endless hallway?

Elisiah's bedroom door?

The questions evaporate from their mind as a bright white light flashes to their right side. Orien turns her head to try and see what it is that passes her, but nothing is there by the time she turns her head. Giving permission to the thing inside her, it takes over her eye so it too can try to see. Another white light zips past them again, this time on their left. Then again on the right, one becomes two, two becomes four until Orien is swarmed by thousands of the streaks of light.

Nox transfixes on the things, and another part of Orien begins to simmer in her middle at the sight of them. Longing fills her veins, and it swims perfectly with the shadows in her as well. Her breathing evens out as her heart rate slows to a more normal level. One by one, the lights die out, and in their place, she can see stars, thousands of shimmering stars.

Cool air flows past her as the smell of grass and dirt make their way to her nose. Nox is just as confused as she is as they try to put the puzzle pieces together that could possibly tell them where they are.

The smell is nothing like Thundaria and not even close to that of Univier. The feeling in her middle begins to rise until it sits in the center of her banded chest. Turning her head to the right, she is met with dozens of tall trees until her back slams into a solid surface. The air is pushed from her lungs as her eyes close. As she inhales, her eyes open to the unknown around her, but it also all seems familiar to her as well. It is like she has been here before or that she is meant to be here.

Nox looks around, and the smell of burning wood makes them look behind them. The knot that was in her chest now lodges in her throat as she stands from her spot.

"Nox?"

I see him.

Orien does not let her eyes leave the males that stand in front of her. As she straightens herself to her full height, the man in front of her has to tilt his head just a inch to meet her eyes full on. Nox still holds its place in her left eye as the man lets out a shaky breath and his shoulders slacken slightly.

"Or–" The man's voice is one of the deepest she has heard but his cadence is nice to her ears. "Orien?" His dark brown eyes quickly switch between hers as he says her name. How does he know who she is? Has she met him before?

She cannot tell him she cannot answer. All she can do is point to the muzzle on her face with her finger. The man follows her finger, and a low growl leaves his mouth. Nox perks up in her head at the sound just as the dim orange glow of the fire behind him makes her catch a glimpse of what flows from his back.

Two wings stretch out from behind his shoulder blades. They are massive compared to the body they fit on even though this is one of the biggest men she has ever seen. Orien takes note of the way they move with his body, and a pain between her own shoulder blades grows. If he has wings then she cannot possibly still be in Thundaria.

"You cannot talk?" His voice radiates anger as he studies the black muzzle on her face.

Orien does not feel any threat to herself as she studies the man. Nox feels the same as it notes every small twitch that occurs on his face.

Do you think we could get into his head? It feels like we know him.

Nox is still wary of the person in front of them, but they also know that they have no other way to ask how he knows of her or where they are exactly. Orien gives the thing in her the go ahead just as it tries to speak directly into the man's head.

She cannot talk, but I can.

They watch for any reaction but get nothing in return.

"And who are you?" The male's voice is soft as it floats into her head.

I am called Nox.

"Are you the one responsible for the black eye?"

Yes, that is me. Orien is the brown.

Nox is skeptical, so is Orien.

"I would know that color anywhere." A small smile makes its way to the man's face for just a second before it falls.

How do you know our name?

Orien shifts her body so that her right hand hovers over the dagger that hangs at her chest.

"Because," the man pauses as he watches her hand. "I helped name you." Something like longing fills his eyes.

What does that mean? Alister Altair named us, the King of Univier.

Nox spits the words out like they hurt to be said. The man notices.

"No. We named you." The wings behind him tuck into his sides as he says the words to her. "Your mother and I. We named you."

Nox snarls in her head as Orien matches the sound, the pressure in her throat moving to her head. This man is a liar; she has no mother, and Alister is her father.

"Let me explain, Orien." His hand raises slightly in front of him as a peace offering. "Please just let me explain." Each word is a plea for her to allow him to straighten everything out, but Orien cannot make out anything that is happening. Nox spirals in her head at the sudden presence of the new thing in their space, and the new thing is terribly bright.

Orien's hands move to cover her face as the light behind her right eye starts to burn. The feeling filling every inch of her is rage. Every ounce of rage she has bottled up over the course of her twenty-seven years is expanding. The man in front of her who claims to be her father steps towards her as she falls to her knees.

Her shoulders shake from the overwhelming amount of emotions she feels at once, and as her fingers trail down her cheeks and meet the leather material of the muzzle, the new part of her loses itself.

A scream rips itself from the confines of her throat as her fingernails grip into the top of the leather, and a single, blinding light takes over her right eye just before the material is shredded by her nails. The light that ripples through her body is the perfect match for the shadows.

Nox shares the space in her head with the other like they have worked this way for years, and Orien feels like she was always meant to have this other thing as well.

Looking at the ground, the first thing she sees is what is left of the muzzle. Her fingers move to where the thing once covered her face, and all she can feel is her skin. The shape of her lips is nothing like she remembers them, but she does not care. All she can care about is the fact that it is finally off. Her face is free. Nox sits behind her eye as it says.

Orien, you can talk.

She sits with the idea for some minutes before she looks at the man that still stands in front of her, only now his hands cover his eyes, and four other men do the same.

Orien gets back to her feet as she looks at each of them just for a moment before she says, "That fucking thing has been on my face since I was four." Her mouth feels unsure of the movements, her tongue is dry in her mouth, and her teeth feel too big for her head. Her words come out as she means them to, and it shocks her that she still knows how to speak.

"What sick fuck puts a muzzle on a kid?" The one that asks the question has a long braid that hangs over his right shoulder, and his wings, from what Orien can tell, are tucked in close to his frame.

"The real question is why did they put a muzzle on her?" This question comes from a man to the right of the one with the braid. His arms are crossed over his chest as he looks her up and down.

"I ate someone." Orien holds the man's eyes that study her. It is all she can think to say to give a quick explanation as to why she has had to wear the muzzle. The one with the braid laughs as he hits the other on the shoulder.

"Fucking sick!"

Nox laughs in her head at the response because the thing feels the same way.

"Who are all of you, and where am I?" Orien's hands rest on the daggers across her chest to give her hands something to do as she grows comfortable with the feeling of her freed jaw. The first man that she saw looks at her as he takes a step closer.

"I am Bashtian, your father. This is your birth world, Arugo."

Orien looks the man over as his words rest on her shoulders. All she wants is to go back to Elisiah. Everything in her tells her that the longer she is here, the more danger her mate could be in. If this is her birthplace, and the man in front of her is her father, then everything she knows about her life is a joke. Elisiah would know how to help her right now.

"I need to get back to my mate." Orien ignores the man named Bashtian as she makes her statement, the ones behind him seem to stiffen at her words. Nox takes back its place over her eye, and the light that awakened in her sits back and watches everything happen. She feels like she is finally full. No part of her is missing now.

"You have a mate?" Bashtian looks at Orien's face as he asks her the question.

"Yes."

"That is why I have been catching your scent." The man smiles slightly as a small laugh leaves him. "Your mate is a World Walker."

The men behind him startle with the information, but all Orien can do is look at him. She does not know what that means. Catching her confusion, he explains.

"A World Walker is someone who can open the doors to the other worlds. They can move freely from place to place and can go unseen if they have enough experience. Your mate, on the other hand, left her scent and yours when she came the last time."

Nox takes in the information just like Orien does until an eternal voice rings in their head.

"It is true, but Lixtis did not make any. Other than themself." Orien freezes, not only with the information, but at the name of the God of Souls. Nox twists from the spot it is in, looking at the ball of light in the corner of her head.

You talk too?

The light scoffs.

Of course I talk.

Orien can feel the annoyance flowing from the new part of her. She looks to Bashtian as she asks him how she can get back to Elisiah.

The man looks her over one more time before telling her to follow him. As he moves deeper into the trees around them, the other four men part so she can follow. All of them stare at her, and she stares right back and bares her teeth enough to get her point across.

Orien may be in their world, but she is still the deadliest out of all of them.

44

ELISIAH

Elisiah saw everything that ran its way through Orien's head, and she felt every emotion that came along with it. A gentle warmth blossoms over her body as the image of her mate being torn open and used permanently burns itself into her subconscious.

She is unsure how long they stood there, lost in the memory, or when she managed to send Orien to the only other place Elisiah has traveled. She cannot be sure that is where Orien has gone, but something in her knows. It feels like a call is being sent out into the atmosphere, and she is the one to answer.

The last thing she can remember is seeing Fredrick carry out a small, broken Orien before Erwin's shouts filled the throne room. The Queen of Thundaria, Aneira, stood wide-eyed beside her husband, and when Elisiah came back to her senses, so was she.

The gentle warmth grew in intensity as each minute passed, but she could not find it in herself to say anything. Elisiah felt like something was working its way across every crevice of her body and painting it anew.

The time passed by in a flash after her mate left from her side. Unease filled the room like a solid brick as the seconds turned to minutes, minutes to hours. It had been two whole hours since her mate vanished into thin air. In those two hours, she has felt every range of emotion, some of them brand new to her.

Erwin has been pacing the floor, rotating his fingers until he has eaten away at the skin from every possible angle. Aneira disappeared without saying a word not even five minutes after the disappearance. The Queen returned some time after with more books then Elisiah cares to count, and the woman has not moved an inch as she flips through various pages, her nose nearly touching the fibers of the parchment.

"How long have you known that you can walk across worlds?" The question makes Elisiah sit up straight in her seat, her nerves on fire. How can she be sure she can trust either of them? She does not know them except for the time she spent traveling with the male. How short is too short to tell someone your secrets? Elisiah does not know the answer because she has only built a relationship of trust with Fredrick.

Orien still does not even know her. She still does not know Orien. It is something that she has been blinded by due to the mating bond, and they have not completed that tethering of souls yet.

"You can trust us, Elisiah. We are all on the same team here." Aneira has broken her concentration from the text in front of her as she looks at Elisiah. The look in her pale green eyes is one of understanding. Elisiah does not understand though. She does not understand anything that has happened to her in the last month. She feels like her body has just been moving with the moment all this time, and now it is like something has clicked into place inside of her.

"What team is that, exactly?"

Aneira looks over to Erwin who has slowed his pacing and finger chewing.

"We need Orien back here with us. We need you here with us. The power Orien has could change the outcome of any war, and that is something we see value in." Aneira gently sets her hand on the top of Elisiah's who sits to the woman's right side.

"Who said anything about a war?" Elisiah is confused because she had not heard anything about a war when she was in Univier or on their way to Thundaria. Is he recruiting for a war? Erwin sits across from the two women as he clears his throat.

"Elisiah, I want to make a change. I want Sytherac to be what it was originally meant to be: peaceful. The Kings that rule over each region have grown set in their ways, and it has marked the people of Sytherac. The original laws have been abandoned. Humans are starting to be considered lesser than cattle, power has been craved more with each new King. I cannot stand by and see our world be destroyed by our own people. Something has to change. Someone has to be the one to make that change."

Elisiah watches the young King as he speaks, and the reality of the situation is something she did not think she would be dealing with.

Her feelings were numb with the absence of Orien by her side; all she can do is stare at the man across from her. Roe raises its head of shadows from where it rests on the floor beside Elisiah. The mention of war must have sparked an interest in the beast.

A fucking war.

Did Altair know this information awaited them when they made it to Thundaria? She was not sure why her train of thought immediately trailed to the rancid man that rules over Univier.

It could be from the fact that he took Orien's womanhood. Or that he tried to destroy her mate every chance he got.

Elisiah thinks to herself as she tries to focus on the statement Erwin just made. She knows that this information cannot make it to Altair's ears. None of them will stand a chance if he knows. Well, Orien most likely could, but that is something Elisiah will not let stew in her mind. Not when she is not even in here with them.

Turning her head to look into the eyes of the Shadow Hound beside her, an ache settles in her chest, followed by the same scorching sensation in her eyes that she felt an hour after Orien vanished.

The pain in her eyes left shortly after starting, but the heat under her skin only grew. Roe was the one who helped her to her feet when the pain from her eyes brought her to her hands and knees earlier. This time, she manages to blink through it. The royal couple that stood in front of her at the time tried to help her from the dark blue floor, but the only part of Orien left with her would not let them move from their spots. Now, as she stared at the steady stream of black leaving the animal's eyes, she knows what she needs to do.

Mariem taught her that all she needs to do is think of something that can guide her soul back to her body, so it should be the same to get to the place she visits against her will. She hopes so anyways, just like she hopes it is enough to get her physical body there as well.

"Erwin, I hear what you are saying, but right now I need to find Orien. I have to get her back." Elisiah looks back towards the male as she speaks to him. He only nods his head at her before looking at his wife.

"I think I can get to her." Aneira looks at Elisiah as she makes the statement.

"You know where she is?"

Aneira holds Elisiah's eyes, her face not showing any kind of emotion.

"Yes. I have a good idea." She reaches for a book to Aneira's left labeled, The World of Creation. The label makes her think about Mariem and the strange place where she has been a recurring visitor.

The weathered book is light in her hands with its minimal pages. As she flips through the stained, torn pages, she stops at the back where a map sits. It shows the supposed other world that was once the home of the Gods, Lixtis and Etbris, and a name stands out in solid black letters.

Arugo

Elisiah knows instantly that is the place her mate has been sent to by her own hands. She also knows that as long as she is there she is in danger. It is a constant reminder in her head, especially as the look of fear on Mariem's face plants itself at the back of her eyes. If that stoic woman could have such a reaction to just a name, then Orien actually being there would not be good for any of them. Elisiah will find her. She will not give herself any other option.

"Give me a knife." Elisiah looks at Erwin as she closes the book, sitting it down back from where she picked it up. He looks her over before he rises to his feet. Roe rises as well, eyes locked on the King moving across the table.

"Do you know how to use one?" His question is one she knows he is right to ask because she looks like she has never used a knife for anything other than chopping vegetables in the kitchen with Fredrick. Just thinking the old man's name makes Elisiah feel like she is missing another part of herself.

I miss you, Fredrick.

The flash of the small space of the kitchen makes her wish the old man was here with her. He would never question her abilities, not like the King across from her. He would help talk her through what she is feeling, but she is glad he is safe in his small space in the castle.

"The Carotid Artery rests on either side of the neck. Pointed end of the knife to the side of the neck almost even with the adam's apple, you will bleed to death rather rapidly." Elisiah's face is set like stone as she speaks the knowledge she has stored away for a moment like this. Her time in the library has benefited her more then it may seem.

Erwin looks pleased as he nods his head with the piece of information, his hand reaching down to his waist to pull out a single long blade dagger.

Roe snarls silently at the sight of him, but as Elisiah places her hand on the vibrating back of the hound, it relaxes slightly.

"Do you think you can find it in yourself to actually kill someone? You cannot second-guess your decision if you are being attacked." Elisiah looks to Roe as Erwin asks her. She knows what it means to take a life, but she has never experienced the feeling for herself.

Would she know that feeling by the time she made it back to Thundaria?

"If it comes to Orien, I will kill anyone or anything to make sure she is safe." Her eyes meet with the bright blue of Erwin's.

"She has been through too much, and I will die before she goes through anymore."

With that, the King of Thundaria slides the dagger across the table to her. As her hand lays across the hilt, a chill runs down her arm from the cool metal. It is welcome from the heat she has been feeling.

Aneira grabs her hand as she lifts it from the table and says, "Elisiah, the only World Walker that has been recorded in our history is Lixtis himself. I do not know what that means for you, but I do know that Lixtis kills out of fear. Of what he cannot control."

Elisiah places her free hand on the woman's. "He will have to catch me first." A small smile spreads on Elisiah's face as the danger she is putting herself in settles in her stomach. There is no light in her eyes as she steps away from the table.

"Roe." Sticking out her arm to the Hound, she takes in a breath, and the beast does not hesitate as its canine body turns to a thick line of shadow in front of her.

Elisiah feels an added weight in her veins as well as strength she did not have before. Looking down at the spot on her palm where the Shadow Hound sank into her, she is met with pitch black veins where blue ones used to be.

She can do this.

She has to do this.

Elisiah closes her eyes as she replays the memory that she saw with Orien. Her eyes open as every part of her awakens with the rush of unknown power.

Her teeth are bared, her breath is quicker.

The dagger in her hand feels weightless as the seconds pass by. The King and Queen in front of her shield their eyes from a light that Elisiah cannot see, but her skin swims in warmth. Elisiah feels like she is alive for the first time in her life.

The girl she once knew who was too scared to speak up to her mother. The one who froze while the King put his unwanted hands on her skin is not in her anymore.

No, Elisiah feels like she could tear the throat from anyone that crossed her path, anyone that harmed the ones she loved.

With the feeling running through her, she finally had clarity on what her eyes were too blind to see from the first time she found herself in that dream.

She was meant for more.

She was born for more.

With one final look towards her black vein-covered hands, she says to the room, "Let the Gods find me." The sound of her voice is not hers. It is a voice so soft, so light it could only be described as Angelic.

It was a voice she has heard before.

Looking in the direction of Erwin and Aneira, a pain slices its way down each of her shoulder blades but she continues with not even a flinch as the room begins to fade from her sight.

"I will be their destruction."

BASIC CLIMATE AND TRADING

Central Climate

The Kingdom of Univier is in the heart of Sytherac. It is a dense forest with seasonal weather and climates. Home to a vast mixture of Humans, Fae, Witches, Spritefolk, Fairyfolk, and different animal species.

A popular travel destination for the surrounding territories. Home to a vast number of great waterfalls and rivers. The common magic for the royal line is emotional manipulation and healing.

Traditions tend to be less cared for and the Royals only think about them as suggestions and not law. Textiles include a variety of different crops, healing herbs and flowers, pelts, and basic animal meats such as beef, pork, and chicken.

Arctic Climate

North of Univier sits the Kingdom of Thundaria. A year-round frozen and frosty climate. The castle rests in the vast barren snow plains, and shifters Fae are found living there.

Ice and water magic is the common trait of the royal lineage. These royals hold their traditions closer to their heart and do not tend to stray from that.

Textiles include many diverse types of wool. What they lack in the textile trade, they make up for with their vast library which is home to all the original texts of the founders.

Desert Climate

West sits the Kingdom of Desitae. Known for its vast sand dunes that are home to the giant Sand Wyrms. The natives of this region tend to only partake in nightlife as it is too hot during the day. The royal line has thrived in this climate due to their shifter traits.

Many of these likes can change their characters to that of the Sand Wyrms, some even choosing to live among them in their Fae form.

These creatures do not mean any harm unless threatened. The main trading source being minerals, spices, and metals.

Tropical Climate

South sits the Kingdom of Runearied. This Kingdom is known for its constant rain as it also shares a smell of wood rot.

The main species in this territory are Trolls, Druids, and Demonic beings. Because of these beings, this is also where the underground economy for buying and selling is found. This

Kingdom is found underground away from the constant downpour of rain and severe thunderstorms. Reptiles thrive in this area and Dragons are not uncommon in the upper mountains.

Trading sources being lumber and mud, typically used as bonding agents. Though most of the fallen timber is normally full of water, the lumber is still used in a vast amount of ways. Through the centuries the people of Runearied have found techniques that work not only for the dry wood but also the wet. It is because of their techniques that the entirety of Sytherac has parchment to write on.

Oceanic Climate

East sits the Kingdom of Octovah. This Kingdom is found under the waters of the great ocean of Orical.

Merfolk are found here, and the royal line is said to have adapted to living in the water after the first settlement was eaten by the vengeful sea. Those who cannot live underwater reside in anchored trading ships.

This area is extremely hostile to outsiders as they believe any upset from the creatures they reside with will cause another fall of the Kingdom.

Trading sources are vast from fish, loot, shells, reef, pearls, and scales from the elusive cousins of the dragons that reside in the mountains of Runearied.

PRONUNCIATION GUIDE

<u>Worlds</u>

Sytherac- SYTH-ur-ac

Arugo- ARR-u-go

<u>Kingdoms</u>

Univier- YUN-ah-veer

Thundaria- Thun-DAR-ee-ah

Desitae- DES-ah-tae

Runearied- Ru-NEER-ed

Octovah- Oct-TOE-vah

<u>Places</u>

Xaxteen- Ex-AX-teen

Hedeft- HE-dith

Buron- Burr-on

Anona- Ah-NO-na

Plants

Callamon- CAL-uh-mahn

Woodsorrel- WOOD-sore-uhl

Popitee- POP-ah-tee

Hollowsroot- HAH-lows-root

Wilier- WILL-ih-puhr

People

Lixtis- LICKS-tis

Etbris- ET-bris

Morzon- MOOR-zon

Altairien- A-TARE-ee-en

Hartland- HART-land

Sandur- SAND-uhr

Nepatae- NEP-ah-tay

Kav- KAHV

Vanora- Va-NOOR-ah

Bashtian- BASH-tee-en

Mariem- Mar-EE-uhm

Hinchy- HIN-chee

Torrein- Tor-EE-en

Matryles- Mah-TRA-ells

Zorro- ZOR-oh

Juroco- Juh-ROH-ko

Alabastor- Al-uh-BAST-or

Alister- AL-iss-tur

Altair- ALL-tare

Orien- Or-EE-en

Elisiah- Ee-LEE-see-ah

Fredrick- Fred-rick

Evadne- EV-ahd-een

Hershel- HER-shull

Erwin- UR-win

Edmon- ED-mun

Aneira- Uh-NEER-ah

Blythe- BLEYETH

Rissa- REE-suh

PRONUNCIATION GUIDE

Neo- NEE-oh

Nox- NOX

Kemp- KEMP

Neo- NEE-oh

Nox- NOX

Kemp- KEMP

CHARACTER GLOSSARY

Light and Shadow are nothing more than a great expanse of power that can be found in everything. They have no face, nor do they communicate to anyone except the ones they create every ten thousand years.

Lixtis – The first-born of the pair of brothers made from Light and Shadow. Also known as the God of Souls. He is the creator of all things pure of heart or soul.

Etbris – The second-born of the pair of brothers made from Light and Shadow. Also known as the God of Death. He is the creator of the Demonian race and all other creatures of the night that roam the world.

Morzon – First Demonian cast to Sytherac after being accused of trying to start a revolution against his own creator. There is no known information about the way he looked or the exact extent of his crimes. Morzon died with the first mass extinction of Sytherac.

Altairien – One of the first founders of the Five Kingdoms after The Endless War started. He claimed the forest of Univier for his home and helped the others build the Laws of Sytherac. Altairien is the oldest of all of the first fallen Demonians and Archangels.

Hartland – Another of the founders of the Five Kingdoms. Hartland claimed the tundra of Thundaria for his home and played a major part in the trading system that was established between the Kings. He is the second oldest of the fallen.

Kav – Another of the founders of the Five Kingdoms. Kav claimed the wetlands of Runaried for his home. He was the youngest of the five as well as the most rebellious.

Sandur – Another of the founders of the Five Kingdoms. Sandur claimed the deserts of Desitae for his home. He was the same unknown age as Hartland and they both favored each other. Sandur was said to stand by his companion, Hartland, during every meeting with the other founders. He was another one of other major deciding factors for the trading system.

Nepatae – Another of the founders of the Five Kingdoms. Nepatae is said to have stayed to himself once he fell from Arugo. He is said to have wandered the grounds of Sytherac until he finally claimed the waters of the Orical Ocean. Nepatae built the underwater Kingdoms of Octovah and would refuse to leave the confines of his coral castle.

Nox – The beast that resides in Orien. It has no gender and does not like being referred to as anything but a part of Orien. It has protected Orien from the emotional toll of some of the abuse the pair have undergone. Nox has never loved anyone as much as it loves Orien.

Roe – Shadow Hound that resides in Orien. It is made from Etbris but has chosen to instead live within Orien along with the others in its pack. Roe can change into anything while in its shadow state but chooses its hound form more often then any.

<u>The Kingdom of Univier</u>

Alister Altair – King of Univier

No Queen/No Mate/One child

Direct descendant of the first founder of Univier, Altairien.

Full-blooded Fae whose powers consist of emotional manipulation

Age – 415

Original Region being Univier

Orien – Heir to the Univier Throne

Father – Alister Farkle Altair

Mother – Unknown

Partial descendant of Altairien

Powers include shadow welding, but the rest is unknown.

Partial High Fae with unknown lineage from mother.

Mate – Unknown

Age – 27

Original region being Univier

Elisiah – age 24

Bloodline – Human/Witch

Powers include Seer, World-Walking, Basic Healing, Spell work.

Mother – Evadne Moon Reindale

Father – Unknown

Mate – Unknown

Age – 24

Original region being Univier

Evadne – age 60

Bloodline – Human

Powers include Seer, Spell Work

No husband/No Mate/One child

Personal Seer to the King Altair

Original region being Desitae

Fredrick – King's Royal Chef/Retired Commander of the Univier Royal Guard

No partner/No kids/No mate

Full blooded Fae, lineage unknown

Powers include Healing and Mending

Age – 657

Original region being Thundaria

Hershel – King's Royal Guard Commander of Univier

No mate/No kids/No mate

Half Fae/human, lineage unknown

Powers include Wind Manipulation

Age – 500

Original region being Univier

<u>The Kingdom of Thundaria</u>

Edmon Hartlander – Previous King of Thundaria/Father to Erwin

Deceased

Direct descendant of Hartland, the founder of Thundaria.

Full-Blooded High Shifter Fae whose powers consisted of water manipulation/control.

Widowed/No mate/One Child.

Age when passed – 542

Original region being Thundaria

Blythe Hartlander – Previous Queen of Thundaria/Mother of Erwin

Deceased

Direct Descendant of the third queen of Thundaria

Full-Blooded Fae who did not have any known powers.

Widowed/No Mate/One Child

Age at death – 115

Original region being Thundaria

Erwin Hartlander – King of Thundaria

Prefers being called Hartlander like the ones before him.

Direct descendant of Hartland, the founder of Thundaria.

Full-blooded High Shifter Fae whose powers consist of water and air manipulation/control.

Married/Mated to Aneira aka his Snowflake.

Age – 30

Original region being Thundaria

Aneira Hartlander – Queen of Thundaria

Full-blooded Fae, lineage being from the second royal family of Thundaria.

Powers include photographic memory and memory reader.

Married/mated to Hartlander aka her Harty.

Currently with child

Age – 28

Original region being Thundaria

Rissa – Personal servant to the King of Thundaria

Full-blooded Fae, lineage being from the second royal family of Thundaria.

Powers include particle manipulation, such as melting solids.

Widowed/Mated to Neo (deceased)

Mother to Aneira and one son, Kemp

Age – 375

Original region being from Thundaria

Neo - Bookkeeper for the Thundarian Library

Deceased

Full-blooded Fae, lineage unknown.

Powers included mind-reader.

Married to Rissa/Mated/One child

Age at death – 382

Original region being from Univier

Kemp – Lead commander of the Thundaria Royal Guard

Half-blooded Fae, lineage being half from the second royal family of Thundaria, as well as from the first recorded warlock coven of Sytherac.

Main power being shapeshifting, followed by a variety of smaller gifts from his warlock blood.

Not married/No mate/No children.

Age – 145

The original region being from Octovah

Demonians of Arugo

Bashtian – Commander of Etbris's army in The Eternal War

Full-blooded Demonian made by Etbris.

Powers – Shadow-wielding, soul-searching, strength.

Mate – None

Wife – None

Children – None

Age – unknown

Mariem – Head healer of Etbris's army in The Eternal War

Full-blooded Demonian made by Etbris.

Powers – Healing, Energy reading.

Mate – None

Spouse – Zoe (deceased)

Children – None

Age – Unknown

Hinchy – A part of Bashtian's inner circle of Elite Warriors

Full-blooded Demonian

Powers – Unknown

No mate/Not married/No children

Age – Unknown

Matryles – A part of Bastian's inner circle of Elite Warriors.

Full-blooded Demonian

Powers – Unknown

No Mate/Not married/No children

Age – Unknown

Torrein – A part of Bastian's inner circle of Elite Warriors.

Full-blooded Demonian

Powers – Unknown

No Mate/Not Married/No Children

Age – Unknown

Zorro – A part of Bastian's inner circle of Elite Warriors.

Full-blooded Demonian

Powers – Unknown

No Mate/Not Married/No Children

Age – Unknown

Astrial Angel of Arugo

Vanora – The first Astrial Angel made by Lixtis/Lead commander for The God of Souls in The Eternal War.

Full-blooded Astrial Angel

Powers – Direct source of Light energy

No Mate/Not Married/One Child

Age – Unknown

ACKNOWLEDGMENTS

First and foremost, to **the reader**: I want to start off by saying thank you to everyone that picks up Ruptured Light. It means the world to me that you are willing to take time from your life to read my book.

Now, with that out of the way, I want to thank **my husband, my rock, my life preserver**. You have saved me from myself since the first day that we met in middle school. If it wasn't for you, my dream of becoming an author would not have been possible. Thank you for believing in me even when I couldn't.

My three heathens, I want to thank you for holding me accountable on this writing journey.

Levi, If it wasn't for you, the days when I became my biggest enemy would have made me give up on all of this. You pushed me to continue writing with each different plot idea you threw my way and even the names for some characters. Son, you made Alister Farkle Altair and now I can't help but laugh every time I read his name.

Lance, your personality and creativity help give these characters their quirks. Each one has a different struggle, but they still live everyday, just like you!

Lucy, you are so much like me but even more like your father, and I want to tell you that I do not have any trouble loving you. You make me realize that I can be the mom I need to be. You make me realize that I was never hard to love.

To my three babies, I will love you until my heart stops beating and thereafter. Always follow your dreams and NEVER say the words, "I can't."

If it wasn't for my best friend and alpha reader, **Courtney McGlothlin**, I would have never been able to organize my thoughts long enough to keep all of these characters straight! She not only threw her computer at me so I wasn't writing on my phone anymore, but she also saw everything for what it was before anyone else. Thank you so much for keeping me on track and not letting me trash everything half way through.

To my **Mother-in-Law and Father-in-Law**, thank you for raising your son to be the man he is. I cannot thank either of you enough for taking me in when I needed a place. Thank you for loving me and allowing me to be myself. Most of all thank you for being that mom and dad for me. I love you guys.

Rachel Richard! Mrs. Rachel Richard. I love you! You have been my crutch through so much, and I know it was never your responsibility. I appreciate everything you do for me. That goes for Pop too. Pop, I love you, and spending the weekends with you is always the highlight of my week. I always look forward to good cooking and good company. Thank you for everything that you do for us.

I want to thank a variety of others who have helped me along the way with their words of encouragement, so I want to list them or this will run on for ages.

Blake Byles and family, thank you for not only supporting my husband and seeing how great he is but also for supporting me on my way to becoming a published author. You are one in a million and you have a beautiful family. From my family to yours, we love you all and appreciate everything you all do for us.

Caitlin Richard, you will always be more than just my sister-in-law. You will always be my sister, and you can't change it. You are stuck with me, and I am worse than Gorilla Glue.

Marcus and Heather Richard, even hours away you guys still find ways to make us feel included and loved. You guys have always been welcoming to be and have never once not loved me like one of your own. I am so grateful to have your little family in my life. I always miss you all.

I think that gets just about everyone out of the way except for just a few who took on the challenge of turning my manuscript into what it is now, a book.

Beth Hudson of Beth Hudson, Ink, you are a beautiful human! You not only corrected my mistakes but helped me grow as a baby author. I understand now what changing just a few words can do for a story. I am extremely grateful I found you and we clicked so easily. You will always be my go-to from now on, and I can't wait for you to work on the next book in the trilogy. Thank you for taking my mess and cleaning it anew.

Amanda Johnson, I want to thank you for even getting connected with Mrs. Beth! You are another beautiful human that I am so glad I got the chance to meet. The words of encouragement and the guidance you have given me along the way is more than I have expected. Even when I was just an ARC reader for Warlock, you still encouraged me to write my story. Thank you so much for all that you have done for me.

Thank you to every single person who loves me and supports me. I will forever be grateful for the impact you have made in my life.

Until my last breath and thereafter I will always love you.

XOXO - K.R. Richard

ABOUT THE AUTHOR

K.R. Richard writes epic fantasy novels with massive worlds and intricate characters.

Writing has always been her safe space, and words began to make their way from her imagination to the page at the early age of 9. She didn't know how to cope with feelings that seemed insurmountable, so she wrote about them instead.

After her sister passed, she picked up books, but when she couldn't find the one that said what she wanted to read, she decided to write her own.

She lives in the south with her high-school sweetheart, where they raise three kiddos and remember the one with angel wings.

facebook.com/k.r.richard.author

instagram.com/k.r.richard_author

tiktok.com/@krrichard_fantasyauthor